ECHOES

LAURA TISDALL

TIZL PRESS

Published by Tizl Press

Copyright © 2015 Laura Tisdall
All rights reserved.

The right of Laura Tisdall to be identified as the author
of this work has been asserted by her.

ISBN: 978-0-9933443-1-2

Typeset in Minion Pro 10.5/13.5
by Mike Butcher Design - mikebutcher.com

www.lauratisdall.com

For my parents

Loopholes

Mallory Park hunches forward over the desk, icy blue eyes glued to the screen of the laptop, a single glow in the otherwise darkened room. Numbers and letters filter through her mind, faster than most people could read, let alone make sense of. The digits on the screen appear jumbled, random, but there is always a pattern, always a solution – and she always finds it in the end. She watches as the code expands, letting herself sink into it, becoming immersed in it, sorting and searching

Searching for…

Loophole.

She spots it. Her pulse lifts a notch as everything clicks into place; a beautiful, crystalline stillness inside her mind. She checks it again, breaths coming a little faster.

Yes, she thinks. There it is, hidden within the programming; a way in, a weakness everyone had claimed didn't exist. Adrenaline ripples through her, elation coupled with the underlying urgency she always feels this close to the end of a hack. Her thin, black-gloved fingers stir to life and race across the keys, the tips just poking out of the cut-off ends and clicking softly against the plastic. With each stroke, she starts to edit the code, starts to mold it, to persuade it… and she begins to ease her way through. Her pulse is racing now; she is alive and surging and *powerful…*

The minutes tick by.

A strand of dark hair falls down across her face. She flicks it back with a jerk of her shoulder, barely lifting her hands from the keys. Everything is slotting into place, fitting deliciously into a pattern with design and logic and cohesion…

It's going to work.

Finding the password had only been the first step. Now, after layers and layers of security, after bypassing hidden traps and authentication checks, she is almost there. She can almost feel it…

Almost…

She types the last few strokes, blood pumping in her ears…

And she slips through.

The screen changes, the code disappearing to reveal the flying bird logo of Harrison Copeland Pharmaceuticals – the final layer of security bypassed with no alarms triggered. That's the key; soft and silent, not loud and damaging.

A needle, not a knife.

Something inside of Mallory releases – both a rush and a kind of relief – and it's as if in that moment everything around her feels clear, where usually there is so much noise. Her lips quirk upwards at the corners. Even Warden had warned her off this hack when she'd told him she'd accepted it. Too many layers, he had said, too many things that could go wrong. He'd kind of sounded worried for her. Her smile widens a touch.

There is always a loophole. You just have to look at things the right way.

She stretches out her fingers, flexing each joint with a sharp, controlled energy, then uploads the program she built to locate the content The Asker had requested. She watches as it starts sifting through the network, searching for the relevant files. He had given this hack specifically to her, specifically to Echo Six. He had said it was important, and Mallory doesn't screw things up.

Echo Six doesn't make mistakes.

She taps the middle finger of her left hand on the desk while she waits – four taps, three taps, four taps, two – watching as the status bar slowly fills, empty black to shimmering green. She rechecks for any signs that she might be being traced…

Careful, careful, careful…

But there is nothing untoward. No one even knows she's there.

The minutes tick by, then finally; SEARCH COMPLETE. Two hundred and forty-six files have been identified as mentioning the initial round of testing for the newly approved cancer drug Estalan, eighty-seven of which are marked with the highest security clearance; files that someone tried to bury. She copies them all. The transfer window counts down from one minute, fifty-four seconds as the status bar refills.

Mallory starts tapping again.

She checks for traces.

When all the files have copied, she opens one, a high security one. A quick skim confirms it is what The Asker was after; results Harrison Copeland didn't want anyone to see, evidence of mistakes, fixes and side effects. Results they had tried very hard – and, from the looks of it, paid a lot of money – to hide.

It was a waste, she thinks, feeling the slightest rush again. They couldn't hide them from her.

She closes the file and wipes her search algorithm from the HC network. Then she rewrites the system logs to remove all memory of her actions, before hacking her way back out, closing all the loopholes behind her. In a few days, when the files turn up leaked on the net, the techs at HC won't have any idea how they got out. There will be no recorded log off or log on, and no recorded search; no evidence she was ever there at all.

Just silence.

There's a knock on the door. Mallory starts out of her chair.

'Mal?' calls a voice, as the latch clicks open. She slams the laptop closed.

'Shit, Jed!' she snaps, yanked harshly back to reality as her little brother peeks into her bedroom, yellow light from the landing spilling in with him. She blinks in the brightness. 'I told you to knock.'

'I did,' he says.

'But you didn't wait for an answer!'

He seems to shrink under her glare. He's eleven, five years younger than she is, though he doesn't look it yet. He's short and skinny, seeming even smaller draped as he is in his oversized red Falcons jersey.

'Sorry, Mal,' he mumbles. She feels a tug of guilt. She shouldn't have sworn in front of him.

'What is it?' she asks, trying to keep the irritation out of her voice.

'I just wondered about dinner.'

She glances at the clock – she doesn't like watches, tight and restrictive – it's nine thirty.

Shit.

That one was only in her head. Her eyes flick back down to the laptop. The Asker will have to wait.

'I won't be long,' she tells Jed, but he's not looking at her any more. He's staring at the desk, where her finger is now tapping furiously. She self-consciously scrunches her left hand into a ball. 'You finished your homework?' she asks. He nods, looking back at her. 'And you wrote down all your workings like it asked?' He nods again. 'Okay,' she says, 'just… just read something else for a few minutes. Maybe sit with Roger.' He hesitates.

'I could start – '

'Not by yourself,' she stops him. 'I told you before. Just wait, okay, kiddo.' Mallory keeps her expression firm, clenching her fist tighter to keep it from twitching. Jed hovers a beat longer, then leaves, closing the door as he goes.

Nine thirty, she thinks. *Damn it, Mallory.* She feels a fresh prickle of guilt. He'll be late to bed now and it's bad to sleep on a full stomach. She'd read that and she knew it and she should have thought better. She should have.

She bites her bottom lip and sits back down in the frayed grey office chair, wheeling it back to the desk. It's almost pitch dark inside her room now. Barely any light from the street lamp outside her window makes it in through the blackout curtains. She sits for a second, just breathing into the darkness, trying to resettle herself, then she reaches for her laptop, flipping open the screen and letting out its pale glow. Slowly, she unfurls her left hand, rests it carefully back on the keypad. The new files are still displayed on the desktop. Her muscles relax a little.

She did it.

She knew she could, but still…

She runs her usual system checks and scans. Every step must be careful, especially the last… She is clear, though; nothing new on her computer but the files The Asker wanted. No traces running.

Safe.

The smile returns. She wants to log in to the Forum right now, to share the files with The Asker, to tell Warden. She *wants* to… but it will have to wait. She glances back at the clock. She taps the pattern once, slowly.

Four, three, four, two.

She powers down the laptop.

Locking her bedroom door behind her, Mallory heads downstairs to the living room; a twenty foot by sixteen rectangle with a dark green carpet and fading olive wallpaper that her mom Jeanie had picked out when they'd first moved in and her dad Roger had hated but put up anyway because it was after that point when he'd stopped saying what he thought. He's sitting, now, straight-backed in his usual spot on the left seat of their too-flowery wicker couch, jeans and *Iron Maiden* T-shirt ironed to lines of military precision. It's a Monday, so he's re-reading the latest edition of Watertown's literally-named *Town Times* with a focus he rarely bestows on anything else besides ironing, Falcons football and the slowly dying engine of his '71 Chevy Nova.

They'd moved to Connecticut from North Carolina six years ago, after he was discharged from the Marines with post-traumatic stress disorder. Mallory had never liked the moving that had come with her dad's assignments – what with all its inherent uncertainties, and different people touching and boxing up her things – but that last time had been the hardest; so much more than the usual changing then, so much there was no control over. They had stayed with Jeanie's mom Ruthie the first few months before they'd found this house. Jeanie had grown up in Watertown and Roger had started reading the *Times* after she'd told him he should get more involved in her local community. He reads it twice through every week now, cover to cover, even the classifieds – and never goes anywhere beyond his twenty-six hours portering down at the hospital.

Jed is perched silently beside him, NFL sticker book resting in his lap. The kid wants to play, but he's so damn small. Mallory's started going running with him twice a week; if you're small, you've at least got to be fast. It's startling how similar they look, her brother and her dad side by side like that, and it catches at her a moment because when it's like this you could almost imagine nothing was wrong. They look kind of like scaled versions of the same person – the same contented person – both with light brown eyes and thin mouths made thinner through pursed concentration. Their short hair curls in just the same way too, only the color different; Roger's a greying brown, Jed's jet black.

Jet black just like Jeanie's had been, before she'd started dyeing it.

Jet black like Mallory's.

The memory of an ache she usually keeps buried tugs deep inside, and she blanks it out sharply. Remembering doesn't change a thing. Whatever it seems, Roger still looks old, older than he should just sitting there. Where Jed doesn't quite match his eleven years, their dad appears well beyond the thirty-six he was last February, cheeks beginning to line like Grandpa's back in Atlanta. His eyes are tired too. He always looks tired.

Mallory bites down once on her lip. It's grating.

Jed looks up as she comes down the stairs, his solemn little face smiling at her before he gets up. He carefully folds his book closed and rests it on the wicker coffee table that matches the couch. Roger nods and says, 'Evening, Mal,' in his quiet gravel tone, still with a trace of its original Southern twang. His eyes don't quite meet hers, though, and he soon returns to the *Times*' stories of potholes and council meetings.

'Evening, Roger,' she replies, then crosses the room, tapping the pattern against her leg. No, remembering doesn't help. She'd started using first names for her parents shortly after her mom had left, four years ago, now. With everything that had happened… something about Mom and Dad had just started sticking in her throat, like it almost hurt to, like she *couldn't*… First names were more practical anyway. Roger hadn't even commented on the change.

Mallory heads through the glass double doors into the narrow kitchen-diner on the side of the house and Jed follows, coming to stand beside her as she takes their well-worn copy of *100 Healthy Recipes* by Irma Pardy off the shelf by the microwave. All of Jeanie's old recipe books are still there too, gathering dust, somehow having evaded the garage boxes that have long since swallowed the rest of the things she never came back for, but Mallory only ever uses the *100*. Jed looks up at the week's meal plan, tacked neatly to the yellow tiles above the basin. They work it out together every Friday night, ready for Mallory to buy at the store after her Saturday shift.

'Red meat yesterday,' he says, meticulously washing his hands twice – soap, water, soap, water – scrubbing under the nails, just like she'd showed him. 'That means veggie today.'

Mallory nods. That's what Ms Pardy recommends. It's tofu stir fry this evening, a quick one, thankfully. She thinks of the new files, just sitting, waiting for her, upstairs…

Shouldn't take too long…

She flicks to page forty-six without needing to look up the recipe number and Jed starts getting the ingredients out of the fridge. Mallory isn't the best cook. Things often seem to burn, even when she follows the instructions to the letter – and she does follow the instructions to the letter – and the phrase 'season to taste' is like her nemesis, but Jed never complains. Roger certainly doesn't. The important thing about it, though, the *important* thing, is that she makes sure Jed eats healthily. Jeanie was a good cook. Mallory had loved her lasagna and the banana bread she used to make on Sundays, but her food wasn't good for you – for all her talk about them staying slim. Mallory had found that out when she'd had to start cooking for them instead. Roger had tried, at first, but his concentration was shot and he dropped whatever he was holding every time the oven timer went off. She'd banned him from the kitchen after he'd given Jed chicken that was still pink in the middle and made him sick for a week. She'd looked up how to cook online. That was when she'd realized how bad for them all the things Jeanie had made had been, seeing all the stats by the recipes. She had found the *100* on Amazon, buying it for $5.78 after spending four hours reading reviews for cookbooks with the word 'healthy' in the title. Now, Jed gets a varied diet, a better diet. That's what matters.

She looks down at the sink and slowly eases the black gloves off of her hands, placing them on the window sill beneath the gauzy net curtains that let you spy on your neighbors, but not them on you. Her skin feels cold and naked without them, all tingly out in the air, and the whiteness of the backs of her hands and fingers stands out starkly against the summer tan on their tips and her arms. She's worn some variance of them almost every day since her parents realized they helped to calm the panic attacks she got when she was little. Sometimes noticing so much, her brain cataloguing every single detail around her whether she asks it to or not, it could be overwhelming, make her feel vulnerable – and touch has always been the *loudest* sense for her. It is intrusive and unpredictable, and the sensation of it can light up her mind like a blinding flare. When she was five, the gloves had felt like armor. Now, she's better at dealing with it all herself, but… well, she keeps wearing them.

She turns on the tap and starts washing like Jed – soap, water, soap, water. Under the nails. Thorough. Beside her, he has already started to chop vegetables. It still makes her slightly uncomfortable, him using a knife that sharp, but he's good at it now, each cut considered. She picks up a pepper and begins to do the same, its silky texture not as bad as the onion he is working on. He knows she doesn't like doing those. She imagines it on her skin then, fingers sticking together…

Stop.

She checks the clock on the wall, making herself think about the Forum instead, and wonders who's online yet. She hates waiting between doing a hack and sharing it. It feels unfinished, somehow precarious.

It won't be long, she tells herself. *Not long.*

She works out the timings in her head; eight minutes to prepare the vegetables, seventeen to cook, fifteen to eat, then another seven for clear up. Then she can log in – her door shut, her curtains shut – and she can talk to Warden and show The Asker just what she found for him…

Not long, she repeats.

The Forum

The laptop whirrs, booting up. The exposed tip of Mallory's re-gloved left middle finger taps restlessly against the desk. Jed is finally in bed and Roger fell asleep on the couch after dinner, the pages of the *Times* rising and falling against his face with every breath. She types her password into the startup prompt. Her room is locked and she's sitting in near-darkness again. She prefers the night. Real life goes silent, the dark dispelling pretensions and conformities and all the rules that people live their days by and that you can try to learn but never seem to quite make sense. The laptop finishes loading. She stares at the new files, breathing in, breathing out.

The tapping stops.

She launches her internet browser, typing in the address of the Forum's back door entrance, and enters the first password. It still feels a little strange, logging in this way. Most members have to hack their way in every time. The Forum is always moving, slipping like a computer virus between poorly protected cloud-based hosts to avoid detection, but there's always a trail set up for members to follow to find the current IP address. It's pretty much impossible to locate if you don't already know what you're looking for, and it's invite-only the first time – invite-only from The Asker himself. Mallory had had to follow that trail like everyone else for the first two years after she joined, but she's a moderator now, someone The Asker has truly decided to trust. He gave her the address to the back door entrance five months ago, right after he upgraded her account.

She types her personal authentication code and answers the subsequent encrypted question that only moderators have the response key for. The screen goes blank, then the familiar message flashes up;

Greetings, Echo Six. Welcome to the Forum.
There is truth to be shared.
Let us begin.

She's read the words a thousand times, but they still fill her with the same mix of relief and anticipation she'd felt the first time. They had been a lifeline back then. She'd been fourteen and Jeanie had been gone almost two years. Roger was at his lowest, shutting himself away and hardly speaking, and they'd almost lost the house because he kept missing work. Mallory had tried everything she could to help him, looked up everything she could find out about what you were supposed to do, but nothing made any difference. It was like he didn't see her. She'd never felt so alone, or so powerless. Then The Asker had sent her the invite. He'd noticed some of her hacks – random ones she used to do, just because coding was something controllable and defined, every cause and effect predictable – and he had left her the trail, offering her a place where the things she *could* do could have direction. She remembers clear as glass the first time she spoke with him after following it, the first time she saw the boards and started to understand what the Forum could really mean... It was like part of her had clicked back together again. She'd finally found somewhere she could exist without limits or strains or the fears that could cripple her in real life, where she would never be helpless and where it didn't matter if she struggled to fit in because what she could do *did* matter, and wasn't considered strange there.

And all of it was behind the safety of a screen.

She closes the pop-up, revealing the Forum itself; a simple black background, the message board threads outlined in blue and titled in white text. Down the right-hand side are listed the names of all twenty-two current members, divided into two boxes depending on whether they are on or offline. Hacker names only. The Forum survives on anonymity and anyone caught trying to hack another member gets a lifetime ban. No one can know who anyone else really is. It's not safe to and it's one of The Asker's most important rules, there to protect them in case the group is ever compromised or infiltrated. Not everyone would agree with what they're doing and it's not exactly legal.

She scans the current online list; Case_X, FreeLoader, Jericho, a few others... Queen Scarlet's there too, the so-called reigning bitch herself and the Forum's other moderator – one of its few downsides. Talking to her usually gives Mallory the urge to punch her laptop, but The Asker values her. She was one of the first to join him when he created the Forum four years ago. His own name is marked in yellow on the list, second from the bottom. The Asker is always online, almost like real life somehow doesn't exist for him.

You're late. The words appear in a new chat box. It's from Warden, the final name on the list. Mallory finds herself smiling. ***Gotta admit***, he continues, ***I was getting worried. Had a search party ready and everything.***

She's usually online way before him. From what she can figure out, he lives somewhere on the West Coast; three hours behind her.

Lucky me, she types. Warden is one of the few people she'll reply to in chat. When she'd first introduced herself on the message boards, Scarlet had promptly replied with, ***Oh great, another newb. Try not to shit on everything.*** Warden had then opened up a chat box to Mallory and said, ***Hi, I'm Warden. Don't worry, Scarlet's a bitch.*** Something about that had sort of begrudgingly endeared him to her. He'd also turned out to be one of the smartest people on there – she never has to dumb down or wait for him. His one problem, though, is his almost complete inability to filter what he says; the guy talks *a lot*, seemingly spouting just whatever comes into his head. It's not a safe trait for a hacker. As well as the time difference, things he's given away to Mallory over the past two and a half years include that he must be a senior in high school, that he lives with his parents and at least one older brother, and that in his spare time he enjoys – as in, *really* enjoys – taking apart safes that he buys off eBay to see how they work. He's thankfully more restrained on the public message boards with regards to his real life, but he's still managed to irritate pretty much every other member at some point with his particular brand of unabridged honesty. Mallory tells him to shut up almost daily – but then, somehow, still ends up reading every single word he writes to her.

I was busy, she tells him now.

Ah, busy, he responds, *I hate it when that happens.* There's a pause. *So, you did it then.* It's not a question. Her smile grows. *I knew it*, he continues, apparently taking her silence as a confirmation. *I knew you bloody could.* Warden says bloody a lot. Sometimes his phrasing makes her wonder if he's spent time abroad – but it's another of the things she shouldn't know about him, so she hasn't ever asked.

You told me not to try, she replies.

I said it was dangerous. Which it was, he adds. *Doesn't mean I didn't think you could do it. You're like a freaking ninja.*

I have to go post it, Mallory types.

Harrison Copeland... he replies. *I know you're used to it, but get ready for some serious hero worship. Jericho's probably going to crap himself.* She goes to close the chat box. *Oh*, adds Warden, *and when you're done being famous, I've got a good guess for you today.* He's been trying to work out the meaning of her hacker name since they met. She's had to limit him to one guess a day, but after nine hundred and sixteen days he's now tried everything from theories about sound waves to six being her golf handicap.

Lucky me, she says again.

She heads into the message boards, clicking on the ACTIVITIES section where The Asker leaves his information requests and the members post their hacks in response. The latest in the COMPLETED area is one of Scarlet's, posted yesterday; documents from a private security firm that implicate them in the extortion of clients. Scarlet had laid claim to that request last Tuesday, while Mallory was at school. The Harrison Copeland one, though, *that* The Asker hadn't posted on the boards at all – he'd just given it to Echo Six. A buzz trickles down Mallory's spine. He'd chosen her.

She sets the HC files transferring into his account, then she begins typing up the hack in a new thread. She doesn't give all the details of how she did it, those she reserves for The Asker only – and possibly Warden, if he doesn't piss her off too much later. She does warn about a new tripwire she encountered on the company's system, though. It was hidden in a second layer of security, right after the password, and designed to do an instant trace. If she'd missed it… things could have got messy. The design will likely spread over the next few months and the other members should know, should watch out for it. That's why they share their hacks.

Jericho is the first to respond to her post – with a whole load of swear words, followed by numerous comments about her hacking technique. Mallory thinks of what Warden said and resists a sudden urge to laugh. She doesn't reply to Jericho, though. She doesn't post much on the message boards, apart from her own hacks or to yell at people when they're being dicks or posting up something about their real life that they shouldn't – part of her job as a moderator. She reads a lot more than she writes. She looks at every other hack the members have done, assessing the pros and cons, always looking for ideas, or mistakes to avoid.

Especially mistakes; they can cost everything.

Hello, Echo. The words pop up in a new chat box. It's from The Asker. Mallory feels the buzz again, stronger this time. *You've been busy, I see*, he continues. *That was faster than I expected – for a system everyone seemed to claim was unbreakable.*

Mallory flexes her fingers against each other, feeling the pressure on the tips, and takes a slow breath.

I try my best, she says.

Yes, you do, he replies. *I'd like to hear about it, if you don't mind.*

She starts writing, taking him through each level of the security design in detail, especially the tripwire. She answers his questions – questions that show that he understands, that he *gets it* like she does – and, as she talks to him, everything about the day that wound her up, that tied her up in knots inside, seems to fade away.

And no lingering problems? The Asker says, when she's finished. *Clean in, clean out.*

He doesn't respond for a long moment, then, *Alarmingly good*, he writes. *I shouldn't really be surprised any more, but let's just say, I'm glad you're on our side.* The buzz, again. *It will take a while to sort what you sent, but what you've discovered is important. It really matters, Echo. I hope you know that.*

Mallory bites her lip.

Yes, Asker, she answers, because that's what she responds when he says things like that.

It's sort of true... but she doesn't always like to think about the specifics of what she retrieves for him. She prefers to just do it – and she doesn't want to stop doing it. Of course she can see the good in it, but when her mind does wander into *all* the rights and wrongs, well, they feel too complicated to her, too shifting and changeable depending on who you ask or even when you ask them. The Asker, though, The Asker really believes in what they do, in exposing the hidden truth, in holding corrupt people to account. He sees what he believes to be good and right, and he acts upon it – and that is more than you can say for a lot of people. And so Mallory trusts his judgement on the big picture instead. He'll never request anything he doesn't think is important, for some greater good, and that part of him – that conviction that has never waned in all the time she's known him – something about that latches onto her. He has a clarity about those things that she struggles to find. He gives her purpose.

The Asker's name switches to grey in the chat box, showing that he's left the conversation. When he's done sorting what she sent, he'll siphon off the documents anonymously, through multiple different sources, and, in a few days' time, Harrison Copeland's hidden test results will turn up on anything from conspiracy theory websites to mainstream news outlets. None of the Forum's members ever take credit for their work outside of the message boards and the hacks they undertake are so disparate and diverse that they have never been linked together as the work of a single group. Corporate corruption, worker exploitation, falsified drugs tests – they go after anything The Asker hears rumor of and thinks people have a right to know about. They go after it, and no one but them knows they exist. Mallory likes that about the Forum; potent, but secret. The truth about Harrison Copeland will seep, not blast, its way onto cyber space and, once there, will spread like a virus, even in the face of the obligatory denials that will come from the company. What people then do with that truth is up to them.

She closes the empty chat box and reopens her conversation with Warden.

What did I miss? she asks.

Well, your prestige score's going through the roof, he replies. *You've been given over thirty-eight... wait, thirty-nine extra points already – probably about half of those from Jericho. He's definitely fangirling. Four replies and counting. Oh, and Scarlet's already posted her standard snarky comment. This time she went with her classic 'you got lucky' theme song. I think you're getting too close to her prestige score. Jealousy is a dark, dark thing. She needs help.*

She needed help before I ever got here, writes Mallory.

Having endured six months of her before then, I can attest to that, Warden agrees. *On to more important things then; did The Asker give you a badge this time? You know, like a merit or something... a certificate? He really should have. Maybe you should ask him? Or I could ask him for you, if you want?*

Oh really? Mallory types, the edges of her mouth pulling upwards again. *You're a dick.*

People keep telling me that. There's a pause. *So, are you going to tell me how you actually did the bloody thing, or do I have to beg...*

Life Outside

Mallory pulls into the school parking lot, Roger's navy blue Nova rattling to a halt. The exhaust is getting loose again. It regularly costs them more than it's worth to fix, but it was his first car and keeping it going is one of the few things that focuses him, so she never mentions it. He's working a night shift later, meaning it's hers for the day. Despite its faults, she's been taking it to school whenever she can since term started. At only sixteen and five months, technically she shouldn't be driving with Jed in the car yet, but none of the teachers have questioned it because she's a senior now. She hates the bus; sticky and crowded, with screechy brakes that make you want to claw out your own eyeballs, and that loudmouth jackass Bobby Dahn boasting daily to his friends about a whole load of exploits she does *not* want to hear about. Exploits she does not want her brother to hear about. She glances across at him, wrapped up in his coat, since the Chevy's blowers are busted again. It's only September, still comfortable outside, but the kid can turn blue in summer. He's made no move to get out the car, looking down and picking at the seam of his backpack.

'Stop it,' she tells him. 'You'll make it tear.' She bought it new for him at the start of term. He's just moved up to the middle school next to her high, and you have to be careful how you start out at a new place. Kids make fun of kids with old stuff. He stops the picking, but the seam is already fraying. She gets out the car, scuffed black boots firm against the pockmarked tarmac. The lot's already beginning to fill. Her nerves flutter. She clenches and unclenches her hands, clamping down on the feeling, the soft fabric of the gloves sliding against her skin.

Jed's still dawdling.

'Come on,' she says. 'You are not getting a tardy in your second week.'

He finally starts walking and Mallory leaves him with a warning that she's got a shift at the store later and isn't going to wait around if he's not in the parking lot on time after school – which, of course, is a lie, but he hasn't tested it yet. She wouldn't leave him just because of lateness. That's something Jeanie would have done.

She crosses the lot and walks up the high school's front steps, trying to ignore the growing tension in her stomach as other students pile in around her, laughing and talking and shouting. She hates crowds, hates their unpredictability and the way they can assault all your senses at once, too much to keep track of. There's a ninth grader to her right, swinging a yoyo... A group of girls from tenth on the left, snatches of conversation about a movie they saw last night... A blonde boy yells up ahead, making her jump... A baseball whistles above, though you're not allowed throw them out front...

You're okay, Mallory tells herself firmly, as if by thinking it she can make it true, can flat out overrule the alarm her body is feeling. She repeats it over and over in her head, forcing her legs to keep moving as the noise grows – chatter, chatter, chatter on all sides. Someone knocks into her. It sparks up her arm like an electric shock. She locks her jaw and pushes forward, left hand drumming against her leg.

You're okay, you're okay, you are fricking well okay.

She makes it through the entrance hall, then hurries away down the nearest emptier corridor. She takes a harsh, shaky breath, and the panic slowly lessens. Not so bad today.

You're okay.

She heads to biology, sitting down in the seat she'd claimed last week, middle right of the classroom. People trying to go unbothered often think the back is best. It's stupid; teachers watch the kids who choose the back. Middle right is not in anyone's direct sightline, but close to the door if you need to leave.

Mrs Trioli tells them they're doing lab work this morning – dissecting sheep eyeballs – before echoing her spiel from last lesson about the importance of their grades senior year and the impact it will have on them getting into college. Mallory shifts uncomfortably, eyes tracing the desk's wood grains until the teacher stops and instructs them to move into partnerships she's pre-assigned them to. Eddie Prang is visibly disgruntled at having been paired with Mallory. She ignores him and starts setting up. It's not like she's happy with it either. Meat-stacked football player or not, he's a definite possible fainter, turning a special shade of pale as she retrieves their eyeball. With Eddie clinging to the accompanying worksheet like a security blanket, she carefully exchanges her gloves for latex ones and starts working purposefully with the scalpel. He audibly shudders. Mallory watches him warily, sure he throws up a little in his mouth – but, to his credit, he swallows it down instead of barfing on the table. She moves her chair as far away from his as possible and works fast after that, finishing the dissection quickly to spend most of the lesson filling in the worksheet, interspersing some of Eddie's depressingly inept answers with her own correct ones. They'll pass with Bs.

Spanish follows biology, then English with the reliably dramatic Mr Cartwright. At lunch, Mallory sits down at a near-empty table, a chair away from Darlene Overton and Heidi Balinski. Darlene eats with her mouth open and has a disconcerting habit of blinking far more than is necessary. Her conversation topics are usually limited to 'things that Heidi has done wrong' and *America's Next Top Model* – current and reruns. Heidi, for her part, stares at you too hard when she talks, though that isn't much at all. People call her Batty Fat Heidi because her eyes aren't set quite straight and she has a weight problem. At least, that's what she calls it. Darlene calls it making a show of eating salad for lunch, then stuffing her face with Twinkies in the bathroom between classes. Mallory doesn't comment. She's never found regular friendships easy to navigate, usually opting for the much less stressful route of avoiding them altogether – but Heidi's parents own the general store on Main Street where she's worked three times a week for the past year, and she sits with her every indoor break because she and Darlene act as a kind of buffer to anyone else coming over. The cafeteria is a teeming mess, too full of people all too close together, all talking so loud it feels as if the walls are constantly pushing in. Mallory normally eats outside on dry days, but they're banned this semester since someone – Bobby Dahn, she knows it was him, the asshat – set the walkway roof on fire during the first lunch of term.

She leaves the cafeteria at the first bell, darting out to her locker before the corridor becomes busy again. One of her books falls as she slides a pile into her backpack and, as she bends to grab it, someone wolf whistles. She starts back up straight, turning to see the very same asshat Bobby standing across the corridor, hair so slick with gel it looks like he's been swimming in it. Aaron Wendell and vomit-risk Eddie Prang are hanging back beside him. She blanks them, going back to her books, but Bobby saunters over, leaning against the locker beside hers. Her muscles tense uncomfortably. He's so close she can smell all that stinking gel.

And she can feel his eyes looking down at her.

She can feel them wandering in a way she doesn't like. People used to look at Jeanie like that all the time, and she'd liked it, but Mallory doesn't. She doesn't.

You're okay, she thinks, forcing herself to concentrate on what she needs from the locker. *Math this afternoon, then history…*

'Looking hot today, Park Rat,' Bobby crows. His friends laugh and Mallory makes a mental note to let Eddie cut up his own damn eyeball next time, let him barf all down his new letterman jacket like a kindergartener. 'Though, you do seem kinda tense,' Bobby continues. 'What you hiding under that baggy tent of a sweater? You even got any tits? I heard your momma had real good ones.'

Mallory slams the locker door shut so hard he actually jumps.

'Got any balls?' she snaps. 'Didn't fucking think so.' She re-zips her backpack and walks away. Bobby Dahn has been a jerk since her first day at middle school in Watertown, back in sixth grade – an irritating practice he's kept up all through high school too – but he's sunk to a new level of mental blacklisting since his idiocy forced her to have to eat in the cafeteria every day, with Darlene the food-spitter for protection.

'I'll show you if you like,' he shouts after her. 'Fancy a quickie under the bleachers?' Mallory turns out of the corridor, refusing to look back at the hoots of laughter. Her heart is pounding, her skin creeping all over. She grits her teeth.

You're okay, she tells herself.

He is beyond contempt.

* * *

'Miss Park.' Mallory looks up from her desk. Mrs Fraser-Hampton is watching her as everyone else files out the classroom. 'Would you come here a moment?' says the math teacher. Morgan Hale – the narcissistic cheerleader who has definitely had a boob job – makes a loud, squealy oohing sound, inspiring a chorus of similarly unpleasant noises from surrounding squad members. Mallory shoots her a murderous glare and the girl seems to choke on her laugh. She distinctly catches the words, 'Like, actually, crazy,' as she hurries out of the room.

'*Miss Park.*'

Mrs Fraser-Hampton is frowning now, dark eyebrows arching heavily. She's new at Watertown this term, a replacement for the now-retired Mr Ortega, and still a fairly unknown quantity – other than that she chose to give them a spot test in their first lesson and so far everything about her seems neat and precise, from the pant suits she wears to the considered touch of powder on her ebony skin. She's real clever, too. It's there in the way she watches the class, the way she notices who understands and who doesn't, and doesn't let it slide.

Mallory crosses the room, her face a practiced neutral. She stops beside the middle front desk, not too close, finger beating absently against the plastic chair back. Mrs Fraser-Hampton picks up a brown file.

'I've been going over your academic record,' she says. Her eyes skim across the pages of the file. 'I like to do that with all my new students, make sure I'm up to speed with where they're starting from so I don't miss anything.' Her face softens and she smiles, looking back at Mallory like she wants a response, so Mallory nods. 'You had three different schools in your first five years of education,' she continues. She closes the file. 'I was an army brat too. It's tough.' She says it like she's doing that thing teachers sometimes do where they try and make a connection, show you they're not that different; something everyone else at Watertown has long since given up attempting with Mallory. She just nods again.

The frown reappears.

'You skipped second grade,' she goes on, 'and up until you moved to Watertown, your marks were near perfect. Then they slipped during sixth – steadily down to Bs – which you've been getting ever since. Most army kids find it tough while they're moving, not when they stop. Did something happen? You didn't like your new school?' Mallory swallows, thrown a little off guard.

'The work just got harder,' she says.

'Okay,' the teacher replies carefully. She pauses, then, 'The reason I wanted to talk to you, Miss Park, was because of your spot test result from last week.'

'Did I do badly?' Mallory asks. She knows she didn't; sixteen out of twenty. She got a B.

'You got a B,' Mrs Fraser-Hampton says. Mallory nods again, tries to look as though she's pleased, but she's starting to feel distinctly unnerved about where this is going. 'However,' continues the teacher, 'what I wanted to talk to you about was not your overall mark, so much as which questions you got right and which you got wrong.' She lifts up a small pile of white paper from her desk, stapled at the corner; Mallory's test – she can see her name scrawled on the front in the rough little letters of her handwriting. 'Questions four, six and eleven were fairly simple; basic algebra, long division… you got them wrong. Questions seven and fourteen; complex simultaneous equations and two of the hardest to answer… those, you got right.' Mallory swallows again, the tapping speeding up.

Four, three, four, two.

Four, three, four, two.

'Now, the one that really interested me,' says the teacher, 'was question seventeen.' She smiles. 'I slipped that one in from a college-level advanced calculus paper, just to see if I had any smart alecs who might need further work to keep them engaged. And you know what, you were the only one who got it right, and without a single crossing out in your workings.'

Mallory's left hand clicks sharply into a ball. Her mind flicks back through the paper's questions. She still remembers each of them, but she hadn't even noticed the difference in level. All of the answers had been obvious. Revealing things like that, though, it draws attention to you. When people realize you're able to do what most can't, they either think you're odd or they start watching you too closely – neither of which is a comfortable or desirable thing, so she's learnt how to avoid it.

'Someone who gets that question right,' Mrs Fraser-Hampton goes on, 'well, it's… *unusual* for them to get a simple long division wrong. Can you explain that?'

'No,' Mallory says. 'I just did the ones I could.' She makes herself not look away – people notice if you look away – all the while silently berating herself and wishing the math teacher would shut it with her needling. 'Have I done something wrong?' she asks. Mrs Fraser-Hampton holds her gaze just a second longer, then shakes her head. She looks disappointed.

'I'm on your side, Miss Park,' she says. 'I just want you to achieve what you can. This year is important. The grades you get are what'll get you into college, and that affects the rest of your life – I think you're smart enough to know that.' Mallory doesn't respond. The teacher sighs. 'Do you know where you're applying?'

No, Mallory thinks. She doesn't even know if she will, if she wants to, what she'd do, if she could leave home, leave Jed… Her insides twist. She hates this damn question.

'I've got some ideas,' she answers.

'Well, don't leave it too late. Some of the deadlines are only a few months away. Anything I can do to help…' Mrs Fraser-Hampton finishes, leaving it open.

Mallory nods, fourth time.

'Can I go now?' she asks. The teacher's face seems to drop a little.

'Yes, you can go,' she says. Mallory leaves, trying not to walk too quickly. People notice that too.

Shit, she thinks.

She'll have to be more careful in future.

Jed is in the parking lot on time after school, just like she asked – which is good because she is very much ready to leave. The seam of his bag is frayed even further. She tells him, again, not to pick at it. She asks him how his day was and makes a mental note of all his new homework as she drives, planning out in her head how they can fit it in before the deadlines. She helps him with English and Spanish because he's dyslexic. He finds math hard, too. It's not that he's stupid, it just takes him longer to get some things, that's all. Once it's clicked, he's fine.

When they get in, Roger's sitting in his usual place on the couch. There's a book on his lap, but his eyes aren't moving. Mallory's chest tightens.

No, she thinks, an unspoken, automatic request. He has a shift tonight.

He's staring at the page in silent contemplation, like he's mulling over some deep existential question. That's not what he's doing, though. She can see it in his face, in the taut lines around his mouth. The book is one of Jeanie's, one that he must have got out of the boxes in the garage. She should just pack that damn stuff up and drive it over to her nana Ruthie's across town – be done with it. She should have done it right away when she passed her test last month... but she doesn't want to go to Ruthie's. She hasn't been in years, hasn't let Jed go either, though he used to ask. She doesn't trust her and the things she says any more, and she'd start asking to see them again and trying to explain and...

Mallory bites down on her lip, feeling the flush of anger she gets every time Roger takes out Jeanie's old stuff – feeling it and hating the underlying pang it brings with it.

He's just sitting.

Just *sitting.*

Probably has been for hours.

She balls her fists – closed, open, closed, open – trying to keep control, and asks Jed to go upstairs and start on his science. He hesitates just a second, eyes flicking from their dad back to her, then he goes. She waits.

Then, 'Roger,' she says, loud and sharp. He gasps, just like she knew he would. The book falls from his hands, fear flashing across his face, fear of something that she can't see. '*Roger,*' she says again. He blinks, coming back into himself, slowly seeing the room he's really in. He looks at her. She tosses him the car keys and he catches them automatically – reflexes still good, at least. 'Exhaust's going again,' she says. 'Can you fix it for me?' She holds his eyes while she says it, her gaze unwavering. After a moment, he nods. She goes upstairs to change into her work clothes, all the while willing him not to go dark on her, willing him to have shaken off whatever crap he's got stuck on by the time she comes back down…

She finds him standing up, the tool box on the floor beside him, the book gone. The tension in her chest loosens a little.

'I'm on it, Mal,' he says, and he nods again and his mouth purses in real concentration, and for a moment it tugs at her.

'Right,' she manages. Then she reminds him she's got a shift now. She reminds him *he* has a shift tonight, starting at seven. He's already had two cautions for being late and he can't do it again. He tells her he won't miss it. She goes to leave.

'It's good,' he says, as she reaches the front door, 'it's good you working like this, saving for college.'

What is it with everyone and that today?

Mallory stops. It's something he started saying over the summer, though they both know that's not what she saves her money for. She looks back.

'Yeah,' she tells him.

'College'll be good for you,' he says. 'You're a smart kid. You're gonna do well. I know you will.' Mallory bites her lip again. He knows she hasn't applied anywhere. He picks up the post from the mailbox every morning like clockwork and he *knows* she hasn't been sent anything. 'You want to go through any brochures or what, sometime,' he adds, 'we can do that…' She bites harder. He sees it and stops, voice trailing away.

'Sure,' Mallory says. 'Sure, Roger,' and she walks out the door real quick. She's not saving for college. Half her money goes on groceries and bills because his hours aren't enough, and he knows that too. The rest she's saving because it's good to save, and, well, she doesn't trust him not to lose his job. He'll work up to saying stuff like that every now and then, like he thinks he can just say it and make everything else all all right, but he can't. He says it and then he zones out and disappears on them again, and she's left with…

She's…

Jed's left.

She shuts the door harder than she needs to and starts walking. It's over a mile from Oakville, the Watertown neighborhood where their house is, to the Balinskis' store, but Mallory doesn't mind it. She cuts off road where she can, walking down through the woods past Echo Lake Brook, the trees just starting to show signs of the coming fall. She's found she likes the open air and the feel of stretching her legs out running with Jed, something relaxing about the rhythm of it. She'd run now if she wasn't headed to work.

As it turns out, she spends most of the afternoon working up a sweat anyway, cleaning half-congealed ice cream out of the chiller cabinets. They broke that morning, but no one noticed until the shelves were already covered in melted gloop. Mrs Balinski has Mallory clearing, then washing, then drying them; Heidi panting beside her, arms jiggling away as she scrubs at the surprisingly resilient cream. It's not so bad, though. Heidi talks every now and then – mainly about the upcoming episode of *Next Top Model* and something Darlene had said earlier that was 'just down right mean bean' – but she's careful to keep to her own space and she doesn't mind that Mallory mainly stays quiet. Her own voice is soft, too, not abrasive and painful like some people's, like Mallory always imagines Scarlet's to be. After the chillers are done, Mallory's stacking shelves alone, perfectly lining up tins of corn, pinto beans and spaghetti hoops. Bobby, Aaron and Morgan come in around six, but they don't see her down at the back, and Mrs Balinski soon shoos them out for knocking over some sodas and generally making their usual asses of themselves. Mallory's glad of that. Her patience is already almost expired for the day and she couldn't be sure she wouldn't have ended up yelling at one of them. Mrs Balinski does not like any yelling at customers, unless she's the one doing it. By the time the clock on the wall reaches seven thirty, she has stacked two hundred and twenty-one cans, and only had to talk to two customers. She buys Jed some NFL stickers on her way out, then runs the whole way home, fixing her mind on claiming a new hack later, wondering what Warden's next crappy guess about her name will be and hoping, really damn hoping, that Roger did leave for his shift like he said he would.

Missing

Mallory scans through the ACTIVITIES section of the Forum again, but The Asker hasn't posted anything new since she last checked. Her brow creases. She's done three more hacks in the sixteen days since the Harrison Copeland one. They were fast and, for the most part, frustratingly easy. All that's listed now, unclaimed, are a small number of similarly dull ones – nothing large-scale, nothing like the kind The Asker usually gets passionate about, the kind that can take Mallory out of herself.

Nothing like the kind she *wants*.

She glances at her profile. Her prestige rating has risen to more than fifteen thousand over the past two weeks, higher, now, than even Scarlet's – a source of seemingly unending amusement to Warden. Mallory is kind of indifferent. Scarlet's good, but she was only ranked so highly in the first place because she's been there so long and she flirts alarmingly in the role-play threads – the same way Warden's ranked lower than he should be because he pisses people off all the time. People seem to think Scarlet's some gorgeous blonde, fawning over her like they do. She's probably nothing like that, like she's compensating, the way she goes on. Mallory's sometimes tempted to hack her for a real photo, just to prove it to everyone; one picture showing her conceited, likely overly made-up face, snorting into her webcam beneath a crappy red dye job…

She looks at the sparse list of threads, feeling jittery. The Asker gives every hack a prestige rating so newbies can't take on something they aren't ready for and get caught and cause a whole shitload of problems, like them having to reset the entire login trail. There have been no new requests marked above ten thousand for several days, though. His name in the right-hand window has also been set to **Do not disturb** far more than usual. It makes her nervous because it makes her wonder if maybe something's wrong in his real life and she really doesn't like that thought. She doesn't really like thinking about him outside of the Forum at all, and it's not just because of the ingrained rules against actually knowing. Her mind has almost subconsciously imagined what the other members might look like – Nexus is a skinny brunette with glasses, Case_X dresses like he thinks he's in *The Matrix*… but she never does it for The Asker. It wouldn't feel right, like it would make him seem somehow less than what he is.

She taps on her desk.

Four, three, four, two.

She looks at the bottom right-hand corner of the screen, where Warden's name remains written in the annoying, dull grey that marks him as offline. When she thinks about it, she doesn't have a mental image for him either; she gets an impression of him – a kind of feel – but never a face. Warden is just Warden. She glances at the clock. And he's late. He's usually on by now and she wants to ask him what he thinks about the lack of requests. He'll tell her straight up if she's reading too much into it. Maybe she's just over-tired. For the briefest second, she hovers her cursor over The Asker's name instead. She could just ask him.

She could…

She doesn't.

It doesn't work that way. Maybe it could, but she almost doesn't want it to. She wants him to be separate, wants him to remain that little bit apart from everything and everyone else. She moves the cursor away. The last time they spoke was two days ago, after her last hack. He'd thanked her, briefly, and sent her a link to another leak of some of the Harrison Copeland documents. It had made it onto *CNN* now. He'd told her, again, about the difference she'd made, the good she had done – and she'd said she understood, because that was what he wanted to hear. He believed it, and maybe she did too…

She *does*.

But the article had said people had lost their jobs in the wake of the leaks. Her mind flicks to what would happen if Roger lost his job… She shuts that line of thinking down. Too many angles, no absolutes. Maybe those people deserved it. They were probably bad people, involved in what they were. The Asker believes it was the right thing – and she believes in him. That's enough. She flexes out her gloved fingers. She just needs another hack, something to focus her.

A *good* hack.

Hello, Echo. She starts as the new chat box appears. Her eyes flick to the corner, but Warden is still offline. It's from The Asker.

Hello, she replies, sitting up straighter.

Oh great. The words flash up as Queen Scarlet's name appears in the box too. *So when you said we needed to talk, you meant a 'team' meeting. Does she really have to be here?*

Bite me, Mallory thinks, feeling a sudden surge of satisfaction about her new rating.

Yes, she does, The Asker replies. *Please be civil.* Mallory's lips twitch upwards.

What's going on? she writes.

Assuming you hadn't noticed, sugar, Scarlet responds, *some of the children are getting antsy with hardly any new hacks. No new hacks means something's up.*

Mallory frowns; she wasn't reading too much into it then.

Before we proceed, continues The Asker, *I need your assurances that what I tell you will stay between us.*

Of course, she answers.

You betcha, adds Scarlet.

Very well, he writes. Then, *Have either of you heard of Cyber Sneak?* The question takes Mallory by surprise.

Yes, she replies. *She's a black-hat* – a hacker whose activities strictly aren't the legal or 'for the greater good' kind – *runs elite-level hacks, seemingly just for kicks. She's the one who cracked the Pentagon last year.*

How do you know that? Scarlet asks. *Even the Feds don't know who did it.*

I wanted to know how it was done, Mallory answers, *so I looked into it. All down to a malware virus from a phony defense contract email, if you're interested.*

Just full of tricks, aren't you, says Scarlet. Mallory doesn't respond, just imagines her version of Scarlet, sitting in front of her computer, scowling and picking cracked nail polish off her stubby little fingers.

Echo is right, The Asker replies. *Cyber Sneak is the one who hacked the Pentagon.* There's a pause.

Why do you ask about her? Mallory writes.

Because she's disappeared.

Mallory wavers.

Disappeared? responds Scarlet. *As in, how?*

As in, says The Asker, *none of her regular contacts have heard from her since September fourteenth. That's eleven days now.*

How do you know?

It's my job to listen for rumors, he answers, *and anything concerning elite hackers concerns me. I keep a close track of a number of them.*

So, she's not been online for a while, Scarlet writes, *but I'm assuming no one knows who she actually is in real life – unless dear Echo's figured that out too – maybe she's sick or moved or went on holiday...*

There are people she would usually give warning to, The Asker responds. *She has a network, just like you do. Would either of you ever leave the Forum without telling anyone?*

No, Mallory thinks, she wouldn't. Not unless something was wrong.

So a hack went bad and the water got too hot, responds Scarlet. *She's lying low. Hell, maybe she's a depressive and killed herself. Hate to sound insensitive, but I don't get what this has to do with us and what we're doing here – and there being no big new hacks.*

Because she's not the only one who's missing, The Asker replies. *Usually, I'd agree it's not our concern, but two of the other elites I watch have gone AWOL since Sneak.*

No one says anything for a moment. Mallory is unsure what to make of it.

Who are the others? she asks.

A hacker called Weevil went second, on September eighteenth. Then the third was Tower, a grey-hat who likes to crash clothing chains linked to sweatshops. He disappeared four days ago, on the twenty-first.

Mallory has only vaguely heard of Tower, but she definitely knows the name Weevil. He's been responsible for a number of particularly irritating viruses over the past couple of years.

You think they're connected, she says, frowning again. On the face of it, it seems a little far-fetched... but then, this is The Asker – he doesn't ever say anything he isn't serious about. Maybe he knows more than he's letting on.

Maybe, he responds.

Some kind of crackdown by the Feds? says Scarlet. *Were they working on something together?*

It's all possible, but not that I know of, The Asker replies. *There's been no chatter regarding the FBI and, as far as I'm aware, our three missing hackers never crossed paths. I'm looking into possible connections at the moment.* The box goes silent, then, *I know how this sounds. I'm fully aware that each case could be harmless and unrelated. I hope they are. I hope they all resurface again like nothing was ever wrong – but I don't* know *yet. You asked before what it has to do with us, Scarlet; every hacker in the Forum is an elite grey-hat.* Mallory shifts, a little disconcerted by the direction he's taking. *I believe in what we're doing*, he goes on, *but I'm also not naïve to the fact that I put each one of you at risk every time I ask for a new hack. Without you, I wouldn't be able to release a tenth of the information we currently do – and so I keep asking – but I also do everything possible to ensure you're all kept safe. The Forum is as secure as it can be, but if elites are disappearing from the web, I want to know why and I'm not sending anyone out on major hacks until I do.*

Another pause.

No major hacks.

Mallory's discomfort rises at the confirmation.

You say you've been watching them, Scarlet writes, *did you ever invite any of them to join the Forum?*

No. That reply comes quickly. *I never made any of them aware of us. All are extremely talented, but they're also too high profile. We can't hold egos and stay anonymous. Hitting the Pentagon is an ego hack.*

So what do you want us to do? Scarlet asks. *Do you need help? You want us to check something out?*

No, replies The Asker, *I don't want you involved. That's why I haven't told anyone else, and why you mustn't either. But it will take up more of my time. I need you to watch the Forum more closely while I am busy, look out for anything unusual, any comment that could relate to this. I'll keep posting low level hacks where I can, things that will fall under the radar, but you might need to smooth the waters for me. Of course*, he adds, *if you do hear anything yourselves, let me know.*

I will, Mallory replies.

Sure thing, says Scarlet. Then, *I still think you're chasing flies, though.* Mallory shifts again. Part of her can't help but agree, though she doesn't say it. When hackers disappear, it's for any number of reasons. Sneak's probably holed up in a motel room with a crate of Red Bull and a month's supply of Cheetos, thinking the Feds are finally onto her for the Pentagon. Weevil and Tower are probably unrelated. Probably.

But it's The Asker, she thinks. And she trusts The Asker.

Thank you, he replies. *And, just be careful, okay. I know you are anyway, but humor me.* Then he leaves. A chat box alone with Scarlet is not exactly Mallory's favorite place to be. She goes to close it.

Well, that was weird, Scarlet writes, sending before she can. *Honest opinion?*

Mallory hesitates.

It's probably nothing, she types.

Check it out, sugar, you said something smart. The Asker always was a little paranoid. Still, he's kept us safe a long time. We do like he says. We watch the Forum, Echo, watch it tight.

Yes, Mallory replies.

Right then, Scarlet goes on, *you check the threads for anything odd, and I'll keep the kids happy. I can wrap most of them round my little finger if I need to.*

And then she leaves, without waiting for a reply. Mallory watches the empty chat box, not quite certain how she feels about what just happened other than she doesn't like that it did. Her room is silent, the house is silent – everything is silent – but she feels tied up inside in a way she never usually does on the Forum. She's not really worried about the missing hackers... but it's disconcerting that The Asker is worried.

And there won't be major hacks till he works it out. There's the briefest flare of frustration... *I need –*

She shuts it down, slamming her eyelids tight closed until it subsides. The Asker knows what he's doing. She just has to be patient, and has to watch the Forum like she just promised him she would. She takes a deep, slow breath, and looks back at the screen, consciously relaxing her shoulders. Her eyes flick automatically down to the bottom corner – but Warden's still not online. She feels a sinking disappointment. She knows she can't talk to him about what The Asker said, but... she just feels disjointed without him there, without having spoken to him at all that night. She glances at the clock again. It's definitely late, even for him. Her finger itches to start tapping, but she holds it still.

We watch the Forum.

That should be her focus. She clicks into the message boards and starts checking through all the threads, reading everything new. No one else has mentioned any missing elites – but that's not exactly surprising. Outside of the ACTIVITIES section, there's just the usual stuff; coding chat, role-play threads, conspiracy theories, arguments about the correlation of the latest Marvel movie to the comic books... One thread catches her eye, though. The Forum's newest newbie – Spyder – has dredged up an old discussion on the hacker Daedalus.

Crap.

Mallory grimaces. Someone brings up that damn topic every couple of months, despite the fact the guy's been dead for going on two years now. Spyder's asking if anyone thinks his last virus is real. Mallory presses her fingers against her temples. It's amazing what supposedly smart people will believe. It's a waste of time. Soon Case_X will re-post his ridiculous 'rumors always have a basis in truth' speech and the thread will explode again for another few weeks – which would be fine, except Mallory will have to read and moderate all of it because people get so stupidly heated about the subject. She'd delete the whole, pointless thing if she could, but The Asker won't let her scrap threads just because people are being inane. She's asked. He says that any discussion is important.

She rubs her eyes and clicks out of the thread. Another half hour has passed and there's no Warden. She should just go to bed, instead of getting all riled up. It's already too few hours until she has to be up for school.

Where the hell is he? The question nags. He always tells her if he won't be on the next night, like she always tells him. She thinks of The Asker's missing hacker concerns and feels a small pang of worry. Then she dismisses it. The chances of Warden being involved in whatever that is – if it's even anything – are miniscule. But what if something has happened to him? What if he got hit by a car – because she can seriously imagine him just walking out into the street and not looking…

You're being absurd, she tells herself.

He'll just be doing whatever it is he does in the evenings in real life when he's not online. Maybe he got so wrapped up in the latest safe he was trying to crack that he lost track of time – and then just went to sleep like a *normal person.* The Asker's worry seems like it's catching, messing with her tired head and making her nervous online, where she usually isn't ever nervous. She just wants to talk to Warden, talk about whatever dumb guess he's come up with for her name today, about the next safe he's saving to buy – she doesn't care – she just wants to talk. It's been a frustrating day. Math sets her on edge now, what with Mrs Fraser-Hampton and all her noticing, and she had to endure two hours of gym class with Bobby and his friends staring at her, and talking and laughing while they played volleyball. She normally just ignores them, but today it had seriously pissed her off. They shouldn't have been laughing. She's good at sports, good at the hand-eye coordination, just like Roger. They shouldn't have damn well laughed. The only plus had been that she'd managed to hit Morgan Hale dead in that smug, glossy face of hers with one smash. It was deliberate and had felt incredibly good.

She looks at the clock for the millionth time. Warden will be back on tomorrow. She should stop. She doesn't. She clicks back into the message boards and starts reading through the older stuff too, going back over all the past two weeks' posts in case she might have missed something before, even though she doesn't really ever miss things. She tells herself that's why she's staying up.

* * *

Echo? Echo, are you there?

Mallory starts, her eyelids flickering up from where they had drooped, slowly taking in the words flashing at her from the chat box on screen.

Warden. He's been sending her messages for the past five minutes.

Where the fuck have you been?! she writes, fingers slamming against the keys, a jolt of relief fizzing through her.

…And hello to you too.

She hesitates, blinking as her heart settles a little. She probably should have thought that one through more. The level of relief had taken her by surprise, though – which was stupid because she'd known he'd be fine and there was nothing to be relieved about.

You're late, she adds, by way of inadequate explanation. She blocks out the itch to tell him what The Asker said, to ask what he thinks.

I'm sorry, Warden replies. ***I had to go to this thing at my dad's work. It overran.***

See? Mallory berates herself. *A perfectly normal, human thing.*

Did you miss me then? Warden adds. ***You're not normally on this late. I only logged in to send you a message.***

I wept over my keyboard, types Mallory.

Knew it, Warden replies. ***This place would be dead without me.*** Mallory rolls her eyes, though she finds that comment weighs a little. ***Trust me, I'd rather have been here***, he continues. ***It was supposed to be this party for clients, but it basically meant standing in the corner next to my mother for three hours, making awkward small talk and eating mildly undercooked seafood canapés, while she steadily made her way through two bottles of cheap Champagne. Now, I'm not a fan***

of seafood at the best of times – too slimy, with little bones or shells everywhere to remind you you're eating something that once wiggled and jiggled about – but when it's half cold in the middle...

Mallory feels herself relax a bit as she reads, something about the rambling familiarity of his rhythm softening the edge of a disconcerting night. She should tell him to stop, though; in one paragraph alone, he's given away multiple facts about himself in real life. Most of it she'd figured out already and the chat box is definitely secure – her own encryptions running on top of the Forum's in-built security – but still... There are always loopholes.

She lets him talk, just a second longer.

Then, **You shouldn't tell me all this.**

Why? he answers. *Would you really want to try and find me?*

I suppose not. She hesitates. **As long as you don't talk like this to anyone else.**

Jealous?

Mallory's cheeks redden.

Hell, no, she replies, too quickly. Warden goes silent, something it's usually hard to achieve. **Just,** she adds, **you are careful, aren't you, in other chats, or in whatever else you do online?**

Sure.

I'm serious, Warden. I mean it.

Yes, I'm careful. He pauses. *Is everything all right, Echo?*

She stares at the words. She wasn't expecting them and she realizes then that it's a long time since she's heard them from anyone – though he's asking it because of her questions about security, not about her, not really. For the briefest moment, though, she has the sudden urge to answer 'no', to tell him that no, everything's not all right – and not just because of what The Asker said, because that's probably nothing, but because of everything else; because today was difficult, and sometimes so much seems difficult and she just wants it to stop, wants her mind to *stop* going on at her...

To just stop...

Because...

But...

No.

Everything's fine, she says. She is Echo Six in the Forum. Echo, not Mallory. Echo, who is strong, who is solid. *You're just a dumbass sometimes and I didn't want you to do anything stupid.* She swallows, agitated, her tiredness stripped away. He doesn't reply for a long while and Mallory wonders if she pushed too hard.

You can trust me, you know. The words appear, unexpected again, and Mallory's skin flushes strangely warm as she reads them. *I know you won't*, Warden adds, *and you probably shouldn't because it's online and, yes, being careful's important and trusting people from the internet – especially hackers – is a dumbass thing to do… like something I would do. But I just want to say it anyway, for the record. You can trust me.*

She takes a deep breath and it comes out a little shaky. She rereads the words. Then, of all things, she finds she wants to smile. She's not really sure why, but she does, it's there, that feeling… and, with it, she doesn't quite know what to say to him in response.

You said you logged in to send me a message, she writes, changing the subject. *What was it?*

Something to make you feel better from whatever the thing is that you feel fine about anyway, he replies; *today's guess. I know it's technically tomorrow already, but I haven't been to sleep yet, so it doesn't count.*

Okay. What is it then? she asks.

A bit out there, he begins, *but I'm going with you picked Echo Six for no reason other than you liked the sound of it. Can't believe I haven't tried that one before.*

Mallory's lips pull upwards again. She waits, just a moment longer than she needs to.

Not even close, she replies.

Bugger.

She properly smiles then.

You're right, she answers, *that did cheer me up.*

Parking Lots

Six days later, Mallory sits impatiently in the driver's seat of the Chevy and checks the clock on the dashboard for the ninth time. Jed is late. The school parking lot is already half empty. She's tried his cell, but he's not answering. If he doesn't come soon, she'll miss the start of her shift. Her finger clicks against the wheel. It's a Tuesday. Jed knows she has a shift on Tuesdays. She reminded him this morning.

Damn it.

She gets out of the car and heads up towards the middle school, slamming the door shut behind her. She goes to the science lab first, where his last class was, but it's empty. She tries his cell again, then checks with the school nurse, but he's not there either. She walks back out front, hoping he'll be waiting by the Chevy, already wondering about hacking into the GPS on his phone… She's just through the doors when she hears the shout. Her heart skips, irritation flipping to apprehension. It was too distant to make out any words, but Mallory knows it was him. It wasn't a good sounding shout. She starts forward.

Round the side of the school? she thinks. *The bike park, maybe…*

It sounds again. Her feet speed to a run and she half trips down the front steps, adrenaline surging. She sprints along the school front, the few remaining kids watching as she passes, heading for the bike park. She doesn't slow when she reaches the gate, hands smacking into it as she shoves it open. She rounds the last corner, and she sees him. Jed is trapped against the back fence, held down by a boy twice his size and struggling uselessly to free his arms. For a second, Mallory's racing heart seems to stop. Then he tries to kick back, and a couple of other kids standing by and watching *laugh* as the boy holding him dodges.

'That all you got, squeak?'

Rage floods through Mallory. She doesn't think, just runs right at the kid holding Jed, though he's a foot taller than her too. One of the others shouts, but too slow, and she punches the boy in the back of the head before he can turn. His skull is rock hard and pain ripples out through her hand, but his face smacks into the fence with a sharp thud. He stumbles, letting go of Jed.

'Mal?' He looks up, eyes wide, but she just pulls him back, her focus elsewhere. Fortunately, the big kid's friends are still only laughing, just at him now – at him rolling on the floor, holding his head. He rolls onto his back and…

Shit.

Mallory goes cold. She recognizes him now; dark hair, pinched face. Just what she needs; Connor Dahn, Bobby's brother.

Shit, shit, shit!

There's blood on his forehead where he hit the fence. There's fucking *blood* on his forehead… Connor Dahn…

Connor fricking Dahn!

He starts to get to his feet and she backs away, pushing Jed behind her.

'You hurt my brother again,' she says, trying to keep her voice even, 'and I will kill you.' Then she grabs Jed's arm and starts walking, forcing herself not to run. His friends whistle after them, still laughing, but she doesn't look back. 'They're just stupid boys,' she mutters, to herself as much as to Jed. 'Stupid jerk ass boys.'

Jed is silent as they walk back to the car. She can hear his breaths, though, quick and ragged. She glances over at him. A bruise is already beginning to show around his right eye and her chest tightens so sharply she has to look away. Her free fist is still smarting, but she clenches it anyway – open, closed, open, closed. Jed's been at middle school barely a month. Four weeks – four damn weeks – and he's already getting beat on. She'd thought he was just being quiet in the mornings because he was still settling in. It's not like their family's ever been especially confident. She didn't realize…

She *should* have realized.

She balls her fist even tighter, gasps at the pain. Jeanie would have.

She'd have noticed that. But Jed doesn't have her any more, does he? All he's got is Mallory and she should have done better.

'Are you all right?' she asks, trying to keep a handle on her raging emotions. Other kids are staring at them. They must have heard the shouting and they can see the marks on Jed's face. He nods, but as Mallory makes herself fully look back at him, she can already see tears forming in his eyes. 'Don't cry,' she snaps. If he cries now it'll just make it worse. They reach the Chevy and she yanks open the passenger door, pushing him inside before running round to the driver's side. She starts the engine and pulls out too fast, the wheels screeching against the tarmac.

Connor Dahn. Damn it... Fricking damn it!

'That the first time?' she asks. Jed shakes his head. 'Shit, Jed.' She shouldn't swear in front of him. She tells herself off for it, but, 'How long?'

He hesitates, then, 'Since before summer,' he says, 'after that trial football day I went to, they... I thought it might stop after the break.' His voice trails off.

Not just four weeks... No...

'Those bruises you said were from tackles?' Mallory asks. Jed just nods. She feels sick.

'You stay away from him, okay?' she says. 'You damn well stay away from him.'

'Okay.' His voice cracks. His eyes are still glassy, but she can see him pursing his lips, trying not to cry. That's good. You can't cry at things like that. But his expression...

'Look, it'll be okay now,' she tells him. 'You get any more trouble, you just let me know right away. Then we can fix it. I'll fix it, I promise.' She will. She'll do whatever the hell she has to. 'We look after each other, all right, you and me?' Jed nods again. They're almost home by the time he speaks.

'Thank you,' he murmurs. She bites her lip until it hurts.

* * *

Mallory runs down the street towards the Balinskis' store. She's already late. After they'd got home, she'd filled a bag with ice cubes and told Jed to hold it against his face. Roger had hovered, looking upset, but too indecisive to do anything much to help beyond getting a glass of water. She'd called Mrs Balinski to tell her she wouldn't make it in on time and Heidi's mom had yelled. Afraid of a caution, Mallory had offered to stay longer and help finish the after hours stock-take. It meant she wouldn't be back in time to cook dinner with Jed, so she'd got a pizza out the chest freezer in the garage, having to push past boxes of Jeanie's forgotten crap and an old police patrol uniform half out on the floor to reach it – Roger must have been in there again recently. It's unhealthy, but circumstances were what they were. She'd left Jed with explicit instructions of what to do, and Roger with explicit instructions to watch him until he leaves for his own shift at the hospital – which he must not damn forget. Then she'd had to go. There are lots of kids in town who want money and not many after school jobs. She needs it. They need it. Jed had promised to keep his cell by him, to call her if he felt sick and to not go to sleep until she's home. She still feels uneasy leaving him, though. He'd been hit in the head. That's not good, real not good.

She reaches the store forty-seven minutes after she should have, hot and breathing hard from running. Mrs Balinski shouts a little more but, after that, things pass fairly normally. Mallory stacks shelves with Heidi, and Jed doesn't call. The stock-take takes way longer than the time she had missed at the start, but she stays until it's finished.

The fall weather is beginning to turn and, by the time she gets out, it's dark and drizzling. She pulls up her hood and checks her phone. Almost eleven. Late to bed for Jed. She starts walking across the parking lot, frustration blossoming. Her left middle finger taps idly against her thumb. Her sore right hand is tucked gingerly into her pocket. Her muscles feel tied in a whole load of knots and she just wants to be home, to be inside with the door to her room shut and locked, with her laptop and no damn people...

Something clangs behind her. Mallory starts. She turns and looks, but the lot is empty, the staff door still closed from where she shut it.

Probably a cat or a fox. She shakes off the small spike of nerves and walks a little faster…

Another noise.

'Who's there?' she demands, turning again. She sees them now, tall and standing in the shadows over by the dumpsters. They step towards her and she reaches for the pepper spray in her bag. For the briefest moment, The Asker's worries about missing hackers flash up in her mind, his plea that she be careful…

'I got spray,' she warns.

'Hey, Park Rat.' Bobby Dahn steps out into the light from a street lamp. 'It's only me.' Mallory lets out a sharp breath – just jackass Bobby who, in that moment, is better than what her mind had started making up.

Stupid, she thinks to herself. Nothing else has happened in almost a week, no other disappearances and The Asker is struggling for a connection. Even he had started to admit they were probably unrelated. She shakes her head. She just needs to get home. She takes her hand out of her bag and starts walking again, flat out ignoring Bobby. She has really had enough of the damn Dahn family for one day.

'Come on, Park Rat,' Bobby calls, jogging to catch up, 'I thought we were friends.' Anger flares and Mallory stops. She spins round to face him. A light flashes in her eyes; a camera flash from his phone.

'What the hell do you want, Bobby?' she snaps. 'I'm really not in the mood.'

He reaches her, an irritatingly knowing smile on his face.

'Heard you beat up my brother today,' he says. 'Had to go to the ER for stitches on his head.'

She tenses slightly.

'He was beating on mine,' she says.

'Hey, all credit to you.' Bobby lifts his arms in apparent surrender. 'Little dickweed had it coming. Oh, and don't worry. He didn't tell anyone *else* who did it, though there are rumors. Too embarrassed, he was.' He pauses, and the smile grows. 'Still, told him I'd get you back for him, didn't I.'

She registers the words just a moment too late. Bobby lunges, grabbing her before she can reach the pepper spray. She cries out, reeling at the touch, but one hand smothers her mouth.

'Easy now, Park Rat,' he grunts, pushing her down towards the damp tarmac.

What's he doing, what's he doing, what's he doing?! He's never touched her before. Only words, only…

Her back slams against ground, the wetness seeping through her jacket. She jerks upwards, her body flooding with adrenaline, fighting against him, but he kneels down on top of her, pinning her arms with his knees.

'I'm not gonna hurt you,' he says, 'just humiliate you, like you did my brother. Family is family, after all.' With his free hand, he takes his phone out of his pocket again. Mallory tries to shout, but the sound is muffled by his palm, his horrible hot, sweaty skin pressing down against her face… He unzips her jacket with the phone hand. 'Always did wonder what you were hiding under those big, baggy sweaters of yours. Well, now everyone can know.' He slips the phone under her top, his hand pressing against her stomach. Horror sears through her and her eyes blank out for a moment. Her whole body feels like it's screaming, like the skin is screaming… 'Just a few snaps,' he says, lifting the sweater higher.

No, no, no…

There's one flash, then another. His hands reach higher. Her head starts to spin, her vision blurring…

No!

A fire courses through her. Mallory opens her mouth, but this time she doesn't try to shout. She bites his hand, bites down as hard as she can. Bobby cries out and the pressure on her eases. She jerks her right leg upwards, kneeing him in the groin. He gasps, rolling off of her and onto his back on the tarmac. His phone clatters to the floor, but Mallory doesn't stop. She yanks the pepper spray out of her bag and blasts him full in the face. He screams – and that is where she should run, but she doesn't. She is so damn furious. She jumps on top of him, pressing one knee down at his throat. She looks down at his face – at his ugly, scrunched up face that has laughed at her and *looked* at her like he shouldn't have for six damn years – and she just wants to hurt him. She reaches down and grabs his balls, digging her fingers in so hard she hopes it tears something. Bobby's streaming eyes go wide. He looks like he's going to throw up.

'Just a joke, Rat,' he gasps. 'Just a joke. Wasn't gonna do anything with – ' Mallory digs her nails in harder and Bobby actually squeals. 'I wouldn't have done it!'

'Shut up,' she spits. 'You…' she begins, struggling to get the words out, 'you sick little bastard. You touch me again, *Rat*, and I'll rip these off. I'll come into your house at night, with a five inch kitchen knife my *momma* used to use to cut up steaks, and I'll fucking rip them off.' His eyes are round circles. All the bravado is gone. He looks terrified.

Good.

'You're crazy,' he gasps.

'Rip. Them. Off.'

She digs in harder. He cries out and nods frantically. She lets go and gets to her feet, leaving him moaning on the ground. She can feel herself shaking, her skin crawling and burning and… She zips up her coat. Her back is soaked from the ground, hair and face damp from the drizzling rain. Then she sees his phone lying beside him. She picks it up, wipes off the screen.

The pictures…

'I'm taking this,' she hears herself saying, 'and hiding it somewhere you don't have a chance in hell of finding, so don't try. I don't give a shit what you said this was, I could sure bet what it looks like. So,' she continues, trying for all the world to keep her voice steady, 'if anyone so much as says an unkind word to my brother again, this goes to the cops.' Her stomach squirms at the words, but she holds herself firm. 'Your dickweed of a brother, someone else, I don't care – Jed gets hurt, it falls on you, *Rat.*'

The staff door bangs open. Mallory spins round, pulse jumping again. There, in the doorway, is Batty Fat Heidi, silhouetted against the fluorescent tube lighting with a Twinkie halfway to her mouth.

'I heard shouting,' she says. She stares at Mallory, then at Bobby, her wonky eyes settling on his, red and raw from the pepper spray. Her face crinkles up in shock as understanding seems to dawn, as she sees the can still gripped in Mallory's hand. She doesn't back away or run, though. She takes a step out the door towards them. Then another. 'You all right?' she asks Mallory, barely more than a whisper.

Mallory nods quickly.

'Just a kid from school,' she says.

'Yeah, I know *that* kid,' Heidi replies, eyes narrowing at Bobby, who's now whimpering on his knees. 'He's the one who started everyone calling me Batty Fat in fourth grade.' Heidi looks back at Mallory with that intense gaze of hers. 'You sure you're okay? If,' she hesitates, 'if he did anything, you know you should... You want me to call somebody? The pol – '

'*No*,' Mallory says, voice snapping into the quiet. She thinks of the last time she spoke to a cop and, despite her threat to Bobby, her face burns. She imagines the car and the flashing lights turning up there, imagines talking to them, imagines them looking at her and remembering, and knowing who she is... and she can't. She *can't*. 'No,' she says again. 'I just want to go home. It's late,' she finishes lamely.

Heidi nods, but she doesn't seem sure and she doesn't move. Bobby tries to rise to his feet, face still twisted in pain, and Mallory instinctively backs away, sharp and jerky, like she was stung.

'You stay right there, Bobby Dahn,' Heidi says, her soft little voice somehow carrying in the still night air. 'You stay right there till Mallory's gone, or I'm calling 911 right now and telling them what I see, I don't care what she says.' He stops, swaying where he stands.

'It wasn't – '

Heidi yanks a cell out of her pocket.

'Right there,' she says, staring him down.

And Mallory thinks, *thank you*... and she starts to back away, to walk away; slow, then faster. She glances back and Heidi is still watching; watching her, watching Bobby. She keeps watching until she's safely out the parking lot.

Don't cry, Mallory tells herself, over and over. It's worse if you cry. She bites down hard on her lip. *Don't fucking cry.*

The tears are falling before she turns the corner.

And It Shatters

Mallory knows something is wrong the moment she steps in the driveway. The Chevy is still there, which means Roger hasn't gone to work.

Not today, she thinks. For a moment, she just stands on the gravel, feeling like she could break, like maybe she would fall apart if someone so much as pushed her. Standing and staring at the car, staring at that stupid blue car and wishing…

Not today. Please, not today…

She stays only for a moment, though, because she can't… she can't break. She takes a deep breath, then opens the front door. Roger is sitting on the couch, eyes fixed on the wall, the *Times* resting unopened in his lap. Not a good sign. Jed is beside him, watching a repeat of the Falcon's game from two weeks back – the only one they've won this season – with the volume down low. He must have put it on to try and coax Roger out. He looks up when Mallory enters, the skin around his right eye all swollen and purple now, but Roger doesn't even move and something about that seems to cut at her.

Of all the days he could have picked…

'Mal?' Jed stands, brow furrowing with concern, and she realizes…
Shit.

Her eyes must be red, though she stopped crying on the way home. She never cries. Jed knows she never cries.

'I'm fine,' she tells him.

'But you – '

'It's okay,' she says firmly, closing the front door and stepping further into the room. 'I'm just tired, that's all.' She swallows. 'How about you? The pizza okay?'

'Yeah, Mal.'

'And how you feeling?'

'I'm okay, too,' he says. 'Eye's sore, but I don't feel sick or have a headache; none of the things you said to watch for. And I did, Mal. I did watch out, just like you said, so you don't have to worry.' He's still looking at her with that concern.

'Good kid,' she says, words a little wobbly. 'You're good.' Roger is still unmoved. 'What started it?' she asks. He's worse than he's been for a while. She can see that already. His shoulders are hunched, not straight. The Falcons are playing right in front of him, but his eyes just aren't there.

'Me,' says Jed, and he falters, expression seeming to crumple. 'He got upset, saying he should have protected me.' Mallory's insides feel like someone wrenched them sideways, sadness followed by this rush of anger. 'I told him I was sorry, that I was all right, but he went dark again, Mal. I'm sorry, he went dark.'

'It's not your fault,' she says, jaw clenching up as she glares at Roger. 'None of this is your fa – ' She stops herself, stopping before she says things she shouldn't. 'Sorry,' she tells him, trying to stall the rage growing inside of her.

Why today? Why the hell today?!

'Just go to bed, hey?' she says. He doesn't go though. She looks back at him. His little blue eyes are still watching her, searching.

'You sure you're okay?' he asks. For a moment, she feels it again, feels Bobby's hands on her stomach, feels him touching her and she almost…

'I'm okay, kiddo,' she says. 'Now, bed.' He doesn't look quite like he bought it.

'I can help with Dad,' he says.

'Go upstairs.'

'But Mal – '

'Upstairs!' It comes out a horrible, nasty sound, but he finally obeys. 'Close your door,' she adds, turning, as he starts up the stairs. 'And if… if you feel sick in the night or anything, you come wake me.' She holds herself steady, like a rigid, coiled spring, doesn't move until she hears that bedroom door click shut.

Then she looks down at Roger.

Damn it, damn it, damn it…

All scraggy and pathetic and old-looking, though he's only thirty-six.

Her *dad*, just sitting there, staring.

Staring, when he should be at work, because if he loses this job, she doesn't know what they…

Staring, when she…

'Roger,' she says, her voice cold and hard. He stirs a little. 'Look at me!' she shouts. He finally does, that same ridiculous expression he always has on his face when she pulls him out of going dark, halfway between startled and scared, though he's only in his living room and she's only his daughter.

'Mallory?' he stammers.

'Shut up,' she says. Whatever he'd been going to say, the words seem to fall back down into his throat. 'So you saw that your son got beat up today?' she continues. Roger's face twists. He glances at the stairs. 'Yeah, that kid,' she says. 'You're upset you couldn't protect him? Well, he's been sitting by you all evening and you looked like you didn't even know he was there.'

'I can't – ' he begins.

'There are things you *can* do!' She's heard it before, so many damn times. 'You just won't. And it's not that you don't see, because you do.' The words start pouring out of her like a stream, all her fury, all her built up tension spilling out on him. 'You aren't dumb. Whatever else you lost, that didn't change. You've never been dumb! You see what's going on. You see everything, but you don't help him, you don't… Your own child.' Her voice breaks. And then, suddenly, it's not Jed she's talking about, 'Right there in front of you…' She sees Bobby's face bearing down on her, feels his hands sliding across her stomach. 'And you don't help, and…' The words choke up.

Don't you cry again! she tells herself. But she can feel it, she can still *feel* it…

Roger is staring at her now, not at the stairs, at her. She blinks her eyes, and blinks her eyes, and blinks…

'There's this boy from school,' she says, her voice suddenly paper soft and trembling. 'And it's been going on a long time, calling names and generally being a jerk... but, today, he actually did something. He did something bad, Roger, and it was horrible. He *hurt...*' Her voice cuts out again.

'Mallory, what – '

And she almost... but she can't, she can't, she can't...

Shut it off. Stop it! Stop it!

'He hurt... *Jed,*' she says finally. She wipes her face, wipes her stupid, watering eyes. Roger's gaze is fixed on her, glistening too. She holds onto it because, for a moment, he's there, he's really there, and her longing for that suddenly overwhelms all else – a longing she never usually lets herself feel any more because it doesn't help, and it hurts. She tries to squash it out now, tries to block it, and grabs hold of his arm, holding on to him though the touch makes the tips of her fingers itch. 'It doesn't matter what you're feeling inside,' she says. 'You hear me? I don't care. But your shift started over two hours ago and if you don't show up at all, you're gonna be fired. You get fired, we lose the house and get the socials on our backs again, just like after Mom left.' He winces, even at the mention of the word and a fresh bolt of fury shoots through Mallory. '*Jeanie,*' she snaps at him. 'Jeanie, who left us because you couldn't deal with your shit, because you were too scared to fight to get her to stay!' The words sting him visibly, and guilt tugs at her. They sting at her too, prickling in her chest and she sees it, sees it in her head, remembers the last time...

Shut it off! Shut it off!

'We're still here,' she says. 'Your son is still here. Jed. Still here. And you need to go to work,' she says. '*Jed* needs you to go to work.'

Roger starts rising, starts doing what she's asking, but he's doing it so slow she reaches out and pulls him up too, dragging him to his feet faster than he'd like. He's heavier than he looks and it almost yanks her shoulder out until his legs start to take the weight. 'You're going to work,' she says, muscles seizing though she doesn't let go. 'You're going to grovel to your manager for being late.'

'Okay, Mal,' he says. They stumble to the door together, her dragging, him following. She grabs the keys from the bowl on the side. 'Okay,' he repeats, finally standing up straighter. 'Okay.' She lets go, flexing her fingers, over and over. She walks him out to the car, handing him the keys as he sits in the front seat. He looks at her, properly looks at her again. And there's that shadow of him again, there in his eyes, and it breaks her heart so hard she almost can't breathe.

'I'm sorry, Mal,' he says. 'It won't happen again.'

'You grovel,' she tells him, and shuts the car door, blinking far too much. She watches from the porch until he's driven away – guilt bubbling again, though she needed to, she *needed* to – then she goes back into the house. She catches a movement from the corner of her eye and sees Jed perched near the top of the stairs. Any strength left seems to fall away.

'You need anything?' Mallory asks quietly. He shakes his head. 'Please, go to bed, Jed,' she says. 'Please.'

He stays a moment longer, before disappearing again. There's a kind of emptiness then, in the silence after so much the noise, as if Mallory's been sucked into some kind of vacuum where everything feels ringing and distorted from what it should be. She follows Jed up the stairs, all her movements suddenly feeling sluggish. When she reaches the landing, her brother's door is already shut. She goes into her room, carefully locking her own door behind her, checking it twice. She double checks her window is held fast, too, then she closes the curtains, right to the top – no gaps, not from any angle. The room is plunged into darkness, but she doesn't turn the light on. Her hair is wet, her back is wet, but she doesn't do anything about that either. She crosses back over to the door and sits down against it, knees scrunched right up to her chest. She takes Bobby's phone out of her pocket and puts it on the floor. Her hand is trembling, though she tries to still it. She should put the cell in a box, in a drawer, hide it, make a copy – it's her insurance for Jed – but, just right then, she can't move. She tries to shut it all out, like Roger seems to be able to do so easily, but all she feels is Bobby, the touch of his skin against hers, the weight of his body on top of her. She starts shaking again, and she can't make it stop. She clenches tighter… tighter… *tighter*… but it doesn't do any good.

She feels helpless, impotent.

She feels alone. And not a good kind of alone, not a safe alone, but one that is exposed and hollow. Almost without thinking it, she reaches up to her desk and pulls down her laptop. She turns it on and types in everything asked of her, fingers moving automatically against the keys. She opens up the browser, goes to the back door address, goes through the security...

> *Greetings, Echo Six. Welcome to the Forum.*
> *There is truth to be shared.*
> *Let us begin.*

The words should release her. This is when everything else fades away and she becomes Echo; Echo who is strong and free and undefeatable... But it doesn't work. She's still there in her room, still just fucking Mallory Park, who's sitting like a scared little child against her locked door, in her wet coat.

Mallory Park, who can't even stop herself from shaking.

Where the fuck have you been?! The words flash up in a chat box from Warden almost immediately.

Mallory starts.

Warden...

That's how we greet each other now when we're late on, isn't it? he adds. He's joking. He's...

Warden, she thinks, *who is always there.*

She roots around in her mind for some sarcastic remark, something that she, as Echo, would usually snap back at him. But there is nothing.

Echo? Warden writes. *Are you there? Hey, Echo! (Echo, Echo, Echo...)*

Nothing.

No clever words come.

Instead, she shatters.

She can feel it happening, feel the walls falling apart as her fingers start to move, and every piece of logic and warning disappears. She pushes enter before she even realizes what she's typed. She reads it back to herself, even as Warden must be reading it, wherever he is.

A boy from school attacked me today. He pushed me down in the parking lot outside where I work and tried to take pictures under my shirt.

Mallory stares at the words. In two sentences, she has told Warden five things about her life. Her real life. She's of school age. She goes to a mixed gender school. She's old enough to work, so likely fifteen to eighteen. She has an after-school job. Where she works has a parking lot. Five things, in two sentences.

I don't like to be touched, Warden, she tells him, more words appearing. *I don't like to be touched at all, not by anyone, but he did.*

Six things.

He touched my face and my arms and he put his hands under my shirt and now I can't stop shaking. I can't stop shaking. I fought him off and took his phone, but I feel sick, even just thinking about it.

Seven things. Seven too many, but she keeps typing.

I have a little brother, and he's small for what he should be.

Eight, nine.

And he's been getting bullied and I didn't even notice. I didn't notice, Warden, when I should have.

Ten. Her fingers keep moving.

And my dad, he's just... He used to be a Marine and something happened when he was on his last tour, six years ago, and he won't ever talk about it, but he's just not right any more and I can't fix it. I tried. I read everything about it I could find, but I couldn't make any difference. And I miss him, she writes, and she feels it again, then. *And sometimes, he just makes me so mad I want to hit him. Like properly hit him. And he's my dad and I shouldn't think that, but I do.*

Eleven, twelve.

Twelve things.

Her fingers finally stop. She stares at the screen. Warden hasn't responded. It doesn't even say he's typing. Twelve things that Echo wouldn't ever say look back at her, typed beside the name Echo Six. Twelve things about who she really is. Some are obvious, some he'll only figure out if he looks closer, but they're there and she couldn't take them back, even if she wanted to.

And she's not sure she wants to.

And that in itself is wrong, because she should want to. She should be panicking. But she's not. Because it's Warden, and, right now, he feels like safety, like something she needs. He finally starts typing. Then he stops. He must have deleted it. He starts typing again. Mallory just waits. She realizes she isn't shaking any more. Her heart is pounding in her chest, but her body is still. She taps her finger slowly against the desk.

Four, three, four, two.

Four, three, four, two.

Four, three, four –

I'm so sorry, Echo. The words flash up on the screen. Then, **Are you okay?**

Even in her cold, wet coat, for a moment, she feels a warmth. And it's not just the relief that he didn't comment on the fact that she'd suddenly spoken honestly to him after years of hiding.

No, she answers. She's not okay.

I mean, bollocks, of course you're not okay, Warden types. **That was a stupid thing to ask. I'm sorry. I just mean… I don't know, is there anything I can do?**

They talk for most of the night. They talk about things that matter, and about things that don't. Warden rattles away in that way he does that's sometimes exasperating but, tonight, makes the tension coiled inside of her slowly release, makes her feel strangely secure. She's careful to never be specific, still – no names, no details – but she is more open with him than she ever has been before. More open than she's been with *anyone* for a very long time. The light of sunrise is just starting to glow faintly along one edge of her blackout curtains when he finally signs off. And she feels better. Despite everything, she feels…

She's just about to leave too, when a chat box from The Asker appears. She blinks, rubbing her tired eyes – and her stomach drops a little as she sees what's written.

Another hacker has disappeared.

Who? she asks simply.

The reply is just one word, but it stops her cold.

Scarlet.

Pulling Punches

Mallory's hand smacks into the punch bag, her skin already stinging, the knuckles still tender from where she hit Connor two days ago. The bag swings back further than it had the last time, but still not as much as she'd have liked. Jed steps forward and steadies it.

'That one was better,' he says, smiling.

Mallory nods. One more go, then it's his turn again. She pulls her arm back, trying to remember everything the YouTube video had said, setting it up perfectly. She swings, fist colliding with rubbery plastic.

Shit! She recoils in pain, barely managing to keep the curse internal. *How the hell do people do this?*

She and Jed have watched that damn clip – supposedly teaching you how to punch properly – three times, but it still isn't working. Mallory shakes out her hand, wincing as the knuckles click.

'You're up, kiddo,' she says, moving back and switching places with Jed. The bruise around his eye is already yellowed and fading, but she still doesn't like seeing it. It shouldn't be there at all. He levels his feet in front of the bag – brow knitted in concentration, mouth a thin, tight line – and bends his knees for balance, just like the video had said. Mallory watches carefully. It's important he gets better. She has Bobby's phone locked away in a drawer in her room, the pictures now backed up on her computer just in case, and maybe it will work for a time – get Bobby to keep Connor off Jed's back – but she can't rely on it forever. Jed needs to learn how to defend himself. He wants to.

And so does she.

She thinks briefly of Scarlet, of what The Asker had told her...

Then she thinks of Bobby. Her skin goose pimples, the memory of hands across her stomach...

No! she tells herself. *No, no, no.* She shuts it off, just like she has been doing for the past two days. She can't let it get to her. She'd almost lost it the first time she saw him at school yesterday, walking down the corridor with his friends, eyes all red raw still… but he hadn't gone near her, hasn't even looked at her since. Warden thinks what she's doing is dangerous, stupid even. He's been on at her to tell the police what happened, saying that she shouldn't hide it, that Bobby shouldn't get away with it. Mallory swallows. Warden doesn't understand. She'd have to go down to the station to do it and they'll know who she is, they'll recognize her, and she can't, she…

She hates that place.

No, she thinks. *It doesn't matter anyway; the threat of the phone is better because it keeps Jed safe too. That's more important.* She tells herself that, at least. Warden had said she should tell the teachers about that fight too, but Connor has steered clear of her brother so far, so it's working – her way is working. It's better, she tells herself again. This way, things are kept under control. She can't risk losing that, can't risk someone else changing it.

Jed swings at the bag, fist connecting with a hollow splat. She'd bought it off eBay, paying an extortionate amount for next day delivery, and strung it up on a willow tree in their back yard that morning. Jed grimaces, rubbing his hand. The bag had moved less than it had for her. Mallory holds in a sigh, fingers flexing.

'You check your weight?' she asks. He nods. 'And your thumb wasn't in your fist?'

'No, Mal.'

'We just got to keep practicing,' she says. 'It'll get easier.'

He nods again and turns back to the bag, small features set with determination. He hits it nine more times and he does seem to get a little better, but the grimace grows with every go too. By the tenth, his face is flushed and his eyes look a little watery. She sees him gritting his teeth against it, though, holding it back – and that's good. They switch places again.

Come on, Mallory thinks, lining up to try with her left hand now. The video had said you should be able to use both. It was very clear about that. She goes through every single step in her mind. *Bend your knees for balance, level your arm just below your face, twist your hips as you move for more power...* She drives her hand forwards with all the force she can muster, imagining the bag as Bobby Dahn's sick ugly face, the face she tries not to see but keeps seeing anyway, all sneery and laughing and...

Pain shoots up through her fingers.

'Crap, *damn it!*' She kicks out at the bag. At least that makes the stupid thing swing more than foot.

'You're doing it wrong.'

She spins round. Roger is standing by the open door. He's back from work; it must be later than she'd thought. He's watching them, eyes squinting against the low afternoon sun, but still seeming more focused than usual.

'You're bending your wrist too much,' he continues, soft and gravely, 'so you're hitting with the flat of your hand. You want to hit with your knuckles, preferably the first two. It's stronger and it'll hurt less.' He sounds direct, clear, and Mallory falters, taken off guard.

'It didn't say that on YouTube,' she says.

'YouTube's wrong then,' he replies. 'And you don't want to pull back so far either. Wouldn't have time in a real fight and it'll give you less force anyway.'

She goes to respond, then hesitates. He's been in real fights, Roger has. He was trained in the Marines, served three and a half tours. Maybe he *does* know... He almost takes a step forward, like he wants to demonstrate and she feels this sudden, unwanted spark of hope.

'Go on, then,' Mallory tells him, voice a little harsher than it needed to be. He's been better the past couple of days, even helping her and Jed with some of the housework last night. Maybe some small part of what she'd said got through, but... well, she can't trust it. A few good days doesn't mean there won't be more bad coming, and any losing sight of that isn't sensible. He moves forward, though. She backs off, going to stand beside Jed as Roger stops in front of the bag. He balls his fists, eyeing it careful like, seeming to try and psyche himself up. Mallory watches nervously. She waits for thirty seconds, counting them up in her head and, by the time a half minute's passed, sweat is already forming on his brow. Maybe this was a bad idea…

'You going to do it or – ' she begins.

His fist shoots forward and thumps into the bag. It swings backwards wildly, chain rattling above it.

'Shit,' gasps Jed.

Mallory doesn't even notice. She's staring at Roger and feeling all kinds of strange inside. When she was little, he'd always seemed so strong; she'd thought he could protect them from anything. It's been so long since she's thought of him as the same person, not since that last tour and…

He knows how to fight, though, she thinks. *He really still does. Of course he still knows.* The problem was never forgetting. There's that ripple of hope again, the one she shouldn't be feeling.

'I'm a little rusty – ' he says.

'You show us how to do that?' she interrupts. Maybe it won't work out, but it's not like they're getting far without him. He glances at her, then his eyes slip down to the ground. The grass is still brown and parched from the hot summer. Knowledge or not, he's hesitating like he never used to, some big internal war going on inside of him that no one else knows about. She stiffens. He's not going to do it…

'Yeah, Mal,' he says, 'I can show you.' He looks up again, holding her gaze, and the words catch in her throat.

'Jed first,' she manages. 'Show him first.'

Jed steps forward, looking at their dad with a newfound awe that somehow makes Mallory nervous. Roger studies him, then starts talking about how he can use his body in the punch, haltingly at first, then a little smoother. He tells him how being small can be an advantage, you just have to use your weight differently to big guys. Jed's next hit knocks the bag back twice as far as his last. He doesn't wince so much either. In fact, he seems to puff up a little and Roger smiles, actually smiles, at him. Mallory bites her lip.

No, she can't trust it. She mustn't.

She decides, then, that she'll see if Jed wants to go running later. It's a Thursday, and Thursday isn't one of their days for running, but he could do with stepping up his training to three times a week, and not just because of his football hopes. She wants him to be able to fight his own corner and maybe Roger *can* keep it together long enough to help with that – but it sure doesn't hurt to be able to run away real fast too.

* * *

I think I've found a connection. The words appear in a chat box from The Asker. It's late that same evening and Mallory's been checking the message boards again, just like she'd promised she would. Everyone seems to have bought his explanation that Scarlet's going to be gone for a while because she's sick in real life – but then, no one does ever question a post from The Asker. *I've found something that links Scarlet with the other missing hackers*, he continues, *something that links all of them.*

Mallory's heart quickens a little. It's not what she wanted to hear. A link makes this all more tangible, less likely to resolve itself or blow over soon. She stretches out her fingers, hands still sore from earlier. The Asker hasn't spoken to her since two days ago when he'd told her that Scarlet was AWOL and, at that point, he hadn't had anything linking her to the other still-missing hackers – other than that she was another elite who had vanished from cyber space without any prior warning. She hadn't logged in for nearly forty-eight hours by the time The Asker had told Mallory, so she's been gone almost four days. She'd not missed a single one before, in all the four years she'd been a member.

Mallory glances automatically to the bottom right of the screen where the name Queen Scarlet is written in grey. She never thought she'd regret seeing that, but she does now. The imaginary, ugly Scarlet – the one with the crappy dye job – flashes up in her mind and she feels a twinge of guilt.

What is it? she asks. She doesn't want there to be a link, she doesn't…

Daedalus, The Asker replies.

Mallory stops. Whatever she'd been expecting, it wasn't that.

I don't understand, she writes. How can a two-years-dead hacker link four current ones?

They were all trying to find his last virus, The Asker responds.

She frowns. No, that wasn't what she'd been expecting. The missing hackers really didn't fit the profile for the people who bought into that.

Daedalus – real name Jeffrey Mullins Jr – had been a black-hat hacker active until October 2011, when, aged twenty-five, he'd shot himself in the head because the Feds had finally traced him back to his mother's apartment in the Bronx. Like a lot of people, Mallory had been in awe of his abilities. The guy had been a genius, no question – his viruses were like little coded works of art and it used to seem like he could crack into anything – but that was tempered by the fact that his actions were also often extremely destructive, and he had some serious ego issues. He posted these annoying little cartoon videos to claim credit for every single thing he did, often leaving online 'quest trails' – his words – hidden within them for other hackers to follow to find pieces of code he'd written or clues as to how he'd done some of his biggest hacks. He also happened to have named himself after the greatest master craftsman in Ancient Greek mythology. He was smarter than everyone else – and he'd wanted them to know it. Before he died, he'd released one final video, entitled *The Reckoning*. In it he claimed he'd left one last 'super virus' for other hackers to find, hidden across cyber space in broken up chunks of code. He'd said that if someone could prove themselves 'worthy' and figure out how to put it all together, it would 'change the world'.

Definite ego issues.

Of course, every hacker under the sun has gone looking for it at some point. Even Mallory did, once. A few crappy viruses called The Reckoning have also popped up since, but they weren't the work of Daedalus unless the guy had had a serious blow to the head first. The reality is that the supposed quest trail he left for it leads nowhere, just dries up. Two years and no one's even got close? The whole thing's bull crap – most halfway decent hackers agree that by now – just a pissed off guy's attempt at some kind of immortality when he realized he'd been made.

Mallory looks down at The Asker's assertion, though, there on the screen in clear white letters. Scarlet was a lot of things, but she definitely wasn't stupid.

Why was she going after it again?

How do you know? Mallory responds.

Scarlet had started asking me about it in chats recently, says The Asker. *She said she'd been looking into it and thought there was more to the rumors than just rumors. I think* – the typing pauses – *I think that she wanted to do something to impress me. I think she was jealous of you, Echo.*

Mallory blinks. For a moment, Scarlet is that real woman in her head again, and not just a name who likes to piss her off.

When she went offline, The Asker continues, *obviously I knew more about her than I had the others who'd disappeared. I tried to match her interests with theirs, see if I could find a connection that way. It turns out Cyber Sneak was also openly after the virus and I'm fairly sure I can link Tower to the search as well. I can't confirm Weevil's attachment, but he's fixated with viruses generally, so it fits that this would be like the grail to him.*

Mallory taps the pattern once, frown deepening.

But, I mean, it can't actually be real, right? she writes.

I think it's highly unlikely, The Asker replies. *I told Scarlet as much, and that I thought she should leave it be, but she must have kept looking anyway.*

So, Mallory says, still unsure, *do you think the four of them might have grouped up, to look for it together or something?*

Maybe, he responds, *but Scarlet would have told me if that meant not logging in. Every time before when she was going to deviate from her usual login times, she would tell me, even if it was just going to be a couple of hours different.*

And, Mallory thinks, *if they were working together, why didn't they all go off the grid at the same time? And why did they even need to at all?* It doesn't make sense. It makes her uneasy.

There is another possibility, The Asker goes on. *While Daedalus was still alive, he had his – for want of a better word – followers. Fans. There were hackers who watched every video he posted, followed every quest, studied every hack and dissected every bit of every virus he ever released. Some of them were obsessive and they didn't just go away because he did, not with that last video dangling out there. I know Scarlet, and I know she wasn't one of them – and from what I've found out, I don't think the others missing were either – but if they were looking for what those followers are almost certainly still looking for, asking too many questions in the wrong places, or getting too close to something those people weren't happy about...*

Mallory hesitates, disturbed by his implication.

You think someone might have done something to them?

I don't know, he replies. *My thoughts are probably running away with me, but there is too much about this I don't know and that is not a situation I like to be in. I am worried, Echo. I've known Scarlet a long time, and I'm worried about her.*

It's such a human thing to say, so unlike how Mallory is used to The Asker being, and her unease grows. He always seems so sure, so in control – and so reassuringly separate from any hint of real life. Her insides flutter, like she's witnessed something personal that she shouldn't have, like she shouldn't be looking... It is vulnerable. And he is trusting her with it. A buzz trickles up her spine.

So what do we do? she asks.

I have to find her. If she has chosen to leave us, for whatever reason, then that is her decision and I trust her to keep the Forum secret. But I don't think she would just go without explanation. In fact, I'm certain she wouldn't. This place means far more to her than that. There's a pause. *I know the rational thing would be to let it go*, he writes, *to hope I'm wrong, hope she still turns up, hope they all do, but I find myself unable to do that. I have to know that she is all right. Echo, I know you two didn't always see eye-to-eye, but she was one of the first to join me here. She risked a lot for me at the beginning, and I can't just leave this now.*

His words stir something inside of Mallory, the way they always do when he talks with such conviction. Unbidden, she imagines the situation switched round, and it being Warden missing, not Scarlet. Her stomach drops and she grips hold of the desk, surprised by the force of it.

How? she asks. ***How can you find her?***

There's a lead I'm following, he responds. ***It has certain difficulties, though.***

Is there anything I can do to help?

He doesn't answer for a long time. Mallory taps nervously on the desk, the rhythm continuous now. She doesn't like not knowing what's going on and she has the distinct feeling there's a lot she doesn't know about this.

The lead isn't online, he finally replies. ***There's a location specific hack I want to do.*** Another pause. ***And, yes, I could use your help to do it.***

Mallory stares at the words. Like most of this conversation, they weren't what she was expecting – and they set her pulse racing. He needs help in real life. He wants to *meet*, in real life; that's what he's saying. Her hand is suddenly tapping like crazy.

And her head is saying, *No. No, no, no…*

Online and real life are two separate worlds and she can deal with one because she has the other. They can't ever cross. Everything would become blurred and confused and –

Echo?

She has to say something…

She has to…

But we can't, she answers. She tries to write it out logically, write out a reasoned answer, so he doesn't see her panic. ***For starters, we could be on opposite sides of the planet. We don't know and we shouldn't –***

I'm in New York City, comes the reply, even as she's typing. She stops. ***That's where the hack would be.***

He's near. The thought blocks out all else for the briefest moment. *All this time, he's been so near to me and I didn't even know…* Not like Warden, far away wherever he is on the West Coast. New York City isn't even two hours' drive from her house. And it gives her the strangest feeling to know…

But…

No, no, no!

He *shouldn't* be saying this. He's The Asker, and he's controlled and sensible and he shouldn't…

I have money, he continues. **Wherever you are, I can pay to get you here and back.**

No, Mallory types, fingertips smacking against the keys, an antsy, griping energy rattling through her, **please stop. You shouldn't be telling me this, any of it. No locations, no real life, that's the rule; your rule!**

I'm sorry, he replies. *I wouldn't ask if it wasn't important, but I don't know who to trust. Echo, this may be bigger than I thought. I need your help.*

Then it's her turn to not reply for a long time. She just stares at the screen. She's never refused a request from him before. Never. She doesn't turn him down. That's not how it works. It's *not* how it works, because she trusts him, because he makes the right decisions, he makes good decisions. He's a good person and she believes in him, believes in what he believes in and, even now, he's doing this for someone else…

She wonders, briefly, what the lead could be. Daedalus was from NYC…

Along with eight million other people…

But, no, that's not what matters. It's not what the lead is…

It's a big risk for The Asker, too, what he's suggesting. His anonymity will be worth just as much to him as hers is to her…

I need your help.

She reads the words over and over…

Over and over…

But she can't…

She *can't*.

There's Jed and Roger, and staying secret and apart is how she keeps what she does safe. It's how any of it is safe; any member of the Forum, any of what they do… It's also what makes Echo Six powerful, what makes her fearless. They can't meet, ever. Mallory isn't Echo outside of this room. She doesn't know how to be. Echo doesn't *exist* outside of this room. She tenses up at the very thought of it, at the nakedness of it, and she wraps her arms around her waist, closing her eyes until the feeling subsides a little. She shakes her head.

I'll do anything else, she writes. And she means it, she would, for him… But not this. It's the one thing she can't. *Any way I can help you online I'll do, but we can't meet. That isn't how it works. It's not safe. I'm sorry. I just can't. I'm sorry*, she says again.

She's letting him down. She's letting him down and it's the worst feeling, like she's falling and reaching, and her whole body is rigid as she waits for his response. And every second feels too long and she wonders what he's thinking, if maybe she's just broken something important and…

Don't be sorry, he replies simply. *It was a lot to ask – too much, really – and maybe I shouldn't have asked at all. Your answer is probably the right one. It is certainly the most prudent.*

A kind of relief trickles through her, but it's incomplete, marred.

I'll watch the Forum, she says. *Whatever else you need. Anything.*

Thank you, he answers. Then, *I've already made you an administrator. I did it earlier. You now have the same control over the Forum as I do. You could even shut it down if you wanted to.* Mallory blinks, reading that again, not quite believing it. *The Forum is secure*, he continues. *Whatever has happened to Scarlet, nothing has been compromised, but, as I said before, keeping the members here safe is my responsibility.*

So why trust me like this? She can't help but ask it.

Because I believe that this place means as much to you as it does to me, he answers. *I wouldn't have made you a moderator at all if I didn't already trust you completely. Others have been here longer.* He pauses, then, *Also, because you are the most talented hacker I've ever met.* The buzz shoots up her spine again, stronger this time. *You don't think quite like other people. You twist a problem around until you find the right angle to look at it to find a solution. I've seen it in your hacks more and more this past year. If the Forum ever does come under attack, there's no one else I'd want running counter-security more. Myself included. I'll still be logged in if you need me, but my focus will be elsewhere for the next few days.*

Mallory's heart is still beating too fast. As she re-reads the words, she almost changes her mind, almost tells him that she *will* go with him…

Almost…

But…

No… No.

I won't let you down, she writes instead, meaning it and feeling it. **I'll keep everyone safe. I promise.**

I know you will, he answers. **Thank you, Echo.**

She bites her lip.

And Asker, she says, **whatever lead you're following, please, be careful.**

Always am, he replies.

Administration

Mallory spends the next few days in a state of hyperawareness, her senses even more wired than usual. She registers every sound, every creak of a floorboard, every scuff of a shoe against the sidewalk behind her. Things that didn't startle her before, now do. It doesn't help that she's pretty much been running off Red Bull and coffee since she refused The Asker's request for help, and he made her an administrator. She's been checking the Forum every free waking hour – and a number in which she should have been sleeping – hoping Scarlet will be back, scanning every new post for any mention of her, Daedalus or the missing hackers, and searching through all the login data she now has access to, looking for any attempt at intrusion, for *anything* out of place. With a member unresponsive for an unknown reason, they can't be one hundred percent certain of the group's secrecy any more and, though it's unlikely anything's been compromised, Mallory isn't taking any risks. She's even set up an alert system to email her cell phone at the slightest discrepancy within the system. She doesn't ever check the Forum on her phone – it would have to utilize different service provider hotspots and that makes her uncomfortable – but, now, if a member so much as accidentally enters the wrong login details once, she will know. She still can't shake a quiet gnawing guilt that it's not enough, though, that regardless of what she does now, she has let The Asker down and can't quite make up for that. It doesn't matter that he told her it was all right, doesn't matter that she still *knows* it was the sensible thing to do, she feels it all the same.

Whatever is going on with Scarlet in real life, she doesn't come back online. Three days pass, then four days, then five… As a precaution, The Asker resets the login protocol for ordinary members. It's what he does if ever any requested hack goes south, or someone's been banned. Every current member, barring Scarlet, will now be sent a new trail start point for logging in, rendering any knowledge of the old one useless. He's also taken away Scarlet's account's moderator status and blocked its access to the message boards. If she – or anyone – logs back in on her profile via the back door, all they would be able to do is send a chat message to The Asker, or to Mallory. It's all fixable when she comes back.

If she comes back.

Just a precaution, Mallory keeps reminding herself, repeating it like deep down she doesn't quite believe it, but doesn't know what to do otherwise. She just wants Scarlet to log in, to tell them she really was sick, or she went on holiday and didn't tell them because… because of something that will make sense and wash the whole thing away. She wants it to just go back to normal. Things rarely work like that though – and thinking otherwise doesn't change it.

The Asker has been posting a few new smaller hacks to help tide things over with the other members, but, though always online, he's been marked **Do not disturb** for more time than he hasn't since he told Mallory his theory about what connected the four disappearances. She keeps wondering what the lead he mentioned could be, but he's asked her specifically not to look into it herself – not to look into Daedalus at all – like he sure knows she wants to now. He said it wasn't safe. It's taking every ounce of her willpower to obey, but she's determined not to let him down on two counts. They haven't spoken much, even when he's not been marked as busy. She's wanted to… but then also been glad, relieved even, every time he hasn't opened a chat with her. There's something wrong about that.

Yes, she just wants things to go back to normal.

By Monday morning, she's exhausted. On top of the late nights and how edgy everything has made her, she went running with Jed twice at the weekend, worked a long shift on Saturday and spent Sunday afternoon having a family practice with the punch bag in the yard. Roger seems to have started retreating again – just like she knew he would, she knew – but at least he's kept helping with that. She rubs her eyes, vision blurring as she stares down at the questions Mrs Fraser-Hampton has them working on – the hawk-eyed math teacher and her damn addiction to spot testing. Mallory tries to focus. She's had to be more careful with her answers since their *discussion* in the second week, but her mind is strung out. Maybe, for once, she'll genuinely get a B. Everything's just wound her tighter and tighter, one thing after another, with less and less to release it. When she's on the Forum now, she doesn't feel the freedom she always has before. She feels a weight; feels a constant, nagging worry at that stupid grey name in the corner… at The Asker being like The Asker less and less. She feels like it's falling away from her; like the one place that is her escape, the one place she actually fits, is slipping out of her grasp and there's not a single fricking thing she can do about it. She hasn't even claimed a new hack since The Asker first told Scarlet and her why he was posting less of them, leaving them for the others who don't know and might start grumbling otherwise.

The one thing left the same is Warden. The last few nights he's been waffling on and on, like he does, about his current favorite subject; a new safe he's been saving up for – a fireproof Lampertz that weighs hundreds of pounds and can apparently withstand a cruise missile attack. There's a particular model he's found on eBay that's ex-military use and, as he's told Mallory repeatedly, is very unusual, not to mention ingenious and, even, just a little bit beautiful. She hasn't told him anything about what's going on, though she wants to, she so *wants* to. The Asker's ordered her not to tell anyone else on the Forum, saying that far from serving as a warning, telling a group of elite hackers that there's something they shouldn't go after would be like lighting a homing beacon – and he's right. She did, however, surreptitiously double check Warden's views on Daedalus and anyone looking for The Reckoning – 'utter rubbish' and 'a bunch of whack jobs' – unable to forget how she'd felt when she'd imagined what it would be like if he ever left too. He knows something's going on, though. He rarely misses things and he doesn't bullshit; that's part of why she liked talking to him in the first place. He keeps wondering to her why The Asker's on **Do not disturb** so much, why he hasn't even replied to the documents he sent him from a hack two days ago. Mallory tries to avoid the subject, but Warden is persistent and, when it comes down to it, she just acts annoyed and says she doesn't know either. She doesn't like it, lying to him like that – which is dumb in itself. They hide things from each other all the time about their real lives – they have to – but this? It makes her squirm inside, makes her face flush up red, though all that's there is a laptop screen.

She stares down at her black-gloved hands, clamped into little fists on top of the white paper and Mrs Fraser-Hampton's tricksy questions. Sometimes she wishes she could just turn it all off, ball herself away like the pale skin of her palms and not know what was happening outside…

Shut up, she tells herself. It's a dumb thing to think.

* * *

At lunch, Mallory sits with Darlene and Heidi, leaving her usual chair's gap. They're already deep in conversation and she makes no attempt to join in beyond nodding hello. She tries to zone everything out, looking intently down at her bowl of ravioli and letting her eyes fuzz out of focus so it all turns into a mushy, beige blur… She can feel herself stiffening up, even so. The cafeteria is too noisy and it's not just Darlene going on about whatever she's going on about. There is so much shouting, so much movement. Mallory scrunches her hands into her lap, pulling her shoulders in. She's aware, too, of Bobby Dahn sat over the other side of the room. She finds she's somehow always aware of where he is now, always checking, just to be sure, though he still hasn't gone near her since… since the parking lot. But she can hear his stupid, sniggering laugh, carrying all the way from where he's sitting to where she is, that same damn laugh she heard when –

Shut up, she thinks. *Just shut up. You're in control. You're the one who's fricking in control.*

'What about you, Mallory?'

She looks up, startled.

'What?'

Batty Fat Heidi is gawking at her expectantly.

'Where are you applying to for college?' she asks.

Mallory looks from her to Darlene.

'Erm,' she mumbles, 'not sure yet.'

'How can you not be sure?' says Darlene, eyes squinting and blinking, blinking, blinking like they do when she's reporting some scandalous bit of *Top Model* news. 'You know the deadlines are coming up. Haven't you been to look at anywhere yet?'

Mallory shakes her head, resisting the sudden urge to throw the bowl at her.

'Where are you applying?' she asks instead – which distracts Darlene suitably. It seems she's made extensive visits, so could give Mallory some pointers… Mallory tries to close out the sound again, to close out Darlene completely, in fact – but then she notices that Heidi is watching her, apparently not listening to the endless virtues of Ohio State either. She feels a tug of guilt. She shouldn't have thought of her as Batty Fat Heidi just then. She'd decided she wasn't going to any more.

The day after the… after what happened with Bobby, the whole school had been talking about how he'd been pepper sprayed. His eyes were so red raw he couldn't exactly deny it, but he claimed his little sister had done it as a joke. Darlene had been going on and on about it, saying how she thought it was a lie and wondering what Bobby had really done to deserve it – and, then, for the first time in the history of them eating together, Heidi had told her friend to 'just shut the hell up'. Darlene had been so surprised that she had, and Heidi had seized the opportunity to then mention how her dad had banned Bobby from her family's store after she'd told him he'd started the Batty Fat Heidi nickname. Mallory had felt a gratitude she didn't quite know how to express, and she'd decided she'd never think that name again.

She looks back at Heidi now and remembers her standing by that doorway, watching till she'd left. She nods because she doesn't know what else to do, and Heidi smiles at her. It's a reassuring smile. And, just in that moment, it somehow makes Mallory feel a whole world better.

* * *

'You think we can win tonight, Mal?'

'What?' It's evening that same day, and Mallory glances across at Jed, hand pausing mid-wipe on the plate she'd been drying.

'The Falcons,' he says, placing another on the drying rack. His brow crinkles. 'They're playing the Jets at Georgia Dome, remember.'

Crap.

He looks up at her expectantly. 'I know we've got a lot of injuries,' he continues, 'but I think the home crowd might help end the losing streak. We've just had a tough start, that's all.'

'Yeah, sure, kiddo,' Mallory says, nodding.

Crap, crap, crap.

With everything else that's been going on, she'd forgotten it was the Falcons' day on Monday Night Football. Her eyes flick to the clock. They've still got half the washing up to do. There'll be no time to log on to the Forum again before it starts. She'd been hoping to not be too late tonight as well; her getting so tired she can't concentrate properly isn't helpful. That's when you get mistakes. She puts the plate away and glances back at Jed. He's already wearing his Falcons jersey. She should have noticed earlier, but he wears it so much anyway. She briefly considers making up that she's got school work to do, but something in her rebels against the idea. They always watch Falcons football together. They always have, and Roger still comes alive when they do. It's one of the few times the three of them really feel united, all rooting for the same thing, like a family should, like they used to… so Mallory doesn't say anything. Jed's had a rough couple of weeks, too, and she shouldn't just go changing something like that. Connor's been leaving him alone – she's been checking every day – but she can see that more than his eye got hurt in that fight. She can see it in the way he takes these deep breaths before they get on the bus or when they reach the parking lot if she's driven. She can see it in the way he focuses so hard on working that punch bag. She'll just have to be late again, maybe not stay on so long.

When they're done with the dishes, she darts upstairs to grab her own jersey. She looks, once, at her laptop, but makes herself ignore it. She'd checked the Forum when she got in from school, before spending the afternoon running Spanish lines with Jed and reeling off her own history essay on Lincoln's inauguration. Nothing had been wrong then, and with her auto-alerts, she'd have had a notification on her phone if anything had gone wrong since. The inbox is empty, so it's still fine.

Her jersey is a little tight for her now, clinging to the sweater she loops it over. Her grandparents had bought matching ones for her and Jed when they'd last visited them in Atlanta and gone to a Falcons home game. That was seven years ago now, not long before Roger left for his last tour. They'd bought them multiple sizes too big so they'd last – so Mallory's still sort of fits, and Jed's still dwarfs him. It was the only NFL game she's ever actually been to. She'd lasted eleven and half minutes before Roger had had to take her out the stadium, balled up so tight she couldn't stop shaking. There were just too many people, and so much noise, the air thrumming with sound. He'd carried her all the way back to his parents' house and she'd been so out of it by that point that she'd let him. When they'd got in, he'd sat with her in his old bedroom with the door shut and the curtains closed, both of them wearing ear muffs until she'd calmed down. She remembers it. She still remembers it. She clenches her jaw, blinking too many times in a row as she heads back downstairs.

It's a good game. Mallory likes watching, likes running all the stats in her head and guessing the plays. She likes how much Roger cheers at the TV with Jed, how his eyes light up whenever they're on offense, and for those three hours she almost forgets about being late for the Forum. The Falcons lose again, though – by just two points – a pair of touchdowns in the fourth not enough to save them after the Jets make a forty-three yard field goal in the final play. Three defeats in a row, now. Roger's excitement falls away like it's something you can feel happening. He doesn't say anything afterwards, just nods goodnight to both of them and heads up to his room. A few moments later, the opening riff of 'Master of Puppets' starts pumping down the stairs.

'It was closer than the Patriots, at least,' says Jed.

'Yeah, kiddo,' Mallory agrees.

It's almost eleven by the time she finally logs in to the Forum. Roger's still blasting Metallica, 'For Whom the Bell Tolls' filtering out through his thoroughly-not-soundproof door, so she wears unplugged headphones to cancel it out. Every other loud noise scares the crap out of him, but sustained heavy metal he can endure. Go figure. She's exhausted, but she has to check in at least once before she goes to bed. She has to speak to Warden at least once, too. If what's happened has taught her anything, it's about the importance of maintaining a regular contact when people expect you to.

She files automatically through the stages of logging in and the welcome message loads up as usual. She closes the box and checks the Forum administration panel she now has access to. The Asker really meant it when he said he'd given her the same powers as he has. She could do anything she liked there; she could access the Forum's code, alter it if she wanted to, even lock *him* out. He really does trust her. The thought gives her a new trickle of energy and she searches thoroughly through the data. There have been no attempted intrusions, nothing untoward, not even a mistyped password today.

And you would have known if there had been, she thinks, *because your phone would have beeped at you, so you shouldn't get so worked up –*

Have you seen the boards yet? The chat box from Warden pops up just as she's finishing. She rubs her eyes, sighing. What crap has someone posted now?

No, she replies. **Just about to. What is it this time? Troubadour and Nexus threatening to hack and out each other again?**

No, he answers. **You need to look, Echo. You need to look now.** Mallory frowns.

Which thread?
You'll see.
Helpful as ever.

She minimizes the box and heads to the boards. There have been fifty-two new posts since she was last on.

What? That can't be right.

She looks down the list of bumped and new threads, and her stomach falls away. Warden is right; she does see what he means. She sees it right away.

'Where is The Asker?'

That's the title of one of the new threads. It has thirty-seven responses and counting.

No, Mallory thinks. *No, no...* Her eyes flick to the bottom right of the screen. The Asker's name is in the second list, below Scarlet's, written in the dull grey it has never worn before.

For the very first time, he is offline.

Offline

It takes Mallory a moment to process.

Offline.

She stares at the screen, feeling as if the oxygen has been sucked out her lungs. The Asker is never offline. **Do not disturb**, yes, but he is always connected, always there in case anyone needs anything. She finally manages to breathe, a sharp intake of air.

He doesn't go offline.

Except, that he is.

Except, he *is*, and he'd been following a 'lead', looking into Daedalus…

Just like Cyber Sneak.

Just like Scarlet, and…

No. Please, no, no, no… Stop it! Mallory tells herself. *Just fricking stop it.*

She doesn't know anything for sure. She clicks on the thread, looks at the time stamp. It was Jericho who posted first, at eight fifty-one – while she was watching the game. Eight fifty-one means The Asker logged out two hours and four minutes ago.

That's all, Mallory thinks, *just two hours.*

Her mind starts whipping through numerous possibilities to explain the absence, each worse than the last. He'd said there was a location hack he'd wanted to do. That was why he'd needed her help and…

Oh shit, oh shit…

Why did she say no? Why the hell did she say no? Why didn't she help? She tries to tell herself she had good reasons, but what if he got caught by security or the police, or something else happened *because* she hadn't?

Get a grip! She closes her eyes, steadying her breathing. *Just calm the hell down.* The Asker could just be offline in order to follow that very same lead. If it was a location specific hack, maybe he didn't have access to a secure connection there. Maybe... *He'd have told me.* The words creep like ice inside her mind. *He'd have told me if he was going offline...* But maybe he didn't know he wouldn't have access there. So many things can go wrong on a location hack. You'd have to improvise, wouldn't be able to plan for everything... *Damn it.* She really hates not knowing. There are so many variables that she isn't even sure where to begin. She opens her eyes again. *You have to work it out then.*

The Asker trusted her. Something like this is exactly where she needs to not let him down. The chat box with Warden is flashing like crazy, but she leaves it for the moment, eyes scanning down the thread, reading every single post. There are lots of questions, no answers. Most people are just wondering why The Asker is logged off – though a few sound a little nervous. A couple have mentioned Scarlet, and some, especially some of the later ones, are addressed directly to Mallory, to Echo Six. As the Forum's other moderator, they're asking what she knows. She clicks out of the thread. Later; she'll deal with that later. The chat box from Warden is still flashing away, five new messages now. He never was very good at waiting.

Do you know what's going on?

I've never seen The Asker gone before.

This isn't good, Echo. It's not good.

Don't fob me off. I know something's been weird these last couple of weeks.

Please sodding answer!

Mallory hesitates. She wants to tell him, but The Asker told her explicitly not to get anyone else involved. Does that still apply now the person who's disappeared is him? Her stomach twists.

You don't know *he's missing,* she tells herself. She needs to think. She needs to... Warden messages her again.

I need to check a few things, she replies. *Just shut it a moment.* Which, of course, he doesn't. If anything, it makes him message her all the more. She tunes it out.

Think, think, think...

Whatever's going on, there's not much she can do to help The Asker directly right now, all she can do is what he asked her to; keep the Forum safe. With him unaccounted for and knowing all that he does, the first thing she should check is security, watch for any attempted intrusion in case their secrecy has been compromised. She goes into the administration panel, pushing aside the prickle of fear that that thought brings, and searches the system logs. She looks through all the logins and log outs, scans every piece of data from around the time The Asker went offline. Then she moves on to the activity from afterwards, then from that afternoon, from that morning. She checks everything. Then she double checks it. There is nothing; nothing strange or odd or that would cause alarm.

That's good, she tells herself. *It's good.*

She wishes she'd had the courage to talk to The Asker earlier today. Maybe then she'd know something. She locks her jaw, then she looks through his account's activity for the past few days; nothing untoward again. He'd even posted two more hack requests just last night. He wouldn't have done that if something was badly wrong then. She looks at the clock; two hours, thirty-seven minutes now.

Not that long, yet, not really, she thinks… *But The Asker doesn't go offline.*

It can't just be a coincidence, not with everything that's happened, but the question is why. Was it something he'd planned or intended… or was it something else?

He'd have told me if it was planned. He'd have told me.

Is it like Scarlet?

Is he going to come back?

Please come back…

Other people are chat messaging her now, people who normally don't try because they know she won't respond. Warden's box is flashing away too. She tries to settle her thoughts; they are running away with her and it's not helping. She needs to order them. And she has to say something. She clicks out of the panel and back into the message boards, back into the new thread. The Asker didn't want other people to know what was going on, didn't want them looking into it.

She has to stop this before it goes any further.

What would Echo Six say? she thinks, because it doesn't come naturally right then like it should. It would be blunt and simple, no room for argument. She starts typing.

The Asker has something he needs to deal with in real life, Mallory writes, **and, no, I'm not going to tell you what it is, so don't ask. He'll pass on any updates through me till he's back. All hacks are suspended until then. Scarlet's still sick; simple as that.** Then she adds, **If anyone shits around while either of them are gone, I WILL come after you. Same rules apply that always have. Don't fucking push me.**

It won't hold things forever, but it will buy some time.

For what? Mallory asks herself. It's not even been three hours. The Asker could come back... *Please...*

Another new message flashes for attention from Warden. This time she clicks on it.

Echo, he asks, **what's really going on?** He hasn't bought it, but then she never quite expected *him* to. She wavers only a second.

I don't know why The Asker's offline, she says. **It's possible that he's missing** – her anxiety flares again as she writes it – **and he's not the only one.** She sends it before she can really let herself think about it. She sends it because in that moment she needs him to know, because she is grasping and he is what she has to grasp on to.

She tells him everything.

He asks a lot of questions, curses a bit, talks a lot, then finally says, **What are you going to do?**

I don't know, she admits, hopelessness surfacing.

This is bloody messed up, Warden replies. **Maybe we should, I don't know, call the police or something?**

Mallory's heart lurches.

Call them? she responds. **Are you fricking high? And tell them what? The founder of our secret grey-hat hacker group hasn't logged in for a few hours and we're worried? Besides, all we have is speculation. Even about the others. We don't even know that any of them are actually linked. In reality, we don't know anything. I don't know anything!** Her fingers slam against the keys in a burst of frustration. She just feels so tense. She feels so damn tense…

Okay, Echo, Warden responds. *Okay.*

It's not okay. It's a pointless statement, but she says it anyway. The Forum is their escape, their refuge, the place where they all fit. Though she's known intellectually that what they were doing there wasn't exactly safe, it's never *felt* at risk before. It was the set thing, like it was something that had always existed and always would. She takes a deliberately slow breath. *All we can do is wait.*

And I hate it, I hate it, I hate it…

Right now, she continues, *that's all there is. If he's not on by tomorrow…*

An idea stirs.

Mallory stops. It's an idea she really, really doesn't like the sound of, so she pushes it away and she doesn't even write it down.

If he's not on by tomorrow night… She looks down at the words. If it's not just a temporary absence, explained by the location hack, or any number of ordinary, okay things…

She doesn't want to think about it…

She doesn't want to…

We just have to wait, she repeats, and she makes a decision. Twenty-four hours. She'll give him twenty-four hours to come back. Then, she'll go looking.

Trail

'So that one's the adverb then?' Jed asks. Mallory places the potato she's peeling into the pan and walks over. She glances down at the workbook in front of him on the table.

'That's right,' she says. He's finally got it. He smiles and it breaks through some of her nervousness. 'You got this. Next set?'

He looks down at the page again, forehead creasing as he concentrates. He tries so hard.

That's good, Mallory thinks. *It's good.*

She turns back to the cooking; potato and bean pot pie today, page nineteen. She tries to focus on the chopping and the measuring and the simmering, letting the rhythm and detail of it fill her mind instead of all the worries that have been swirling around since last night. She had stayed up way past midnight, hoping and hoping, and then she'd logged in again early before school, but The Asker hadn't come back online. Neither had Scarlet – although she wasn't really expecting that any more. It made her antsy to consider it but, just to be thorough, she'd also checked local NYC news sites for stories of arrests. Thankfully, nothing had remotely matched. By the time she'd checked the Forum again after school, before her shift, most members seemed to have accepted the explanations in her post – or they were too afraid of Echo Six to argue. Either is fine, for now. Warden seems to have taken it upon himself to personally berate anyone who has even vaguely challenged her. She's glad she told him. They had talked for a long while afterwards – gone through options, shot down most of the ridiculous theories fizzing round in her brain – and it had helped to calm her a little. He seems to be increasingly good at that.

She glances at the clock – five past eight; twenty-three hours, fourteen minutes since The Asker went offline. The idea she had yesterday flutters up again. Warden won't be happy about what she's planning on doing… but then, there's not exactly anything he could do to stop her. As it is, they just don't know enough. They're sitting blind. It makes her want to hit something. Very hard. She throws the next potato into the pan. It's not like she wants to do it. She's fully aware of the repercussions, and there's a flicker of fear beyond just her Forum concerns, a fear she tries to quash because it asks what she could really be getting herself into by doing this… but it's for The Asker, and if he isn't on by the time she logs back in later, she can't hesitate.

* * *

You're going to do **what?** Warden writes. She can almost hear the shocked tone of his voice.

I'm going to hack The Asker, Mallory repeats.

But you can't, Echo.

I can't?

No, Warden replies, *I don't mean you can't as in you're not able to – please DO NOT take that as a challenge; let's put it this way, you're the person I'd least like to attempt hacking me – but if you're wrong about all of this and he comes back…*

Mallory's insides knot. You try to hack another member and you're out, no exceptions. It's only happened twice in the whole time she's been in the Forum. The last time, she was actually the target; a newbie called Igor had tried to hack her account back at the start of term. He hadn't got very far before Mallory had stopped him and counter-traced – some kid out in Pennsylvania misguidedly attempting to gain a shed-load of prestige by breaking Echo Six – but The Asker had been furious when she'd told him. He'd apologized to her, over and over – he usually vetted newbies so well, watching them for months before he left them that first trail in. Igor had been permanently banned with a warning that his true identity, along with enough evidence of his illegal hacks to send him to jail, would be leaked on the internet if he ever revealed the Forum's existence. The login trail was reset too, so he could never find it again.

Would it be the same for me? Mallory wonders. Surely it wouldn't, not if she did it *for* The Asker, not if it was because she was worried about him. He'd given her control of the Forum, after all, had asked for her help in person. *He wouldn't throw me out,* she thinks. *He wouldn't...*

She's not sure, though. If she's honest, she's not completely sure. You don't hack another member. It's their first and most important rule. If she attempts to hack The Asker, even for a good reason... But then, if she's right about something being wrong, what does it matter what the rules or punishments are?

Whatever happened to Cyber Sneak, she replies, **whether she went off the grid by her own design or... or because of something else, she's been gone well over three weeks.** Mallory doesn't have The Asker's connections, but she's been checking various grey and black-hat forums to see what she can find out about the first three missing hackers – not much, other than that they don't seem to have resurfaced and more people are starting to notice their absences now. **What if The Asker never comes back?** she goes on, this hideous dread of it rushing over her even as she types it. **What does it matter if I'd get kicked out, if he isn't even here anyway? There is no Forum without him, Warden.** He finds the hacks, finds the new members, gives what they can all do purpose. **None of this means anything without him!**

And there it is, out in the open, the selfish fear underlying everything else. If she loses The Asker, she loses the one thing that is her escape. It would be like falling with nothing to hold on to, and it wouldn't just be losing him; she'd lose all of it, lose this whole half of her life that feels just as real as the part outside her room. She'd lose the Forum, lose Echo, lose Warden himself – *can't he see that?* He goes quiet for a long while.

So, he finally answers, **say you do it, and you get his last login location – which is probably all you'll get, if you manage it at all, again, NOT a challenge – what are you going to do with it? From the things you've said before, I assume you're somewhere in the US – well, what if the trace leads to Hong Kong, or Delhi, or London?** She doesn't think it will, though, she thinks it'll be New York City, where The Asker had asked her to meet him. *And, you know what*, Warden continues, *say you even do get there, what can you do? It's like you said with the police, you can't exactly waltz up and say, 'Hello, my secret hacker friend went missing a couple of days ago. I don't know his name or what he looks like, but have you seen him?'*

Mallory's jaw clenches in frustration. Her finger taps against the desk.

Of course I wouldn't, she writes, almost hitting the keys because he's right, isn't he? He's right and she knows that and she's thought about it too, of course she has, but she doesn't have another option. *So we should just leave him?* she asks. *Hope he reappears?* Scarlet may have flitted off to goodness knows where without telling anyone, but The Asker wouldn't. He spent four years building up the Forum. It means too much to him.

No, Warden answers. *I mean, I don't know.*

Well, that's great, very helpful. You don't know if we should leave him?

No, he repeats, *of course I don't mean that, it's just…*

Just what? Mallory asks, when he stops typing.

Just that you'd be risking a sodding lot for someone you've never met, he responds. *I care about him too, but people have disappeared, Echo. Real people. Cyber Sneak, Weevil, Tower, Queen Scarlet – there's a real person behind every one of those names and we have no idea what's happened to them. This isn't some online hack or game you can just outsmart because you're cleverer than everyone else.*

Mallory's cheeks flush, but it stops her cold. It full well stops her cold, because he's right there too, though she tries not to let herself feel it, tries not to feel what those sentences really mean, what they imply. They've been using this word *disappear*, but skirting around voicing what it could mean for the missing hacker themselves, skirting it because there is one very important distinction they don't know; was it their choice, whatever the reason – or did something happen *to* them? Mallory bites hard on her lip.

Four, three, four, two.

Four, three, four, two.

But it's The Asker, she types, like that's an answer, because even in spite of all that, she can't let him go. The Forum saved her. *He* saved her, when she was at the lowest point she had ever been. He believed in her, gave her back control when her life was spiraling. She has to know that he's all right.

Exactly, replies Warden, **and whatever is going on, he couldn't avoid getting caught up in it – The Asker, Echo. Whatever safeguards he put in place looking into this stuff, they weren't enough. What if**, he pauses, **what if Echo Six is the next name to disappear?**

The fears she's been trying to push down blossom again. She swallows, then she re-reads, trying to stay calm… and something else hits her.

You're worried about me, she writes, of all the things she could write.

Of course I'm bloody worried about you! Her skin seems to tingle, almost like when someone's close, though she's still alone in her room. **Say you disappear next, who's going to have to come looking for you? Me. Bloody I would have to.**

Mallory stares at the words, feeling all kinds of strange.

You wouldn't just leave it? she asks.

He doesn't answer for several seconds, then, **You won't leave The Asker.** Mallory swallows again, and she knows – she *knows* – she wouldn't be able to leave Warden either. She wouldn't, not if she didn't know the why of it, and she'd hate it even if she did. She'd do whatever it took to find him, to make sure he was okay… but she doesn't say that. Just realizing it makes her feel oddly vulnerable in a way she never normally does with him. Her fingers seem tied.

You wouldn't be able to hack me, she writes instead.

Maybe not, but I could bloody well try. Then, after another pause, **Echo, this is going too fast. We need to cool it down; it's all just going too fast. Look, you said yourself you don't even know if why he's gone is related to the others. I'm not saying we leave him, I just think you shouldn't rush into anything you might not be able to back out of.**

A wave of exhaustion seems to hit her then. She's been running on adrenaline and too much caffeine too long. The fight falls away and she says something she would never usually say.

What do you want me to do? she says. ***I don't know what to do, so tell me.***

Would you wait one more day? he asks. ***See if he comes back. Give yourself one more chance to avoid getting mixed up in whatever this is?***

One more day, she says, ***and then?***

Then you try and hack him, and I'll do whatever I can to help, even join in shoveling duty when whatever shit it throws up hits the fan.

She tries to make herself think what The Asker would do. He cared about the Forum, but he also cared about its members, about ensuring they were safe – it wasn't just what he'd said to Mallory and Scarlet about that, you could see it in his posts, in the way he interacted with newbies, always trying to build them up and bring them on. Each member mattered. Even if there is a reasonable, non-sinister explanation for why he is away, the protection of those people has fallen to Mallory now.

What would The Asker do?

The Asker is careful. The Asker doesn't take risks. So, Mallory can't take any, not now.

Okay, she tells Warden. ***I'll wait one more day.*** But there *is* something else she needs to do in the meantime.

What would The Asker do?

No, she thinks, *what did The Asker do?*

She looks down at the bottom right corner of the screen, where the name Queen Scarlet is still written in grey above The Asker's. He'd made Mallory an administrator, said there was no one he would trust more to protect the Forum. That means he trusts her instincts.

Just fricking do it, she tells herself – and then she does to his account what he did to Scarlet's. She downgrades him from an administrator and shuts off his access to the message boards. She resets the login trail again – maybe people will ask questions about that, but it's necessary. This is what he would do. Any account you have a doubt about, you have to shut it off. If anyone ever found the Forum who shouldn't, the repercussions… Now, if he comes back, he can message her, and her alone – and she can reinstate everything. She also adds both The

Asker's and Scarlet's accounts to her notification settings, so she will be emailed immediately if she gets a message from either of them.

It's all fixable, she tells herself. She still feels hollow. She clicks out of the administration panel and back into the message boards. *It's fixable*, she repeats.

* * *

Another day passes, going both slower and faster than Mallory wants it to. She had stayed up late again, then repeated her early Forum check before school. The Asker's still gone and her apprehension has been building steadily throughout the day. She logs in straight after she and Jed get home, her brother starting on his math without her, though she doesn't feel good about that. With the second login reset, one or two members on the boards are getting a little more agitated about The Asker's absence, but Warden has been keeping up his crusade against anyone who argues with her.

Of course I'm bloody worried about you.

That's what he had said, and the words have been bouncing round in her head a great deal since. She kept finding herself thinking about them through school, wondering if he was wondering about her too, wherever he was, wondering if he was *right* to be worried…

She logs out, and then goes through the motions of the afternoon, churning out an English essay on Emily Brontë and filling in a bio question sheet, before checking Jed hasn't gone too far out on his math. He hasn't and she feels a glow of pride for him. Afterwards, they cook pesto chicken pasta together – page eighty-two – Jed carefully chopping the onions so she doesn't have to touch them.

And all the while the clock ticks on and she wonders… She wonders… And her nerves grow and grow till she can hardly swallow her food, though it doesn't taste half bad…

And then she's there, online again, and it's been another twenty-four hours and The Asker's name is still written in that foreboding grey.

I'm doing it then, Mallory tells Warden, her heart beating all fidgety.

I know, he replies.

It's been two days.

I know.

I can't leave him. She should have helped when he'd asked, but she didn't, and now this is all she can do.

I know, Echo, Warden says. *I'll help, if you need it.* Mallory feels the tingle again, running across her arms. *Not saying that you'll need it,* he adds quickly. *It's just, it is The Asker.*

Thank you, she writes. *I'll let you know.* She minimizes the chat box.

Just calm yourself down, okay, she thinks. But it's hard, because whatever happens, wherever The Asker is, what she's about to do will change everything. She taps the pattern once, slowly, carefully.

Four, three, four, two.

Then she begins.

She heads into the admin panel and starts searching through the system logs, pinpointing the exact time of The Asker's last login. When she tries to look further, though, to locate details of the device used or the IP address, she hits a wall; an error message. She tries a few different things, all of which fail. The Asker had really meant it when he'd said about safeguarding their real identities – even from administrators of the system. He's probably got his own additional security set up on top of it as well, just like she has. Even with her account's new access privileges, this is going to be a challenge. She presses her fingertips against each other, feeling a little rush that isn't down to nerves or worry. Despite everything, something like this is what she's been yearning for.

She starts trying to crack her way in. It's complicated and clever. Scarlet had been dead right when she'd said The Asker was paranoid. Regular status-requesting interruptions from Warden don't exactly help – he really doesn't know the meaning of the words *I'll be quiet now*, even when he's said them – but Mallory finds herself relaxing as she does it; her shoulders, her neck, her whole body loosening from where it's been screwing itself up into since everything started to go so wrong… This, this is good, it *feels* good. She is finally doing something, facing something she understands and can solve, instead of sitting and waiting. Her room fades away around her as she disappears into the characters on the screen. And it feels right and ordered and comprehensible... And, strangely, calm.

It takes a long time but, eventually, she breaks through, manages to find her way past the twists and turns to what she is looking for; an IP address. Her hands pause on the keypad. A rush of triumph trickles down from her neck to her gloved fingers. The address might not tell her exactly where The Asker was when he disconnected, but it should give her the general geographical area. She actually smiles, then runs the numbers through an online IP search. A location appears on the screen.

The smile falters.

It is in New York City, just like she'd expected; an area of Port Morris on the southern edge of the Bronx. There's a fresh sting of guilt. *Did someone discover him doing the very hack he'd asked her for help with?* She types the location into Google Maps, setting it to the satellite image. It looks mainly industrial, like warehouses or factories, all nestled along the bank of the East River.

Crap.

There's nowhere obvious that The Asker might have been; why would there be a hi-tech secure network – somehow connected with Scarlet and Daedalus – just for a bunch of derelict-looking buildings? She zooms in as far as she can, scanning any labels that appear, but there's nothing, just street names and...

Her breath catches.

One of the buildings is labelled *Labyrinth*. In Greek mythology, the Labyrinth was a maze built by the original Daedalus. Sure, the name has since also been used in a whole load of movies and books and media, and she could be massively extrapolating a connection... but still. Mallory clicks on the link. It's a nightclub, built inside a converted warehouse complex. Not exactly a smoking gun, but better. At least it's a place where people generally go.

And the name...

She starts running background on the place. Nothing pops out, other than some seriously bad taste in décor and a penchant for alarmingly heavy techno music. The club was given its name by its current owner of three years, Evan Seable, who made his money on Wall Street and now seems to be having some sort of midlife crisis. From recent photographs, he actually wouldn't look too out of place in the eighties *Labyrinth* movie. Somehow connected to the disappearance of five of cyber space's most elite hackers, though? Mallory finds nothing linking either him or the club back to the more recent Daedalus.

If there *was* a closed network The Asker wanted to hack, the club's security feed would be the most likely target in that area, but it still doesn't feel right. When he'd said a location hack, she'd expected some big corporation or something… But then, if this *was* the lead The Asker had been following to find Scarlet, and she'd been following Daedalus the hacker… well, a seedy-looking nightclub in New York would sound about right. Jeffrey Mullins was from the Bronx, after all, though no way near Port Morris…

If, if, if.

More questions again.

She clicks back to the map. She's zoomed in so far she can see streets, cars, tiny people even. It's strange thinking that's where he was – the actual person who is The Asker – that's where he was last logged in. She could drive it in under two hours, go look around. She shivers. It's so very real, seeing it like that, thinking that. She takes a slow breath and notes down the coordinates. Then she checks through the Forum data again for any other connection details, but there is nothing there for The Asker, nothing apart from his last log off. She can't even find the type of device he was using. The history is clean. The Asker probably wiped it as he went. In which case, Mallory realizes with a chill, the only reason there's one traceable position at all is that he was interrupted mid-session.

She backs out of the system logs and runs her usual checks. There are no traces running, no alarms she can find, though. The fact he hasn't tried to stop her… She closes her eyes.

You don't know anything for sure.

All she has is one single clue. She looks down at the address scrawled on her notepad. The last place that The Asker was The Asker.

Best Laid Plans

You want to go there, don't you, says Warden. It's not a question. Mallory has told him what she found from The Asker's account. She didn't give the details, just that it had led to an area of NYC, probably a club. Her stomach flutters.

Warden's wrong.

She doesn't *want* to go there. She wants to stay in her room with the door locked and the curtains shut, but the location is the only lead they have on The Asker. Mallory had hacked Scarlet's account too, after she'd hacked his – she'd done one, she might as well do both – but it had been completely wiped clean. Whether Scarlet had done that herself before she left, or The Asker had done it later to protect her, she doesn't know, but it means she has no other options left to find them electronically. If Labyrinth was where The Asker was when he logged off then maybe, just maybe, the security footage could tell them why. The place will likely be crawling with CCTV cameras and, with access to its archived footage, Mallory could search for someone actively using a phone or tablet or laptop at the same time he was – someone perhaps interrupted at that exact moment. *Something* happened in that club that caused him to log off for the first time in four years. She just needs to find out what.

But there's no way to reach the footage remotely. The club runs a closed network. She'd have to be there to do it; a location hack.

She starts tapping on the desk.

I have to go, she replies. *I need to tap into the security feed and it'll have to be on site.*

I can't convince you this is a bad idea, can I? says Warden. *I mean I could tell you that it could be dangerous, that you have no idea what you're walking into, or even if it will be of any use at all, but I don't think you'll listen.*

Mallory taps faster. Does he think she doesn't know all these things? It doesn't help him saying that, it doesn't damn well help, because they have nothing else and she can't contemplate that being it…

I'll leave my 'I'm a hacker' T-shirt at home, she replies. *It'll be fine as long as I don't go round shouting, 'Hey, everybody, I'm Echo bloody Six.' I'll just be some girl no one will see.*

Okay then, he answers, surprising her. She had expected more argument than that. *But I'm coming too*, he adds. Mallory's heart seems to skip a few beats.

No, she replies, almost automatically.

YES, Warden answers. *Two things. One; believe it or not, I care about The Asker just as much as you do. This Forum kind of changed my life and if he's in trouble I want in with helping him out of it. Two; you don't seem to grasp how serious this is and I really don't trust you not to do something stupid.*

Mallory stares at the words.

I get that it's serious, she replies. *That's why I'm going.*

And that's why I'm going too, he answers. Mallory starts typing another response, this one ruder, but Warden's addition appears before she can post hers. *If you go and then you disappear, I told you, I'll have to come looking for you anyway, so we might as well just get it over with together.*

That tingling feeling floods through her again. She tries to shrug it off, but part of her wants to say yes, wants to go into this with him and not alone – it really fricking does – and that, in itself, is unnerving. She doesn't want to go to the club at all, but if she can go with Warden, who's smart and who understands and who she… who she trusts? But the idea terrifies her, too. Not just the logical, sensible caution against taking that huge risk to meet someone from the internet, but also just a very human fear of having the actual person who is Warden standing right in front of her, having him see her as she actually is, with no screen between them and…

Damn it.

She had turned down The Asker because he wanted to meet in person. It's something she told herself she would never do. She doesn't know who Warden is, not really, no matter how much she feels like she does. That's the thing with the Forum; no faces, no accountability, and she likes that about it – but it also means you can't verify anything. That doesn't make a difference when the only place you interact is online and who you are *there* is what's important. But it matters in person. Mallory doesn't like to entertain the idea that Warden has ever really lied to her seriously, but he could have. He *could* have, and she shouldn't forget that, no matter how much she recoils from it. All the things she thinks she knows about him could be false and…

Crap, crap, crap…

She doesn't know what to do again. She's had enough of feeling that way.

I can help, Warden adds. **Point number three. Maybe that should have been number one. I should have started with that. Hacking security on site, downloading a shedload of files** on site, all that has risk to it. But it's actually something I know a bit about. I may not see code the way you do, but with this, I think I can help. I've got an idea.

An idea? Mallory pauses. *Just write something,* she tells herself. *At least ask him what it is. Write something!*

But she doesn't. She feels frozen.

Are you freaking out? Warden asks. He really doesn't know when to stop talking. Maybe he just can't. Maybe that's how he copes with things. Maybe in the same way she can't get a word out now, he can't make himself stop. **Is that why you're not saying anything? Hey, I've got no confirmation you're not a serial killer either, and you are definitely the more volatile of the two of us online. I'm still offering to do this, though.** He's getting worked up, she can tell. The words are coming faster and faster. **I told you before that you can trust me. I don't know what else to say other than I meant it, Echo. I bloody well meant it. Please don't do this by yourself.**

And that's what it comes down to.

Does she go to the city alone, a place she's only been twice in her whole life, or does she believe him, *let* herself trust him? Her skin tingles again. She wishes it would stop. There is worry in his words. She can see it as she rereads them. She didn't trust The Asker – that was the choice she made before, and now he's… now he's… she doesn't damn well know, does she? What she does know is that if she could change it, she would.

Your idea, she says finally. **What is it?**

* * *

It's Friday afternoon, and two days have passed since Mallory found out about the nightclub and told Warden. She's been twitchy all through school, more so than usual. Mr Cartwright even sent her out of English for ten minutes because she couldn't keep still. She didn't mind – they were still doing Emily Brontë, and pretty much all the characters in *Wuthering Heights* were dicks who deserved what they got. Plus she's had it with Mr Cartwright claiming he *knows* what Emily thought, when there's not a way he could. Her head is too full to concentrate anyway. In every class, she's been thinking about what's happening later, what they're going to do…

She and Warden had spent yesterday evening researching all they could on Daedalus. They were still wary of The Asker's warning about looking into it, so they went carefully, but given what they are planning, the possible danger had seemed fairly insignificant. They had split up the task to save time; Warden examining Daedalus's life, and Mallory, The Reckoning and the events that had followed his death.

At first, she had found little she didn't already know. Jeffrey Mullins Jr had shot himself in his mother's North Bronx two-bed on October fifteenth, 2011, after being traced there by the FBI. Next Tuesday will be the second anniversary – but then that didn't feel too significant given that it was already four weeks since whatever was going on had started with the disappearance of Cyber Sneak. Daedalus had been dead by the time the Feds had found him but, before his suicide, he had released that stupid final video introducing The Reckoning and baiting other hackers to try and follow this final quest trail, to find his swansong 'super virus' and use it to 'change the world' – though no one seemed to be able to agree on what that actually meant in practice.

Mallory's next move had been to watch the video again herself, but nothing had stuck out. Like in all of his videos that she'd seen, it had featured a seriously freaky talking cartoon Minotaur – more mythology – with a capital letter delta seared into its chest. The delta looked like an isosceles triangle, with the right-hand line drawn thicker, and was the first letter of Daedalus's name in Ancient Greek. He used the symbol in everything he did. The voice the Minotaur spoke with had managed to drip with pretentiousness as it described The Reckoning, despite having been electronically altered, but no new angle had presented itself to Mallory on re-watching, nothing that she'd missed when she'd first watched it two years ago like everyone else. She had spent countless hours trying to follow Daedalus's last quest then – creepy Minotaur or not, it was impossible not to admire his abilities, and hard to ignore such a beckoning challenge when everyone in the hacker world seemed to be talking about it. The clues ultimately led nowhere, though. If The Reckoning was hidden online like Daedalus had claimed it was, *someone* would have found it by now, or at least some part of it – hence, why most adept hackers had long since stopped trying.

So why were all these extremely smart people looking for it again, and why now? That was what Mallory needed to find out, what she had looked into next, and The Asker had been right when he'd said that there were people who still followed Daedalus – although idolized was maybe a more accurate description. It was kind of disturbing. Mallory had found numerous online groups dedicated to him. They ranged from forums and chat rooms discussing his hacks and quests – complete with heated arguments over what was a 'genuine Daedalus' and what wasn't – to cybergangs with names like New Daedalus or the anarchic We Are the Reckoning (a.k.a. WAR). Warden's personal favorite had been the Children of Daedalus, because their acronym spelled out CoD – a point he'd seemed to find disproportionately amusing when she'd told him. The CoD were based in New York, but then so were a lot of the groups she'd traced. Daedalus's old stomping ground was a popular location. Nothing that came up had been especially useful, though. Yes, there were people still seeking after The Reckoning and, yes, several of them seemed to be in NYC, but Mallory hadn't found any overt threats against rival searchers. In all honesty, most of the groups seemed fairly harmless in that regard. Weird, yes – downright creepy, a few – but she and Warden were looking for something that could have compromised five of cyber space's most formidable hackers, causing them to disappear. None of the websites for the groups or gangs she had looked into had had security setups good enough for the programmers behind them to be of any real danger. In a way, it had backed up what she had always thought; that serious hackers didn't give The Reckoning much credence any more. The trouble was, there was also such an indecipherable mishmash of rumors that had sprung up since Daedalus's death that it was hard to be sure of anything.

Warden hadn't had much luck either. He'd reported that before going solo, Daedalus had first surfaced in 2003 as part of the Finders Reapers, a cybergang he'd co-founded with another hacker called Apollonian. The group ran anything from denial of service attacks, to stealing data, to repeatedly crashing the networks of various companies, causing enough havoc to get themselves officially branded as cyberterrorists. Mallory had vaguely recognized the group's name, but she hadn't known Daedalus was one of them – all of their activity had been long before she'd started hacking, coming to an abrupt end in July 2005 when six of the members, including Apollonian, were caught in an FBI sting. According to Warden, Daedalus had acrimoniously parted ways with them a few months before, and managed to evade it. None of the other Finders Reapers had given him up, claiming to not know his real name. More likely, he had enough dirt on each of them to send them away for longer if they snitched. Warden had looked into where the other Finders Reapers were now, wondering if they might somehow be involved in what was happening, but he'd met only dead ends. Some of them had never been caught, like Daedalus, but none of their monikers had been heard of since the arrest of the others. Of the members Warden did find real names for – and could track down – most had now gone straight, working legally as white-hat programmers or internet security experts. Or they'd got out of the internet game entirely. More than that, it seemed their animosity towards Daedalus was well documented – they had publicly washed their hands of him – so, it's unlikely any of them would care for completing his legacy.

Mallory felt like she knew a little more about the background to whatever was going on after they'd shared what they'd found – but that was all it was, background. Nothing either she or Warden had discovered had told them any more about why hackers might be going missing now, and nothing really seemed like it would help with what they were going to do later. It hasn't stopped her obsessing over every detail all through school, though, nerves growing and growing as it nears the final bell…

On Wednesday night, she had told Warden yes. His idea for hacking Labyrinth's security system had been a good one – safer than what she'd been planning – and so she had gone for it. It needed both of them to work, so she'd told him where the club was and they'd arranged where and when they were going to meet; nine blocks west of the warehouse, eight thirty tonight. They'd decided to wait an extra day until the weekend, Warden suggesting Labyrinth would be busier on a Friday, easier to blend in to. Mallory's been trying not to think about what it will actually be like with all those people inside… She's so tense by the time school does end that her jaw is aching from how much she's been clenching it. There are no message notifications on her phone. As she was really expecting, The Asker hasn't come back, and neither has Scarlet. That means the plan will be going ahead.

Roger had taken the car for an early shift that morning, so Mallory and Jed have to ride the bus home. She can tell her brother knows something's up, but he doesn't say anything till they get in the house. She's gone back and forth over what to tell him. She can't tell him nothing because, actually, she needs his help. She wants to trust Warden like he'd said she could, but with everything that's been going on, she's not going to take any more risks than she has to. She looks down at Jed. No, she's got to be careful.

'A friend of mine is having some trouble,' she says, after he finally asks her what's wrong, 'and I need to go out tonight and give them a hand.' His brow furrows, maybe because she's never exactly had a lot of friends.

'Okay,' he says, though.

'I need you to do something for me too,' she continues. 'It's important.'

''Course, Mal,' he nods. 'What is it?'

'Give me your phone,' she says. He takes out his cell, the screen scratched from where he dropped it on the gravel out front a while back. She flicks through his menus, sliding across to a new page, blank apart from one app; a new app she'd added to it last night. She shows him. 'You see that,' she says, tapping the icon and opening it up, 'it's a tracking program. I put it on there for you.' Jed glances up at her, light brown eyes going a little wider. There's a GPS map and a button saying on or off. It's switched to off right now. 'Watch,' Mallory says, and she taps the button. After a few seconds, a red arrow appears in the center of the map and starts zooming in. The screen stops moving, now showing only Watertown, Connecticut. The little arrow is pointed right at their street in Oakville. Jed looks up at her again.

'A tracker to our house?'

'More specifically, me,' she answers. 'My phone.' She takes it out her pocket. 'Now your phone can find my phone if it gets lost.' She turns the app off and hands Jed's cell back to him. It stays sat in his palm. His lips purse.

'Where are you going, Mal?' he asks.

'To New York. To help a friend, like I said.'

'What kind of trouble are they in?'

'Nothing bad.'

'Is it dangerous?' His eyes hold hers, searching, and she feels a tug of nerves. She taps the pattern on her leg.

'No,' she says firmly. 'But look, you've got this now, and the thing I need you to do…' She hesitates. 'It should be fine, but if I'm not back or haven't messaged you by the time you get up tomorrow… you'll know how I can be found if anyone needs to.'

Jed's eyes really do go wide then.

'Mallory – ' he says, voice rising in alarm.

'It'll be fine,' she says sharply, as much to herself as to him. It's just a precaution, only there because there are so many unknowns in this and it's stupid not to always have a back-up. She has a fairly tight window to get everything ready and drive in to the city to park. She doesn't have time for questions. 'Look, it'll be fine,' she repeats, 'I just need you to do this for me, okay? Trust me, Jed. Can you do that?'

'Mal – '

'Can you do that?'

There's a pause, then he nods.

'Thank you,' she says.

'Be careful.' His tone pulls at her.

'Of course.' She taps the pattern again. 'You don't turn that on unless you need to,' she says. 'That's important.' Jed nods again. 'Now, I gotta leave as soon as Roger gets back with the car, so I won't be able to get you dinner. You'll have to do a pizza again.'

'Okay, Mal.'

It's not good, him having pizza twice like this but, well, things are what they are. She heads through the kitchen and into the garage to get one out. As she does, her eyes fall on the boxes of Jeanie's stuff and she stops. She still remembers exactly what's in each of them. She looks down at the one to the left of the freezer – the one with all her work things, her uniforms, old patrol gear – and an idea pops into her head that she both likes and doesn't. They'll need to blend in at the club. She reaches out, hand wavering just a little bit, and opens the box.

Gilbert

Mallory is seated in a silver plastic chair by the front window of *Stevie's Space Age Diner*, looking out on the street corner where she's agreed to meet Warden later. Labyrinth is still several blocks away, just a few buildings out from the East River. She hadn't known about the space age theme when she'd looked up the diner online and decided to wait there. She'd picked the place because of its view of the street, but it must have had a refurbishment since they last updated their website. Apparently, 'Space Age' to Stevie means everything is painted in cheap silver and blue, with flashing fairy lights hung around rubber UFOs. Mallory's table is right next to the door, a perfectly-positioned spot she'd had to wait a quarter hour for, deliberately staring out the couple who were sitting there when she'd arrived until they left. She's been there nearly an hour now, just watching people go by and checking, checking, checking… She'd driven into the city as soon as Roger had got back at five. She looks at the time on her phone. Eight-oh-one. Twenty-nine minutes until Warden shows – or doesn't show. He'd confirmed he was coming last night, agreed everything again, but it's still possible he could get cold feet…

And then, what if he *does* come?

Other kinds of worries surface. For the first time, he will see her and not Echo Six, whatever idea that name conjures for him. Is she going to lose something by doing this? What if she isn't what he expects? What if it changes things too much? Are they giving up something important?

Four, three, four, two.

Four, three, four…

A sparkly-clad waiter with blue face paint and fake antennas comes over to refill her coffee for the third time. His gaze wanders down to her finger, beating out a positive tattoo against the table. She makes it stop, but the jitters continue flitting round inside of her.

She wants to run away.

She wants to stay.

She wants her mind to shut up a moment.

She drinks the coffee too quickly, eyes locked on the street corner. The minutes tick by and she stays watching. She hasn't seen anything strange during the past forty-four she's been sitting there, just lots of people. Lots and lots of people. It makes her skin prickle. No one's been loitering, though. She's scanned the area systematically, making a mental note of anyone who's stood in the same place for more than ten minutes. Apart from a guy flogging beanies and scarves from a stall, the only ones to hang around that long were a clearly tourist family of three, who really didn't know how to hail a cab. Mallory's nerves have spiked every time she's seen a boy around high school age pause and look around. Each time she's wondered if it could be *him*, and then the boy will have moved on or she'll have noticed he's already with friends.

She had refused to tell Warden what she looked like over the internet, and she'd stopped him before he could tell her. Maybe it was paranoid – she knows the chat was secure, she knows it – but still, she couldn't do it. They'll just have to go on what they've already figured out about each other, look for someone the right age and gender, who's clearly looking for someone else too… She stares out at the vast throng. Maybe it was damn stupid as well as paranoid. She'd forgotten how busy New York was, how fast everything moved compared to home. Still, like with The Asker, she's almost avoided imagining Warden's face before. To her, he is his name, lit up in a chat box, the constant stream of words that flow out from him, paragraph after paragraph of streaming babble that just appears – paragraph after paragraph that she always reads all of. He is the hacks he does, the neat little twists he thinks of. And that is how she feels comfortable with him. That, not this.

She swallows, and checks her phone again. Eight thirty-one. She starts, and looks out of the window with renewed intensity. It's beginning to drizzle. There really are a lot of people and they really are moving so very quick. She watches as they exit to the subway, watches as cabs pull up, but their inhabitants turn out to be older or female...

She watches and watches, but no one looks right...

It passes eight forty-five. More jitters begin to grow in her stomach, the ones asking what if he's not coming? What if she has to go to the club by herself? What if she's all The Asker has? What if...

She feels disappointed.

She feels it more intensely than she'd thought she would. She knew a no show was a possibility – she's thought of backing out herself a hundred times. She knew and yet still...

Another cab pulls up on the street. The back door opens and a teenage boy clambers out, awkwardly dragging a small, paisley-patterned wheelie suitcase with him instead of getting out first and then reaching back in for it afterwards. A green satchel is looped around his shoulder, just the right size for a laptop.

Mallory's heart skips.

He's medium build, not especially tall, and wearing a short-sleeved brown shirt, navy sweater vest and black cord pants. His hair is a short, dark and sandy blonde, growing darker as the rain dampens it. He pays the driver and then just stands like a lemon on the sidewalk, with suitcase and satchel, getting wetter and looking thoroughly lost.

It's him, Mallory thinks. She's not sure how she knows, but something about him just clicks. Her pulse is rising in a way that isn't just too much caffeine and her mouth seems to have gone dry. The urge to run away grows stronger, but she stays glued to her seat, watching.

Watching Warden...

It has to be...

He squints up into the rain, trying to both shield and partially unzip his suitcase as he pulls a parka out of the top. It takes him a further minute to navigate putting the coat on without letting his satchel fall on to the wet ground. It is only when his hood is up that he really starts looking around him. Mallory can see him taking in the passers-by, can see on his face that he is wondering where she is, if she's there yet, if *she* is who she said she was...

Warden, who is nothing more than he said he was...

He looks across at the diner.

And then he sees her, sees her watching him.

Their eyes meet through the glass and, for a moment, she can't really move. Then her finger starts tapping on the table again, even as she sees the question now in his eyes, eyes that don't move on from her like they did from everyone else.

This is it, she realizes, the last moment to back out. She could turn away. She could get up and leave.

She could…

She nods once, small.

His face breaks out into this smile. Mallory clenches her hand to a stop, pins and needles rippling all over. She stays watching him as he waits at the traffic lights, as he crosses the road, as he walks to the diner door, as he opens it, chiming the bell above and pulling down his hood…

As he stands in front of her.

Her mind seems to go both very blank and very noisy at the same time. His eyes are brown, like the shirt. There's a light sprinkling of freckles across his cheeks. Mallory feels herself standing too, not knowing what else to do, and her heart is beating so damn fast, and it takes her aback how strongly she's feeling it all…

'Echo?' he asks, sort of mouthing it like he's trying to be secretive, and her face flushes because it's him, it's really…

'Warden?' she replies. The word catches. Why is her mouth so dry? He nods, but… 'What was your first guess?' she asks, trying to stay calm, to keep control though it feels suddenly hard to speak at all, speaking to him with her actual voice and not just through the keys and…

'What?' he says.

'If you're really Warden,' she tells him, 'you'll know what that means.' Damn it, she wishes her heart would slow down a bit. He seems to fit, but this is important. She has to focus.

His forehead scrunches up into a frown, then, 'That E six was your favorite chess square,' he answers, 'identified using the phonetic alphabet.' He's right. It is really him. She nods, adrenaline fluttering irrationally inside of her. 'So, what does my name mean then?' he asks. 'You know, if you really are Echo.'

'Warden of the internet,' she replies, 'guardian of truth, upholder of all that is good; some cheesy crap like that. I got it on my second guess.'

'Yeah, you did.' And he's smiling again.

'Dorkiest thing I'd ever heard,' she says, her eyes never leaving his. This doesn't feel real. He's just looking at her and grinning this stupid goofy grin like he's really damn happy, his mouth hanging slightly open.

'Erm,' he stammers, as if remembering himself. 'Well, Echo, it's nice to meet you. Ward,' he adds, holding out his hand, 'Warden. I mean, Gilbert Ward. I'm Gilbert.'

His name, she realizes. *That's his real name. Crap, this is weird...* Then; *his surname's Ward?* Mallory raises an eyebrow. He actually used his real name in his pseudonym. *Wow.*

His face crinkles a little as he sees her disbelief.

'Yeah, I know,' he says, misinterpreting, 'Gilbert. I blame my mom for that one. She's got a thing for old names. Could have been worse, though, my big brothers are called Rex and Diggory, so...' He swallows, though he's still trying to hold the smile. There's something unusual about his accent, like he's British, but with some definite West Coast added in. Maybe she'd been right to wonder before about him spending time abroad. 'I prefer Gil,' he adds, 'but most people call me Bert, I think just to annoy me. My dad goes with Bertie, but... that's irrelevant. Right, well.' He swallows again, and Mallory feels the strangest sudden urge to smile back because he *sounds* like Warden.

His eyes drop, looking down at his offered hand, the one she still hasn't taken.

'Crap,' he says, 'sorry, the touch thing. I forgot you – ' He starts to lower it. She reaches out, though, jerkily, her gloved hand grasping his, surprising even herself. The material takes most of the contact, but the tips of her fingers touch his skin for the briefest of moments. His hand is warm, soft...

What are you doing?!

'Mallory Park,' she hears herself saying. She hadn't been sure, before, whether to tell him her real name or not, but there it is, out in the world in front of him. His smile returns, so utterly genuine, reaching right up to his eyes…

The door to the café swings open again, chiming the bell. Mallory starts and lets go of Warden's hand. The new entrant, a woman, almost trips over his suitcase.

'Bugger, sorry,' he says, pulling it away and tucking it under the table. The woman glares at him and walks past. 'Sorry,' he calls after her again, definitely sounding British that time. 'There sure are a lot of people here, aren't there?' he says, looking back at Mallory. 'The airport was packed, but I thought maybe out here the city might be better.' He sits down in the chair opposite her.

She sits, too. Beneath the table, she scrunches her right hand into a ball in her lap, fingers still tingling oddly from where they touched. Warden, right there, in front of her. No chat box. No screen. She doesn't say anything, just stares.

'Well, this is nice,' he says, starting to look a little uncomfortable.

No Echo to hide behind…

Nothing to hide behind…

She feels herself flush again…

'You're late,' she says, unable to think of anything else. His face falls slightly.

'Well, I had to pick up that… that *thing* we talked about,' he replies, bobbing his head covertly. 'And you said I needed a false ID. That took some doing. It's not like I just had one lying around.'

'Sure, you did,' Mallory tells him. 'Just like I did. I know you've been seeing new R-rated movies since way before you could have been seventeen and I'm fairly sure you didn't take your mom. It was definitely at the movie theatre you saw them, too, because you've told me several times that 'certain things like that have to be experienced a certain way.''

A small frown wrinkles Warden's forehead again.

'Okay,' he replies, 'so I left my wallet on the plane and had to go back for it and then security got funny about letting me through, even though I told them I really needed it. I mean, have you ever even tried…'

So this is Warden in real life, Mallory thinks. He's still talking. *Definitely, definitely Warden.* The corners of her mouth tease inextricably upwards again and he stops.

'What?' he asks, but the blue-faced waiter chooses that point to return with the coffee jug and an extra mug for Warden.

Warden who is sitting smack there in front of me…

'Oh, no thanks,' he says, 'gives me indigestion. Have you got any mint tea?'

'We got Little Green Martian Tea,' drawls the waiter.

'Is it really made of little green Martians?' Warden asks. 'I'm not sure that makes for good intergalactic relations.' The waiter stares at him, blanked-eyed.

'We got soda,' he says.

'Oh, no, I did want the tea…' Warden begins. He stops. 'Soda sounds perfect.' The waiter nods and wanders off.

Warden finally takes his coat off, then, though he still looks freezing. His skin is tanned but his cheeks have gone pale. Up close, the brown shirt is crisscrossed with narrow cream lines, dividing it into check. It's buttoned right to the top. His hair looks like it was once neatly combed, but is now ruffled and sticking right up at the back, maybe from the airplane seats.

'So you flew here?' Mallory asks.

'Yes,' he replies, 'landed at JFK an hour and a half ago.'

'Where are you from?'

'California. Sun City, to be precise. Although, originally England. That's why my voice is weird, if you're wondering. I'm half and half; my mom's from Guildford and I grew up there till I was twelve, then we moved to California, where my dad's from.'

That's why he's cold, then, she thinks, and she was right on the time zone. *He came a long way for this.* Her eyes flick down to the suitcase. *A long way.*

'You?' Warden asks.

'Connecticut,' she says. 'I drove down, parked in a garage up the street.' It's deliberately vague and she feels briefly bad about that. 'You did bring an ID then?'

Warden nods. He reaches into his pocket, pulling out a black wallet before slipping out a driver's license. The name reads 'Jacob Tyler' and the age puts him at twenty-one. Warden doesn't look anything near twenty-one, but the picture is his, hair there combed into a careful side parting. He's wearing a tie.

'I suppose that's what you should call me,' he says. 'Or maybe Jake,' he adds, 'you know, make it look like we've known each other a while.' He slips the wallet and ID back into his pocket. 'And you would be?'

'Abigail Smith,' she answers. 'Twenty-two.'

'Right, got it. *Abby*,' says Warden, grinning. Mallory doesn't respond, fighting the distinct urge to roll her eyes. His soda arrives. 'So,' he begins, expression becoming more serious as the waiter walks away, 'what now?' Her nerves spike again as she remembers what they're actually there for.

Focus, Mallory.

'I guess we start by just going in, looking around,' she answers. 'And then we see if we can...' She looks at him meaningfully. 'You brought the bug?'

'Yep,' he says, patting the satchel. That was his big idea – place a physical tap into Labyrinth's security feed so they could download the past week's footage later, off site. He was right, it is a much safer way of doing it, but Mallory didn't have access to a bug herself and she hasn't really looked into that physical side of hacking much. Warden had said he did, said he had.

'And you're sure it'll work?' she asks.

'I made it myself.' He says it like that's an encouragement. Mallory tenses.

'You *made* it?'

'Yes,' he replies, a little defensively.

'And you've tested it?'

He nods.

'Been tapping into the CCTV at my high school for the past three months. I'd found a hair in my macaroni one lunch time and I did not trust the cafeteria hygiene levels after that.'

'So you *bugged* it?' Mallory asks – though, it does sort of sound like something the Warden she knows would do.

'Yes. And I was right to, too.' He makes a face. 'I now know which dishes to avoid.'

'You're telling me,' Mallory responds, 'we're going to attempt to bug a New York nightclub with something you've only previously tested on your school cafeteria?'

'Well, no one found it in all the three months it was there,' he replies. Mallory gives him a look that she hopes reflects how little that reassures her. 'It'll stand up to a lot more than that,' he insists. 'No one will be able to trace it.'

'You're sure?'

'I'm sure.' He holds her gaze.

It's Warden. Warden knows what he's doing.

'Okay, then,' she agrees. 'So, I was thinking about possible ins. I hacked the club's blueprints from the Department of Buildings – '

''Course you did.' His smile is suddenly back like it hadn't ever gone and, even amongst all the anxious energy, Mallory feels that stupid urge to return it again. She bites her lip instead.

'I had a look,' she says, 'and, if it seems okay once we're there, I think there might be a way we can get you to their server with no one seeing...'

Into the Labyrinth

'I can't believe you're bringing a paisley suitcase to a nightclub,' Mallory says, as the wheels of Warden's bag clunk along the sidewalk beside her. She's found if she doesn't quite look at him it's easier to talk like she would online. It's almost nine thirty and they're walking the last block towards Labyrinth, the nightclub's lights flashing garishly further up the street. She can already hear the thud of the bass. A different, gnawing worry is beginning to grow in the pit of her stomach, biting sharply as she sees the queue of people lining up to get in. How many more will there be inside? She shifts her gloves, feeling the reassuring fabric against her skin.

'I came on a plane,' Warden replies. 'The flight was nearly six hours long and I had no idea what one I'd be getting back. I didn't even know how long I'd need to be staying, just that we needed to go to the place where you-know-who disappeared and put in the you-know-what.'

She should have thought of that before. She knew he was West Coast. Still…

'It'll stand out.' And when they know so little about what's going on, what they might be looking for, standing out is not a good thing.

'I'm sure they'll have a cloak room.'

They walk to the end of the queue in silence. Mallory subconsciously brushes her hair lower over her face, pulling Jeanie's black leather jacket tighter around her. She'd taken it from the box by the freezer in the garage before she left, and it had fitted exactly. Jeanie had used to wear it over her uniform on cold nights when she was on patrol. Mallory had brought it with her because judging by the club's website pictures, it mainly catered for techno-loving goths. She'd put heavy eye makeup on in the diner's restroom before they left. She doesn't usually wear it, hates the feel of it – sticky and thick whenever she moves her face – but it at least makes her look less like her usual self, like someone who might actually go here. Which is why the suitcase isn't so damn unhelpful.

'I feel like a wally,' Warden mutters. 'Sunglasses when it's not sunny.' She'd brought them for herself, but made him wear them for the same reason she's in makeup. 'I mean, who does that? I look like a – '

'Just shut the hell up,' Mallory snaps, nerves making it come out harder than it should. The girl in front of them glances behind her, studded eyebrow raised in obvious appraisal. Warden smiles uneasily.

'Hello,' he says. 'Nice evening.' The woman turns back without a word, and Mallory steps, quite deliberately, on his sneaker.

'What?' he mouths, scratching at his new black beanie hat, just purchased from the street seller outside the diner. He didn't like wearing it without it having been washed, but she had insisted, again; partly because he looked so damn cold, partly because sunglasses weren't enough to hide the fact he was wearing a sweater vest to a nightclub.

Oh crap.

They're going to stand out a mile. More people join the queue behind them and Mallory feels a sweep of nausea. She takes a deep breath.

'Are you all right?' Warden asks.

'Fine,' she says, making herself step closer to the club as the queue moves forward.

You're okay, she thinks.

'It's going to be okay,' he says beside her. He nods encouragingly, even though she just yelled at him, and she suddenly feels very glad to have him there, ridiculous suitcase and all.

It takes them ten minutes to reach the end of the queue. There are two bouncers on the door, both well over six foot and with arm muscles bigger than Warden's head.

'IDs,' one of them grunts. He's dressed in black, the word SECURITY written across the front of what Mallory realizes is a stab vest. His neck is completely covered in tattoos and a vicious looking spike is poking out of his chin. She tries not to stare at it as Warden hands over his card. The bouncer's brow furrows into hedgerows, like he doesn't quite believe the age. Warden lifts the sunglasses and smiles awkwardly, matching the picture. The smile falters as the bouncer's gaze bores into him, but then the man hands back the card and nods him past.

'Thank you, sir,' Warden says. 'Thank you.' Mallory squirms.

He's faster okaying her ID. Maybe the makeup makes her look older. The second bouncer is checking bags, already unzipping Warden's suitcase as he hovers beside it, looking like there's nothing he would want less than this man going through his things. The lid flips open, revealing the most painfully neat packing Mallory's ever seen. Even the underwear is folded. Unperturbed, the bouncer's clumsy hands rifle through the contents, dislodging the perfect lines.

'You're touching my underwear,' says Warden, appearing genuinely disturbed in a way that clearly shows *no one* touches his underwear. The bouncer gives him a *look*.

'Don't be a dick, *Jake*,' Mallory mutters, mirroring it.

The man hands back the suitcase, leaving Warden to zip it back up as he moves on to the satchel, and then Mallory's backpack. Finally, he waves them through, telling Warden he'll have to leave the suitcase in the cloakroom down the hall. They nod and hurry past, Warden somewhat reluctantly then depositing the case and parka in exchange for a cardboard tag. He keeps his satchel, though, and Mallory her backpack, and they carry on down the corridor.

'Did you see the way they looked at me?' Warden says. 'You could tell they thought I looked stupid. The sunglasses looked stupid.' He goes to take them off, but Mallory stops him, her hand stalling just before it touches his. He notices.

'Fricking keep them on.' She jerks her hand back, pulling up the hood of her jacket. The music they could hear from the street is getting oppressively louder the further they go. Her insides roil with apprehension.

You're okay, you're okay...

The walls look like they were once purple, but sections of the plaster have chipped away and the paint is now discolored with patches of mold and darker stains Mallory seriously tries to avoid, shrinking her arms in against her body. Her boots are sticking to the floor, peeling off with each step. They reach a pair of double doors at the end.

You're okay.

She pushes them open and steps through.

She freezes.

The assault on her senses is overwhelming. Labyrinth is huge, like the original main warehouse space has just been gutted, but it's already packed and heaving with dark-clad people, pierced faces everywhere. The room is filled with platforms on different levels and a huge balcony overhangs the bar on the distant back wall beyond a sea of dancing bodies. Everything is black and red, or silver metal. The lights are flashing like they're trying to give somebody a fit and the bass reverberates through Mallory's skull with each thudding pulse.

'Do *not* touch anything!' Warden yells beside her, voice several tones higher than before. 'We're going to get tetanus. That man had more tattoos than face!'

Mallory doesn't answer. There are so many people, so many... Someone knocks into her and she shudders with alarm, the touch sending rivulets of shock shooting through her. She tries to back away, but new people are pushing them further in. There are people *everywhere*.

' – all right?'

'What?' She looks back at Warden beside her. She can barely hear him above the noise. He sticks his thumbs up, face questioning. Mallory nods, forcing her feet to move further into the club. They have to keep going. She tries to concentrate, tries to remember what their plan was... but all she can think of is the people around her, so many – too many – and the pounding of her heart in her ears, almost as loud as the music, and far too fast...

'Maybe we should dance,' Warden shouts. He starts to sway in a way that is definitely not normal, bobbing his head with the music. 'You know, blend in!'

A cheer goes up behind them. Mallory turns to see another new group of revelers enter through the double doors, these a swathe of black and neon. There are eighteen of them, all piling onto the dance floor at the same time, and forcing her and Warden forwards in front of them. She stumbles, trying to get away. It feels like hands are touching her from all sides. The room starts to swim.

You're okay, you're okay, you're okay, she tells herself, but she knows this feeling, knows she is definitely not okay… *Get a grip!* she orders desperately. *Get a…*

But her eyes start to fuzz up and…

Oh shit.

'Abby?'

Where's the door? Where's the fucking door…

She tries to run one way, then another, but the room won't stop spinning.

No, no, no, not here…

She feels like she's going to be sick. She tries to slow her breathing, but the air is so fuggy, so full of sweat…

Oh shit! Shit! Shit!

'Abby?!'

She looks to the side. Warden is still there, his forehead now crinkled with concern.

Abby? Then, *The ID,* she remembers.

'I can't,' she stammers, feeling her body contract, and being utterly helpless to stop it.

What was she thinking? That she'd come here as Echo Six and somehow be able to do this? Somehow not be who she really damn is? She can't help The Asker… She can't do anything! She shouldn't have come… She can't…

She *can't!*

Someone smacks into her from behind, hard, and Mallory lurches violently towards the ground…

No, no!

She doesn't hit though. An arm catches her, pulling her back. For a single still moment, her face is buried against navy blue wool, still damp from the rain.

Warden smells like soap.

Her heart is thudding in her chest.

'Hey, watch it!' she hears him snap above her head, apparently confronting whoever knocked into her. She pulls away to see a massive guy in leathers glaring down at them – and Warden's expression quickly changes to reflect the realization that this is not a guy you should ever snap 'watch it' at. It's the man with more tattoos than face. 'Look – ' he begins.

Tattoos steps forward and Warden suddenly looks very, very small in comparison...

No. The single thought breaks through the panic in Mallory's mind and she grabs his arm before he can say anything else, yanking him away and plunging deeper into the crowd of dancing bodies.

Her head is screaming.

There are hands touching, hands reaching, people pressing up against her... It feels like her skin is crawling, *burning*... But she keeps pushing on, dragging Warden away until she physically can't any more, until her hand just lets go and her muscles have seized up so tight her legs won't step again.

'Abby?' she hears. 'Abby, are you okay?' Warden draws level. Thankfully, Tattoos is nowhere to be seen. Warden is watching her and she must look bad because he looks worried – really, really worried.

His face is so open, Mallory thinks. *So very open, just like when he talks and doesn't hold things back...* Her fight seems to disappear. She shakes her head. She's not okay. She doesn't want to be here. She wants to be back at home, in her room where it's quiet and safe and ordered...

He nods and looks around like he's trying to decide what to do. He reaches out, as if to take her hand. It's deliberately slow, but Mallory flinches, so taut she can't help it. She tries to say sorry, but it's lost in the noise and the tightness of her jaw. It feels like every single muscle is turning to stone. Her fists are clenched so hard that it hurts where her nails are digging in, even through her gloves, but she can't get them to release...

What is she doing here?

What the hell did she think she could do?

Don't cry, she tells herself, *don't...*

But there's no way out... There are too many people... There's no way...

Warden steps in front of her then, careful not to touch. He's speaking, but she can't really hear him or even see him properly. Everything feels blurred, her senses fried and overwhelmed.

'You can do this.' She catches it that time. 'Hey, Echo,' he says, using the name he really knows her as, though he shouldn't, he shouldn't... 'Look at me.' She finally does, away from the people seeming to crush in on them from all sides. 'You can do it,' he repeats. 'This way.' He starts walking backwards through the crowd, clearing a path for her. Dancers knock into him, but he keeps looking back at her. 'Come on.' He holds his arms out around her, still careful not to touch, but trying to stop others from getting near her – and something moves inside of her and, somehow, she follows. 'You're all right.' She can see the words, even though she can't always hear them. She stares at him, holding on to them, grasping... 'You can do this.' He says it over and over as she follows after him, as he shields her with his body until they make it to the other side of the dance floor. He heads quickly to an empty booth by the far wall, and they both break his suggested rule of not touching anything and sit down. Again, he leaves that careful space between them. The music is still loud there, but it's bearable, and the booth is dark and sheltered. Mallory curls up against the leather, shrinking back into her hood, trying not to shake. She closes her eyes.

She feels stupid.

She feels so damn stupid.

Don't cry, she tells herself again. *Don't you cry.* People go to night-clubs all the time and they don't freak out like idiots. She had known it would be crowded, had deliberately agreed to this time because of it, so they wouldn't stand out. She'd known it would be hard, but she'd thought she could control it, like at school. She'd thought...

She hasn't been this bad in a long time, even at what happened with Bobby. She'd nearly passed out.

If Warden hadn't been there...

She opens her eyes and looks over at him. His hands are clasped tightly over the satchel now on his lap like he really doesn't trust the floor.

'Would you like a sick bag?' he asks. 'I have one in my pocket from the plane.' His face is still full of that concern. She notices, again, the gap he left between them and feels an intense gratitude.

'Thank you,' she says. He reaches into his pocket, misunderstanding. 'No,' she stops him. 'I don't mean that. I just meant,' she nods towards the dance floor, 'thanks.'

'Oh,' he says, 'no worries.' He flaps his arms in this little shrug. 'How are you feeling?'

Like I want to scream.

'Better,' she says instead. He doesn't look entirely like he buys it.

'It's the touch thing, isn't it?'

She nods. *And the lights,* she thinks, *and the sound, and the fact that there's no fricking air in this place...*

'Is it always this bad?' he asks.

'No,' she says, 'not like this.' The room is spinning a little less and, hidden in the booth, her breathing is slowing closer to normal, but she still feels light-headed. She grits her teeth.

'Have you always been like it?' he asks. If he wasn't Warden, and she wasn't used to him asking questions that people should stop before asking...

'I didn't have some kind of childhood trauma if that's what you're asking. No one hurt me or did anything... this is just me. For as long as I can remember.'

And I don't need people telling me it's wrong or messed up. I deal with it. Usually, I can control it and it's fine... and it's...

But he doesn't tell her it's messed up. He doesn't.

'We can just sit for a bit,' he says. He even half smiles. 'Enjoy the music, you know.' Mallory nods again, but she looks down at the floor. What must he think? He's flown halfway across the country to meet a crazy person...

She's stupid, so stupid!

It's not something she's used to feeling, but she's so far out of her depth, it's absurd. Did she really think she'd come here and somehow be able to *hack* her way on to the next stage of finding The Asker, just like she would online? It doesn't work like that in real life. All of her assumptions suddenly seem so juvenile. They could get the footage, but he might not even have been at the club at all; the name Labyrinth could just be a coincidence. He could have been at some other warehouse, or the IP could have been registered incorrectly. They have the bug and their plan but, really, she doesn't know what to do, what to look for… She glances at her shaking hands.

And she couldn't even do it if she did.

'I'm sorry.' The words seem to fall out, just loud enough for Warden to hear. Her eyes glass up, even though she wishes they wouldn't. 'I'm sorry.'

This is a mess.

'Hey,' he says, doing the shrug again. 'Hey, it's fine.' She looks down at the table in front of them, wishing for all the world that its shiny surface was a screen that could hide her, trying to pretend…

'I'm not so good as myself,' she says, and she *feels* it as she hears it. 'Echo is good, but me – ' She cuts off.

Stop it, stop it…

'But you are Echo,' he replies.

'Don't you feel different as Warden?'

He pauses, then, 'Maybe. A little. But the person who looks after your family, that's you. The person who stood up to that kid beating up your brother, the person that fought back against the prick with the camera phone, that was all you.' She remembers, then, the fire she had felt… but she can't feel it now. 'And coming here, looking for The Asker like this,' he says, 'that's Echo and it's all you. She's in there.'

'But Echo doesn't make mistakes.' Mallory's hands clench in her lap, still trying to stop the damn shaking. 'She's never afraid.'

'Well, this is a scary place. I mean, I'm terrified too. Seriously. We get outside and I'm emptying a whole bottle of antibacterial gel on my hands. And these pants,' he adds, 'I'll probably burn them.' Bizarrely, something about that almost makes her laugh. 'You think I'm joking. That's the funny part.' He stops, and grins back at her. Then, 'We could go,' he says. 'We don't have to stay. This was always a long shot.'

Mallory feels herself agreeing, even as she hates herself for. She looks out at the wall of people beyond the booth. She can't do this. She'll have to find some other way to help The Asker because she can't do *this*. She's almost going to do it, to back out, to tell him yes… when she sees it.

She stops.

There, in the whirl of mess and noise outside, she suddenly sees something that makes sense – an isosceles triangle with the right-hand line drawn thicker than the other two. It's a capital of the Greek letter delta; Daedalus's symbol.

And it's tattooed on the back of someone's hand.

Delta

Mallory's head snaps up as the woman walks past, the inked triangle swinging with her left hand, its top point angled down towards her fingers.

'What?' Warden asks.

'Her hand,' she tells him, nodding towards the woman. They watch as she slides into the crowd of dancers, arms rising, the delta arcing into the air as she disappears.

'Oh,' he says, eyebrows rising above the frames of the sunglasses. Then, 'Crap, this is really real.'

It can't be a coincidence, not when The Asker came to this area investigating Daedalus ties, not coupled with the club's name. Hackers know that symbol. It was all over Daedalus's videos, all over the message boards dedicated to him.

I was right, Mallory realizes – and a bolt of adrenaline trickles through her. She thinks about what Warden said. Maybe, just maybe… She tries to seize on it, tries to use it to regain her control.

Come on…

'Watch,' she says. Within minutes, they've spotted two more marks on people's left hands; on a woman with a stud chain running from her ear to her nose, and a man with a blue Mohican.

'Why do they all have it?' Warden asks. Mallory shakes her head. She doesn't know, but if The Asker's warnings and their own research told them anything, it's that there are people out there obsessed with Daedalus…

This is it, she thinks; a sudden, icy clarity. *This is where The Asker really was.*

No, it isn't just a coincidence. Whether something to do with the location hack he'd wanted her help for, or just another lead he was chasing – *a hell's hornets' nest of leads* – four days ago, he was in this very room, logged in to the Forum. Mallory stares at the man with the Mohican.

Does he know where The Asker is? The thought is both energizing and frightening. She tugs her hood down lower over her face again. Just like Warden had said, this is *real*. It's suddenly very damn real, real beyond just being in a club with all these people.

About that, though, she doesn't panic.

She holds it back and, instead, she starts to feel focused. She has a new clue now, a lead of her own – something to hold onto and follow and figure out – and, with it, a new determination begins to build up within her, a drive that she only usually feels when she's hacking, when she's Echo Six and she's on to something, chasing it down…

She's in there. Warden's words reverberate in her mind.

Her eyes dart around the room, searching. She spots the first security camera, blinking red up above the bar. It doesn't take long to locate more; several over the dance floor, one above the door to the restrooms, another looking down on the booths. They're everywhere, just like she'd guessed they would be. And they are always watching, always listening, always recording – just like they would have been four nights ago, recording The Asker.

The answers are here.

Mallory looks up at Warden. She swallows.

'I'm not going,' she says.

You're okay, she tells herself, no room for argument. She starts loosening her muscles, forcing them to move. Focus of Echo or not, she's still fricking Mallory Park in fricking Mallory Park's stupid body. *Get up,* she thinks. *Get up!*

'Are you sure?' Warden asks. She shoots him a look that says she damn well is and he shouldn't argue either. That's more Echo, at least.

She stands, somehow managing to stay on her feet, though her legs morph right from stone to Jell-O. Her whole body is crawling with a fidgety, skittish energy. She takes a step forward, willing herself to not be her real self, just for a few moments. She tries to stop fighting against the sound still pounding in her ears, tries to just go with it, to let the beat of the music start to infect her instead of battering against her. She takes another step, slamming down any threatening panic with every ounce of willpower she has.

You're Echo, she thinks. *You're Echo fucking Six.*

Someone stumbles into her, clearly off their head, but she glares at them with such a wired ferocity that they are the one who backs away. She feels a rush. She glances back to check Warden is following, then starts walking, fists balled solid, skirting around the edge of the dance floor and heading towards the glowing neon sign indicating the restrooms. She dips her head as they hurry under the camera and pushes open the door, trying not to freeze up at the sticky feel of the handle against her gloves. Thankfully the music drops a notch as they go through, but she doesn't stop. There are three doors in the corridor beyond; men's, ladies' and a separate disabled bathroom down the end. That's what she heads for, darting quickly inside. As she goes to close the door, a guy with a neon blue jacket enters the corridor. His eyes fall on Mallory, then flick to Warden behind her – and he grins like he thinks he knows what they're doing. His eyes start to wander… Mallory's skin crawls and she slams the door shut so fast Warden jumps. She locks it.

You're okay.

It's quieter still inside, so much calmer, so much safer. Relief shudders through her and she takes a long, shaky breath. Warden is watching her, brow all wrinkled up in concern again. He opens his mouth like he's going to ask her if she's all right, but then he stops, apparently thinking better of it. Mallory takes one more deep breath.

She takes in the room. It's small and dingy, lit by a single strip light. The floor is a disturbingly damp beige, littered with paper and bottles and a load of other junk she really doesn't want to look too closely at. A toilet and basin are pressed up against the back wall, hand rails drilled into the tiles on either side. Most importantly, a large metal air duct runs across the ceiling – just like it had said on the building's blueprints. The bathroom is one of the few places in the club with no camera. Warden eyes the duct nervously. His hands are shoved firmly in his pockets and he's started rocking back and forth between feet. He looks like he would pay serious money not to have to touch anything in this room. He really does have a thing about hygiene. He wasn't just saying it.

'Worse than the school cafeteria,' he mutters. Mallory feels this strange rush of warmth for him. They both had their own additional reasons to fear tonight, and they both came. She walks to the toilet, puts down the lid using paper, then covers it in the stuff before perching down.

You're Echo.

Echo who is fearless, who gets things done.

She slips her laptop out of her bag and boots it up. Warden comes to stand beside her, pulling off the sunglasses and hooking them onto his sweater vest. He watches as she selects the club's secure network, as she starts hacking her way into it. Even locked away in a damp, dingy bathroom, Mallory starts to slip away from herself as she watches the screen, as her mind twists and turns and she sinks into a place she understands. A couple of minutes in, she notices something odd, though, something not quite right in the code she's looking at... She stops.

'What's wrong?' Warden asks.

'An alarm,' she responds. 'There's an alarm built in to warn the operators if anyone tries to hack the system. It's not like I haven't seen that sort of thing before, but it's not where I would have expected it to be hidden. Crap, that was clever.'

'Can you bypass it?'

'I think so,' she responds – now she's seen it. It takes several more minutes, going cautiously – there are a few more pitfalls and snags built in – but she makes it through. And she doesn't trigger the alarm.

'Bloody hell,' breathes Warden, 'remind me never to piss you off.'

Mallory clicks through menus until several different CCTV feeds are displayed. She scans them quickly.

'There,' points Warden.

Her eyes follow his finger to the feed from what looks like the club's security office, where a woman in a black staff shirt is fixated on a bank of screens. The woman doesn't seem to have noticed the invasion of the system, but Mallory can't see her left hand from this camera angle, can't tell if it's marked with Daedalus's symbol. She taps out the pattern once, her own left-hand middle finger against her thumb, watching for a further few seconds, just to be sure…

Nothing. They're in clean.

She searches the different feeds until she finds the room the server is in. It's thankfully empty, and she starts recording the footage from it, ready to be looped. Technically, Warden doesn't need access to the server itself to place the bug, just a connected cable, but the server room seemed the quickest way of finding that without knowing the wiring layout.

'You're up,' she tells him.

'Right, yes.' He glances anxiously at the air duct again, then starts rummaging around in his satchel, taking out a pair of latex gloves. His fingers fumble against the plastic as he tries to pull them on. He swears and yanks off the beanie hat, claiming he's too hot and it's making his hands clammy. He shoves it in his satchel, hair now completely sticking up at all angles. Mallory bites her lip, sympathy eating at her.

'You don't have to do this.' She says it before she really thinks it. He stops, looking back at her. 'You don't have to,' she repeats, though part of her wishes she'd stayed silent. Maybe it's just because he gave her a get-out too. 'I can download the footage from here…' She trails off. Warden hesitates, just for a moment, then he shakes his head.

'Safer this way,' he says, 'off site before we download anything, and we'll have more time so the bleed can be slower and they'll be less likely to notice.' It's what he'd said before. He nods at her, once, a little more sure.

'We need to hurry, then,' Mallory says. She glances at the clock on her laptop.

Crap.

Too long already. Her own nerves flutter. There's only so much time they can stay in a club bathroom before someone else will want to use it. Warden nods again, and finally manages to pull on the gloves. He turns to the sink and begins attempting to climb it in what appears to be the most uncoordinated way possible. After several failed attempts and a series of panicky grunting noises, he's standing with one leg balanced precariously on the basin, the other on a hand rail. He does not look stable.

'Looping the feed now,' Mallory says. She sets the recorded footage playing back, overwriting what the camera will be seeing live. A quick check tells her the security woman didn't notice a glitch as it switched. 'We're good,' she says.

Warden mumbles something that may or may not have been 'brilliant', and unclips the access panel on the side of the duct.

'Is now a bad time to tell you I'm afraid of heights?' he says.

'You're three foot up.' Mallory glances at the clock again.

'And germs, I don't like those either.'

'Just do it already!' Adrenaline makes her voice come out harsher than she'd intended and she feels a flush of guilt. They're taking too long, though. 'If you're going to go,' she adds, more evenly. 'Just, we can't stay in here forever.'

'Right,' he gulps. 'Yes, absolutely.' He reaches upwards, hooking both arms into the opening and trying to pull himself up.

Trying.

Oh hell…

Mallory rises, pushing her laptop aside. She reaches up, trying to help balance him, her hands buzzing where they touch.

'Don't kick me!' she yells, as a flailing sneaker almost catches her in the face. 'I'm trying to help you.'

'Sorry,' he calls down, voice muffled from the duct. 'This is harder than it looks in movies.' Eventually, he makes it in and brightness flares beyond him as he sets his phone to flashlight. 'Oh, good grief,' he gasps, 'you would not believe how dirty it is in here.'

'*Warden.*'

'I'm just saying, do *not* be encouraged about the air you're breathing right now.'

She hears scuffling then, though, as he starts making his way along the duct, following the path she'd shown him on the blueprints back in the diner. She returns to check the laptop. The loop is still running, the woman in the security office still unaware. Sixty seconds pass. Ninety.

One-twenty. The room where the server is stored is only fifty-three feet away; he can do this, they can…

Someone bangs on the door. She jumps.

'Speed it up,' they demand.

Crap.

'Just a minute,' Mallory answers.

Come on, Warden, come on…

Her finger starts tapping as she looks back at the screen. She has both feeds of the server room displayed – the looped one that will be playing on the security office's monitor, and the real, live one. Finally, Warden appears in the second, clambering out of the vent. He dangles there for at least ten seconds.

Come on. Come on!

He drops to the floor, collapsing in a dusty heap of awkward landing.

'Look, lady, hurry up!' the door shouts again.

'Just a *minute*,' Mallory snaps. Warden is now crouched down behind a desk, fumbling with something…

The guy outside keeps yelling, gradually becoming more irate, his language more colorful. Warden slips his laptop out of the satchel. It's connected to the internet via a portable Wi-Fi dongle he'd brought with him – something Mallory doesn't entirely like, but it's way more secure than using the club's. He'll be checking the connection to the bug, checking it's all linked in… He turns and looks up at the camera, giving a thumbs up. She feels a rush of relief, but at the same time, *fricking come on!*

'That's it,' states the door, 'you don't come out, I'm calling security!'

Oh crap, crap, crap…

Mallory unleashes a venomous stream of profanity at whoever's out there, hoping to scare them off. They stop talking, at least. Warden is standing on the desk now, trying to pull himself back into the vent, but it looks like he's struggling, legs dangling wildly into the open air…

No, no, no…

Two painful minutes later, he finally makes it up. There's a bang on the door.

'This is security,' a new voice says. 'Everything all right in there?'

Shit.

'Yes,' Mallory yells, her already racing pulse jumping further, 'yeah, just coming!' With Warden out the server room and the vent that end shut, she types quickly, shutting down the loop, hoping he's moving his ass real fast down that duct…

'We operate a strict no drugs policy,' the voice continues, 'and I got a guy here saying you been in there near on twenty-five minutes.'

'I'm not doing drugs!' she answers, which is probably exactly what someone doing drugs would say. 'I'm just…' Her mind goes helpfully blank for once. 'I'm just coming.'

Come on, Warden. Come on!

She stands beneath the opening, laptop stashed away back in her bag, willing him to get there faster. She can hear him clunking closer…

'Ma'am, let me be clear. You don't come out, I'm going to have to open that door.'

Warden's face appears in the vent, flushed and covered in dust.

'I think I burst a blood vessel doing that,' he gasps.

'*Get the hell down here,*' she hisses.

'Ma'am!'

Warden's head snaps towards the door.

'Oh bollocks.' He slides his way out of the duct, in what is the fastest, but definitely most ungainly maneuver so far, Mallory having to grab his arm to stop him falling after he closes the vent and drops down from the sink. 'So… dirty…' he breathes, quickly peeling off the now black-tipped latex gloves, before trying to brush the grime off his clothes.

'Ma'am, I'm coming in!' shouts the man outside.

'What do we do?' Warden asks, paling.

Mallory's mind flicks back to the man with the blue jacket who first saw them go in, to what he had thought… She looks back at Warden, hesitates just a second, then clears the distance between them and grabs his hand. Her skin beneath her gloves tingles at the touch, but she makes herself interlace the fingers.

'What – ?' he begins. There's the sound of a key turning in the lock.

'Just follow,' she says. 'Glasses back on.'

He obeys and she yanks the door open herself, just as someone else pushes it in from the other side. A thickset bouncer stands in the doorway, arm still raised. He looks momentarily taken aback. Behind him peers a red-faced squirt of a man with badly-dyed black hair.

You're Echo Six, Mallory thinks.

She smiles at the bouncer – smiles in the way Jeanie always smiled at guys when she wanted something – and exits the room, pulling the still-breathless Warden after her.

'All done,' she says, running her free hand through his hair with a wicked grin.

You are damn well okay.

Warden helpfully smiles like an idiot, though she's not quite sure it was intentional. She walks past the stunned bouncer and the little squirt man, not waiting for a response, then she pushes open the door back into main club, bracing herself against the assault of sound. She steps out, her hand gripped like a vice onto Warden's, a shadow of Echo pumping in her veins.

Trust

'I can't believe we just did that,' Warden mutters. They're three blocks away from Labyrinth and he's been repeating it solidly for almost two minutes whilst lathering his hands in antibacterial gel, as promised. 'I can't believe we bloody did that.' His eyes are wide, but he's sort of smiling, like he's just been given a present he doesn't quite trust is real. It *is* surreal. All of Mallory's senses are still buzzing, this bizarre and twitchy combination of feeling like she's escaping from something, alongside coming off the high of a hack. 'I mean, bloody hell,' he goes on. 'We just bugged a New York nightclub. I actually went *into* a night-club, for starters... And then we bugged it. We bloody bugged it!'

'And now you're telling everyone,' Mallory says. Warden glances behind him, startled, but the street they're on is fairly empty and no one's looking at them.

'Sorry,' he says anyway. 'It's just, *we did it*. And it was way cooler than hacking from my bedroom with my mother coming in every half hour and asking me where she left her foot massager.' He smiles at Mallory then, a full smile, and some of his relief seems to seep into her – though it almost hadn't been a clean out. When he'd gone to pick up his suitcase, it had looked as if a drink had been spilt down it. Even in a club they were trying to leave quickly and without notice, he'd almost had a fit. 'It's bad enough,' he had said, 'that I had my things manhandled by that giant on the door, but this? My *granny* gave me this suitcase!' At which point Mallory had given him the adrenaline-fueled glare of a lifetime and told the cloakroom lady he'd had too much to drink, drag-ging him away before they could become reacquainted with security. He'd calmed down a bit once they'd got outside, once they'd put a block between them and the club and he wasn't quite so jumped up. He'd moved quickly from anger, to disbelief, to wonderment. Hence, why he's now grinning at her like a total dumbass. In spite of everything, in spite of how simultaneously wired and exhausted she is, Mallory smiles back at him. She shakes her head, not quite believing it either, especially after how it had started out. She smiles because they did it – and she smiles because the things that make him angry or excited, and the way he talks about them... it's all just so familiar, even though in one way they've only just met.

'Who do you think they were,' Warden asks, 'the people with the tattoos?'

'I don't know.' Her mood drops a notch.

'Do you think that was the hack The Asker wanted you to help with? Maybe he thought Scarlet had been there. Maybe' – he pauses to hold his breath as they walk past a steaming manhole cover – 'that hidden alarm could have caught him.'

'I don't know,' Mallory repeats. It was tricky, certainly, and, if she's honest, the alarm had almost caught her... but it was a one person hack – breaking into the system itself required only one laptop and one hacker. Why would The Asker have needed her help? Unless he'd been after footage specifically as well, and had wanted to do a similar thing to what she and Warden had just done to avoid detection. Did he know hardwire bugs too? Maybe without Mallory, he'd had to download the large video files quickly, on site, and someone had noticed the data spike and...

Not helpful, she tells herself, shutting off that train of thought. It's all ifs and maybes and a whole shedload of unsubstantiated assumptions until they can actually watch the footage from Monday night.

'Or maybe,' Warden says, 'The Asker had found out about the delta people, just from looking into Daedalus and that was why he was there – nothing specifically to do with Scarlet – and the hack he wanted your help for was some other completely different lead?' He looks at Mallory expectantly, then hesitates, seeing her downcast expression. 'Or maybe you don't know that too,' he adds, 'and I don't know it either and I should just stop making suggestions until we do.' He takes out his phone – the universal gesture for *I feel awkward.* Gaps in conversation are much easier when you can minimize a chat box. Mallory focuses on the paving stones, suddenly self-conscious. They walk in silence for a while.

'Hey, check this out,' Warden says, a few blocks later, 'I did a web search for delta tattoos on the left hand and guess what it came up with?' Mallory glances up. 'Children of Daedalus.' His eyebrows rise meaningfully.

'What?'

'The *cod* people,' he elaborates.

'I know who you mean.' She takes the phone from him, acutely aware of their fingers touching. It's open on a Daedalus forum, this one entitled *Save The Minotaur*.

How many of these things are there?

In the selected thread, someone's asking about the exact same tattoo they saw in the club.

'The capital delta tattoo,' Warden recites, even as Mallory reads the first response, 'drawn on the left hand, with the point facing the fingers, signifies membership of the cybergang Children of Daedalus. An official tattoo can only be applied by an existing member and incorrect application results in complete ostracism.' She scrolls down, but the discussion then diverts into the generic merits and hindrances of membership tats. She hands the phone back to Warden, frowning.

'It doesn't make sense,' she says. 'CoD looked harmless. I mean, really harmless. It took me less than five minutes to crack their message boards and, aside from the fact there was no mention of missing hackers, it was mainly just some seriously disturbing Daedalus role-play and gushing discussions of anything from his video editing skills to his hacks.' Warden looks questioning at that, so she adds, 'But not in a way that made me think they really knew what they were talking about.'

'Maybe that was a front,' he suggests. She hesitates. She doesn't think so – she should have been able to tell if there was something hidden in the architecture, even if she couldn't access it right away – but she'll check it again tomorrow. They finally reach the twenty-four hour parking garage where she left the Chevy. She stops. It's not raining any more, but the ground is still damp.

'This is you?' Warden asks.

'Yes.' He already looks cold again, though they've only been outside twenty minutes. He glances at his watch, then nervously around the street – and she realizes something. 'You don't have anywhere to stay, do you?' she says.

'Not technically,' he mumbles, freckled cheeks flushing a little redder. 'Everything was a bit of a rush making it here at all; getting the bug back from school and the flight booked, then packing and getting to LAX in time for check in. I mean, I guess I was thinking I'd just try and find a hotel…' He sort of shrugs, looking distinctly unnerved as he takes in the dark, empty street. 'Do you know any? You know, preferably nice, definitely cheap.' She can just imagine him wandering round the Bronx looking for one at this time of night, with that damn wheelie suitcase and his laptop slung over his shoulder in a bright green satchel…

He'll get mugged.

He'll damn well get mugged.

All because he flew right across the country to help me, she thinks. She bites her lip.

'Echo?'

She makes a decision.

'I live just under a couple of hours away,' she says, 'a place called Watertown. We need to go through the footage together anyway, and we don't know where that'll lead and I can't keep driving back up here.' Her hand taps furiously against her leg, part of her wondering just what in the hell she is doing. 'You can stay with us, if you want to.' The words come out anyway. She watches him carefully, notes that *he* hesitates, and feels her own cheeks redden. It obviously wasn't what he was expecting.

'Are you sure?' he asks.

Maybe she shouldn't be. Her doubts get louder. She has crossed all kinds of boundaries she said she never would tonight, but spending two hours alone in a car with a hacker from the internet – no matter how familiar he feels – taking him back to her house, back to where her dad and her brother are sleeping?

Still…

'If it hadn't been for you back there…' If it hadn't been for him, she'd have probably passed out right in the middle of that dance floor and she doesn't know where she'd be right now. She certainly wouldn't have made the hack. He came through for her; him, in person. For a moment, they watch each other, both wondering, both assessing.

Can they trust like this?

Can Warden go with her somewhere *he* doesn't know?

Should she let him?

When she looks at the boy in front of her, she sees a stranger – a stranger she could never trust this quickly – but when he talks, she hears Warden. Her mind seems to squirm, arguing with itself, because it doesn't matter how much she *wants* to believe all he's told her about his real life, how much she *feels* like she can. It's about what's logical, and sometimes your feelings can be wrong about even the people you trust the most. She knows that. She thinks of his name on the screen, that voice she's spoken to every day for more than two years. They have never really minced their words before. Why start now? She wouldn't as Echo.

'I've not lied to you,' Mallory says. 'Everything today has been straight up. It's up to you if you trust me on that, but if you're not who you've said you are, this is your last chance to back out.' Warden's eyes widen again and he starts to shake his head.

'Echo, no – '

'Because if you come back with me,' she continues, cutting him off, 'and you're not, and anything happens to me or my dad or my brother, there won't be a single place you can hide on this whole planet that I won't come find you and destroy you.' He stares back, mouth hanging open just a little. It was kind of harsh, and probably unnecessary, but it's Jed's safety she's banking on him. 'Plus,' she adds, a little self-consciously, 'my dad was a Marine Sergeant, so you try anything, he'll rip you a new one.' She doesn't mention that that second part's not exactly true any more.

'Right,' Warden says, after a moment. 'Destroying, and a ripped new one.' Then, 'For the record, I'm just Warden. I haven't lied either. I'm rubbish at lying face-to-face anyway; you'd be able to tell. The only person who ever believes me is my mother and that's usually because she's already had a couple of Tom Collinses by the time I'm back from school. I'm just Gilbert Ward from Sun City – well, and Guildford – but I already told you that. Nothing else. I wouldn't – '

'So are you coming then?'

'Just to check, you'll only destroy me *if* I do something wrong, right? Otherwise, I'm safe?'

'As long as you don't piss me off.' Mallory turns, resisting a sudden urge to smile again, and heads into the garage. 'I make no promises.'

'That's a joke, right?' he calls after her. She can hear him following, though, wheelie suitcase rattling against the concrete, and something about that makes her disproportionately pleased. Whether she should be or not, she's glad that he's coming. 'Right? I'm taking that silence as a yes.'

She pays for the ticket and they take the elevator down to the basement floor where she left the car.

'Whoa, a seventy-one Chevy?' says Warden, when he sees Roger's blue Nova parked in the bay. 'Proper old school.'

Mallory gets in, dumping her bag on the back seat, while Warden puts his suitcase in the trunk. She starts up the engine. It makes an unhealthy rattling sound. The exhaust is coming loose again. The one Roger said he'd fixed.

Damn it.

'Exhaust's going,' Warden says, getting in beside her. A trace of anxiety wells as he does; cars are small and enclosed, and she's not used to being stuck in one with anyone other than Jed. She tries to shake it off. She knew this was part of asking him. 'I could fix it for you tomorrow,' Warden adds, as Mallory pulls out of the space, 'if you want.'

'You know cars?' she asked, trying to distract herself.

He nods.

'Work most afternoons in my dad's dealership. I help fix them up, then he and my brothers sell them on to unsuspecting customers. You would not believe the dregs they give me to start with.'

'Do you like doing it?' Something about his tone makes her ask.

'It's not so bad, I guess. I like seeing how things work.'

'Like safes.'

'Like safes.' He grins. Mallory turns right on to the street. 'I suppose I'm not such a fan of cars if I'm honest. I like motorbikes better; more compact, neater. But my dad doesn't get many of those in.'

'Have you got one yourself?' The image of him on a Harley in his sweater vest doesn't exactly gel.

'A bike?' he responds. 'Hell, no. Sodding death traps. I would not want to go seventy with nothing on either side of my legs but leather and air... That sounded weird. I just like the engines.'

'Okay.' Mallory focuses on the road, not knowing what else to say and trying not to think about how close he's sitting to her, trying not to notice every single tick or movement he makes. She opens the window a crack, letting in a blast of cold October air.

You hacked a nightclub, she thinks, *you can manage two hours in a car with Warden.*

She merges onto the interstate and accelerates, careful to keep to the speed limit – the last thing she needs is to be stopped, driving this time of night on a learner's permit with a passenger.

'It's what my dad wants me to do,' Warden says softly. 'Fix cars,' he adds. 'Wants me to join the family business full time after high school.' Mallory glances over. He looks about as morose at that as he sounded. She notices him shivering and reluctantly closes the window.

'And what do you want?' she asks.

'To go to college,' he says, 'MIT, if I can get in. Massachusetts is suitably far away from California. Major in electrical science and engineering, or something like that. You don't have to decide right away there. Dad doesn't like it, though, says he won't pay thousands of dollars for me to learn 'all that computer shit' and end up working for the 'pothead Democrats in government'. I'd have to get a scholarship, or work while I'm there and have no social life. So, not too much different from now then.' He laughs, but it's kind of forced. Mallory feels like she wants to say something helpful, but doesn't know quite what. She becomes deeply engrossed in checking her mirrors instead. 'How about you? he asks. 'How old are you actually, by the way?'

'Sixteen,' she says, 'but I skipped second grade.'

'So it's senior year for you too?' She nods. 'Got any plans for college?'

Mallory feels the same, trickling disquiet she gets whenever anyone brings that up. She grips the wheel a little tighter... but she doesn't lie like she usually does. Something about it being him asking just then makes her want to tell the truth.

'No,' she tells him. 'I mean, I don't know. Everyone keeps asking that, saying how all the deadlines are coming up, but I don't know what I want to do. I don't know how you do know. And, plus, with my dad and my brother needing help and stuff...' She stops.

'That's okay,' Warden answers, 'the not knowing.'

'You're the only person who's said that.'

'I know you,' he answers, shrugging – like it's not a big thing he's just said, though it sets her cheeks going all warm again – 'you'll figure it out. You figure out most things.'

'I'm not sure with this. I don't know how to start.'

'Well, what do you like doing the most? What gives you, I don't know, purpose, meaning, er, that kind of thing?'

'The Asker,' she says, a little too quickly. She feels a pang of worry, but pushes it down. 'He's so sure of everything, so sure of right and wrong, and when I'm on a hack, it's like nothing else matters and all the other crap that's going on just gives it a rest for a second. ' She cuts out.

'You ever thought about doing computer science?' Warden asks. 'Now I'm not saying specifically MIT' – though it sort of sounds like he is – 'but the place is pretty much at the cutting edge of anything new in CS. From there, you could get into security or software development. It's not like you could stay a grey-hat forever and live off it – unless you go full black-hat and start stealing money, which is kind of a sucky thing to do.'

His phone buzzes then, making him jump and thankfully stopping the conversation. He takes it out of his pocket. 'Friend from home,' he says, though she hadn't asked. 'Not a girlfriend or anything. I don't have one,' he adds, then goes bright red like he isn't sure why he did. Mallory feels a kind of flutter of jitters at that, though she isn't sure why either. It's not like it matters. She glances at the clock. It's late, but then back home for him means three hours behind.

'Where do they think you are?' she asks – in New York to hack a nightclub seems unlikely.

'Visiting MIT, as it happens.' He starts typing out a reply. 'Seeing the campus, checking out the general area.'

'I thought you said you couldn't lie convincingly.'

'This is text,' he answers. 'I said I couldn't lie face-to-face, except to my mother, and she's not so set against college. She believed me when I said I was visiting, even called me in sick with school so I could get here in time.' He puts the phone away. 'I don't know what she'd do if I told her the truth.' His voice drops. 'She thinks I spend all that time at my computer online gaming. I've never actually told anyone what it really is. Have you?' he asks. Mallory shakes her head. She's not exactly sure what Roger and Jed think, but the thought of them knowing the truth… In the same way as it feels vulnerable to have someone from the Forum see her real face, having those in her real life know about Echo Six would be equally… unsettling. 'I suppose it's not exactly a thing you just say, is it?' Warden says. Then he frowns. 'Do you ever think about how it's all illegal?' Mallory glances over sharply. 'I mean,' he goes on, 'I think we do a lot of good stuff in the Forum, but it's technically against the law – like, very much so.'

The other reason she's never told her family. Her fingers stretch against the wheel.

'I don't know,' she says. 'I… well, of course I know it nominally, but it doesn't really feel like that, not when I'm doing it.' It's true. She just feels this driving urgency, like she is trying to win at something – like she *should* win at it. It feels right, if there is a right or wrong about it. It's not like there aren't rules they follow, they are just The Asker's. They don't ever steal – not money or real things – and they don't set out to hurt people, just to show the truth. It jars, thinking about the actual legality… not getting caught is just part of the hack. She doesn't often think about what would happen if she did, just focuses on it not happening.

'I was fourteen when The Asker invited me to join,' Warden says. 'I didn't really consider it being illegal so much then. I was just excited. It was kind of like, well, like it *was* an online game. Like I said, I've always liked working out how things work – that was why I started hacking at all – and the Forum... the Forum was like a doorway into the ultimate puzzles.' He pauses. 'I guess that sounds stupid.' It doesn't, though, not to Mallory. 'And then,' he goes on, 'the more I did, the more I began to realize that everything The Asker ever asked me to do, every hack I ever took, it exposed some really bad thing that needed exposing. It was humbling and overwhelming to realize the extent of it, of what people will hide, what they'll do in the first place, to end up needing to hide it. I started to feel like maybe we were doing something about it. Like it meant something. But lots of people would say that's bull, lots of smart people who have their own, very sensible ideas about right and wrong. And sometimes, if I'm honest, I don't quite know myself, because we could really go to prison for it, and if the internet *was* just a free-for-all – everyone knowing whatever they wanted – well, I'm not sure that would really be better, and who are we to choose what gets released and what doesn't?'

Mallory shifts uncomfortably, these kinds of questions exactly why she normally tries not to think about this stuff.

'Are you saying you think we should stop?' she asks.

'I'm not quite sure,' Warden sighs. 'No. I don't. It's just... it's made me think even more about it with him gone. We're minors, but we're legally culpable, Echo. We could go to jail for what we did tonight, for any one of our Forum hacks. Are you really saying that never occurs to you?'

She falters, her mind feeling too crowded. She's just tired, that's what it is, making everything heightened...

'I guess sometimes,' she responds. Then, 'The FBI tried to trace me once, about a year back.'

'They *what*?'

'I thought about it then, I suppose,' she says. 'It was after the Roberson hack. The Feds were already monitoring the system when I got in and someone tried to piggyback out. I never told anyone that, not even The Asker. I thought he might freak and ban me.'

'Bloody hell,' breathes Warden. 'How do you know it was them?'

'I counter-traced back to an IP address at the Javits Federal Building.'

'And didn't that scare you?'

She doesn't answer for a moment. It had made her think, but the real answer was, no, it didn't scare her, not as much as maybe it should have. It didn't, because she'd dealt with it. It had actually kind of made her feel *good*, sort of unstoppable…

'They hadn't got very far,' she says instead.

'But if they'd caught you – '

'They didn't. They didn't even get close.'

'Wow,' Warden says simply. He sounds half impressed, half a little frightened. He goes silent for a while then, and she's glad of it because she doesn't know how her answers sounded to him, but they didn't seem quite good enough to her and she doesn't want him to push into that. She just wants things to go back to how they were, where these questions didn't feel like hers to answer. She stares at the road, trying not think about all the things he's stirred up, the doubts she usually suppresses about the potential consequences of the Forum, possibilities she tries to never fully acknowledge because she doesn't *want* to stop, doesn't ever want it to end… But she can't quite shut them off, not after everything that's happened, not after what they've just done.

This is really real.

That's what Warden had said back in the club, when she'd pointed out the first delta tattoo. It's real. And real life is more complicated than online. It is somewhere that maybe Echo Six can never fully exist, whatever glimpses there may be, because there are too many facets of it that Mallory doesn't understand, too many things that, however much she tries, she can't predict or control. There are no clear cut rules. It is flowing and unwieldy. Yet, in what they have done tonight, they have stepped out of their comprehensible online world and exposed themselves to the real risks outside of it. They have done something illegal, in person, and they have done it looking into unknown *circumstances* that have already caused five other hackers to go off the grid. Mallory Park has, not Echo Six. Gilbert Ward, not Warden.

No, she can't turn off the thoughts he has stirred.

We had to do it, she thinks. They couldn't leave The Asker, they couldn't... but going to the club, that had been her idea, and as she drives the long way back to the real house she shares with her real dad and her very real little brother, she can't help wondering what she might have got them all into by doing it.

Welcome Party

By the time they reach Oakville, Mallory is shattered. She is edgy and riled, and her mind would not shut up its second guessing the whole time Warden wasn't talking – which, admittedly, wasn't that much in the end. She checks the dashboard clock as they pull into the driveway.

One fourteen.

They get out of the car and she gulps down the chill night air like there hadn't been any inside the Nova. She feels a little calmer now she's home, the strangeness of Warden being there less apparent than she'd been expecting it to be – although what Roger and Jed will make of her new 'friend' and why she wasn't back till the early hours remains to be seen. The house is dark and she signals Warden not to speak, not wanting to wake anyone. Those problems, as least, can wait until morning. They creep down the driveway as quietly as they can – almost impossible given that it's gravel – and she puts her key in the lock. The front door opens before she can turn it, jerking it out of her hand.

'Mal, is that you?'

'Shit, Roger!' she gasps. He's standing in the doorway, curly hair sticking up like he's been repeatedly running his fingers through it. 'Damn it…' She takes a deep breath, switching on the porch light. Her dad blinks in the brightness, his newly illuminated face so filled with concern that it cuts right through her alarm.

'Sorry I startled you,' he says. 'You were just so late back.'

He stayed up for me, Mallory realizes with a jolt. *He actually stayed up.* She feels an odd kind of elation.

'Jed had said you'd gone out,' he continues, 'but then – ' He stops mid-sentence, eyes falling on Warden behind her.

Oh crap.

'Er,' Warden mumbles helpfully. 'Hello, sir, Mr Park.' He moves forwards, holding out his hand. 'I'm Gilbert Ward. It's nice to meet you. Sir,' he adds again.

For a moment, a hardness enters Roger's eyes, a glimmer of something that demands, *Who the hell are you and what are you doing with my daughter at one in the morning?* Something inside Mallory knots up as she sees it, there so unmistakably that Warden's feet shuffle like he wants to take a step back.

Say it, she finds herself thinking at Roger, finds herself almost hoping – though she shouldn't, because of course she doesn't want him to say it and cause problems. Why would she want that? But, for a moment, just a moment, she even actually thinks he might…

And then it falls away.

She sees that happen as well, the fight dissipating as quickly as it had come, lost in some secret internal struggle.

'Nice to meet you too, Gilbert,' he says softly, shaking Warden's still outstretched hand. Unexpected disappointment seeps through Mallory. Roger doesn't even ask where she's been, just holds the door open for them. She probably looks terrible, too. She's dirty and tired and her eyes are caked in makeup, but he doesn't even ask, though she sees him taking it all in, sees how it hits him. And she knows what he'll be thinking, too – thinking how Jeanie always used to wear makeup and Mallory never does, so why is she now? And she's still wearing Jeanie's jacket, and she looks so much like her anyway and it must be hurting him… But he doesn't say any of that, does he? And something about that stings. She yanks her keys out the door and walks past him into the living room, anger flaring in place of her surprise.

What was the damn point in him staying up then?

Warden follows her, Roger shutting the door behind them. He *should* have asked and, in her tiredness, it makes Mallory suddenly so mad that she turns and glares at him so hard he seems to shrink back.

'My room's upstairs,' she tells Warden, making it very clear that he should go.

'Okay… right,' he says, glancing from Mallory to her father, clearly not understanding what's going on. She hears him cross the room, suitcase clunking into the coffee table. 'Goodnight, sir,' he adds, feet creaking on the stairs. She waits a moment longer.

I'm sixteen, she thinks at Roger, still wanting him to act, and not, at the same time. But she waits, daring him on, grasping… *Sixteen years old and there's a boy you've never met going up to my room…*

But the spark is gone, only ever a shadow of someone she remembered when she saw it and that she latched onto because of all the stressful and unnerving things that have happened that evening. That person isn't there any more. She knows that. She knows it and she shouldn't have… Roger drops his gaze to the floor and it hurts in a way she shouldn't let it be able to by now.

'Goodnight,' he says. 'Glad you're home safe.'

'Goodnight, Roger.' She heads for the stairs. She's just tired and him waiting up has set her off kilter, set her thinking things there's no point thinking. She can feel him watching her again as she hurries after Warden.

Let him think what he thinks, she tells herself. *And let him feel real bad about it.*

Warden is waiting on the landing, clearly unsure which door to open.

'Here,' Mallory says, unlocking her bedroom and turning on the light. He follows her inside and a slight apprehension stirs as she watches him take it all in; the bookshelf that lines almost the entire back wall, the single bed with the blue spread she's had since she was thirteen, and the pink children's flowery wallpaper that Jeanie picked and she's had for even longer. She watches him seeing for the first time the things that make up the place she feels most at home – and she feels self-conscious, like a deep part of her has been exposed and she didn't quite mean it to be.

It's just a room.

She rubs her eyes. It's tiredness, she thinks for the millionth time. That's all any of these strange, wound up feelings are.

Warden's gaze flicks to the wooden desk where her laptop usually sits, its position marked out by the power cable still resting there. He half smiles and, for some reason, she feels embarrassed.

'We should start the video files downloading,' she says, stopping any comment on what his judgement might be, 'set them on a slow bleed overnight like you said before. You know, so there are no sudden data surges they could notice their end.'

'Sure,' he nods, 'yeah.' He looks taken aback by her abruptness, but he reaches for his satchel. 'Is it all right if I...?' He indicates her bed, the only other place in the room he could sit. She taps out the pattern once on her leg and tells him it's okay. He perches on the very edge, like he sort of realizes he's in a personal space for her and it's something she might not be fully at ease with.

'I need to check on the Forum,' she adds. They load up their laptops, Mallory retrieving hers from her backpack. The welcome message pops up on her screen and her eyes flick automatically to the bottom right corner – no Asker online, no Scarlet. They're doing something about that, though, she tells herself. Warden is, right now. She can hear him typing away. There have been no notifications sent to her, but she sets about double checking all the login data for the past evening anyway – and finds nothing odd. Afterwards, she scans through the message boards, quieter today. Everything has been quieter the last few days, what with no new hacks.

'It's all set,' Warden says. 'Downloading all the footage from the last five days. Should be done mid-morning.'

'And it's still secure?' Mallory asks, glancing back.

'Still secure.'

'You're sure?'

'Yes, I'm sure. It may shock you, but I do know what I'm doing, Echo.' There's a half smile on his face again.

'Sorry,' she says, any other reply drying up. She looks back at the message boards. He does know and she knows that. She knows. She starts scanning, reading through everything new. There are a couple of threads she should post in, a couple of arguments she should sort out, and Case_X is still kicking up a fuss in the thread about The Asker...

Are you all right? The question pops up in a chat box from Warden. She stares at it, the room silent apart from the soft whirr of their laptops. She stays facing the screen, a kind of unexpected release in just seeing the words there.

I'm not sure, she answers, writing it out instead of saying it. Then, *Are you?* She hears him typing before the words appear.

I think so. It's been a strange day, though, I'll admit.

Do you regret it? she asks, everything easier to say in that little box. More clicks against the keys.

No, he answers, *not yet, anyway. I reserve final judgement until I know whether you're going to destroy me or not, though.* Her lips tease upwards.

Still pending. She pushes enter and hears him laugh.

So, he writes, *this is where you were, all that time we spent talking, this little room. I like it, though I always pictured you with an AC/DC poster on the wall, not sure why. Who picked out the wallpaper?*

You don't think I did then?

You don't exactly strike me as the pink flowers type. I may be wrong.

She hesitates, then, *My mom chose it*, she says, *when we first moved in.* She taps the pattern once more.

Four, three, four, two.

Warden begins typing a response, then he deletes it. Then he types something else.

Where is she? The question flashes up. Mallory's hands flex stiffly in front of her. She could shut it down, shoot down the question. That's her normal response.

Four, three, four, two.

Four, three, four, two.

She could… but she doesn't. Like before, some part of her wants to tell him.

She left us, Mallory types, focusing only on the screen, just the screen, not on him being there really – and not on what any of the words really mean, *four years ago.*

Don't ask for more, she thinks, unsure she could cope with relating it all just now, the memory of it already needling at her from that. *Don't ask for more.*

Oh, he replies simply. *I'm sorry. That really sucks.*

Mallory swallows, grateful. He's leaving the door open, for her to take it further or not. Maybe at some point she will with him, eventually. Not tonight.

What about you? she writes, diverting away. *What's it like where you log on normally?*

My room, you mean?

I guess so.

A little bigger than this, he answers, *at the back of our house – it's only single story. The walls are green.* Like his satchel. It's his favorite color; she recalls that from somewhere. *The bed's against the left wall when you come in and my desk is at the far end, beneath a double window. It looks out onto a fence, but the light coming in is still nice. That's where I sit and talk to you. And hack into some of the world's most secure systems, of course.*

Most secure? Mallory raises an eyebrow, the hint of a smile returning.

Definitely, he replies. *Didn't anyone tell you, I'm the best?* She actually laughs then. *Okay*, says Warden, *that was a little harsh. FYI, I just rolled my eyes at you.* Mallory hears the creak of the stairs outside; Roger going to bed. *Hey*, writes Warden, *sorry if I made things weird with your dad.*

It wasn't you, she answers.

My mom would have gone mental if I'd brought a girl home this late.

Mallory doesn't quite know quite what to respond to that… and he can obviously hear her not responding, not typing.

Not that that sort of thing really happens, he adds quickly, *and I didn't mean it was anything like that with us, just that it might have looked like it to your dad.* Then, *Sorry. I said that all wrong.* A pause. *You know what I mean, right?*

Yeah, I know what you mean.

She hears him let out a breath, and she does smile then. She listens to the silence after, to the ongoing whirr of their computers – to his, already beginning to download footage that could tell them where they might find The Asker, where he might have gone. She listens, and she's glad he is there.

Thank you for coming tonight, she writes.

Hey, I got to go to a nightclub, he responds. *Thanks for letting me.*

Warden, she writes, after a moment, *what if we can't find him?* What if he's really gone? What if she never talks to him again, and the Forum goes after – because it will without him – and they all just… She feels suddenly cold. What does *this* mean, her and Warden, without that to keep them together? She doesn't want to lose it either. She feels it then, sharply. She doesn't…

We will, Warden replies.

You don't know that.

Well, he writes, *he's got you looking for him. I would never bet against you.*

Mallory shakes her head, worry bubbling beneath the surface, and turns to him in the chair, almost like she needs to see him then. He looks up from his laptop and holds her gaze. He nods, his face firm, believing.

'We'll find him, Echo,' he says.

Worlds Collide

Mallory wakes to the sound of muffled shouting. Then she hears footsteps running up the stairs. It takes her a moment to fully register, by which time someone is already banging on her door.

'Mallory!' It's Jed. 'Mallory, there's a guy in the living room!'

'I told you,' says someone behind him, voice all panicky, 'I'm her friend.' It's Warden.

Shit.

After they'd logged off, she'd got him a pillow and blanket from the closet and he'd slept downstairs on the couch.

'It's okay, Jed,' she says, stumbling out of bed, still half asleep and tripping over her own damn duvet as she goes. She unlocks the door and light spills in, stinging her dark-adjusted eyes. 'It's okay. This is...' She steps out onto the landing to find Warden looking equally bleary-eyed in *Iron Man* pajamas. '...Gilbert,' she finishes. 'This is Gilbert. He *is* a friend of mine and needed a place to crash. I didn't want to wake you last night to say.'

Jed stands beside her, eyeing Warden like he's still not sure of him.

'He's the friend you went to help?' he asks – the friend Mallory had been worried enough about meeting to give Jed a tracker... She hesitates.

'Yes,' she answers. She doesn't want to open a bigger can of worms. 'It's okay, Jed,' she repeats. 'It's all fine now.' Her nerves flicker, though, even as she says it; the footage must be nearly downloaded. Jed nods, but he's still frowning. 'Go get showered,' she tells him. 'I'll start breakfast.' It's pancakes on Saturdays, with blueberries and little pieces of banana mixed into the batter because he likes both.

'Okay,' he says finally. 'I'll be down quick to help with the chopping.'

With perfect timing, Roger emerges from his room just as Jed leaves, rubbing his eyes and mumbling something about having heard shouting. He sees Mallory, then, standing alone with Warden in the doorway of her bedroom, and seems to spark right awake.

'Morning,' he manages.

'Morning, Roger.'

'…Hello again, sir.'

'Come on,' Mallory tells Warden, and heads downstairs.

* * *

'Where are you from?' Jed asks, black curls now dampened and sticking up from a poorly-executed towel dry.

'California,' Warden replies. He's dressed now too, a mustard yellow sweater vest clashing violently with a short-sleeved navy shirt, buttoned right to the top. In contrast to Jed, his sandy blonde hair is combed into a neat side parting. 'Sun City, to be precise.'

'Why's your accent all weird then?'

'*Jed*,' Mallory says. He only looks a little chagrined.

'I lived in England till I was twelve,' Warden answers. 'My mom's from there. Then we moved to California. Been there ever since.'

The four of them are sitting having breakfast together; Mallory, her dad, her brother – who seems hell bent on some kind of inquisition – and the boy she's only ever spoken to online until she met him last night to hack into a nightclub. The two very separate aspects of her life are suddenly intermingling around their little, plastic-topped kitchen table. Mallory's not sure she's ever felt so disconcerted.

'So why were you in New York?' Jed says.

Warden falters.

'He was visiting a school,' Mallory says. 'Cornell Tech. Gilbert's a senior, like me, trying to decide where to apply for next year. The hotel he was staying at lost his booking and had no rooms left. I was the only person he knew nearby.' It sounds kind of weak, even to Mallory. The frown reappears on Jed's forehead and she sees his jaw tighten. Roger seems to be finding the pancakes of infinite interest.

'How did you know him?' Jed goes on. That one stumps her. How could she know someone from California, who's seventeen and never lived anywhere else besides England?

Thanks for that little detail...

'Online gaming,' Warden answers. 'World of Warcraft.'

Jed is silent a moment, then, 'You shouldn't meet people you've met online,' he says quietly. Roger's fork stops halfway to his mouth. 'We had a whole seminar on it at school. There was this kid in Missouri who had his insides – '

'Okay, we get it,' Mallory says. He looks back at her.

'Is that why you gave me the – '

'I've known Gilbert a long time,' she interrupts, giving Jed a look that in no uncertain terms means he should zip it about what he was just about to say. He does, but his forehead creases further.

'Cornell Tech,' Roger says, unexpectedly cutting in. 'You into computers then, like Mallory?' he asks Warden.

'Yes, sir, very much,' Warden replies, seizing on the change of topic. 'My first choice is MIT; Massachusetts Institute of Technology. Their electronic engineering department is one of the best in the world. It's like a hub of all the things I'm interested in.' His mouth opens and closes like he's fishing for more things to say before Jed can start questioning him again. 'Mallory should apply too.'

Her eyes snap to him.

What in the hell?

'Someone as clever as her,' he adds, 'I'm sure she'd get in.'

She glares, fingers flexing.

'Is that one of the ones you're thinking of, Mal?' Roger asks.

'Maybe.' She swallows, her own jaw clenching a little. Roger just nods, though, and goes back to his pancakes, that one burst of interest thankfully all he can muster this morning. She tries not to think about last night and the feelings it brought up.

After breakfast, Mallory calls the store. Heidi answers and Mallory tells her she's ill and won't be able to make her shift later. It grates to do it, knowing Mrs Balinski still won't have forgotten her recent tardiness, but some things can't wait. Heidi is the model of sympathy, offering to smooth things over with her mom, and Mallory feels bad for lying to her, but there's no other choice, not today.

While the files finish downloading, Mallory and Warden recheck the Children of Daedalus message boards, but it's like she'd told him yesterday; nothing connecting them to the disappearances and a whole lot of stuff that seems to be shouting out that this group is not who they are looking for. There are a few oblique references to membership initiations and marks, though – references that make a lot more sense now they know what they're referring to – and they find a couple of other outside sources more blatantly corroborating that the delta tattoo, drawn like that on the left hand, is definitely CoD. Mallory hunts around for restricted areas or hidden links that might be on their site, but if anything's there, she can't find it. Warden has no other suggestions, so it's a dead lead for now.

The files finish downloading at five past nine and he copies half over to Mallory's laptop so they can split the searching between them. He cuts off the live link to the bug, but says he can re-establish it whenever, if they need it again. He's still certain no one's found the leak. There are hours and hours of footage to go through, from numerous different cameras hidden all around Labyrinth. It's daunting, but they start with the recordings closest to the time of The Asker's log off on Monday night.

'So what are we looking for exactly?' Warden asks, perched on the end of her bed again. 'A guy using a phone or laptop, then stopping or being stopped at exactly eight fifty-one? There's just a lot of people, now it comes to it…' Mallory knows what he means. Even looking through the first couple of videos, it feels like she's already seen more than two hundred faces, several using smartphones. 'And what if he was in the bathroom then, like we were,' Warden adds, 'or in another camera blind spot?'

'Then,' Mallory replies, 'we'll have to look at who had moved out of shot at that time. No one can have entered the club without being seen and, with the Daedalus connection, that must have been where he was. The reason he logged off is in this footage, we just need to find it. We'll follow every single person if we have to. Just take it slow. Slow the videos down if you need to, just don't miss anything.'

'Right, don't miss anything,' Warden says lightly. 'Don't miss a needle of unknown size and shape in a whole barn full of hay… On it.'

'What happened to, 'We'll find him, Echo?'' Mallory asks, quoting from last night.

'I don't know.' He flushes a little. 'I was still jumped up on the high of success?' he suggests. Then, 'Sorry, I *am* on it.' He looks purposefully at the laptop. 'We should mark up any images we find of the people with the tattoos, too, could be another way to go.'

'Good idea.'

It *is* slow going. Even starting with just the footage from eight forty onwards, there's still masses to trawl through. Plus, the club's lighting is a frustrating mix of dingy and sporadically bright – which does not go well with the cameras' fuzzy night vision. They start off working in silence, but silence never did sit well with Warden. Mallory can hear him fidgeting for a good few minutes before he speaks. Then he starts talking, going on about random things he likes, like he does when they're online. He talks about TV shows and movies, and his favorite methods of breaking into dial locks, stopping only to answer another buzzing text on his phone. It actually makes Mallory feel better, helps her focus more. There are certain rhythms to his speech that are just so familiar to her from his words in text. She lets it all sink into the background as she watches the slo-mo dancing, as she marks anyone using a device, or anyone with a Greek delta on their hand. There are a few… not many, and they're mainly just clubbers – only two members of staff with it so far.

Mallory's so intent on the task that she actually jumps when her own phone beeps, breaking through the temporary calm. She frowns. The only person who usually texts her is Jed, and he's in his room playing his DS. Maybe it's Heidi saying her mom got pissed and she needs to go to the store. She pulls the phone out of her bag. It's not a text, it's an email notification from the Forum. Her pulse lifts a notch as she clicks on it, though it's probably nothing more than a mistyped password…

Her heart slams inside her chest.

It's a message alert. Only messages from two specific accounts will send her notifications this way. This one is from The Asker.

'Warden,' she stammers, already closing the footage and heading online. '*Warden*.'

'What is it?'

'He's messaged me,' she says, hope sparking as she begins logging in.

'Who has?'

'The Asker.'

'What the – ' He stumbles over. He sees her completing the last stage of the back door log in, but she doesn't care. The Forum's welcome pop up appears on the screen. She closes it and the chat box is there, waiting for her. The Asker's icon is in grey, so he's not online any more, but he's left her a message.

He's left…

She starts to read and her body seems to go cold, the hope she felt turning to an icy shiver that runs right from the base of her spine to the very tips of her fingers.

'Oh no,' says Warden.

Hello, Echo Six, it begins.

We have The Asker and we have heard he is important to you. This is fortunate as we would very much like to talk with you. You see, we need your assistance on a matter of great importance. We shall be honest with you, we don't know where you are in the world. You are too good for that – which, ironically, makes us want your help all the more. As such, we are giving you twenty-four hours; twenty-four hours in which to reach New York City, USA, and contact us via this Forum so we can arrange to meet.

Be assured, should you comply with this request, you will not be harmed in any way. We are great admirers of your work and simply need your help. If, however, you do not meet this deadline, you will never see or hear from The Asker again. Any attempt on your part to engage the authorities will not end well for him. We have eyes and ears everywhere.

Yours,

Children of Daedalus

Ransom

'What the hell?' whispers Warden. 'This is a ransom note. It's a bloody ransom note. The Asker's been kidnapped?'

Mallory stares at the screen, her mind bombarded with so many different thoughts that she can't seem to grasp hold of any one of them. Of course, they'd known, technically, that it was an option someone had been after him... but the sudden confirmation of it among several possibilities... actual kidnapping? Everything has got a whole shitload worse. Noise is rushing through her ears, even though all she can really hear is the whirr of the laptops and Warden's increasingly fast breathing.

'And they want *you*?' he goes on. 'Echo, why would they want you? I mean, how do they even know you exist? Unless they forced The Asker...' His voice falters. 'I mean they got onto his account and he would never willingly let anyone near the Forum.'

No, he wouldn't, Mallory thinks. What has happened to him over the past five days? She feels sick. And the CoD... who the hell are these people? What did she miss?

'Bloody hell,' Warden says. 'Oh bloody, bloody...' He keeps on cursing, wondering out loud what the hell is going on, but Mallory can't speak, can't take her eyes off the screen, rereading the words, over and over, her insides coiling up and tying themselves into suffocating knots. Part of her doesn't want to fight it. Part of her wants to collapse in on herself, close the laptop, lock all the doors and never leave her room. Never think about...

Words are streaming out of Warden's mouth in a panicked flow. He's talking about the Children of Daedalus now, talking about the tattoos, wondering who at the club knew what, and how it doesn't all quite make sense to him.

'Echo?' he says, seeming to notice, then, that she hasn't said anything yet. 'Echo, you can't just sit there like a sodding prune, we have to do something!'

She doesn't know what, though. She wants to shut it all away and hide, but The Asker, the man who once saved *her*...

The Asker.

Oh no... she thinks, *no*, her eyes blurring with unshed tears that won't help anything. *Get a grip, Mallory.*

Warden starts pacing, repeating the short walk from one wall to the other, seeming to give up on her.

'Maybe we should go to the police,' he says. 'Maybe we should tell someone...'

Mallory finally looks at him, dragging her eyes away from the screen. She can tell from the way he stops that those words have them both remembering their conversation in the car last night about how pretty much everything they've been doing – that The Asker's been doing – is seriously illegal. The weight of it, the reality of it suddenly comes crashing down on Mallory then in a way it never fully has before, because how can they go to anyone for help? And it's not just her stupid personal hang-ups about the police because of Jeanie any more. For starters, what would they tell them? How would they show them the ransom message? They still don't have any idea where The Asker actually is and the only way to communicate with the CoD is through the Forum – and the Forum could land twenty-two different people in jail, *especially* The Asker and...

And...

Any attempt on your part to engage the authorities will not end well for him.

And that's the crux of it. Mallory chest's tightens so much it hurts.

'We can't,' she answers, voice cracking. They're alone.

'No, Echo, this is bigger than us,' Warden says. 'It's got so much bloody bigger than us, it's ridiculous.' His voice is rising in pitch, freckle-dusted cheeks blotching red. 'It isn't going to a club, looking for where someone we know has just *gone off* to, or disappeared to, or even been scared off to; it's a full, bloody kidnapping!'

'I know, Warden! But you saw what they said.'

He shakes his head.

'They can't be watching everywhere,' he says.

'But we don't know what they *are* watching.'

'The FBI will have back channels, protocols for anonymous tip offs.'

'These are hackers!' Mallory replies. 'Just like us. Fucking brilliant elites, in fact, given the people they've already managed to locate.'

'But – '

'If we do this wrong, The Asker could end up *dead*!'

Warden stops. His face is pale and he looks so damn scared...

'That's what it means,' she goes on, willing herself to just *keep it together*. 'What they said, that's what it means. If we don't do what they want, they're gonna kill him.' She swallows. 'And we've got no idea where Scarlet is,' she adds, 'though they could have her too, probably do. And Cyber Sneak, or Weevil, or Tower. Real people' – her eyes lock to his – 'just like you said.'

Warden's shaking a little. She can see it as he rubs his eyes with rough, angry hands as if he can make it all go away by closing them. And it's like something moves inside her at the sight and she almost steps towards him...

'You're not thinking of going, are you?' he asks suddenly. 'Doing what they want?'

Mallory hesitates, just the briefest second where she thinks, *What if it's my fault? What if it is my fault The Asker got caught, because I didn't help...* And the sick feeling inside grows and she wishes, she *wishes* so badly she could change what she did, so badly that for a second, she considers...

Then, 'No,' she says, but Warden saw it, saw the pause.

''Cause that'd be bloody stupid,' he tells her.

'I'm not going.' She holds his gaze and he looks away, down at the floor, wringing his hands out in front of him.

'What do we do?' he says. 'If we can't go to the police and we can't go ourselves, then what?'

Mallory looks back at her laptop, rereads the message for the umpteenth time, her skin prickling as if she's surrounded by people, though there's only Warden and he's sat back down on the bed, away from her.

'It takes around two hours to get to the city,' she says carefully, 'three max, if traffic's bad. They don't know how close I am already. That gives us time. It gives us twenty-one hours to figure out something else. We need to think. We just need to think.'

And be really damn careful.

She saves the CoD's message so it won't be wiped clean like chat box conversations usually are when you close them, then shuts it.

'Check the live feed from the security cameras again,' she tells Warden. 'Check no one's picked up the bug.'

'I would know if they had – '

'*Check*,' Mallory repeats. 'We can't take anything for granted now. Anything.' She hears him begin typing. 'Then we keep doing what we were doing, looking through feeds from around the time The Asker logged off. If we can find out exactly what happened, maybe we can work out where they took him and…' She trails off.

And then… I don't know, I don't know!

She needs to calm down. She needs to think rationally. She clenches her fists, hard, nails digging deep into her palms like she's trying to pour all of the tension out into them. Then she releases. She does it twice in a row, breathing deep and slow.

She looks back at her screen.

Careful. Think.

Regardless of whether Children of Daedalus had looked harmless earlier, it seems they are anything but. There must be other members behind the operation, other members a lot smarter than those on its boards – or maybe the boards are no more than a front, as Warden had suggested.

And they logged in to The Asker's account.

That thought is so unnerving that Mallory has to lock her fists again because she is certain The Asker would not have given up how to log in willingly. She's not even sure he'd have given it up if he thought his life depended on it. The Forum is everything to him. The most likely thing is that, if they have Scarlet too, she was the one who told the CoD about its existence... but if that was the case, then why didn't they log in on her account instead?

No, she thinks. Whoever did this was sending a message greater than the literal one. They used The Asker's account for a reason. Either it was as proof they had him and they *did* manage to force him to log in for them... or they hacked his account, and if they did that, then – *hell* – who are they dealing with? And what do they want with elite hackers when they're obviously more than proficient themselves? They said they needed Echo Six's help.

Just work it through, Mallory tells herself. *Go over everything again, step by step.*

Technically, it's still guesswork that the CoD have Scarlet at all – and they didn't mention her in the ransom message – but it does seem likely. It also seems likely they were behind the disappearances of Cyber Sneak, Weevil and Tower – and now they want help from Echo Six, who had just started looking into Daedalus too. She starts tapping on the desk as her mind turns it over.

Four, three, four, two.

Four, three, four, two.

None of that can be chance. Those hackers are specific, talented. Either the CoD are a bunch of psychopaths who just don't like anyone else good looking into Daedalus and the 'help' request is just in the message to lure her in, or – way more likely – there *is* something specific they need an elite hacker to do, something that they haven't been able to do themselves, something *no one's* been able to do yet. The obvious answer is find The Reckoning. Mallory can't think of anything else, but it doesn't make sense. The quest trail doesn't lead anywhere and if the missing hackers had suddenly figured out something everyone else had missed, why wouldn't they have released it themselves?

And how would the CoD have known about it anyway?

And why would they think Echo Six could help? What do they think she can do that the others couldn't?

And what if she can't?

And, and, and?!

Fear ripples through her. She feels tangled up, caught in a web that's so much bigger than she thought, that she still can't see the edges of.

'It's fine,' Warden says, breaking into her thoughts. 'The connection wasn't traced.'

Mallory nods, frustrated with herself, with the situation.

'We go back to checking the feeds then,' she says. Warden doesn't argue. Maybe he can't think of a better option. She goes into the admin panel, a few other things to make sure of before joining him. The Forum site is secure as far as she can tell – The Asker and Scarlet's accounts are still blocked from the boards and only able to message her – but she checks everything she can think of regarding its defense. Nothing is wrong, nothing is compromised. However the CoD logged in, it appears that was all they did. She minimizes the Forum window and goes back to searching the feeds like she'd told Warden. They have to find something. They need to know more. They *have* to... She looks through video after video, studies a thousand different faces, and finds nothing. All the while, the minutes tick by.

What if you don't find anything in time? a growing voice asks. *What if you miss it, or you're wrong and there's nothing there to find at all?* If all they want is for her to hack or code something, then maybe... *No!*

Warden's right, this is too big, and she suddenly feels very small; very human and very vulnerable. She can't go to New York like they want. Their only option if they run out of time would be the police, some back channel like he'd suggested... but then The Asker...

No, no, no, The Asker...

Tears prick infuriatingly at her eyes again and, for a moment, her breath catches as she thinks of what might have happened to him and what it would be like to really lose him, what it would be like to know he was never coming back. He's a good man, a good man who does good things, who tries to help people and show up what's rotten – and now someone is threatening to hurt him. She tenses up, fighting against the emotion threatening to overwhelm her, because he doesn't deserve it, and because she can't... she *can't* lose him.

And it's my fault. If I'd just gone with him...

'Echo,' Warden says.

She can't…

'*Echo,*' he repeats and she finally turns, blinking too fast. His eyes are fixed on his laptop. 'I've found something.' He looks up sharply and Mallory crosses to him. His screen is paused on the footage of a camera in one of the booths. He pushes play. Mallory glances at the time stamp.

Eight thirteen; thirty-eight minutes before The Asker disappeared.

No, she thinks, *not disappeared; before he was* taken.

A man enters the booth alone. He's dressed in a plain shirt and suit pants, and his hair is dark and shaggy. He seems wary, careful to keep his head angled downwards, as if he knows there will be cameras and he doesn't want them to get a good look. He sits, and takes out a phone. It's hard to see in the grainy image, but it looks like his fingers start moving across the screen. Warden scrolls the footage forwards then, to eight forty-four. The man is still in the booth, still on his phone.

Is that him? Mallory thinks, adrenaline spiking a little.

As it plays, the man looks up as if he was startled by something, tilting his head and giving the camera a better view, though it's still an angled one. Best Mallory can make out, he looks about thirty. His face is smooth and clean shaven, his eyebrows dark over hooded eyes. Three new people walk into the shot then – two men, one woman – and position themselves around him, remaining standing, as if to block any exit. They talk to the man with the phone for a minute or so, then he starts typing. One of the new guys – big and bald, with a shedload of tattoos – dives for the device. He punches the shaggy-haired man right in the face and Mallory flinches, even just watching it. A few moments later, the phone is surrendered, its owner apparently having succeeded in whatever he was trying to do. Mallory looks at the time again.

Eight fifty-one.

The exact moment that The Asker had gone offline.

'Echo,' Warden says, 'the time.'

'I know,' she answers, blood pulsing.

It's him, she thinks. *It's really The Asker. It must be.* And it's the strangest thing, seeing him there, the real him. He's somehow younger that she expected – though she'd never really thought of him in person

– younger even than Roger. He just seemed older, maybe, from the things he said, the conviction and authority he had. She stares down at his stoic face. Even in the grainy, poorly-lit image, she can see his nose is bleeding. He'd taken that punch without trying to defend himself, taken it in order to try and finish whatever he'd been doing on that phone…

In order to finish logging off.

He was stopping whoever those people are from gaining access to the Forum. He was protecting everyone else on there – protecting her, protecting Warden. Mallory's insides twist. The bald man puts an unsubtle hand on The Asker's arm, pulling him to his feet. There's a tattoo on the back of it; the black outline of a triangle. Then they exit that camera's field of vision.

It takes Mallory and Warden a while to find the right places on each of the proceeding cameras' recordings, but they finally manage to follow The Asker's journey from the booth, across the club floor and on through a small warren of corridors and storage rooms out back. It ends at one near the far left side of the warehouse complex.

A room without a camera inside.

They spend another half hour fast forwarding through the footage of the feed from the corridor outside of it, covering the time now lapsed between Monday night and earlier this morning when Warden had cut off the link. As far as they can see, The Asker never leaves the room. They check the club's blueprints, but there isn't another way out.

Does that mean he's still in there?

Throughout the week, only four people ever go in and out of that room. It's never left unguarded and there are never less than two people present, even overnight. There are the original three who took The Asker – the bald guy who threw the punch, a scrawny man with so many piercings his face looks like a pincushion, and a woman with dark skin and spiky hair. Then there's also another woman, blonde with glasses. All four of them have Daedalus's symbol marked on their left hands. The blonde had arrived that first evening, carrying two bags, both the right size for laptops – further supporting the theory Mallory now voices to Warden, that the CoD were after elites to complete a specific task, possibly to do with finding The Reckoning – though what that could entail, she has no idea.

'And now they want you,' he says slowly, 'Echo Six. If you're right, that means none of the others have succeeded yet, even The Asker, even the people good enough to *catch* The Asker.' Mallory nods, feeling a weight of expectation that is frightening, feeling that smallness again, like she's one tiny, blind piece in a much larger game she doesn't know the rules of yet. 'It would also explain why they didn't send a ransom note right away,' Warden adds, 'to give him time to attempt whatever it was.' Mallory nods again, trying not to wonder what might have happened to the other hackers who failed. They haven't seen any sign of them on the feeds.

We still don't know for sure they took them too, she tells herself, though it feels a hollow reassurance.

'I could be wrong,' she says. 'It's just a theory.'

'It is,' Warden replies, but neither of them voices an alternative.

She looks back at the screen. Apart from various apparent laptops, all The Asker's captors have brought in and out throughout the week has been food and drink. And a bucket. Those are good signs, though, Mallory tells herself, good signs – signs that reinforce the assertion that he is still in there and currently unharmed. If that's true… Her nerves flutter at how close they were to him last night – and how close to his captors. If they had slipped up…

Focus, she tells herself, stopping any panic at that thought before it can start. They didn't. The ransom note admitted that the CoD had no idea who or where she was – and there would have been no point sending it if they had. It would have actually been a risk; a risk they didn't need to take. No, she and Warden were in and out clean at Labyrinth.

The strange thing is that none of the club's uniformed staff ever go near the room where they're keeping The Asker, though she and Warden have now seen three with the tattoo. In fact, the four kidnappers have interacted with no one else all week – not the CoD on staff, nor any tattooed clubbers. They go in and out through an alley side door that no one else uses, and the whole back section of the complex seems otherwise abandoned. Only the main warehouse space and a few adjacent rooms have been converted for the club.

Mallory shows Warden the few recent photos she had found of the owner, Seable, but he's wearing leather gloves in all of them, so they can't tell if he's marked. In fact, he's wearing a lot of leather in them, period. The photos before his techno goth reinvention have him in a suit with no tattoo on his hand. Mallory's seen him in the club's footage a few times but, like the staff, he never goes near where The Asker is being held. She can't quite work it out. Maybe he just doesn't know what's going on. Maybe only some of the CoD's members are part of what's happening, not all. Whoever's involved, someone at the club must be helping the kidnappers, though, because they're there on the security monitors and no one has questioned it. Mallory wonders, briefly, about trying to run facial recognition on them, but she doesn't have access to a database herself and trying to 'borrow' a federal one quickly, and with no prep, would be like asking to get traced and arrested. Truth be told, she's not even sure the images are good enough quality to get a match. They're blurry and, like The Asker, it seems everyone is careful to keep their heads down, so there are no direct shots.

'We should reconnect to the bug,' Mallory tells Warden, her voice coming out a little hoarse. 'We need to see what's happening now, what's happened since the footage ran out.' He nods and begins typing, the live video feed soon appearing on the screen. The pincushion is stationed outside the room, the others likely inside.

'I'll start downloading – ' Warden begins.

There's a knock on the bedroom door. He starts, the laptop teetering precariously on his lap until Mallory's hand shoots out to grab it.

'Mal?' It's Jed. Hearing his voice then hits her, jarring with everything that's just been going on. The two things shouldn't be in the same place. She slams Warden's laptop lid closed and darts back across to her desk to do the same to hers.

'Come in,' she calls, trying to keep her voice even. Her brother enters, giving Warden a slightly dirty look.

'I just wondered about lunch,' he says. It's so normal. It jars again. Mallory glances at the clock. It's a half hour past meal time. Here they are trying to save The Asker's life and Jed needs a sandwich.

Of course he needs a sandwich, she tells herself. *Of course that's all still real and still matters like it always has.* They're in her room, in her house. That stuff doesn't just stop because of all the crap that's coming down from that *other thing* she does in her life, the thing Jed doesn't know about and shouldn't know about, and shouldn't even be near – now, more than ever...

He seems to sense he's interrupting something.

'...I could do it by myself, Mal,' he suggests. 'I can see what's on the chart.'

In spite of everything, she hesitates. She knows it's stupid, because of course he can do it by himself, use a knife by himself. She knows he'll be fine. She knows it. But she still gets this irrational fear with him, because if anything ever happened to him... Guilt bubbles up from somewhere deep inside of her. She has to protect him. She is all he has to look out for him, and whoever's fault that it is, it certainly isn't his. The laptop hums, warm beneath her fingers.

'Okay,' she says. Jed wavers, like he isn't sure he heard her right. 'Just be careful.'

'Course, Mal, course,' he nods, a smile breaking out. 'Do you want one too... you guys?' he adds, glancing at Warden.

'That would be great,' Mallory says.

'Yeah, thanks,' Warden agrees, though he looks confused. He's still looking oddly at Mallory when Jed leaves.

'What?' she asks.

'How old is he?'

'Eleven. Looks younger, I know.'

'Why did he ask if he could make a sandwich, can't he just do it?'

She shifts uncomfortably.

'I don't want him to cut himself,' she answers.

'He's *eleven.*'

She swallows. Maybe her approach doesn't quite make sense from the outside, and maybe it isn't perfect, but it's the way she knows how to do it and it's worked so far.

'I got to look after him the best I can,' she says quietly. 'He's my responsibility and if anything bad happens to him it's on me. So you can stop about things you don't understand.' She crosses to the bed and sits back down, pulling open his laptop screen without looking at him. 'We got things to do, okay,' she says.

They spend the next hour or so sifting through the footage of The Asker in detail on Warden's laptop. Jed comes in after about ten minutes with the sandwiches, perfectly made, breaking an initial awkward silence. He tells Mallory he's going out in the yard to practise on the punch bag with Roger.

It's good, she thinks, as he goes, *it's safe,* and that's a thought she shouldn't even have because none of this involves Jed and it shouldn't. *But they want me, and I'm his sister.* She tries to shut it all out, tries to focus only on the footage. That's what will help.

There is no sound with the video, so they try to lip read what was said before The Asker was punched, but the image distorts too much when they zoom in. When the most recent footage from the corridor downloads, they check that too, but it doesn't tell them much else, other than that at one point the blonde woman with glasses came out the room looking angry and started talking hurriedly with the spiky-haired woman who was guarding outside at that point. Then she'd gone back in with her, and the pincushion guy had taken her place in the corridor. According to the time stamp, it was about a half hour before the ransom message was sent.

'What do you think that was about?' asks Warden, but Mallory just shakes her head, unsure.

She glances at her clock; one fifty-five now. It's twenty hours, thirty-four minutes until the CoD's deadline – sixteen hours and thirty-four minutes until they'd have to leave to make it back to New York in time. If she was going to go, which she isn't, which she can't…

Damn it.

She gets up from the bed, stretches out her legs. They do know a lot more – know what The Asker looks like, where he's likely being held – but no miraculous plan is presenting itself in her head yet. If it reaches that sixteen hours, thirty-four minutes, when she'd have to leave, or not, and she still has no other option…

She wonders, again, about telling the police. She keeps going back and forth on the idea – thinking they have to, then thinking they can't. Now they know where The Asker is, surely there's at least a chance of getting him out safely that way... but then she thinks of the warning in the ransom message and changes her mind all over again.

None of the options are good.

Plus, they've never seen the feed without a guard in that corridor, and the blonde and at least one other usually inside the room with The Asker on top of that. Even if they did somehow manage to tip off the police and the CoD *didn't* get wind of it in advance – and the police took it seriously and sent in some kind of SWAT team – there's still no guarantee The Asker would be alive by the time the officers reached him.

And he can't die. He can't...

She can't let that happen. She rocks back and forth on her feet, trying to release some of the taut energy rattling within her.

Come on, think, she tells herself. *You always find a way past, always find a loophole. That's what you do, what you're good at. Just fricking think!*

'Hey, Echo,' says Warden. 'We've got movement on the live feed again and...' He stops talking.

Mallory turns to him.

'What?' she asks.

'Shit,' he says, his voice disturbingly quiet.

'What, Warden?' she snaps. She looks down at the screen of his laptop –

and her heart feels like it stops, like someone's shocked it with one of those defibrillator pads and it's just shut off. She blinks like she can't be seeing it right...

All four of the captors are stood back in the corridor now, talking. The door to the room where they're keeping The Asker is left open but there isn't enough of an angle for the camera to see inside. That's not what really matters, though, it's not... because the pincushion man is now holding a piece of paper, a printed picture.

He's holding a photo of Mallory.

A Thousand Words

It's me, Mallory thinks dumbly. The image is dark and grainy, taken from the club's CCTV, but it's definitely her; her face looking upwards beneath the hood of Jeanie's jacket. *They know what I look like.*

She half sits, half drops down onto the bed. First the message, now *this.* After years of hiding, there she is in a stranger's hands, just Mallory Park, all the Echo Six stripped away.

She feels naked, violated.

'How?' she gasps. Everything is moving too fast. The rules and problems are changing and developing, all of it too fast.

'I don't know.' Warden's eyes are wide, his mouth open. Mallory's mind starts to race with the question, like it's burning, searing her…

'How did they know I was even there?' she says. 'Did they trace your connection?'

'No.' He shakes his head.

'You're sure?'

'You can check it yourself.' He offers his laptop, but she doesn't move.

'It doesn't make sense,' she mutters, her heart racing now. This doesn't feel real. It feels like everything's warped, like it's a nightmare she should be able to wake up from. 'Even if they were looking for Echo Six, how did they know that *I'm* Echo Six?' They evidently do, from the photo – and it frightens her in a way she's not really felt before. There is no backing out now, no way she could just walk away any more, even if she wanted to. 'How did they even know to look for me at the club?' she goes on. 'No one knew we were going to be there!'

'I don't know,' Warden repeats. 'I don't… I mean, if they found out about your connection to The Asker, maybe they thought you might try and trace him, and so they were looking out for someone?'

'But they'd still have had no idea *when* I would go,' Mallory says, thoughts piling up inside her head, fingers flexing jerkily, 'or what I would look like if I did.' She gets up again and starts pacing, a hideous energy firing through her veins. 'There must be thousands of people in and out of that place every night and they can't have any specifics on me – they can't even know how old I am. They can't know. They can't know any of it, unless…' She hesitates. 'Unless…'

She stops.

Her eyes flick back to Warden and it's like a physical pain tears open in her chest. The strength of it shocks her and she steps backwards knocking into the book case. She remembers his texting. Everything points to one answer, and it hurts, it really fucking hurts, because he couldn't… He couldn't…

Not Warden…

And in that moment, she suddenly realizes how much he means to her, how much she relies on him – has done for a long time – and…

'No,' he says, seeming to realize what she's thinking. 'No.'

'*You* knew,' Mallory says simply, her hand gripping hold of the book-case. A mole in the Forum…?

Please, oh please, no…

'You were the only one who knew,' she says.

'But I didn't tell anyone,' he replies, eyes wide circles. 'Echo, I wouldn't.'

'How do I know?'

'Because you know me.'

'No, I don't,' she says, shaking her head. 'No, I don't, not really.'

And still, *not Warden,* she begs. *Please not Warden… Oh please, PLEASE!*

'Yes, you do.' He stands, putting the laptop aside, but she backs further away from him, along the bookcase. He stops, looking helpless.

'Have you been lying to me?' she asks, the question biting at her. 'How long has it been a lie?'

'Never,' he says, but she feels so stupid. 'I've never lied to you. My name's Gilbert Ward and I'm from Sun City and we've spoken almost every day for the past two and a half years – '

'Then why is it they only have my picture and not yours? We went there together. Why aren't they holding up your face too?'

'I don't know,' he says. 'Maybe… maybe, well, they're looking for Echo Six,' he seizes. 'They're looking for a woman, not a guy and – '

'Why did you come here?' Mallory demands, cutting across him.

'What?' he stammers. Then, 'You know why.'

'You didn't want me to go looking for The Asker at first,' she says, thinking back. 'You told me to wait, and I did, but then you still didn't want me to do it, did you? So you can't have come because you cared about him that much – '

'I care about The Asker,' Warden responds, a hardness entering his voice. 'I told you to wait because it sounded dangerous and I was worried about you, and as it turns out – '

'So you flew right across the country to meet someone you'd never met, to go and bug a nightclub where we thought someone else had disappeared, even though you thought it would be dangerous. I mean, who does that?'

'Echo – '

'No, it's crazy! And now you're in my house, because *I* trusted you, because I brought you here and now *they* know what I look like and maybe they're even coming here. *Here*!'

'Echo, listen to me, I didn't – '

'Then explain it!' she shouts. 'Because it doesn't make sense.' Her voice cracks and there are tears falling down her cheeks now – and they won't stop though she tells them to – because she doesn't want it to be him, she doesn't, but… 'I should have seen that before,' she says. 'You haven't got a tattoo, so did they pay you?'

'Pay me? No,' he protests.

'So you didn't rat me out?'

'No, Echo!' he says, and he looks angry now, hurt himself. 'Come on, if I was going to do that, surely I'd have done it at the club before crawling through that sodding vent and exposing myself to goodness knows how many bacteria!'

She wants to believe him. She wants to, but…

'Then why did you do it?' she asks, the words streaming out all loud and angry. 'No one would do all that, not for someone they've never met, that they don't know!'

The room goes silent. Warden's eyes drop to the floor. He's gone strangely still, grating against how wired Mallory feels right now

'I know you,' he says softly, barely more than a whisper. 'I *know* you, Echo.' His eyes flick back up to her and they are glassy now, too. Mallory feels like she can't move. 'I know you don't like peanut butter,' he says. 'You told me once that you liked peanuts and you liked butter, but not the two together because of the texture. I agree,' he goes on, 'it's weird.' Then, 'I know you like football, the American kind, not soccer. You talk about the stats sometimes, how you like to run them in your head, and you're always a little more animated after a game night.' His voice gets faster. 'I know you think rom coms are stupid, but you also like watching them because they're usually predictable and that's safe. I know talking about how you really feel makes you nervous.' His voice shakes. 'I know that because you always swear at me in chat when I do, or you just stop talking back. But at the same time I don't think it's because you don't feel – which is what you seem to want to project – I think it's because you feel everything a little bit *too much* and you can't really cope with it if you say it out loud.' Then, 'I know you like solving problems and fixing things, like I do, and that sometimes The Asker and the Forum feel more real to you than your real life does. I know you care about your family, though, so much so that you'd do absolutely anything for them.' He hesitates. 'I know I like talking to you,' he says. 'I may not have seen your face until yesterday, but I know you – Echo Six, Mallory Park, whatever it is you want to call yourself.' Tears are rolling down his cheeks now, his cheeks that are all flushed bright red. 'And you know me.' Mallory stays rooted to the spot, her eyes locked on his, her whole unmoving body feeling like it's pulsing with fiery energy, like what he's saying is reverberating inside of her with a truth she would never have admitted before.

'You want to know why I flew right across the country to help you?' he asks. 'Because you're my best friend.' He lets out a kind of sharp laugh – a laugh with no real laugh in it at all. 'Does that sound stupid to you? But see, I don't have that many at school,' he goes on, speaking a mile a minute, that way Warden does. 'I mean there are classmates I sit with, but I find it hard to get close to people, you know? Well, you do because I never lied to you – though you keep seeming to think I did – and so you know how I have a knack of pissing people off just by talking, so that's school out. And home? My brothers are jerks and my dad wishes I was more like them because apparently that's what being a proper man looks like. My mom loves me, but she's drunk half the time because he's been cheating on her for years and she knows it.' His voice rises. 'So then there's you and the Forum. I care about The Asker because the Forum saved *me* too. It's the best part of my day, talking to you, being Warden and not sodding Bertie. I hate that name, but my dad still calls me it and I bloody hate it. Maybe it is ridiculous,' he says, 'coming all this way because I thought *you* were in trouble – blowing most of the money I was saving for the Lampertz safe on the ticket, because there weren't any economy ones left that'd get me here on time – maybe it *was* even bloody stupid, but that's why I did it.' His voice falls away. 'So don't give me crap about not trusting me,' he whispers. 'Just don't, because I'd never hurt you. I never bloody would.'

He looks like an open book, just stands there, wiping his eyes, everything he's feeling written like sentences across his face – and something in Mallory just can't really bear it, can't bear to see him so upset like that and…

'Warden,' she says simply, a whole lot of meaning scrunched up in that one name. He looks at her and she feels both crumpled up and blown open all at the same time and – for the briefest moment – it has nothing at all to do with her picture on the screen. She steps towards him, her whole body feeling electrified…

Another step…

Then another…

And then she's reaching out to him, pins and needles running all up and down her arms and…

'Warden – ' she repeats.

'Mallory!' The door to her room slams open. Mallory drops her arm like she's been stung. It's Roger, Jed beside him. They're both in their sports gear, sweaty-faced and out of breath. 'What's going on?' Roger asks, eyes flicking from her to Warden. 'We heard shouting.'

'Mal?' Jed asks. 'Mal, are you crying?'

Damn it. Damn it!

She moves to block her laptop from view and wipes her cheeks, looking back at Jed, his small face full of concern, a face – Warden's right – that she would do anything to protect. And then she remembers *her* face in that image from the security feed, and whatever just happened between her and Warden falls away...

And, suddenly, it becomes all about that damn picture again.

She doesn't know how the CoD got it, but she doesn't think it was from the boy standing just across from her. However it happened, though, it could lead them here. A very real and very close fear skitters through her. It could lead the people who kidnapped The Asker, and likely the others too, who implied that they were prepared to *kill* him to get what they want, right here...

To Jed. To Roger.

No.

That thought is solid, unwavering. Mallory doesn't know what she is going to do about so many things, but this one thing is clear. She will keep them safe.

'You need to go,' she says.

'What?' asks Roger. 'Look, what's going on?' He glances at Warden, Warden's own eyes still red. 'Did he hurt you?'

'No,' Mallory says firmly, the same time as Warden. Roger looks between the two of them. Jed is just glaring at Warden. 'No,' she repeats, 'just, something... something has happened and it means you can't be here right now. I need you to go.' She stands up straighter. She wipes her face again and walks towards the door, towards her family.

'What do you mean, go?' says Roger, eyes narrowing as she reaches him.

'I mean you need to pack a bag, now. You got ten minutes. Then you're taking the Chevy, leaving this house and going to stay in a motel for a few days. You drive out northeast and don't stop till you're past Hartford. And you do not stop for gas at all, you hear me? You use the can in the trunk if you need it.' Gas stations have CCTV and she doesn't know what to trust any more. Maybe she's being paranoid, but if they got her image at the club, she doesn't know what resources they have or how widespread they are. The picture was blurry, but if they do have access to a database and manage to actually ID her from it – *no, no, no* – they'll know she has a family. If they were prepared to use The Asker to get her to do what they want, they'd sure use her little brother.

And that sure as hell is not going to happen.

Mallory pushes past them. She heads straight to Jed's room, dragging his old brown suitcase from under the bed.

'Mallory,' Roger says, clearly agitated.

'Go pack,' she orders. There isn't time for this.

'This doesn't make any sense – '

'I said fucking go pack!' She shouts it at him, practically screams it. She hears him gasp, the way he always does at loud noises. 'Just do it!' She doesn't let herself look back to see what it did to him, focusing only on taking clothes for Jed out of the painted blue chest of drawers by his bed and putting them in the case. 'Enough for a few days,' she says and she hears the floorboards creak as Roger walks away, hears him open the door to his room. Jed starts collecting things up himself without a further challenge and she feels a fierce rush of affection for him. 'Sorry,' she mutters. 'Sorry I swore.' Especially *that* word.

Within ten minutes, they are standing by the front door, two small suitcases shoved into the Chevy's trunk. Mallory gives Roger half the cash she keeps stashed in her desk drawer for emergencies, telling him not to use an ATM unless he absolutely has to. Yes, she's being paranoid, but then The Asker was paranoid and that wasn't enough, was it?

'I'll call you when you can come back,' she says. Roger doesn't go though, just stands there in the doorway, fists clenched tight like hers.

'Look, Mal,' he says, 'if you're in trouble, let us help. Whatever it is, it doesn't matter. We can call, we can call the police – '

'No,' Mallory snaps. She takes a shaky breath, knowing what it must have cost him to suggest that, but, 'No, whatever you do, you can't call the police. You can't.'

'But we – '

'You can't!'

'Then let *me* help you,' he says. There's a pleading in his eyes, but also something else, something she hasn't seen in so long it makes her chest tighten… He looks defiant.

'You can help me by looking after Jed,' she tells him, 'by going.'

'No,' he says. Mallory stares at him.

'What – ' she begins.

'*No,*' he repeats, stronger this time. He looks down at her, a full head taller. 'I am not leaving you, Mallory, not like this. This is crazy.' He locks his jaw. 'Now, you're gonna tell me what's going on and I'm gonna help you out of it. No police,' he adds, 'okay, but if you're in trouble, we work it out together.'

Mallory still just stares at him, dumbstruck. He hasn't told her 'no' since Jeanie left and he wouldn't tell her where she went or why he wouldn't fight for her. She's wanted him to, wanted him to tell her off for things, to give her boundaries, to care enough to step in. So many damn times she's wanted him to, and now… now, here he is doing it, this moment of all the moments he could have picked…

The one moment she can't accept it.

Mallory looks into her dad's eyes, light brown like Jed's. The defiance is there still, but she knows him, knows how paper thin it will be, how easy to tear apart… She lets herself feel it, though, feel it just for a second, feel him looking at her with that concern, taking control of the situation and being like the dad she only just remembers, the dad who always protected her, who she *misses*…

Oh shit, she misses him so damn much…

And she lets herself feel it…

And then…

Then…

'You're going to do what I say,' she says, her voice like ice, even as inside it feels like she's splintering.

'Mal, listen – ' he begins.

'No, you fucking listen!' she shouts. She yells it so hard her throat hurts and he flinches back, but she doesn't stop. 'You think you know better than me? I've been keeping this family safe for over four years. Me. *I* have. Four years you had to act like a parent and you didn't!' The words rip out of her. 'So now you're gonna listen to what I say we need to do here, because you bailed, Roger. You backed away every single time.' It's cruel. And it's like she can see him breaking, see his resistance falling away, falling so damn easily it hurts to watch, but she keeps going because he has to listen. It's her fault this has happened and she has to make absolutely sure he'll do what she says. She has to keep him safe, keep Jed safe. 'You want to start being yourself again, start being a father again, then great, but you do it to Jed and not to me, because you're too damn late and Jed's the one who needs you now. You look after him. That's what I want from you.'

He fades away right before her eyes, the spark blowing out as he clasps his fists tighter and bites his lip to keep from crying and…

Shit, shit, shit…

'It's all I want.' She hands him the keys to the Chevy, forcing herself to keep looking at him, though she doesn't want to, she doesn't want…

'I'll look after him,' he says finally, voice hoarse. Mallory nods once. Roger blinks too many times and backs out the door without another word.

'Are you going to argue too?' Mallory asks Jed. She hopes it's a no because she doesn't think she could take that.

'No, Mal,' he says, and she feels it again, that rush of affection.

'Why not?' she asks. 'Why do you never argue with me?' She glances over at Warden, hanging back by the stairs. He's right. Jed's eleven now. He should argue with her, but he never does, not really. She looks down at him.

'Because we look after each other,' he says. Then all of a sudden he's hugging her – hugging her for all the hugs she never gave him, because she couldn't, because she *couldn't*. She feels it, everywhere he's holding her, but she doesn't let herself pull away, makes herself hug him back, trying to tell him in it that she's grateful and she'll sort this out, and that she's so very proud of him…

Jed steps away, into the doorway, then he looks back at Warden.

'You hurt my sister,' he says, 'and I'll kill you.' Mallory is too taken aback to respond.

'I wouldn't – ' Warden begins, but Jed walks straight out to the

Chevy, not waiting for an answer.

Echo Six

Mallory watches until the car turns off the road, exhaust rattling away – no time to fix it now. She can't get the image of Roger's stony face behind the windshield out of her head, even after they've gone. They're safe, though. That's what's important. She wanders back inside, locking the front door, staring at the wood, the varnish scratched and fading like a lot of things in their house.

'Are you all right?' Warden asks. Then, 'Sorry, bad question, of course you're not. Echo, that was… Look, I don't know what to do but I swear to you…' And the words just start pouring out of him again. Mallory closes her eyes as he tells her again how he's on her side, how he wouldn't hurt her. He brings up the safe again and it's almost like she's back up in her room talking to him across three thousand miles of internet. Warden is right, she does know him; his speech patterns, the things he says, the things he likes – that he would never betray her, and she feels ashamed for even thinking it. She *knows* him, and maybe, just maybe, she would have flown right across the country for him too. 'I swear I didn't tell anyone anything,' he continues. 'And those texts I've been getting, they're from my mother. You can look but it's pretty much just her calling me poppet, saying how I'm growing up too fast, looking at colleges and making her feel old, and asking when I'll be coming home.'

'What did you tell her?' Mallory says quietly, turning back to him. Warden pauses.

'…That I needed a little longer,' he says. Then, 'Here,' he says holding out his phone, and he doesn't even sound angry – though maybe he should, he should be mad at her – just determined to prove his innocence, as if what she thinks is all that really matters to him, and it moves her in a way that she doesn't really know how to respond to. 'Here, you can check, and you can look through anything you want on my laptop. And you can search through my suitcase, my coat, my pockets, whatever you need to – '

'I believe you,' she interrupts.

'But – '

'I trust you.'

'Oh,' he says. And he stops. Mallory flushes with guilt again, and so much other pent up emotion, she doesn't know what to say.

What comes out is a very soft, 'It's kind of all snowballed like I didn't expect.' Then, 'Sorry,' she says. 'I'm so sorry, Warden.' She makes herself repeat it, clearer the second time. 'If you want to go back home, I'll understand, with everything that's happened. They only have my picture at the moment. Like you said, it's Echo Six they want.'

'I don't want to go,' Warden tells her – even after everything she said to him – and the words fill her with relief because she doesn't want him to go either, she doesn't want him to. 'I mean,' he adds, 'I'm pretty sodding scared, being honest, but I don't want to go… if you still want my help, that is.'

Mallory bites down on her lip, closes her eyes, just for a moment.

'I'll always want that,' she says.

* * *

Mallory sits down at her desk. Warden is perched on the bed behind her, checking the feed again. She doesn't ask him what's going on in it, though, not just then. Instead, she reaches for her own computer and opens up the Forum window. She doesn't feel like she used to as Echo Six, sitting there and looking at the message boards. She doesn't feel strong. She feels vulnerable… frightened, just like Warden had said he was. And it's like a loss, like something there is already damaged beyond repair. She shuts her eyes. She is Echo, and she isn't. Either way, someone who shouldn't know her face does now, so what they call her doesn't really matter. It was only ever a wall to hide behind anyway…

Echo Six is just a name, she tells herself. *I did everything she did. And, in the club, that was me…* Something stirs inside of her. *And before that, with Connor, and Bobby, that was me…*

She is wrung out, but, as she sits there, a new, driving purpose begins to grow; a desire – no, a solid determination – to fix what has gone wrong. Everything that matters to her is at risk now, both sides of her world and the people in them, and it is not okay. And she is angry.

It is not okay that the Children of Daedalus have taken The Asker – and maybe the others, whoever they are, wherever they are. It is not okay that they have threatened him.

It is not okay that they have her picture.

It is not okay that her family is now in danger.

Echo is just a name.

It is not okay, what she is going to have to do now.

Mallory opens her eyes. What she has to do now is something that Echo never would. It's what she should have done the moment she got that ransom message, but she couldn't even face thinking it. Enough is enough, though. She goes into the message boards and writes out a new post. It is a simple one, and it will be the last from Echo Six.

The Asker is gone and the Forum is compromised. Be careful and check you haven't been traced. Delete your accounts. Do not log in again.

If someone knows her hacker name – however they found it out – then they might already know others too. No one else needs to become involved in this.

'I'm closing the Forum,' Mallory says out loud. She looks across at Warden. For a moment, his face breaks and she feels it… but then he nods, agreeing.

Goodbye, she writes under the message.

She clicks to post. Eleven people are currently online. Within a minute of the message going live, that number is down to six. And they're not just going from white to grey – the online list to the offline one – they're vanishing completely. It's over. It was never going to be saved, from the moment The Asker disappeared. She just hadn't let herself think it consciously. That was a mistake.

As an administrator, Mallory could delete the Forum completely, but she needs to give the other members time to see the warning – and she needs to keep the channel open to The Asker's captors. She hasn't replied to their message and she doesn't know if she will yet, but she doesn't want them to have any idea of what she's doing. Neither The Asker's or Scarlet's accounts can do anything but send messages to hers, so unless they have someone else from the Forum, they won't know what's happening. If they do have... well, then there's nothing she can do about that. Shutting it down is still the right thing. There are eighteen other people on there.

As the number of names in white steadily continues to drop, Mallory goes through the message boards, permanently erasing every section, every thread, every hack... everything that made it somewhere important – everything except her last post. Then she goes into the administration panel. She deletes the accounts of everyone not currently online – apart from The Asker and Scarlet – and sets up the same warning message to show when they next try to log in. At each name wiped, the anger in her grows, but her hand shakes as she reaches Warden's, a deep sadness welling up as she clears away every trace that he had ever existed there. When she's done, she glances at the right of the screen again. There are no names left online, apart from her own. They have all read what they needed to, so she deletes the message boards entirely. After that, she wipes clean every remaining trace of every piece of data or code that isn't essential, until all that's left is the back door entrance and a chat box system that runs between the three remaining accounts. She feels both hollow and utterly, seethingly furious.

'It was the right thing,' says Warden. Mallory turns to see him looking across at her and, even though there are eighteen names she will never see again, there is a relief because, account deleted or not, she hasn't lost him. And she is *not* going to lose The Asker either.

'Are you done?' Warden asks. 'Need to show you something.'

'Are they all still in the corridor?' she says, crossing to the bed.

'No, just the one guard now, the skinny one who looks like a cross between a rat and a porcupine.' He turns the laptop to give her a better view. The corridor is empty apart from the pincushion, the door to The Asker's room shut again.

'The others are inside?' she asks.

'No,' Warden replies, and he seems to hesitate, 'the others just left.'

'Left the club? As in, all three of them?'

Warden nods. That's different; there has never been less than two people left behind before – one guarding, at least one inside the room with The Asker. Warden is already skipping back in the feed to show her, stopping at a point when all four of them are still in the corridor, with that copy of Mallory's picture. She starts tapping steadily against her leg, holding on to her anger. The blonde woman seems agitated. In fact, they all do. The pincushion is gesturing angrily, yelling back through the open door of The Asker's room until the blonde physically pulls him back. Mallory's tapping gets faster. They talk for a while longer – Warden scrolling through it – then everyone nods, some kind of decision apparently made. The pincushion hands Mallory's picture to the bald guy, who folds it and puts it into his back pocket. Both the women enter the room, then re-emerge a few minutes later holding laptop bags. They lock the door behind them, then they head out of the corridor completely, along with the bald man, leaving just the pincushion behind. And that's it; he stays that way until Warden fast forwards the footage to catch up with the live feed.

'Did they leave the club?' Mallory asks, apprehension stirring. 'Did they actually all leave?'

He rewinds again, then starts clicking between different feeds, following the three of them until they do exit the club, out of the side alley entrance. They've never left the room with just one guard before, not once, in five days. And they left with Mallory's picture. Panic threatens then, but she shuts it down firmly.

'Do you think they ID'd you?' Warden asks.

'It's a possibility,' Mallory says, clinging to her anger, not panic, clinging to that cold determination she'd felt. 'I don't use social media and it's a crappy picture, but it depends what access they have to facial recognition software. If they did ID me, they could have this address. They could be coming.' She balls her fists. At least Jed and Roger aren't there. At least she was right about doing that.

'They told you to go to New York, though,' Warden says.

'And I didn't reply,' she answers. 'However they found out I'd been there, however they found my picture, it looks as if they only just did – they wouldn't have sent the ransom note if they'd had it before – but they still don't know what I'm doing now.' Her voice is clinical. 'I could be disappearing. I could be giving up on The Asker.' Mallory taps out the pattern once more, then stills her finger. 'They want Echo Six more than they want to keep him,' she realizes. She glances at the clock; twenty hours, three minutes until their deadline – plenty long enough for them to check out a possible lead in nearby Connecticut and still make it back to New York in time for her to arrive if any ID they'd made proved incorrect. Wherever they've gone, it doesn't really matter just at that moment, because an idea is finally forming in Mallory's mind. What matters is who they left behind.

'What do you think we should do?' asks Warden. His face is earnest, and she sees in it that he'll do whatever she suggests. He really will. That thought focuses the drive inside of her, grinding it down into a diamond point, sharp and deadly...

We will not *lose The Asker,* it says. *We are going to save him.*

And none of their current options are acceptable.

She is not going to sit and wait while a clock ticks down. She is not going to give herself up like some idiot on a plate, losing the one bargaining chip they might have. She is not going to risk a tip-off that could end everything for The Asker before anyone has a chance to act. No, she is not going to do any of those things.

She is going to find a loophole.

Online or in real life, everything is a piece of a puzzle, every action has consequences and repercussions, the results of which can still be predicted and analyzed, just like something you type into a computer. Those results may be more erratic in real life, but Mallory is smart – she is really fucking smart – and they have no idea who they are dealing with.

They wanted Echo Six; they will get Echo Six.

And Echo would not be told what moves she can and can't make. She would create her own option, do the thing that no one else would expect because they look at the problem the wrong way. She would take back control. Other people muddy things, screw them up, complicate them...

Control.

Her thoughts race. It changes things, them having her picture, makes it about far more than her original goal to find The Asker and somehow keep the Forum running the same way it always had. She doesn't know who's seen it, how many people are involved or even who they are, other than the name Children of Daedalus. Her new option needs to be bigger than all of that, bigger than what they don't know; it needs to be able to keep The Asker, her friends, her family, herself safe. All of them, despite the photo.

What she needs is leverage.

Just like the cell phone gave her power over Bobby, she needs something to give her power over the CoD. And there is definitely something they *want*. The missing hackers are not an end game – she is sure of that – they are a means to something else...

And The Asker, she thinks, *The Asker will know what that is.*

Control.

'Echo? What do we do?' Warden repeats. She looks at him, her gaze certain.

'We go and get The Asker,' she says.

Return

Mallory and Warden turn into the alley that runs along the left side of Labyrinth. They stop and Warden takes out his laptop. Mallory glances down at the watch she'd put on back at the house, shifting her wrist beneath the strap, not liking the feel. It's five-oh-three. They'd got a taxi into the city – majorly expensive, but the train would have taken too long. Warden had kept the live feed from the club open the whole way, using his portable Wi-Fi to stay connected. None of the other three captors had returned. Mallory tries not to think about where they might be headed. Before they left, she and Warden had set up a webcam to watch the front door of her house, so at least they'll know if something does happen. Roger and Jed aren't there. That's what important for now. When they have The Asker, everything else will change. They won't be on the back foot any more.

When, not if.

Warden hadn't argued when she'd told him what she wanted to do. He'd looked for the briefest moment like he might – a range of expressions from confused to frightened to angry shooting across his face – and then he'd just said, 'Okay.'

Still here, she tells herself. *The Forum's gone, but you haven't lost him.*

She hasn't told him her back-up plan, though, the last resort she has tucked away in the back of her mind and maybe the real reason she doesn't want anyone else like the police involved – if all goes south and any one of them or The Asker is in danger, she can reveal who she is. She can complete the offered deal and try and do whatever it is they want Echo Six to do. She doesn't like it, but contingency is necessary and not having it is stupid, forcing you into on the spot decisions.

'Still clear,' Warden says, laptop balanced on his forearm. 'Looping the feeds now.' He's been recording footage from the cameras on the side entrance and in every corridor they're going to have to go down, ready to run in place of the live streams that will soon include the two of them. The security office is currently empty, though; the club doesn't open for another couple of hours and no one's monitoring it yet. There are a small number of employees already in the building – cleaners, techies, bar staff doing prep – but they're all in the main club itself. Just like for the past week, none of them are anywhere near the corridor where The Asker is being kept. 'We're up,' says Warden.

Mallory nods and they start down the alley, pulling on latex gloves, and balaclavas bought from the same stall where they'd got Warden's beanie yesterday. Loops or no loops, their faces are not going on camera this time. Mallory's skin chafes as the fabric comes over her head, but once it's on she finds it actually makes her feel safer. She feels focused. It had rained on the drive there and the floor of the alley is wet and glistening. Despite the recent wash, it smells of beer and urine and, even in daylight, looks like the kind of place you'd go to get mugged. Mallory keeps glancing backwards, expecting someone to rush in on them from the street beyond, but no one does. It's empty and quiet, nothing like last night.

They reach the club's side door, grey and rusted, and locked shut. Warden slips the laptop into the plain navy backpack Mallory lent him – less conspicuous than his green satchel – and studies the lock before taking out a small leather wallet. He removes a large needle with a hooked end, and a small L-shaped piece of metal. Earlier, when she'd raised the question of the locked doors, he'd replied, 'You didn't think I'd started with safes, did you?' She feels the briefest hint of a smile.

He has the door swinging open in about twenty seconds. It creaks loudly on the hinge and they both freeze – but no sound comes from beyond. Mallory steps through into a narrow corridor. The floor is smoothed concrete and the walls so smeared with grime that she can't tell what color they were originally supposed to be. They creep along the passage, store rooms dotting either side, until they reach a T-junction. Mallory pauses, checking each branch before looking back at Warden.

This is where they part.

He unzips the bag again and takes out the replica BB hand gun that Roger's parents had given Jed a couple of Christmases back – and Mallory had promptly confiscated. Roger won't keep real guns in the house any more, but at least this looks like one. Warden pales a little as he grips the handle. Everything feels more real and fragile now they're here, but Mallory gives him a nod; they can do this. She turns away to the right and starts walking, drumming the pattern on her leg. The plan is to take two different routes to the corridor The Asker's room is on, so they can come at its pincushion guard from both sides. The door to the room is positioned closest to the end Mallory will come out of, hence why Warden has the BB.

She carefully navigates the maze of derelict storage rooms, the building's blueprint clear inside her mind. She encounters no one and, a minute or so later, is standing next to a small metal trash can at the turning onto the target corridor. She's barely moving, but her heart is pumping so loud she's sure the guard beyond must be able to hear it. She can hear him. He's breathing noisily, sniffling away through his silver-ringed nose and shuffling about every few seconds like he's got ADHD. Mallory glances at her watch.

Almost time.

She crouches down beside the bin, and waits.

Four, three, four, two...

Four, three, four, two...

She looks at her watch again; it's time.

Warden is five seconds late...

Ten seconds...

'Freeze!' she hears him yell.

Seriously? He went with freeze?

She darts her head around the corner. The pincushion guard is only a five feet away, his back to her, facing Warden and the BB – and he's pulling out a gun, a *real* gun, and...

'Who the – '

Mallory leaps forward and whacks him round the head with the metal bin. He collapses, the weapon clattering to the floor. How did they miss that in the footage? She crouches down and picks it up, pulse racing as Warden runs towards her.

'Shit,' he gasps. 'That's a sodding – '

'The door,' she snaps, taking a cable tie out of her pocket with her free hand. There is no time for them to panic.

'Right,' Warden answers, nodding more than he needs to. 'Right.' He turns away, slipping the BB gun into his backpack and taking out the lock picking tools.

'How long do you – ' Mallory begins.

A hand grabs her leg. She cries out as it is jerked from beneath her. She falls and her shoulder slams into the wall. Pain flares and she drops the gun, hears it skittering away across the floor… Then the pincushion man is on top of her, pierced face angry and red, the metal in his skin so much more disturbing close up. Alarm floods through her, but before it can even really register, his fist connects with her jaw. She bites her tongue, stunned, as the taste of iron fills her mouth…

No, no…

'No!' That shout wasn't her.

The man's snarling face disappears as Warden drags him off her, toppling backwards under the weight of him. The pincushion turns – so fast again – and punches him right in the stomach. Warden lets out this horrible, strangled gasp, but the man grabs him, and hits him again, this time in the head…

Mallory's vision goes red.

Rage surges up within her, stronger than the pain in her shoulder, in her jaw. She doesn't think. All she sees is the man raising his fist a third time, and how he is *not* going to hit Warden again…

She launches herself at him, colliding with his back so he smacks into the wall, just like she had. As he lurches, she reaches for his face, grabbing whatever piece of metal she can find – then she pulls, right damn hard. The man screams as his nose ring is torn loose, but Mallory doesn't stop. She punches him in the face, putting her weight behind it and using her front two knuckles, just like Roger had showed her. The pincushion crumples to the ground. He looks out cold this time, but she isn't going to take the chance. She picks up the cable tie she'd dropped and, straining audibly, rolls him over to tie his hands behind his back.

'Echo?' Warden gasps, breaking into her concentration as she moves to do the same with the man's feet. She looks up and sees him lifting himself slowly off the ground. He's blinking a lot. 'Echo, are you...' His voice is high and wavery and muffled through the balaclava, but his eyes seem to finally focus on her. Her chest tightens.

'I'm all right,' she says, though the words shake and her jaw throbs as her mouth forms them. 'Are you – '

He half steps forwards, arms lifting, and, for the briefest moment, it looks as if he's going to hug her. Mallory freezes, a new rush of adrenaline flickering through her... but he stops. He's still only inches from her, though, and their eyes are locked together in a way she can't quite work out how to break.

'Echo,' he repeats, and it's more like a sob of relief than anything else, and she feels it too as he says it and, in that moment, she has the strangest urge to reach out for him too, because she remembers him getting hit, remembers the sound he made and how it felt to see it happen and...

'I'm sorry,' he stammers, pulling away, seeming to remember himself, to remember who she is, what she's like. 'Sorry. I just... I'm glad you're okay.'

Mallory manages to a nod, her veins buzzing. She pulls the cable tie tight on the pincushion's legs, trying to focus on that instead.

'I'll get the door,' says Warden. He leans down to pick up his tools and the balaclava slips a little. His nose is bleeding and she gets it again, that strange impulse to reach for him, but...

No, no, fricking no! Her body seizes up.

'You're sure you're all right?' she asks, holding her arms in against her stomach. They don't exactly have time to stop. Warden nods, still studying the lock. Mallory shifts her jaw, feeling the pain there, her shoulder still aching from where she hit the wall. No time for that either... Her gaze falls back down to the guard. He isn't moving and his face is a mess where she pulled out the nose ring. It makes her skin crawl, but even as Warden scrabbles against the door, she finds can't tear her eyes away from it.

She did that.

He deserved it, she thinks. At the very least he's in on a kidnapping… but still. She shivers, unnerved. She backs a little way down the corridor, past the now-dented metal bin, and picks his gun up. She doesn't like the feel of it, cold and hard even through the plastic gloves. Her eyes flick back to the man's wrecked face.

I did that. The thought comes again, and she feels an odd spark of exhilaration, similar to the kick she gets hacking, like she's strong and powerful and… and at the same time it makes her want to throw up. She flexes her free hand nervously in front of her – then stops, catching sight of something. Two of her fingers are marked with black ink. She frowns, and glances back down at the guard, wondering where it came from. The edge of his left hand is smeared with it too. She bends down and lifts it, using only the very tips of her fingers. The delta symbol on the back is smudged. It was drawn on, never a tattoo at all.

What the…?

The door to the room clicks open, snapping her attention away.

The Asker.

Warden glances back at her and she drops the hand.

Later. She can think about what the hell that means later. She comes to stand beside him and raises the gun because, really, they have no idea what they're going to find inside. Roger taught her how to shoot when they were living in North Carolina, back when seeing a gun didn't scare the crap out of him. They'd practiced on cans in the yard… but that was a long time ago, and he'd given her headphones to wear then so she couldn't hear it so bad. She shuffles her hands against the metal – not liking it, not liking it at all – trying to even out her breathing.

What are they going to find inside? What the hell are they going to find?

'On three,' Warden whispers. She nods. 'One,' he mouths.

Please let The Asker be all right, she thinks.

'Two…'

She tries to hold her hands steady, but…

Please…

'Three.'

Warden turns the handle.

The Man Who Asks

The door swings open. The room beyond is dark, pokey and window-less, illuminated only by the light now spilling in from the corridor and the familiar dim glow of a singular computer screen, faced away from them towards the back. Mallory squints to try and see further, but the place is a mess, a mismatch of dusty boxes and piled cleaning equipment. It doesn't smell good either. She steps inside holding the gun in front of her, but no one jumps out – no one says anything at all. Her heart is thumping wildly and… part of her doesn't want to do this, she just wants to run, she wants to…

You're okay, she tells herself firmly, blocking out the impulse. She steps further into the room, her shadow breaking up the light.

Someone groans.

Warden jumps and Mallory's eyes flick to the back of the room, still cloaked in darkness. The screen she saw belongs to a laptop. She can see its outline now. It's open on a table and, beyond that, as her eyes gradually adjust to the lack of light… beyond that, she sees *him*. He's tied to a chair, with a gag in his mouth; the room's only occupant – the same man they saw being taken in the club's video footage.

The man who is The Asker.

Mallory falters at the sight, suddenly overwhelmed by it all. He looks different, now, to the recording, the shirt and suit pants he came in ruffled and grimy, a dark bruise surrounding one of his eyes, another on his cheek just above new grown stubble. He looks exhausted. Something wrenches inside of her.

'No…' she breathes. He groans again, this time more desperate, more like he's trying to say something, and she doesn't wait another moment. She runs to him, tucking the gun into her waist band. Warden is beside her, both of them moving at the same time.

'Don't be afraid,' she hears him say, his own voice shaking, but the man in the chair seems to shrink as they approach.

'It's all right,' Mallory finds herself saying. 'It's all right. We're going to get you out.' She reaches for the gag in his mouth, her emotions crushing any hesitation, while Warden starts on the duct tape binding his right arm. 'It's okay.'

'Who are you?' The Asker stammers. 'Are you with them? I told them I can't do it. I tried, but I can't...' His voice breaks and it pulls at Mallory. She follows his gaze to the laptop, sat on the desk across from him – apparently set up for him to watch. There's some kind of code trailing across the screen. Whatever it is, it's incredibly complex... but there's no time for that now. No time.

'We're from the Forum,' Warden says. 'We're here to help you.' Mallory turns back to them, but the man shakes his head like he doesn't really hear it.

'I tried,' he gasps, and there are tears in his eyes. 'I tried. I tried, but I couldn't. I – '

'*Asker*,' Mallory says firmly, her own eyes glassing up as she watches him, even as her hands start work on freeing his other wrist. He looks up at her, finally seeming to find a little focus.

'How do you know that name?' he whispers.

'From the Forum,' Warden repeats. This time it seems to register. 'I'm Warden.'

'Warden?' It's barely audible. And then The Asker is crying for real, for a whole different reason. 'Warden... You came for me? I don't understand,' he gasps. 'How did you find me? How did you – '

'I'm Echo,' Mallory says. 'We found you together.' For a moment, The Asker just stares at her.

'Echo Six?'

Mallory nods, biting her lip so damn hard, even though it makes her jaw hurt. She needs to keep a grip.

'I hacked your account,' she says, 'traced you here.' His eyes are glistening.

'Echo,' he repeats, letting out a sharp breath and watching her with a kind of wonder. Then, his face drops, and, '*No*,' he says, eyes widening with fear.

'What?' Mallory asks. 'What is it?'

'You can't be here,' he stammers. 'You have to go, Echo. They want you. I don't know how they knew your name, but they did and they kept asking and asking about you.' He shakes his head. 'I didn't tell them anything,' he says, sounding more certain, 'but they went looking for you. They told me they'd find you anyway. They said they had your picture.' Mallory swallows, ignoring the chill that brings, ignoring the sharp glance she gets from Warden.

'We know,' she says, looking back down at the bindings, her fingers working with renewed vigor. She frees his arm, moves on to his leg…

'No,' The Asker repeats, more insistent. He grabs her wrist with his now free hand. Mallory flinches, but he doesn't seem to notice. 'You have to listen to me. You have to go *now*.'

'Not without you,' she says, loosening his grip with her own gloved hand. She reaches down, fingers scrabbling to get the duct tape off his leg.

'But you have to – '

'No,' Warden interrupts. 'We came for you and we're leaving with you. No argument.' He cuts The Asker's right leg free, using one of the lock picking tools to saw through the tape. Mallory lets him take over on the left, glancing back towards the open door.

They're taking too long.

'Scarlet,' she asks, 'do they have her as well? And the others who went missing, do you have any idea where they are?'

The Asker shakes his head.

'I don't know where, but I believe they have them all,' he says, voice ragged. 'I *know* they have Scarlet. I came here trying to find her. I couldn't get anything off her Forum account, but she'd mentioned Children of Daedalus to me before and I found some intel saying some of them hung out at the club. So I came, but then…' He trails off. They all know what then. 'They told me they had her, that my helping them would help her. When I couldn't… they wouldn't tell me anything else.'

Damn it, Mallory thinks. She'd hoped for something, at least.

Scarlet's a bitch, but… *Could she have been the one who told the kidnappers about me?*

Warden finally snaps the other leg free.

No time to think now.

'Let's go,' he says. 'Can you walk?'

'I think so,' The Asker nods. He stands, shakily though, and Warden has to steady him. He's tall on his feet, almost a half foot above Warden. Mallory crosses to the door, pulling out the gun again. A quick glance outside tells her the corridor is still clear apart from the pincushion guard. He's starting to stir and she considers gagging him – but she doesn't trust how well he could breathe through his nose now. Together, she and Warden manage to drag him inside the room.

'We need to bring that,' says The Asker, pointing at the laptop.

'What is it?' she asks.

'What *they* want,' he says and, for a moment, his tone is clear and solid. Mallory goes back for it, closing the screen on the scrawling code. 'There's a tracker next to the front left foot,' he adds. 'Found it when they had me working on it. Might want to leave that here.' She flips it and finds a small black disk attached just as he'd said. Peeling it off with her nail, she sticks it to the table, then tucks the laptop into her backpack on top of her own.

'Anything else?'

'I don't think so,' he replies.

They exit into the corridor, Warden re-locking the guard inside. Mallory leads them back the way she came, hurried walking soon developing into a full on run. Her adrenaline swells at every intersection or turn, but the halls are empty, silent apart from their pounding feet. They reach the side door and exit into the alleyway, stopping only when they're out of camera range.

'Must do more exercise,' pants Warden, bending over, hands on his knees. 'I mean, I walk my mom's dog every day, but it's a shih-tzu so it doesn't go very far.' He groans. Next to him, The Asker is breathing heavily, dark brown eyes blinking furiously in the daylight, bruises standing out against olive skin, looking so much worse outside. Fear and pity well up in Mallory.

What did they do to him?

'We need to get out of here,' she says, trying to stop herself staring. The other three kidnappers could come back at any time, right down this alley...

'Looking like this?' Warden questions. He's right.

'Clean up best you can,' she says. She flicks on the gun's safety and places it into her backpack with the two laptops. The balaclava and latex gloves follow – swiftly exchanged for her regular cut-off black ones. She notes, again, the ink smears on the white glove's fingers...

Later, she tells herself. *No time now.*

Warden follows her lead, his hair sticking up with static as he yanks off the balaclava. His nose and chin are smeared with drying blood. Mallory's breath catches at the sight and she crosses to him almost without thinking. He's already wiping it off with a handkerchief, but she helps him with the last of it, her hands moving gently so as not to hurt him, fingertips feeling it everywhere they touch his skin...

You're okay. You're okay...

But her heart is beating way too fast. Way too fast...

Four, three, four, two, she thinks.

Four, three, four, two...

He holds stock still as she works, watching her in a way that she can't quite meet. His nose is red and swollen, but it doesn't look to be broken. At least it's stopped bleeding.

'I thought you'd be older,' says The Asker. Mallory turns back to him. 'Both of you.' Of course, he hadn't seen their faces before. Mallory bites her lip, thinking the same of him again, definitely no more than thirty, and...

It's just so strange looking at him, right there... The person behind the name that saved her, who she's spent so long following, and the magnitude of it rises up again. He's tried to brush his tousled hair down across his face. There's no blood, but he looks as if he's been in a serious bar fight. They probably all do. Her own jaw is throbbing.

'Everyone just,' she says, trying to steady her voice, 'just keep your heads down.' They can't stay any longer. She starts towards the end of the alley, turning right at the street and then heading north, at a right angle to the direction of *Stevie's Space Age Diner* and away from where most people will be. She moves quickly, eyes scanning the sidewalks ahead, but no one takes much notice of them. The Asker is flagging within minutes, though, and they have to stop in another alley six blocks over.

They need a plan.

Warden pulls out his laptop.

Checking the feeds, Mallory thinks. *That's good. That's a start.*

'Anything?' she asks.

'Corridor's still empty,' Warden replies. The tension in her chest eases a little.

'You bugged them?' says The Asker.

'Yeah,' Warden begins. It seems like he's going to say more – and then he hesitates. He glances at Mallory, and then says to The Asker, 'Sorry, but we have to be sure before this goes any further. Before I joined the Forum,' he says, 'what was my hacker name?' He's testing him, Mallory realizes, just like they had tested each other when they first met. After everything that's happened, it does make sense. 'These people seem to know a lot about Echo Six,' he continues, 'but no one's interested in me. Only the real Asker would know this.' For a moment, there's silence. Mallory watches the man they just rescued, heart pounding, though she's sure it's him. She's *sure…*

'The Runt,' he says, and there's a shadow of a smile. Warden nods, echoing it, wider and fuller.

'Correct,' he says. Mallory feels a sharp relief. 'Nickname from my brothers,' he tells her. 'I was using it ironically, obviously.'

'My turn, then,' says The Asker – the real, definite Asker. 'Echo, what was *your* name before the Forum? I know it, and Echo Six knows it, but I'm near certain she won't have told anyone else.'

'Sandman,' she says. Warden's eyebrows rise. 'My dad's a metal fan.'

'Good to know, and also correct.' The Asker sighs, and his shoulders sag back against the wall. 'Thank you,' he says softly. 'Echo, Warden, thank you.'

Damn, this is weird…

'Yes, I bugged them,' Warden tells him, finally answering his earlier question, 'a little mite in the server room.' The Asker looks impressed – something Warden seems embarrassingly pleased about – and Mallory wonders for the hundredth time if that *was* the location hack he had asked for her help with, the one she'd turned down. Her face burns and she bites back the question. She doesn't want to ask, doesn't want to know if all those bruises were partly her fault.

It doesn't matter now, she tells herself. *He's safe. That's what matters.*

'Cutting the loops,' says Warden. A few more clicks, then, 'Cutting the connection.' He lets out a slow breath, folding away the laptop. 'When they find the guard,' he goes on, 'they'll know we must have looped the feeds – can't avoid that – but at least they still shouldn't know how. I don't think I should connect again, though.'

Mallory nods. The first thing they'll do is look for a tap.

'What happened with The Forum,' The Asker says, 'after I left?' Mallory stiffens, though the question was always going to come at some point. 'No one else disappeared, did they?' He trails off. Mallory feels Warden look at her.

Four, three, four, two.

'No one else,' she tells The Asker, and his relief is obvious.

Four, three, four, two.

'I shut it down,' she says. She makes herself look at him, even as her muscles squirm. 'I had to.' She explains what happened then – everything she and Warden did, why they did it – as clear and fast as she can. She doesn't quite know how she expected The Asker to react – anger, maybe, disbelief – but she sees none of that.

'You did the right thing,' is all he says afterwards. 'The Forum was compromised.'

'But it's *gone.*' This time her voice comes out shaky. He holds her gaze. He looks sad.

'Yes,' he agrees, 'but we are not, and the other members are not, wherever they are. I asked you to keep them safe, Echo, and that's what you did. I'm grateful.'

Mallory manages only another nod in response, feeling both like a weight has lifted, but also remembering the loss all over again.

You're okay, she tells herself. *You're –*

'Do you have any idea how they used your account?' Warden asks. 'How they sent the ransom message?'

The Asker shakes his head.

'They must have hacked it from outside the Forum,' he replies, 'though I don't know how, and it's alarming to think who would even be able to do that. I've never told anyone how to log in as me. Some of these bruises are because they demanded I do just that, and I wouldn't. I still can't figure out how they even knew about the site in the first place.'

'What about Scarlet?' says Mallory, finding her voice again. 'Could she have told them?'

He hesitates.

'She could have, but I don't think so. Scarlet has a way about her, but the Forum meant almost as much to her as it did to me. She wouldn't have given it up.'

'Even if they hurt her?' says Warden. The Asker licks his lips like they're too dry.

'But you said they logged in through my account,' he replies, 'not hers. And there would have been no reason to ask her about the Forum at all if they didn't already know it existed.'

'Could there have been another mole, then?' asks Mallory.

'I don't know.' The Asker sighs. 'And I hate how much I'm saying that. It's possible, I suppose, but who? I vetted everyone so carefully. I just...' He stops. 'I don't know,' he repeats, running a frustrated hand through his already ragged hair. No one says anything for a moment.

However they got there, what they really need is to work out what to do next. Mallory's plan for when they had made it past rescuing The Asker had been to find out what the CoD really wanted and bargain it back to them on her own terms – keeping everyone else safe. She has what they want now, right there in her backpack, and The Asker is out of their reach, so this is the time to act, to do it... But now it comes to it...

'I think we should call the police,' says Warden. Mallory's nerves flutter, but she stays silent as he pulls out his phone. Maybe that's best now. Maybe they should.

'No,' says The Asker, though, 'you can't.' Warden pauses.

'Why not?' He frowns. 'You're safe now, but we need help. *You* need help – '

'That doesn't matter.' The Asker's voice is insistent. 'You can't tell anyone.'

'But they still have Scarlet and the others, and we have no leads. They have Echo's picture – '

'And they have mine too,' The Asker says, stopping him. 'Those being a few of the reasons why we *can't* call for help.' He holds Warden's confused gaze, his bruised face set. 'The police can't help us with this,' he continues. 'Warden, Echo, you've been trusting me for a long time, I need you to trust me now. What's going on is bigger than you could possibly know and there just isn't time.' Warden looks at Mallory, unsure. She nods. He lowers his hand, tucking the phone back into his pocket.

'Okay, then,' he says to The Asker. 'What do we do?'

The House of Ms Angeline Garcia

The taxi pulls into a quiet residential street in the South Jamaica neighborhood of Queens. Mallory glances at her watch. Hailing a cab had taken several minutes – they probably didn't look like very savory customers – and the ride out to the borough has been a further thirty-three. It's nearly six thirty now, the sun almost completely disappeared behind the tiled roofs of clapboard houses, oak trees and yard fences casting long shadows across the road below. A group of kids are chucking a football around a few houses up. It makes Mallory think of Jed, him and Roger stuck in a motel somewhere, not knowing why, because of what she's got herself into. She clenches her hands; tight, then loose, tight, then loose.

She's fixing it.

They're fixing it.

She had checked the webcam feed from her house right after they'd got into the cab, but no one had turned up there yet. If that was where the three other kidnappers had been headed, then they should have made it by now… unless they'd ID'd her wrongly from that blurry picture. Or maybe they hadn't been going there at all. There are still so many questions. The main thing, though, is that Roger and Jed had done what she'd said and hadn't gone back there either. She's had no more message notifications on her phone from the Forum, which means that either no one's found the injured guard and the otherwise empty room, or they have and the CoD just haven't decided how to respond. At least that gives them a little time to make a plan themselves. They haven't been able to talk openly during the ride, what with the driver right there too. Mallory has spent most of it trying to not touch anyone – squished in the back with The Asker and Warden – and noticing it so very much every time she does…

'Just over there,' The Asker says now. The driver pulls up in front of a pale blue house with a neatly manicured lawn. Mallory gets out quickly, stepping away from the car and taking long, slow breath.

The first thing they'd needed to do was get off of the streets and out of Port Morris. They couldn't exactly go back to Mallory's and they didn't completely trust anywhere with CCTV. The Asker had said he knew a place where they would be safe, though he hadn't been there in a while.

'Is this it then?' Warden asks, looking up at the blue house and reapplying antibacterial gel to his hands as the cab pulls away – he'd already given them a good covering on the ride. The Asker shakes his head.

'Still a few blocks away,' he says. 'Doesn't hurt to be cautious.' He sets off down the sidewalk. He seems calmer now, more alert. More like his voice from the Forum. Three minutes and five streets later, he stops in front of another clapboard house, this one a greying white. It's a narrow detached, separated from the street by a half height wire fence. The place looks like it's been well kept, apart from the lawn is a little overgrown. The Asker seems to hesitate a moment, his expression unreadable, before stepping forward and pushing open the gate.

'This,' he says softly, 'is it.'

Mallory follows, glancing at the name on the mailbox: *Ms Angeline Garcia*. She doesn't recognize it, but that's not exactly surprising. Beside her, Warden is frowning.

'You okay?' she asks. The redness across his nose is already turning to a dark bruise. She can smell the gel from his hands.

'Yeah,' he says, brow softening as he looks up at her. 'Headache, that's all. You?' Mallory's shoulder is sore and the throb in her jaw is kind of making her want to punch something.

'Fine,' she answers. Warden smiles this little reassuring smile, and something inside of her seems to relax, to ease off.

The Asker crouches on the porch and lifts up a large cactus pot to the right of the yellow front door. There's a small hole in the boarding beneath. He hooks his finger inside and lifts the panel.

'Some things never change,' he murmurs, reaching through the gap and pulling out a brass key. He unlocks the door and steps inside. The living room beyond is painted yellow like the door, little pink flowers decorating the border beneath the coving. A few family photos are hung here and there, but all the furniture is covered in white sheets.

'Whose house is this?' Mallory asks.

'My aunt's,' says The Asker.

His aunt's? It's odd thinking of him having a family, though it shouldn't be. Every hacker identity has an actual someone behind it.

Warden asks the question out loud.

'I had to grow up somewhere,' The Asker replies. Mallory wonders if his surname is Garcia too. They haven't done real name introductions and she thinks they probably won't. It's maybe safer that way. 'Stayed here sometimes when things weren't so good at home.' He pauses in front of one of the photographs. He looks so normal. It's all so normal.

Of course he was going to be normal, Mallory thinks. *He's just a person, like you're a person, like Warden's a person...* But he's also The Asker, right there in front of her, and she doesn't know what to say or how to interact with him like this.

'So, I'm guessing she's not here right now?' says Warden.

'Died a few months back,' The Asker tells him.

'Oh man, I'm sorry.'

'Life happens, right?' The Asker replies. 'My cousin hasn't cleared the place out yet. We should be safe here.' He crosses the room, hand trailing absently along one of the dusty sheets, and exits through a door at the back. Mallory and Warden follow him through, emerging into a large kitchen with white walls and windows hung with lace curtains. The room is L-shaped, with the stove, sink and cupboards in front of them, a sheet-covered table off to the right. A door behind it leads out to a utility room, then the yard. The Asker pulls the covers off, revealing a dining table and four mismatched wooden chairs with plump, flowery cushions tied on to make them more comfortable. They each take a seat, Mallory taking the cushion off hers – she doesn't like the way they slide about. Warden is next to her, The Asker sat across.

It's surreal.

A wave of exhaustion hits her. Running on adrenaline seems to burn you out way faster than actual running and this whole week has been a kind of whirlwind. They can't stop yet, though. She loops her bag off of her shoulders and takes out both laptops, leaving the gun inside. She opens her own computer, turning it on to check the feed from her house again – the other, she pushes to the middle of the table. Everyone's eyes fix on it, a single silver rectangle on the varnished wood. There are so many things they don't know, so many things that Mallory doesn't understand, but a lot of it seems to be pointing back to that one laptop.

'Asker,' she says, finally speaking, 'what's on it?'

'The Reckoning,' he replies. 'Daedalus's last virus, the super virus he claimed could change the world.' Mallory's heart skips. Warden's jaw visibly drops. They'd known the disappearances had to do with people looking into it, but the virus itself? Her mind buzzes, trying to make sense of it. The Asker's face is deadly serious.

'But it's not real,' she says, though that's a fairly pointless statement right now. 'I mean,' she goes on, 'you said so yourself. Thousands of hackers tried to follow that trail.'

'I was wrong,' The Asker replies. 'Well, I was right in one respect – it was never hidden anywhere on the web, and that's why no one ever found it – but it does exist. It exists on one, single hard drive.' He reaches out and opens up the laptop's lid, revealing the code Mallory had glimpsed before. 'It exists here, hidden behind an encryption no one can break.'

'I don't understand,' Warden says. 'In Daedalus's final video, he said he'd hidden it in pieces across the internet. Did someone find them all? I thought no one could find *any*?'

'Daedalus lied,' The Asker responds. 'He wanted to be a legend, to be immortal, wanted everyone to keep looking for it so he wouldn't be forgotten. But that wasn't where he actually hid it.' He shakes his head. 'I don't know how the CoD, specifically, got the laptop, only that they said he'd sent it to one of his followers before he killed himself and that – and I quote – only someone Daedalus *deemed worthy* enough would be able to crack the code and release the virus.'

Mallory feels a chill.

'That's why they wanted elites,' she says. The Asker nods.

'And why,' he adds, 'they were initially targeting those already looking into the virus.'

'Daedalus has been dead almost two years,' Warden says. 'Why now? Why only start all this, going after other hackers, now?'

'Because they're running out of time,' The Asker responds. 'Daedalus set certain conditions on the encryption, rules which, if broken, would lead to the deletion of The Reckoning by those unworthy of it. Things like, you try to copy the code from that laptop, it deletes. Try to transfer it, it deletes. Then, just over a month ago, they said a new clock started ticking on the screen – a new rule – counting down to October fifteenth, five thirty in the morning; the second anniversary of Daedalus's suicide. Apparently, he had planned when he was going to kill himself. Along with the clock, there was a video message from him saying they were taking too long and he was only going to give them a Biblical forty days more to complete their trial. They've got' – he glances at the clock on the wall – 'just under fifty-nine hours left, or they've failed. After that…'

'It deletes,' Warden finishes.

'That's why the CoD started getting more reckless,' The Asker explains, 'more dangerous.' Mallory swallows.

'You said you don't know how many of them there are?' she says.

'I only ever saw four after I was caught,' he answers. 'Elsewhere, I don't know, but someone must be holding the other hackers.'

'If they're still alive,' Warden says quietly.

'I don't think they'd kill them,' he responds, 'not before the deadline. Even if they'd failed at first, those are some of the top coders out there – they could still need them. And Scarlet,' he says, more firmly, 'Scarlet was definitely alive when they caught me. That's what they told me.' He blinks too many times in a row.

He really cares about her, Mallory thinks. *Even after what's happened to him, he's thinking about her.*

'She's alive,' he repeats. 'They must just be holding her somewhere else – someone else in the CoD. I know there are more than four because there were others at Labyrinth the night they took me, and someone at the club was either paid off or in on it because they had the room and access to the CCTV. That's why we can't go to the police. They can't protect us from an enemy with unknown numbers and unknown faces, and it would risk retribution against Scarlet' – his voice falters – 'maybe the others too.' The weight of it comes down on Mallory again, then. It's all on them. 'The only way to tell a member is by a triangular tattoo that they have on their left hands,' he goes on.

'A Greek delta,' she nods. 'D for Daedalus. We saw a few of them at the club, too, though we don't know which or how many were actually involved. No one else went near you...' She stops, remembering the pincushion's hand. 'Something strange, though, the guy who was guarding you,' she says, 'the symbol on his hand wasn't a tattoo. It was only drawn on.'

'What?' says Warden. The Asker's brow creases.

'His hands must have been sweaty or something because it smudged onto my gloves – it was just normal black ink. I didn't say anything at the time because, well...'

'There was so much other crap going on,' Warden ventures. The Asker is still frowning.

'Maybe he just wasn't a full member yet?' he suggests. 'Some kind of initiation still to come?'

'Or what if he wasn't really CoD at all?' says Warden. 'These guys seemed pretty serious about their tats. Lifetime ostracism if it was done wrongly, remember.'

'You think the name in the ransom note was false?' Mallory asks.

'Well, it didn't really fit with anything else we knew about them at the time.' He pauses, then shakes his head. 'Just a theory,' he adds. 'Could be bollocks.'

Mallory looks at The Asker, questioning.

'I don't know,' he says, shrugging. 'I knew about the tats, but the kidnappers themselves never told me any names, group or individual.'

'So,' Warden says, 'added to the list of things we don't know.' Mallory bites her lip. 'What do we do now, then?' he continues. He looks at The Asker. 'You said before that we couldn't call the police. I'm guessing that means you have another, preferably brilliant plan?'

The Asker runs a nervous hand through his hair.

'I have *a* plan,' he says, 'but nothing about this is going to be brilliant or easy. The Children of Daedalus – or whoever they are – know our faces. That is a problem. Even if they didn't have Scarlet – and, we assume, the others – we still couldn't disappear. Like I said, the police can't keep us safe if we don't know who they are, or even how many. This new doubt over their affiliation only makes that worse.'

'So what can we do?' Mallory asks.

'Well, the ones I encountered,' he replies, 'they are dangerous, but hurting people isn't their actual goal, just a means to an end. What they *want* is this laptop, unencrypted.' The Asker's eyes fall on Mallory. 'We offer that,' he says, a fire behind them now, 'and we have something to bargain with – *we* become the ones with the power. We give them that and we might just save Scarlet, Cyber Sneak, Weevil and Tower – and ourselves along with them.'

'But you said you couldn't break it,' says Warden.

'I couldn't,' he agrees, 'but I think maybe Echo can.' A spark trickles down Mallory's spine, a kind of heaviness coming to rest with it. 'I don't know how the CoD got your name,' The Asker says to her, 'but I think they were finally looking for the right person. I couldn't do it' – he taps the laptop – 'but you're *better* than me.' The words shock her, but he holds her gaze, like he's trying to make them sink in. 'Maybe you don't see that, but I've known it for a while; the way you look at things, see the angles other people don't, and so lightning fast... you don't think like any other hacker I've ever known, and I've known a lot. You read up on Daedalus, that's exactly what everyone says about him too. If anyone can do this, Echo, it's you.'

All in a Laptop

'Are you sure about this?' Warden asks. He's whispering, leaning so close to Mallory that it makes her skin tingle. The Asker is a few feet away, round the corner of the L-shape, rooting through the kitchen cupboards for any remaining food. Warden had complained quite loudly – and, apparently, fraudulently – about being hungry.

'He's sure,' Mallory replies softly.

'That's not an answer. What do *you* think?'

She shifts awkwardly. It is what she'd originally intended to do when she'd told Warden she was going after The Asker – find out what it was the CoD wanted, find it and then use it to force a way out of this for all of them. It feels different now, though, just like it had back in the alley, now that she's sitting here actually about to do it. So much is different in person, even to how you imagine it'll be – more immediate and loud and pressurized. The Asker's bruises are real. He was really tortured. The thing is, the more Mallory finds out about the people who took him, the more they frighten her – and the more she doubts whether giving them what they want could ever be a good idea. They don't even know what The Reckoning does. If the CoD do, they never revealed it to The Asker while they had him. Still…

'I think,' she says, trying to keep a handle on it all in her head, 'that this will put us in control.' That's what she had wanted, what she had thought could fix this, and maybe it can. Whatever her doubts, it is all they have, and the first part of that growing control has already felt damn good – a message she just sent to The Asker's account via the Forum; ***Now I'm the one with something you want. Fortunate. Back the hell off or I'll smash it.***

Control.

'*If* you can do it,' Warden shoots back, 'and if you then give them The Reckoning. Otherwise it will just right royally piss them off.'

'It's just a computer virus.' The words feel hollow.

'But we don't know what it does.'

'I know that.' Mallory stretches out her fingers, the movement jerky, not likely to be missed by Warden. And it's not like she doesn't remember that most of Daedalus's past viruses had been these nasty and destructive things, malicious even. If The Reckoning is supposed to be his greatest... 'Doing this keeps us safe,' she says, taking the watch off her wrist, the feel of it making her antsy. The Asker knows what he's doing – he always does – and, like he said, there isn't another choice.

So how is that control? She shuts out the question.

'That message will keep Jed and Roger safe,' she goes on, almost like she's trying to convince herself. 'Doing this will keep us safe, and if the CoD still have the others – ' She stops. The Asker is coming back, a big bag of pretzels and pack of cookies in his hands. He drops them on the table, next to the juice he'd already found.

'All there is, I'm afraid. Any reply yet?'

'No,' Mallory answers. It's still silent at her house, too. Warden could re-establish the connection to the club's security feed, see what's going on there now, but they've decided it's safer not to. If the pincushion's been found, whoever gave the CoD access to the system could be actively looking for a tap. The last thing they need is to be traced.

'Are you ready then?' says The Asker.

Mallory glances at Warden, but his eyes are fixed on the table.

He doesn't think I should do it.

She locks her jaw, blinking at the bolt of pain it brings.

'Yes,' she replies. 'I'll try.' They don't even know if she *can* do it yet – Warden's right on that. The Asker himself couldn't and, despite his faith in her, none of this is sure. But she might as well attempt it. Then, if she succeeds, they will know more about what they're dealing with and they can make an informed decision and...

She pulls the laptop towards her, the same code still scrolling across the screen. The Asker's captors had left it running in the dark so it was all he could look at. They'd said maybe he'd get inspired. She shivers.

Beside her, Warden's watching the screen now, ignoring the food he'd requested, mouth pursed into a line. 'Let me know if you notice anything,' Mallory tells him. He just nods. She wants him to smile, to look at her – anything to say he's with her on this – but he just keeps staring at the laptop.

She taps the pattern once.

Four, three, four, two. Focus. Come on, Echo.

She tries to shut everything else out; close off her doubts and everything she's worried about, forget everything that doesn't make sense along with everything she *thinks* she knows. She focuses only on the code, letting the numbers wash over her, searching out the reason behind them, feeling herself becoming lost in it all…

It's the most complex thing she's ever tried to get her head around and she probably doesn't type anything for at least a half hour – she's vaguely aware of Warden fidgeting beside her, eventually breaking into the pretzel bag – but it's definitely not random. It seems that way, but it's not, and her mind starts to see the patterns, see the correlations… numbers grouped in clusters, each cluster relating to the cluster next to it… and, crap, it's a tricksy thing… but, slowly, *slowly*, the meaning of it starts to fall into place…

'Hey, have you noticed – ' Warden begins.

'Shut up.'

'But you said – '

'Yeah, shut up.'

He goes silent and she fades back into the code…

No, it's not random… it's just… it's…

It's incomplete.

At that thought, she suddenly understands why no one else has been able to crack the encryption. It's not really an encryption at all, at least not in the traditional sense. It's more like a puzzle. The numbers and letters form a sequence, but there are gaps in the code and it will only activate when each part of it is completed sufficiently to perform an assigned function. This is not about hacking your way into something, it's not about finding a loophole or breaking something down, it's about building it up.

She begins typing.

It's exhilarating, mesmerizing. It makes her breathing go steady, makes her muscles loosen… And it's working, starting to come together… And it's something beautiful… And it's something she *understands*, that is more comprehensible to her than all the people who have been after it and all of their convoluted whys and hows…

She doesn't know how long it takes, but she finally clicks the last piece of the puzzle into place. The screen goes blank.

'Bloody hell,' Warden breathes. 'You did it, you actually – ' He cuts off. A new code flashes up on the screen. It takes a second for Mallory to see it's like a variation of the last, but slightly altered, a little more complex.

Damn tricksy… But she doesn't feel annoyed. In fact, as she realizes what it is, she sort of wants to smile – which is a strange and stupid thing given everything else, everything that's riding on this.

'What's going on?' says The Asker.

'It's in levels,' Mallory replies. 'Each part of the code you complete loads up the next.'

'How many levels?'

'No way to tell.' She is already typing again, catching the thread of it quicker this time. 'It'll take a while, though.'

She gets through four more stages within the next hour. The patterns become both clearer and more intricate with every level; clearer because she knows what to look for – more intricate because all the elements she is completing are combining together, pieces of something bigger. As it builds, she begins to realize something else, too. The code in front of her isn't just a security system Daedalus designed to protect his work – it actually *is* the virus. It's just all twisted and jumbled up so it's useless unless you untangle it through the levels.

What she's doing is completing it.

And once she realizes that, she begins to see what it is actually designed to do and…

No, she thinks. *That can't be right.*

She knows Daedalus was a genius, but this…

The more she looks, though, the further she gets, the more she realizes that what she is guessing is exactly what it's going to do. Daedalus wasn't exaggerating when he claimed it would change the world. It will change everything, and…

Shit… shit. Shit!

'Echo,' Warden hisses beside her.

'Shut up,' she snaps, still trying to work it through in her mind.

'No, Echo,' Warden repeats. 'I need you to listen to me.'

'*Warden –* '

'It's important,' he says, reaching out to her gloved hands and physically stilling the tapping of keys. Startled, her face flushes. He lets go quickly, but her reverie is broken. She turns to him – her skin needling beneath the fabric – ready to launch into a tirade about why he's a stupid dick for interrupting because she really needs to think right now…

His expression stops her.

He looks scared, really damn scared. She glances around for The Asker, wondering what's going on, but he's not there. She vaguely remembers him going upstairs to the bathroom…

'Echo,' Warden says, drawing her attention back. He's holding his phone out. 'The Asker has been lying to us.'

'What?'

'We have a serious bloody problem.'

Mallory stares at him, not quite processing the words. She rubs her eyes.

'What are you talking about?' she asks.

'The name on the mailbox,' he replies. 'It had been bugging me.'

'Angeline Garcia?' She remembers him frowning when they first saw it, but he'd said that was from a headache.

'Does that surname mean anything to you?' he asks now.

'Not really,' she says, 'a lot of people have that name.' The relative calm she'd felt while hacking is very quickly dissipating. 'What do you mean The Asker's been lying?'

'What about Apollonian, then?' Warden persists. 'Recognize that?'

'Of course,' she answers. 'He co-founded Finders Reapers with Daedalus, got arrested in 2005. You researched it and told me. Look,

I don't get what this has to do with – ' She stops, something clicking horribly somewhere between Warden's intense expression and what he's just said. 'What are you saying?'

'I know Garcia is a common name, but when I saw it on that mailbox… I knew I'd heard it before, in connection with Daedalus.' He hands her the phone. It's open on an article from 2005 about the trial of the Finders Reapers. 'I'd read it here. Apollonian's real name was Nathan Garcia.'

Mallory stares down at the picture in the article, at the picture that is unmistakably the man upstairs, only younger, clean shaven and with shorter hair.

'No,' she says simply.

'He was released from prison in 2008,' Warden goes on, 'a year before the Forum opened, which about matches up with when his parole would have ended. Echo, everyone was someone else before the Forum – The Runt, Sandman. What I'm saying is that The Asker was Apollonian, *is* Nathan Garcia. I'm saying The Asker *knew* Daedalus.'

Ghosts from the Past

Mallory feels dazed. She hands the phone back to Warden, questions filling her mind.

'He lied to us,' Warden repeats. And it wasn't about a small thing, either, it was about having known, in person, the hacker at the center of all of this. Surely that's something you would mention.

And if he lied about that, what else…? Her thoughts recoil from it.

'But it's The Asker,' she mutters uselessly, as if that precludes it from having happened. '*The Asker*. We can trust him. We've always been able to trust him.'

'Then why didn't he tell us this?' Warden responds. 'What else hasn't he told us?'

'How's it coming along?' They both jump as The Asker re-enters the kitchen. He's changed out of the dirty shirt and suit pants, and is now dressed in a faded grey tracksuit that looks too small for him. He really is very tall, his head almost reaching the door frame.

What else hasn't he told us? Warden's words echo inside Mallory's mind. She thinks of what she's realized about the virus, about what it does, and her blood goes cold. *Did he know?*

'Fourteenth level,' she says, finally managing to answer him. Her voice sounds shaky, even to her.

Get a grip, she thinks.

'You okay?' says The Asker. She nods.

It's The Asker. He's still The Asker.

'You startled me,' she explains. 'When I get into the code, I'm not really aware of other things. You made me jump.'

'I'm sorry,' he replies. 'Level fourteen, huh?' He smiles a little. 'How many of these things did the guy leave?' Mallory's insides squirm. That felt like a lie right there. Not just some guy – a guy he *knew*. The Asker crosses the room, leans over the laptop to look at the code. Mallory shrinks into herself. The Asker notices. He hesitates.

Shit, shit, shit… Oh fricking shut up! she tells herself. She's starting to panic – and she can't panic. It's a pointless thing to do. *It's still The Asker,* she thinks again, *whoever he was before. Whatever he knows or doesn't know, it's still him.*

And she trusts him.

She *trusts…*

She tries to speak, but her jaw seems glued.

'She doesn't like it when people come too near her,' Warden intervenes. 'Haphephobia.' Mallory glances at him. 'I googled it,' he adds.

'Oh, sorry,' The Asker says again, leaning back like he genuinely is.

And why wouldn't he be? He's The Asker and he cares about us. He's always…

The Asker stops. His eyes are fixed on the phone in Warden's hand. The color seems to drain from Warden's face, quicker than it should be able to.

'You haven't been contacting anyone, have you?' The Asker says. 'It's not safe.'

Warden shakes his head for no, at the same time as he stammers, 'Just my mother.' Then, 'She worries when I'm away. I have to text her every few hours or she – '

The Asker steps around Mallory and takes the phone before Warden even thinks to close his fingers around it. Mallory's whole body tenses as he looks at the screen.

'Oh,' he says simply.

Everything seems to go still, the room very silent, yet at the same time blood is rushing through Mallory's ears like a torrent so loud it makes her want to clamp her hands down on them.

'Asker?' she says, and her voice sounds smaller than it should. He looks down at her. 'Have you lied to us?' Something inside of her cracks a little at the words, and he looks… he looks sad.

'It's not what you think – ' he begins.

'Do you know what the virus does?' asks Warden, interrupting – and he sounds angry, angry in a way Mallory's not heard him be before. 'That's what all this has been about,' he goes on, 'Daedalus's last virus – and Daedalus founded the Finders Reapers with you, so surely you'd know what it would do. What are you trying to get Echo to do?'

'Hold on,' The Asker says. 'It's not like that. I meant everything I said before. This is the best way to keep everyone safe from the CoD.'

'Really?' replies Warden. 'And how do we know that's the truth?'

'Because Daedalus was an asshole,' says The Asker. 'And I am categorically not in any group named after him. Yes, I knew him, but that was a long time ago. We started out as friends, but we certainly didn't end that way. Call it a difference of ideology. I hadn't spoken to him for years before he died. That's why I never mentioned our connection. It was history.'

'You still didn't answer my first question,' says Warden. 'Do you know what it does?'

The Asker seems to hesitate, running a hand through his hair.

'I know what it does,' Mallory hears herself say, breaking the silence. 'The code isn't just an encryption, it's the virus itself, all hidden and jumbled up and incomplete. Each level is a section that relates to the last, but you'll never see the whole thing until it's finished, until you reach the last level. I'm not there yet, but I've seen enough to figure out where it's headed.' They're both staring at her. 'Daedalus worked out a method of cracking common internet encryptions, like RSA,' she says, 'in *minutes*.'

'What the…' is all Warden manages, apparently rendered speechless for once.

The protection of every single piece of data on the internet – be that emails, bank records, web browsers – relies on commonly-used internet encryption protocols. These codes are built in at a base level and require specific, mathematically-generated keys in order to be decrypted. Without them, nothing on the web would be authenticated, or secure. The keys themselves are usually just very large prime numbers and, theoretically, could be calculated by a malicious third party. The reason they aren't is that the calculation required would be so big you would need an absurd amount of computing power to achieve it and, even then, it would take years to complete. For decades, people have been looking for mathematical ways to do it faster – from black-hats, to Harvard professors, to the NSA – because if anyone did crack it, it would catastrophically undermine the security of the entire web, allowing the user access to pretty much any data they desired. You could break into anything, take or destroy *anything*. People have hacked security companies to steal information on specific existing keys before, but writing an algorithm that can actually calculate them within a reasonable time frame? No one's ever done that.

No one before Daedalus.

No, he didn't lie when he said The Reckoning would change the world.

'He created an algorithm that can crack base internet encryptions quickly,' Mallory explains. 'The Reckoning is that algorithm, encoded within a computer virus that acts like a distributor for it. If it's released, it will disable security on whatever it encounters, leaving it vulnerable to attack. Nothing will be able to stop it from spreading and nothing will be able to stand up against it.'

'Right,' whispers Warden. 'Wow, I mean, shit.' Mallory looks up at The Asker, an underlying hope that he has an explanation still clawing in amongst everything else. He hasn't said anything, his face unreadable.

'I think you should answer Warden's question now,' she says, both wanting and not wanting him to. 'Did you know what The Reckoning would do? Did you know, when you said I should give it to the CoD?'

The Asker licks his lips, then, 'Yes,' he answers, and her heart drops. 'Or I guessed, when I saw the laptop.'

'Bloody hell,' mutters Warden. 'And you still wanted Echo to do it? Just give something like that to a bunch of his nutter followers to release – because you know that's what they'd do with it, and you know it would cause utter chaos. Security would start failing all over the internet and it would be a free-for-all on anything from email accounts to bank details.'

Another silence.

Then, 'At least it would level things up,' says The Asker. His voice is clear, but quiet. Warden stiffens in his chair. The Asker is looking at

Mallory now, his eyes holding her so tight she can't let go. There is an urgency behind them, the fire she had glimpsed before. 'Do you know what I was arrested for in the end, back in 2005?' he says. 'I leaked documents from six different oil companies, exposing a price fixing ring that was crippling ordinary people. I was doing what we do in the Forum. We find truth. We share it where it needs to be heard. Yes, I was Apollonian before I called myself The Asker, but my goal has always been the same; the dissemination of necessary truth, where lies have caused harm – where people have a right to know. You've both seen the corruption that is out there; in individuals, in corporations, in *governments*. Have I ever asked either of you to do a single hack that wasn't to expose something rotten, to try and make things better?'

Neither of them speaks. Neither counters on that point. Mallory isn't sure she could, even if she knew what to say.

'That's why I set up the Forum after I got out,' The Asker goes on. 'I couldn't be Apollonian any more, so I became The Asker, the one who called out the people no one else was holding to account. I found others who felt the same and for four years we've been fighting against every piece of dirt and lies and greed that I can find. Four years and you know what we've achieved? Almost nothing,' he says. 'The more we uncover, the more I realize there is to find. We could release ten thousand hacks a month and still only be a drop in the ocean.

'Daedalus was an egotistical bastard who found it increasingly hard to think beyond his own growing mythology – but he *was* a genius, and cracking the common internet encryptions had always been the holy grail. If he actually did it, then I say let the CoD have it, let them put it out there, and let's see who's on top once all the lies are out. Let there be a reckoning. You can do this, Echo,' he says. 'You can still do this. You should still do this.'

Should.

The Asker believes it, and Mallory has always believed in The Asker, in his choices. He is standing there, telling her that completing this virus, that letting it be released, is the correct thing to do. He *believes* it's good, but…

But…

He lied to us. The words keep going round inside her head. Almost out of everything he's said, that's what matters the most to her. *He tried to use me. He didn't trust me to make the right call.* Though what she would have chosen then…

'Don't do it,' Warden says, cutting into her consciousness. 'Don't, Echo.' She turns to him. 'It's not worth it.' He looks up at The Asker. 'That was a good speech. I believed in you too, you know, believed in what we've been doing. I've been with you longer than Echo, even, but this – *this* is crazy.'

'Listen to me, Warden – ' The Asker begins.

'No, you listen.' Warden stands, the legs of his chair scraping against the tiles, making Mallory flinch. 'Some things are secret for a reason. If this virus can open anything, then we're talking military, too. Ours, theirs, it doesn't matter because *anyone* will have access. You really want launch codes available to some whack job who thinks we've all been overrun by aliens or, better yet, a hacker working for the North Koreans?'

'Warden – '

'It could give away troop positions in Afghanistan.' Mallory stiffens. 'You want to give the truth to ordinary people?' he goes on. 'Well, here's another truth for you, how much do ordinary people's lives rely on the internet? How many livelihoods? How many will lose their savings? Imagine the cybercrime there would be in the wake of it.'

'Sometimes a cost is required to achieve something worthwhile,' replies The Asker. 'I know that more than most. Listen to me, everything I said earlier was true – giving the CoD the virus is the only way to keep us all safe – but this is bigger than that. I didn't tell you before because I didn't want to overwhelm you, but now you know, Echo' – he looks at her – 'will you do it? Help me make the world better.' And Warden is shaking his head, but then, 'If you've ever trusted me,' The Asker continues, insistent, 'trust me now.'

And Mallory's insides seem to twist apart.

It's The Asker. The words repeat yet again in her mind. *The Asker, and he's asking for help.* And the last time she turned him down…

But another voice is shouting for attention too, Warden's voice, his words. One line in particular; *troop positions in Afghanistan*. And, of all things she could think of in that moment, she thinks of Roger. She thinks of her dad and what it was like during every tour he was out in Iraq, the fear she felt every time the phone rang or the door went. He would never lie to her back then, even when she was little, and so every time he went away, he wouldn't promise her that he'd come home. Instead, he'd tell her that he would try to, and then he would hold her hands – the only time she'd ever let anyone hold her hands – and he would promise that while he was away, he would make it worthwhile by doing the good he believed in, doing good as best as he could see it. He'd said that that was what was important in a person, wherever they were, and even after he was sent home early from that last tour, even after *he* lost that himself – Mallory had tried to hold onto it, grasped it like it was her lifeline, her one way of making sense of a whole lot of things she couldn't make sense of…

And she had found The Asker.

The Asker, who believed in things so much.

But now two people she has trusted, who both believe they are right, disagree on what is good and it is finally up to her. *She* has to choose. It's not about what they think, but what she does. It's not about what she can or can't do, but what she should. What does she believe is right?

Mallory?

'No,' she says quietly. 'No, I won't do it. Asker, we should tell the police about the CoD, get them looking for Scarlet and the others, and protecting us. Whoever those people are, we can't give them this.' The Asker's face falls. 'It wouldn't be some kind of victory for freedom,' she tells him. 'It would be anarchy, and that is not better. You need controls, at least some, but we *can* keep doing what we always did,' she says quickly, still trying to hold on to him, trying to get him to understand that this isn't a choice against him. 'We'll keep finding truth that way. Set up a new Forum. I'll work harder,' she pleads, 'try harder, do more hacks.'

'It's not enough,' he says, shaking his head. 'Echo – '

'I won't do this,' she says.

'I need you to.' His phrasing jars.

Need?

'No,' she says, and she turns off the laptop. The code disappears. The Asker stares at the screen, like he can't believe what she just did.

'*Echo –* '

'She said no,' Warden tells him, and he steps backwards towards the kitchen counter.

'What are you doing?' says The Asker.

'Calling the cops.' The Asker is still holding his cell, but there's a phone on the wall by the fridge. 'That's what she wants to do. They can look for Scarlet and the others, raid the club. You can tell them what you know. Help ID the kidnappers – '

'Warden,' says The Asker firmly, 'I need you to stop.'

'No.' He takes another step. 'You know, we risked a lot for you, coming for you.' Another step.

'I know you did.'

'And I'm glad you're okay,' he continues, 'but I don't trust you any more and I'm not going to listen to your reasons. We should have just dialed 911 back in that alley. I'm sorry, Asker, but I'm going to do this.'

'We have to,' Mallory says. Warden reaches the phone.

'I'm sorry, too,' says The Asker, barely more than a whisper. 'I really am.' He picks up the cushion Mallory took off her chair, then he pulls the gun out of her backpack.

'Wha – ?' Warden begins.

The Asker flicks off the safety, holds the cushion in front of the gun, and shoots him.

The Children of Daedalus

Warden screams.

The sound cuts right through Mallory. She didn't seem to register the bang, but every part of her felt that scream. He drops to the floor, the phone tumbling from his hand. Mallory dives towards him, her chair clattering to the ground behind her. Her knees thump into the kitchen tiles.

The bullet hit him in the left leg.

Only the leg, she thinks wildly, but blood is blossoming out from his thigh around a horrible little hole in his pants.

'Oh shit,' she stammers, unable to really process what just happened… Warden is moaning, his eyes wide brown circles. She presses her hands down on the wound, trying to stop the blood, but it seeps out around her fingers, soaking her gloves. She doesn't know what to do. 'Oh shit!'

'Quiet, or I'll shoot him again.'

Mallory looks back to The Asker, a million questions and hurts and accusations flooding her mind.

'What the fuck did you do?!' she shouts. '*Asker*!' Her voice cracks. It feels like she's falling.

'Quiet!' He raises the gun again, but he won't meet her eyes. He drops the ruined cushion. There's foam all over the floor. 'You both be quiet.' She obeys – though inside she is seething and raging and yelling, and afraid – and Warden's moans cut out to ragged breaths as The Asker walks over. Mallory tries to put herself between them, but all The Asker is interested in is the phone Warden dropped. He stamps on it, crunching it against the tiles. Then he does the same with Warden's cell. 'Yours too, Echo,' he says. She takes it out of her pocket and slides it over, careful to keep her other hand on Warden's leg. The Asker smashes it like the others. Then he opens a drawer in the kitchen counter and takes out another cell, one that Mallory wonders how he knew was there because he'd said he hadn't been to this house in a while. He puts this new phone – the one that he shouldn't have – against his ear.

Warden moves and a gasp escapes him. Mallory turns back to him, away from The Asker and the gun, and thoughts of what the hell is going on. He looks so scared, his face contorted in pain... And her hands are still pushing down against him, warm and wet...

And she feels it against her skin – she *feels* it – but she doesn't care because all she wants is for him to be all right...

But she can't get it to stop...

The bleeding won't stop and...

Oh shit, oh shit, oh shit!

'Change of plans,' she hears The Asker say down the phone. 'Come now. And have her check local police chatter about a gunshot.'

And Warden's looking at her, his scared, wide eyes are looking at her...

'You're going to be okay,' she says, and she doesn't know why she says it, because she doesn't know if it's true. There obviously aren't any organs in your legs, but there are arteries and he's bleeding a lot... Enough to have hit an artery?

No. No, she doesn't think so. *That would spurt. Arteries spurt.*

'You're going to be okay,' she repeats, pressing down harder on the wound, and he winces, and, 'sorry,' she tells him. 'Sorry.' And he's still watching her, and he's being so brave, not making a sound...

Somewhere behind her she hears a door slam, then another, but she ignores them.

'Echo,' The Asker says, but she ignores him too.

'You're going to be fine,' she tells Warden. 'You're going to be – '

Hands grab her from behind, pulling her away from him. She cries out, thrashing and kicking as she's yanked to her feet.

'Hold still,' someone snaps – a man, not The Asker. Mallory fights all the harder. Her fist connects. 'Little bitch!'

Something hits her in the face. She gasps in pain.

'Don't hurt her!' That was The Asker. Then, 'Echo, listen to me.' He comes round in front of her, the other arms still gripping her from behind, so tight it feels like they're crawling across her skin, and she wants to scream, she wants to… 'That shot was a warning,' he says. 'I didn't want to do it, but if you don't stop fighting, if you don't be quiet, I will shoot him again. Somewhere that matters this time.' He finally looks her in the eye and, though he's blinking too much, she knows he means it.

And something inside of her crumples.

It's as if in that moment all she thought she had had in him and the Forum is physically ripped apart and shown to be pathetic and worthless – and she still doesn't understand why, or what she did wrong, but it feels like the part of her is torn apart with it. And she bites down on her lip, and she stops struggling – she forces herself to stop. She wants to cry, or to strain or to just start yelling… but she doesn't. She looks down at Warden, who's still looking up at her, and she makes herself stay still. He's got his own hands holding down the wound now, and they're already smeared with red.

'Let her go,' The Asker says, talking to whoever's holding her.

'But – '

'*Let* her go.' The hands release her and she stumbles away, shivers passing through her body, even when they're gone… As she stumbles, she turns… And she sees her assailant… And it's like something hits her all over again – because he's short and scrawny, his grimaced, rat-like face pierced so many times it looks like a pincushion. There's a bandage taped across his nose.

Mallory tries to speak, but no words quite make it out.

Behind that man stand three others; a bald guy stacked like a brick wall, a woman with dark skin and spiky hair, and a blonde woman with glasses. The last is leaning against the door frame, smiling this nasty little smile like she's in on some joke Mallory doesn't quite get yet.

'That's her?' she asks, and The Asker nods. 'Well, isn't this a treat.'

'Clean him up,' The Asker tells the woman with spiky hair, and she walks towards Warden. Mallory moves to block her, some instinct kicking in – but The Asker tells her no, and she stops because he's still got the gun. 'She's a doctor,' he tells her. 'She'll take care of him. There's something else we need you to do.' The spiky-haired woman crouches beside Warden, starts talking to him in a voice that sounds too gentle in this room, starts taking things like bandages and bottles out of a bag she's got with her…

'Wash your hands, Echo,' says The Asker, pulling her attention back. No explanation of what's going on, just 'wash your hands'. And she does, she steps over to the sink, because The Asker's still got the damn fricking gun and Warden's still been shot and nothing is quite making any sense because the woman with him and those people over there – standing beside The Asker like there's not a thing wrong in the world – those people are the very same ones they *rescued* him from just five and half hours earlier. 'Turn off her laptop,' he tells someone else. Feet move.

And they're taking orders from *him*.

'There's another in that navy backpack, make sure it's off too.'

Mallory stares down into the basin and turns on the tap, leaving her gloves on. She watches as Warden's blood rinses out of the fabric and runs away from her skin. She washes twice – soap, then water, soap, then water. The air smells like iron and vanilla. 'Towel in the drawer in front of you,' The Asker says. She opens it up takes out a dishcloth covered in pictures of herbs. 'Now over to the laptop.' She starts going, still trying to sponge out the gloves. 'You'll have to take those off,' he adds, and her chest tightens. 'They'll be damp. We can't have them near it.' Her muscles begin seizing in on themselves…

This, even now, she thinks at herself. *Even now, you can't fucking hold it together?* But she feels like she's going to throw up, and…

'No,' she says, 'I can't, please,' and to her shame, her voice breaks.

'Take them off,' repeats The Asker.

She looks towards Warden, now mainly obscured by the woman and the counter, though she can hear him gasping. She slips them off. The bare skin of her hands is cold and prickling, and she clenches them into tight balls against her stomach.

'What's the matter with her?' says the pincushion.

'What the fuck is going on?' Mallory shouts, the tension inside of her finally ripping out.

'Well, isn't that a sight,' says the blonde woman, still smiling that smile, 'we've found something our little Echo can't figure out.' Mallory's gaze darts to her. 'What's the matter, *sugar*,' she says, and the word stops her dead because... 'don't you recognize me like this?'

Because...

'*Scarlet*?' she stammers.

'There we go,' the woman drawls. 'Reigning bitch herself and all that.'

'I don't understand. I don't...' Mallory looks back at The Asker. 'You said – '

'Oh, honey,' Scarlet interrupts, 'he said and did a lot of things to get you in the same room as this here laptop.' Mallory's blood turns to ice. She finally sits down in the chair.

No...

'And here you are supposed to be the smart one,' Scarlet continues. 'We played you, sugar. I was never missing, he was never missing, *no one* was ever missing – we got Weevil, Tower and Cyber Sneak right here, safe and sound.' She points respectively to the pincushion, the bald guy and the woman tending to Warden. 'Along with yours truly, meet the Finders Reapers who never got caught. They've been going solo the past few years, but they came back for this.' Her face hardens a little. 'Some things are important like that.'

No, Mallory thinks again, biting her lip so hard it splits. They're all looking at her. The pincushion smiles. *No, no, no!*

'Why?' she asks, though she thinks she knows.

'Because The Reckoning could achieve all we were ever working for before,' says The Asker. 'I was the one Daedalus sent the laptop to before he died. I spent nearly two years trying to crack it, until thirty-seven days ago I got that automatic video message saying I was taking too long. I needed help, so I got in touch with others I knew I could trust with it. They all tried it, numerous times, but...' He shakes his head. 'The Reckoning was too important to lose, but we couldn't save it. What we needed,' he looks at Mallory, 'was you, Echo – you, who thought like no one else did, who thought like *Daedalus* had. You reminded me so much of him in the way you saw things, the way you could hold all the pieces of a puzzle in your mind at once and see it working in a way other people couldn't – see the loopholes, as you say. You were our only hope.

'But you guarded your anonymity so fiercely, never gave away anything about who you really were. Most people do – little slips here and there – but you didn't, not with me anyway. I knew you'd never agree to meet in person and I didn't think telling you the truth about why I wanted to would help. I wasn't sure you would choose to assist if you knew what the virus did – turns out I was right about that. So I had to try and find you, bring the laptop to you, persuade you somehow. Remember that newbie hacker who tried to trace you in the Forum; Igor? That wasn't a kid in Pennsylvania, it was me. You were too good, though.' He pauses, and he can't quite meet her eyes again, like he knows what he'll see and doesn't have the guts to face it; like he knows what he's doing to her, each word feeling like it's tearing her into these tiny little shreds… 'How do you find a hacker no one can hack?' he asks softly.

'You take away something she cares about,' finishes Scarlet, moving forward and draping an arm across his shoulder. It was a trap. Mallory feels hollowed. She feels cut open and, of all things, strangely embarrassed, like a child being publicly shown the naivety of having believed in something so fully.

'Everything was set up to make you think something had happened to me,' explains The Asker. 'I chose Labyrinth because of its name and because it had a closed network, so you'd have to come in person. It was public and busy – somewhere you wouldn't feel exposed – and the owner, a Wall Street hack called Seable, just happened to be in Children of Daedalus. You were right, Warden,' he tells him, 'the real CoD weren't involved.'

'Just helpfully-named, harmless little yuppies running around giving themselves tattoos,' says Scarlet, wiping her left hand and letting the ink smudge just like it had on Weevil's.

'But Seable gave us use of the club,' says The Asker, 'and a blind eye when I told him who I really was.'

'Fangirled worse than Jericho used to over you,' Scarlet tells Mallory.

'That name and that CoD connection,' continues The Asker, 'plus the trail I left from my account... I didn't know for sure if you'd come, but I hoped. Sneak, Weevil and Tower all went offline as planned so I could set it up that hackers were disappearing. There were clues there and I didn't think you'd be able to leave them unfollowed. I knew the Forum meant a lot to you and I could tell you felt guilty about turning me down.' Mallory's face flushes, her fists clenching tighter and tighter, so tight it's painful. 'I set up a silent alarm,' he says, 'to catch anyone logging on to the club's system – so if you came, we'd know. We'd staged the kidnapping footage for you to find, so while you were downloading and checking it, we could work out who you were. We were waiting, watching the security feeds from laptops in the room where you found me. The plan was for Scarlet to catch you then, and blackmail your help in exchange for both of our freedoms.

'It got to five days, though, and we were running out of time. Maybe I was wrong, maybe you weren't coming. We started double checking everything this morning, just in case we might have missed something. Tower was the one who spotted it.' He glances at Warden. 'We never found your bug, but he noticed the increased data usage – someone was downloading from the system. You'd already been the night before,' he tells Mallory, 'and you'd done what Echo Six does and got in and out without a trace, found a loophole. We didn't know what you'd seen yet, but we couldn't risk you going to the police.'

'So we sent you a little encouragement not to,' says Scarlet. 'It was all or nothing then.'

The ransom note, Mallory realizes, *no one needed to hack The Asker's account because he'd sent it himself.* And her face burns again because, *Stupid, so stupid...*

'After that,' says The Asker, 'we started searching through the footage for you. Still took hours, and an incident report about a locked bathroom, before we thought we'd found you. You'd brought a friend, boyfriend maybe, but it was only Echo Six we needed.'

'No offense.' Scarlet smiles at Warden.

'Fuck you,' Mallory hears him grunt, and she feels a jolt of both relief and pride.

'By then, you still hadn't replied to the ransom message,' The Asker goes on, 'but I knew you would have seen it. I started thinking... you had bettered us before. Maybe trying to trap you was the wrong way to go about it. Maybe the way to get you was to give you what you wanted. We knew you were watching now, but we didn't look for the bug or try to stop you. Instead, we left me with only one guard and we waited.'

'I could still have called the police,' Mallory says, struggling to process it all.

'But you didn't, did you?' Scarlet answers. 'Because you're arrogant, Echo, and with that ransom message... well, you care about our dear Asker here, don't you? A *lot*.' The words seem to cut Mallory, slicing through her.

'You damn – ' she begins, rising.

'Stop,' The Asker orders – and Mallory does, because he's still got the gun, hasn't he? Scarlet smiles. 'You hadn't so far,' he says softly, 'and I know you, Echo; you always try to fix things yourself. You don't trust other people to do it. That's why you'd never do co-op hacks. You need control.' Mallory sits back down. She feels so fricking small. 'Sneak was monitoring various police tip lines just in case, but, as Scarlet said, it was all or nothing. The picture we had of you wasn't good enough for any facial recognition software we had access to. Weevil flashed it at the camera to give you a little extra incentive, though, I wasn't so happy about that. I thought it might scare you off.' Mallory remembers the shouting in the footage.

'Worked, didn't it?' says Weevil.

'You were never going to my house,' she realizes.

'Sugar,' says Scarlet, 'we don't even know your real name. You could have disappeared and we'd never have found you. But, again, you didn't,' she grins. 'That's the beauty of it. You came and rescued The Asker like two budding little heroes and then – well, you kids know the rest.'

The Asker was never in any danger – and neither were she or Warden, until she had put them there. Every single part of it was a trap to get her to access The Reckoning for them. And she fell for it. And Warden...

Oh, damn it, Warden...

Warden, who was cautious and sensible, and shouldn't even be there, but came because of her, and who's now been shot because she didn't see it, because she was too stupid to see it, because she *trusted*…

'I need you to try again,' says The Asker. She looks back at him, filling her gaze with every piece of anger and rage and hurt that she's feeling. Everything she ever did for him, every conversation they ever had, every time she justified what she did because he said it was the right thing, all of it has become this tainted and twisted mess – maybe it always was, she just never knew it.

'I came for you,' she hisses, and he flinches because he *knows*. And it makes it all the worse because he knows what he's done in betraying them, and he still did it, like they didn't matter. '*We* came for *you*!' she shouts, and her voice breaks, and then she's crying because it hurts, even though she's so fricking angry. She's still crying, even though she doesn't want to, not in front of them, not for him, not now. And, in that moment, his face is pained and awful, and she can see that some part of him *is* sorry – but it's not enough, it's not near enough.

'I never wanted to hurt anyone,' he says thickly, 'but I need you to do this, Echo. Please,' he tells her, walking over, crouching beside her chair like you'd do with a little kid. The smile is gone from Scarlet's face now. There is no snide remark. 'I need you to do this,' The Asker repeats, 'and I know you can, and if you do, we'll let you go, both of you.'

'Like hell – ' she begins.

'I *will*,' he insists, definite. 'Like I said, I don't want to hurt you. That's not what this is about.' And, even after all that's happened, deep down something inside of her still believes him on that. He hesitates. 'This is more important than what I want, though, so whether you trust me on that, or not, is irrelevant. What you need to know is that if you *don't* try, Echo, if you fail…' He glances at Warden.

The meaning is clear.

Jeffrey Mullins Jr

Mallory stares at the blank screen of the laptop. The kitchen is strangely quiet now. Warden has been taken down to the basement, his leg strapped in bandages and an old T-shirt. Sneak said she'd staunched the bleeding and cleaned the wound, but he'll need proper medical attention eventually. The bullet went right through, but she thinks it cracked his femur. He'll be fine for the next few hours or so at least – again, she *thinks* – enough time for Mallory to break the unbreakable encryption and release the most destructive and insidious computer virus the world has ever seen. The whole thing makes her feel sick and it's not just because she's fairly sure she can do it. Warden would hate what she's doing to save him. Guilt wells up within her. Whatever she does, it is going to hurt people. He had looked so pasty pale when Tower and Weevil had carried him away. They wouldn't even let her get up to go to him, had taken him out all too quickly, his face scrunched up in pain. All they'd given him was Tylenol. Two stupid pills when they'd probably shattered his femur…

Assholes. How could The Asker do it? How could he? *Because he isn't who you thought he was.*

The Asker shuts the kitchen door. He's sent Tower to guard the front, Weevil out back into the yard. It doesn't seem like anyone reported a gunshot – the makeshift silencer seeming to have done enough. The cops would have been there by now, but they're still being careful. Sneak is with Warden.

'There's a bed in the basement,' The Asker tells Mallory. 'Warden should be more comfortable there.' He says it like he still cares what she thinks, and it makes her insides twist. It's like he wants her to know that he's thought about that, like he still thinks he can convince her that he's not a bad person and that what he's doing is right and all for some greater good.

He can go to hell.

She doesn't even look at him, just stares at the laptop. It's just him and Scarlet in the room with her now; The Asker armed with the gun, Scarlet with the BB she'd found in Warden's backpack and said was 'cute'.

'What I don't get,' says Mallory, eyes still glued to the screen, 'is why Daedalus made it so hard. Why all the rules, the encryption, the time limit? I thought he wanted The Reckoning to get out, but he knew you, so he knew you weren't smart enough to crack this on your own. Why set it up that way?'

'Because he was a dick,' says Scarlet, and, for once, there isn't any trace of sarcasm. 'He couldn't see anything beyond his own ends, beyond what he wanted, couldn't see anything greater.'

'He did it,' says The Asker, '*because* of me. I'd known him since we were kids. He was a couple of years younger, lived on my block till his parents split and his mom moved up to the Bronx. We got into coding together, but everything was always a game to him. Everything was about winning, being better and proving it – not that there was ever any competition. I was well aware of how beyond me he was. When we started the Finders Reapers, all I hoped was that I could help him use it for something worthwhile, give him a direction.' He pauses. 'He didn't want direction, he wanted victory. I didn't lie when I told you things didn't end well between us. I told him he was wasting his gifts and he didn't react well. He left us – took on increasingly reckless hacks to feed his ego, started releasing viruses that stole and damaged and destroyed, started releasing those ridiculous videos. After I got out of jail, he'd email me every single one before he posted it, like he wanted me to be impressed, and at the same time was trying to say he didn't care what I thought because *look* what he could do.

'The Reckoning was his final salvo in the game he thought we were playing. He made it everything he knew I'd always wanted him to do – breaking the common internet encryptions had always been my holy grail, not his. And then he hid it, just out of my reach, before blowing his brains out with a 12-gauge.

'The video he'd released online, the one claiming the existence of The Reckoning, containing the quest instructions that ultimately led nowhere – that was for him, to make sure people wouldn't forget him, to make him into some kind of myth because people would never stop looking. But the virus itself? That was for me. He knew no one would try harder to break it and he knew I would probably fail. He won either way. If I cracked it, I'd release it and everyone would know he'd done it. If I didn't, he'd still be infamous and he'd still have won because he'd beaten me. I think he knew the FBI were closing in on him long before they actually traced him. He could have run, but he didn't, because that would have been defeat.' He shakes his head. 'He could have done so *much*, but he just – ' He cuts off.

'Now all that's left of that is this laptop,' he says, 'a ticking time bomb of the idea that could save the world.'

Or break it, Mallory thinks, but she stays silent. The Asker pushes the power button.

'You'll have to start from scratch, I'm afraid.'

Mallory feels numb. All this because of a friendship turned sour?

A home screen finishes loading on the laptop; a delta drawn in black on a silver background. In the top right corner is a timer, counting down the days, hours, minutes and seconds until Tuesday morning's deadline. In the very center of the delta is a large, cartoony red button reading, *Try Again?*

'Click it,' says The Asker.

Mallory does and the screen goes blank. A fanfare begins to play, blaring out tinny and electronic, like the soundtracks to the video games she and Jed used to play on the fossilized Atari at Ruthie's house. The volume is set so high it's distorting the laptop's speakers, but nothing happens when she tries to turn it down. The backdrop disappears, replaced by a webcam view of a guy sitting at a desk in a bedroom, a topless Lara Croft poster tacked on the wall behind him. He looks in his mid-twenties, with broad shoulders and short, fuzzy brown hair. Mallory recognizes him as Jeffrey Mullins Jr from the pictures in the news stories about Daedalus's suicide. He smooths out the *Pac Man is My Homeboy* T-shirt he's wearing, like he's about to give some kind of address, then he looks dead at the camera and smiles. It's an unnerving smile, dangerous.

'Hello,' he says, clapping his hands together once, loudly. 'Hello, Apollonian. Oh, sorry,' he hesitates, brow creasing, 'would you prefer The Asker now? Either way,' he smiles again, 'welcome to my… video – call it what you like – suicide note, although that is a bit grim.' He pulls a face. 'But whatever, it is my last recorded message to Planet Earth and I have left it for you, old friend. I hope you realize how important you are to me.' He tries to look serious, but a trace of the grin is still there. 'No Minotaur for you; we know each other too well for that. I want you to see my face for this.

'Now,' he goes on, 'thinking about my imminent death has made me reassess a few things, consider my legacy, you know, all that crap you don't care anything for. And you know what I kept thinking about the most? I kept thinking about *you*, and what you said to me before we oh-so-unceremoniously parted ways and you abandoned me. You said, now what was it…? Ah, yes.' He sticks his face right up close to the camera. '*You are a waste. If I had an ounce of what you have* – and then you paused, I remember you paused, and you said – *you could change the world if you weren't such a selfish, egotistical bastard.*' Daedalus leans back, letting out a long sigh. 'Gotta say buddy, that hit me, right here.' He smacks his fist sharply against his chest and, for the briefest moment, his eyes darken. 'I named myself after a genius,' he says quickly, 'but you took the title of a *god* and you want to change the world. I think we could debate which of us really has the ego problem.' He stops. Then he smiles again, holding his hands out in surrender. 'I may be about to depart this earth, but – because of our friendship – I am going to give you what you wanted all along. I'm going to give you that ounce of what I have in here.' He taps his forehead.

'Okay,' he continues, 'now comes the technical part. Pay attention. On this laptop, I have left you a virus. I like to call it *The Reckoning*.' He sweeps his arms out like a banner. 'Too dramatic? Ah well, I've already made another little video about it for everyone else – I think you'll like that one – and I can't change it now. So, anyway, what does this virus do, you ask? Well, I don't like to boast, you know I don't, but I kind of figured out how to crack the common internet encryptions in less than a million years. I know, I know, people have been trying to for, like, ever and no one's ever done it and now *I* have… but there we go, let's get over it, because that's not all, my friend. No. I have encoded this algorithm into a virus for you, the result of which has the potential to hack any system and, once you release it, it will. It will open any door that has been shut. It will find the things people have tried to hide and it will leave them open to the wonderful world of cyber space.' He pauses. 'And it won't stop,' he says quietly. 'It will just keep going and going and going. Daedalus forever… ever… ever…' He laughs.

'Look, I've seen what you've been up to with your little Forum. Didn't invite me to join – even though we both know you based it on my design for a roving Finders Reapers site – but we'll let that go. It's cute, really, what you're doing. This virus, however, will really change things up for you, man, and you can find all the truth you ever dreamed of.' His face darkens again. 'No,' he says, 'I was right with the name; calling it The Reckoning isn't too dramatic. It will be dramatic. It will be everything laid bare; no exclusions, no exceptions and no nepotistic protections. That's what you wanted, isn't it' – and his voice rises – 'for everyone to just tell the fucking *truth*!' he shouts. He looks almost manic, and the words rattle Mallory because she also believes every one of them. 'Maybe,' he spits, 'you'll get more truth than you ever wanted, but beggars can't be choosers.'

The video cuts then, like Daedalus edited the footage. He is calmer again.

'I'm sorry,' he says. 'I got angry. I promised myself I wouldn't do that. I knew how things were going to end. I shouldn't fight the inevitable, just embrace it. Now,' he continues, businesslike, 'you know me, I'm a great believer in the importance of earning what you get. Work ethic matters. So, I'm not going to just give it to you. Harsh, you say? Well, maybe I'm feeling a bit prickly and emotional given that I'm going to kill myself in about' – he glances at his watch – 'fourteen hours, fifty-four minutes. Whatever the reason, this is how it's going to work. I have built a labyrinth for you, just like my namesake. The Reckoning is encrypted within the laptop you'll be watching this on. You hack it, you can have it. Forever,' he whispers dramatically, wiggling his fingers at the screen. 'Use it to change the world all you want.

'Some ground rules, though. I don't want you to cheat. I hate cheaters. Rule one; you try and copy the code – send it, back it up – whatever, and it will delete itself. Two; you try and tamper with the laptop in any way – try to reset the date, the timer, etcetera – and the code will, you guessed it, delete itself. Finally, three; you can't ask me for help. I'll be dead by the time you're watching this.' He mimes shooting himself in the head. 'Oh, and four's not really a rule, but you're going to have to watch this little video every time you try and crack it. I don't want you to *forget* me.' He frowns.

'This is it, Nathan,' he says, 'after everything, this is really goodbye.' He looks away from the camera for a moment, like he's finding it hard to speak. Then, 'Here's another truth for you,' he says quietly, 'one final secret between friends.' His face goes deadly serious. He leans right into the camera again and whispers, 'I don't think you can do it.'

The video cuts out, and the code appears on the screen.

'He was right,' Mallory hears The Asker say, 'I couldn't.' She looks up at him, thoroughly disturbed. 'But you can, Echo,' he says. 'Now it's your turn.'

A Recurring Pattern

It doesn't take Mallory as long, this time, to reach the same stage of the encryption. She makes it past level fourteen by one in the morning. Her eyes are tired and her head is beginning to swim a little, but when she's inside the code, for a time, she can forget where she actually is, forget what it is she's really doing, what she's a part of, forget her fear for Warden...

Forget what The Asker has done.

When she doesn't, when she slips back into herself, this hideous dread comes crashing down on her. Every time she looks at him now, it's as if something breaks in her, and then this searing rage bubbles up and she just wants to hurt him so badly, and she has to bite her already jagged lip just to stop from screaming at him...

They sit beside her as she works – The Asker and Scarlet – kitchen chairs pulled round so one of them is on either side. Their closeness makes her skin creep and she's asked them to move, but they won't. She doesn't know how much of what she's doing they can follow, but they still want to watch. Maybe they're checking up on her – though it's not like she could contact anyone from this laptop. Maybe they just want to see it happen.

With every level, she sees more what The Reckoning will do. It's clever – it's so damn clever – and it will be unstoppable. She tries not to think about that, tries not to think about the chaos it will cause, tries not to wonder how many people will lose their jobs or their savings because of it, tries not to wonder if people will *die* because of it... And then, even though she's trying not to, she keeps thinking of Roger and when he was in Iraq and, when she does, it sort of feels like it cuts her up, which is no fricking help at all because what can she do? Warden is down in the basement with a bullet hole in him and she can't let anything happen to him. It doesn't matter what arguments she gives herself about right and wrong, or good and bad, because when she even thinks about him getting hurt, hurt worse, it's like for a second she can't breathe. She keeps replaying it in her head, the moment when The Asker had fired the gun and for a few terrible seconds, she had thought that maybe, maybe, that was it for Warden, and he was going to be gone, really gone… She'd never felt so afraid. She would have done *anything* asked of her to save him, then, to protect him.

And, each time she thinks of it, it starts her typing again.

* * *

Mallory glances at the clock on the wall. It's nearly two. She rubs her eyes and blinks, forcing herself to look back at the code. Level seventeen now. It's getting harder, though, slower, and she's seriously losing track of time. The Asker's made her three coffees already, but she's still beginning to flag. Just because she can do it, doesn't mean it's easy, and there's only so long she can maintain that level of concentration. She lets her eyes blur for a second, the numbers fuzzing up before her… She blinks again. Twice more. Then…

Wait.

She leans a little closer to the screen. Her brain starts whirring again, filing, sorting. There's a new series of numbers in this level, a new recurring pattern scattered in amongst the others so it's possible you wouldn't notice them at all. It's a date, she realizes. It's written in epoch time, but she recognizes the format. It takes her a moment to calculate, but when she does… A fresh spark of energy flutters through her. It's not just any date, it's Tuesday's date, five thirty in the morning; the two year anniversary of Daedalus's suicide. Mallory sits up a little straighter.

'What is it?' says Scarlet.

'Quiet,' Mallory tells her, in a way that really means shut up, BB gun or not. She looks at how the numbers are positioned, hidden and connected within the code. It's part of the kill switch that Daedalus built in to delete the virus if The Asker didn't make the deadline. She flexes her fingers in front of her, feeling skin rub against skin instead fabric. An idea starts trickling into her mind, the tiniest beginnings of what could maybe, just maybe, be a way out… It would be dangerous though; to her, and, not least, to Warden. She has to be sure.

Four, three, four, two…

She starts tapping on the desk, looking and looking and checking, and the more she does, the more she checks, the more she thinks it could be possible, that it could work… It *would* work. She glances at the clock again. She'd have to time it just right. She thinks of The Asker's threat, and sees the gun firing, sees Warden fall… Get the timing wrong and he could end up dead.

Four, three, four, two…

Get it wrong, and they *both* could. Scarlet is already shifting impatiently beside her; Mallory can just imagine how she would react, let alone The Asker. But if she completes the virus as it is…

All the thoughts she has been trying not to think start piling back up, thoughts about what she is setting in motion, right here in this little kitchen…

And she doesn't know what to do…

She doesn't…

She can't decide…

She *can't*…

She needs to see Warden. It affects him too and she needs to see him.

'I need a break,' she says. The Asker looks up from the chair beside her. The gun is still rested in his hand.

'No,' he replies carefully, 'you need to keep working.'

'I can't,' she says, shaking her head, rubbing her eyes again. 'Crap, I'm tired.'

'Then I'll get you more coffee,' says Scarlet.

'This isn't a joke,' Mallory snaps. 'I need to rest, I need to use the bathroom again… and I want to see Warden.'

'Like hell,' Scarlet answers, heading to the kettle.

'I keep working with no break and I'm going to do it wrong, going to miss things. I haven't eaten since lunch yesterday and I've been staring at that damn screen so long I've already got a fricking migraine.'

'Then we'll get you aspirin.'

'You think I want to make a mistake? You think I'm stalling?'

Scarlet walks back over, staring Mallory down.

'I don't know what you're doing, sugar,' she says, 'but it isn't clever.'

'I'm not screwing around!' Mallory stands, the chair's feet scraping against the floor and making her shudder. 'You already near as told me you're going to kill Warden if I don't get this right. I want this to work as much as you do, and I'm telling you I need a *time out*. And I want to see my friend.'

Scarlet yanks the BB gun out of her pocket and points it right at Mallory's face.

'Just give me a reason, hon.'

'Enough,' interrupts The Asker. 'Come on, Scarlet, that's enough.' She shrugs. She nudges the gun against Mallory's cheek.

'Wouldn't kill her,' she says lightly, 'even close range if I was careful, but I could leave some lovely scars on that pretty little face.' Mallory stays where she is, forcing herself not to flinch.

'I want to see Warden,' she repeats.

'Okay,' replies The Asker, getting up too. 'Okay. Scarlet, just put the gun down.' He sighs. She rolls her eyes at him, but she steps away, tucking it into her back pocket. 'Okay then, Echo. You said you're hungry.' He grabs the pack of cookies off the table. 'Let's go see how Warden's doing, give you some motivation.'

Mallory follows him out of the kitchen, strongly resisting the urge to tell Scarlet just what she can go and do to herself. The Asker leads her through the living room, past where Tower is sat by the front door. Then he takes her upstairs to the bathroom and waits outside while she uses it. She tries to take the moment's solitude to calm herself, but her pulse is all jittery. In the mirror, her jaw is swollen an angry black and blue. Another bruise is showing on her cheek from where Weevil hit her in the kitchen. She looks herself in the eyes and tells herself she can do this. She can hold it together, can still find them a way out. She can fix this.

The basement is dim and cold, with that musty smell of somewhere that's not been used in a while. It looks like it was once a spare room, but has since doubled as a storage space for the old cardboard boxes of stuff that all houses seem to collect. Warden is laid out on a bed against the back wall, Sneak sitting at the bottom of the stairs with a laptop perched on her knees – the only visible chair is missing a leg. Apart from the laptop, the basement is lit solely by a dim floor lamp by the stairs, the beaded shade throwing out odd shadows across the room.

'Main bulb's blown,' says Sneak, by way of explanation.

'How is he?' says The Asker. Warden is watching them. He looks at Mallory, and she takes the cookies from The Asker, walking down the stairs past Sneak without waiting for permission.

'Threw up a couple of times at first,' she hears Sneak reply. 'Seems okay now, though.'

Seems okay? Just seems *okay?* Mallory stops by the bed. He doesn't look okay, he looks really damn pale. Her free hand clenches at her side.

'Hi,' says Warden, and he tries to smile and it pulls at her.

'You've got ten minutes,' calls The Asker. Mallory doesn't respond.

'How are you doing?' says Warden.

'How am *I* doing?' she says. 'Shit, Warden, you were shot. How are *you* doing?'

'Never better,' he replies, though she can hear the strain in his voice. 'Although,' he continues, 'this bed's a little uncomfortable, far too lumpy. I've got this memory foam mattress at home that – ' He stops. He smiles a little again, still trying to act normal, and it sort of makes her want to cry. 'But you don't want to hear about that.' Mallory bites her lip. His smile fades. 'You're doing it then,' he says quietly, 'breaking the encryption for them.'

She nods. She waits for him to respond, to tell her what he thinks she should do, to tell her she shouldn't – but he doesn't. The silence stretches out, and Warden never lets silence stretch out. He definitely looks too pale. He moves, trying to sit himself up a little and she sees the pain flicker across his face as his leg shifts, and she feels so fricking useless...

'Are you hungry?' she asks. She opens the packet of cookies. They're chocolate chip.

'I don't – '

'I think you should eat something,' she says firmly, because that's something she can do, can help with. She hands him a cookie and watches unblinkingly as he eats it on demand. Then she hands him another. Her stomach rumbles noisily and he raises an eyebrow.

'Your turn, I think,' he says, that trace of a smile again, and she finds she has to look away. She does take one for herself, though. They're a little stale, but she really is hungry and they finish the packet between them in a few minutes; a few minutes of eating and not talking. Mallory doesn't know what to say – other than the thing she came to ask – and she doesn't know how to ask that, how to get the message across, or even if she should… but The Asker said ten minutes and time is ticking. If she's going to do it, she needs to do it now, otherwise she'll be stuck back up in that room in the same position, not knowing.

Every time Warden moves, she sees how it hurts him, and it's almost as if she can feel it, and if she does what she's thinking and it goes wrong…

If it goes wrong…

She glances back at The Asker. He's watching her now. So is Sneak.

Damn it.

She'll have to be careful. They can't know, can't suspect. She looks away from them. Warden is watching her too, but it seems an impossible thing to say even one sentence to him without anyone else catching it. They'll know. They'll hear, unless…

Unless…

She sits down on the bed beside him, and inside she's all squirming, but it's the only thing she can think of. She has to do it. She looks down at him, trying to tell him, to show him, to get him to trust her.

'I don't want you to worry,' she says. 'You're going to be fine. I won't let them hurt you.' Then she leans towards him, slowly. He stays stock still and she can see the confusion on his face, but she wills him not to say anything and he doesn't, and her heart starts racing and…

Oh crap, oh crap, oh crap… Just do it!

She leans down and hugs him. Her arms wrap around his back and it feels like fire is radiating out from every spot where they're connected, her bare hands buzzing all over pins and needles. And she can feel him shaking a little beneath her, and then his arms move tentatively around her in response...

And inside of her is this sudden rage of noise...

Of fear and adrenaline...

But also...

Also...

This strange *relief*, and security, and a feeling of not being alone that she's not used to, and it's so strong and overwhelming and unexpected that she feels herself shudder against him...

And, at the same time, she wants to draw away – to *run* away...

And, at the same time, she wants to stay there a moment longer...

And she makes herself stay...

She makes herself...

And she tries to think...

She tries to...

Her face is just by his neck. She lifts it...

'There's something I can do about it,' she whispers, 'but it's dangerous for us.' It's both a statement and a question.

'That's ten minutes,' says The Asker. Warden jumps and Mallory pulls back.

'Echo,' Warden says, and she looks down. 'I know it will be okay,' he tells her, and he holds her gaze, and her skin is hot and her mind is still yelling all sorts of different things at her and... 'I trust you,' he says.

It's a yes.

Better

Mallory re-enters the kitchen. Her body is still buzzing, but her mind is more focused. She knows what she is going to do.

'Got it out of your system?' Scarlet asks.

'I could use that coffee now,' Mallory replies, returning to the laptop without looking up. The Asker sits beside her. Mallory blanks him too. She starts tapping on the table.

Four, three, four, two…

Four, three, four, two…

And she thinks through the plan that's been formulating in her mind. The virus has to work. There is nothing she can do about that. Even if The Asker is going to hold true to his promise to let them go afterwards, he'd be stupid to do it until he was certain he had what he wanted; until he'd seen The Reckoning in action. It *has* to work – but maybe, just maybe, there are two other little things Mallory can add into the equation; timing, and a little extra targeting. If The Reckoning can hack into anywhere… She stills her hand, one specific target in mind.

Scarlet slams coffee number four on the table. Mallory gulps it down in one go, though she's probably already way too jacked on caffeine. She needs to be awake for this. It will push her to the limit of what she can do and she can't make a single mistake. Scarlet sits beside her again. Mallory can feel them both there, feel them too close, hear their breathing, hear Scarlet clicking her nails impatiently…

She starts to type.

She begins filling in the level, just like she should, building up the missing sections of code until it's almost complete – but then she doesn't finish it, not right away. There are certain key requirements you have to fulfil within each level for it to trigger the next one to load. All of these relate to the algorithm that will crack the common internet encryptions and they can't be changed without damaging the function. What can, theoretically, be altered is the computer virus that will act as the delivery system for that algorithm. It would have to be subtle – real subtle – subtle enough not to damage the overall effect of the virus at first, and subtle enough for those watching her not to notice, but if Mallory can do it…

Sometimes the tiniest change is all you need in a hack. The smallest loophole is still a loophole.

She has to test it first, though, test how much The Asker and Scarlet really understand before she gives away what she's going to do. She keeps typing, never breaking her rhythm, filling in the digits as she should… and then she makes a change, alters one number – a single digit – making it what it shouldn't be.

No one comments.

Neither of her observers even moves.

They just sit, watching.

It worked.

Adrenaline ripples through her. She makes another alteration, then another, her heart pounding… The Asker and Scarlet say nothing. Mallory realizes, then, that The Asker had really meant what he'd said before; she *is* better than him. A lot better. She feels a rush, aggressive and driving. Neither of them is following what she's doing, at least, not entirely. They don't understand what's on the screen. Daedalus knew exactly what he was doing when he set this game. He wanted The Asker to lose, wanted him to fail…

And he would have.

He's still going to fail, she thinks viciously. She keeps typing, faster and faster. Once she's committed, there is no going back; she has to time it perfectly. The Asker shifts in his seat at the change of pace, but he doesn't say anything. Scarlet clicks her nails. Mallory puts in another alteration.

And neither of them notices a damn thing.

'What's taking so long?' Scarlet mutters. She's been doing it a lot since Mallory started slowing down. She had realized she was on the penultimate level about a half hour ago – too early. It's only three thirty. She's been stalling ever since.

'Don't speak,' she says, not taking her eyes off the screen.

'You know, I'm real tired of – ' Scarlet begins.

'Please, keep talking if you want me to crap this up. Otherwise let me do what you keep waving a gun at me to do.'

'Cool it,' The Asker tells Scarlet. She backs off, but, 'You are slowing down, Echo,' he adds.

'Well, it's getting harder,' she tells him. 'It's like a video game. Each level is more complicated than the last. You have to keep all the previous parts in your mind, then align the new one to slot in with them. You want to do it, by all means…' She leans back, arms out. The Asker's face darkens, but he doesn't move. 'No? Didn't think so.'

'Be careful,' he warns.

'Always am.'

She looks at the clock. Just a little longer…

* * *

'She's stalling,' Scarlet says.

It's four now. Mallory's on the last level. She can even see what she needs to do to finish it, but…

Not quite time, not quite…

Beside her, The Asker sighs. He rises from his chair and sits on the table next to the laptop. Mallory glances up at him, hand tapping nervously against the wood. He lifts the gun a little, like he's reminding her it's there.

Four, three, four, two…

Four, three, four, two…

'You don't need that thing out,' Mallory says, her muscles tightening at the sight.

'I'm sorry, Echo,' he answers, 'but I think Scarlet's right. I think you are stalling.' He frowns. 'I thought I made myself clear before.'

'You did,' she answers. 'I'm almost done.'

'I could go and get Warden – '

'*No*,' she says. She hesitates. 'Look, just a few more minutes and you'll have your reckoning. Just leave him alone.'

'A few minutes,' The Asker says. 'Then I get him.'

Mallory starts typing again. He's claimed more than once that he doesn't want to hurt them and, despite all he's done, part of her almost does believe him on that – the person she's known for two and a half years wouldn't *want* to – but he's already shot Warden once. She can't push it. She glances at the clock again. It's close enough.

It has to be.

She lets her mind shut them out, ignores The Asker as he sits back in his seat and restarts his pointless staring. She lets herself disappear into the code. She fills in the final gaps, sees how it all clicks into place to form something complex, and beautiful and terrifyingly, wickedly smart. She sees them, the last few steps.

Then the final click.

And even given where she is, even given what it is, a satisfied thrill shoots through her and...

The screen goes blank.

'What's happening?' says The Asker, sitting up abruptly.

'It's done,' Mallory tells him.

'But where's – ' Scarlet begins.

A new video appears; Jeffrey Mullins Jr – Daedalus – in the same bedroom as in the first, in the same *Pac Man* T-shirt with the same *Tomb Raider* poster on the wall behind him. His face is strangely expressionless, though, compared to before.

'Well, well, well,' he says, 'you actually did it. It seems I underestimated you.' He frowns. 'I'm afraid I spent all my time on your consolation video – this was more of a just-in-case after thought – so it's not as good. I'm sorry about that. The other one had music, dancing girls, streamers...' His eyes narrow and he scratches his forehead. 'But you've done it, so this is what you get to see instead.' Daedalus glances down.

He shakes his head and, when he looks back at the screen, his face is serious, somber even. 'I am a man of my word,' he says quietly. 'I give you The Reckoning. Goodbye, Nathan.'

He switches off the camera, all the bravado gone.

'That's it?' Scarlet asks. 'Is that really it?'

The Asker looks unsure, then, 'He lost,' he says.

The code appears on the screen, scrolling in its entirety, faster than you could read. It begins working automatically, opening up other windows, releasing itself onto the internet by hacking into the nearest Wi-Fi network. Mallory locks her hands tight as she watches, watches what she has helped create, all the while knowing the damage it is about to cause.

Not as much as it could have, she tells herself. Lost within that swirl of digits, are the changes she made, including a single, secret marker that's also being sent out. She feels a swell of apprehension as she wonders if it will find its target, if it will be located and understood quickly enough, before everything starts to go wrong and it is too late for Warden, too late for her... *Please, please, please...*

'I knew you could do it, Echo,' says The Asker. There's an intensity to his voice that makes her turn to him. His eyes are glistening. 'Thank you,' he says. 'I'm proud of you.'

Mallory swallows, the words getting to her, even now, words that would have once meant everything...

Screw you, she thinks, but she doesn't manage to say it out loud. She looks back at the screen, just stares in silence with him as The Reckoning begins to take effect. It starts low key, just like it was designed to, entrenching itself across thousands of different computers before it really begins to act.

And it *works.*

The Asker gets up from his seat. He goes to Scarlet and they embrace, Scarlet's eyes glistening just like The Asker's had been.

'We did it,' she whispers to him. 'We did it, Apollo.' When they pull apart, The Asker's face is flushed and damp.

'Tell the others,' he says to Scarlet, resting his hand against her cheek. 'Tell them to stay on watch, but to also set their laptops to start collecting data.' Scarlet nods and heads out of the kitchen. The Asker opens up another laptop, one that she had brought in earlier. He begins searching, begins copying, begins downloading from targets that have already been hit – as others around the world are probably already realizing they can do too, are probably already starting to.

It's going to be a mess.

Mallory checks the clock again; four twenty-one. She completed the code about five minutes ago, so the virus went out around four sixteen. Even with the changes she made, it's still going to be a mess. A lot can happen in seventy-four minutes. Maybe she judged it wrongly...

Maybe...

'I want to see Warden,' she says. The Asker looks up, his face still flushed, eyes still blazing with triumph.

'You don't want to see this?' he says. 'After all that we have worked for – '

'I want to see Warden,' she repeats. 'I did what you asked me to. Now' – she swallows – 'now, let us go. We won't tell anyone what you did. Please, just let us go.'

The Asker watches her carefully.

'Not yet,' he says.

'Warden needs medical help,' she begins. 'His leg – '

'He's had medical help,' he cuts her off. 'I told you, Sneak's a doctor and she's been watching him. He's not bleeding out and the wound is clean. He can hold on for now.'

'But he – '

'Not yet,' he repeats, and it's final. It's the answer she expected, but she still feels herself sag, feels a little of the remaining fight dissipate. 'It's early days,' he tells her, indicating the laptop, 'and I'd like you to stay a short while longer, just in case we need you.' Mallory holds his gaze. 'I *will* let you go,' he promises, 'both of you, in a few hours. I'm a man of my word.'

'Like Daedalus,' she says. The Asker doesn't reply to that. 'I want to see Warden,' she repeats. 'If you won't let us go, then at least let me go check on him myself.' He still hesitates. 'Come on,' she says, 'what am I going to do? I've given you what you wanted. I'm not going to blow that on trying to do something stupid now. I trusted you for over two and half years' – she tries to keep her voice calm, the words stinging – 'and I don't think you want to hurt us.'

Four, three, four, two...

Four, three, four, two...

'I'll wait like you want,' she continues, 'I won't fight you, but I just want to wait with him.' She sees it in his eyes, sees the cogs ticking, his face softening, sees the words working. He cares what she thinks. He still *does* care... 'Please.' She forces herself not to drop her gaze. He finally nods.

'Okay,' he says. Then, quietly, 'I'm not a bad person. I know you must think that now, but I hope one day...' He trails off and Mallory has to clench her fists to stop herself reacting. She wants to both scream at him and break down at the same time.

They find Sneak waiting at the top of the basement stairs now, laptop still open.

'Reception's crap down there,' she says, then she looks at Mallory. 'Thank you,' she tells her, and it sounds like she really means it. Mallory just nods.

'Lock her in with him,' The Asker tells Sneak. 'There's only junk in the boxes.' He looks again at Mallory. 'What you've done tonight has fulfilled everything we were trying to do with the Forum, but never could. I know you don't believe me, but you've made things better, Echo. You will see that,' he says. 'Eventually, you'll see.'

No, she thinks, stepping through the door, *no, I won't. And, in a few minutes, neither will you.*

Touch

Mallory stands just inside the doorway. She feels the air move as it shuts behind her, hears the key turn in the lock. The basement is even darker than before, the yellow light from the beaded lamp now the only illumination, casting its strange mottled shapes against the walls and boxes. She walks down the stairs, floorboards creaking beneath her feet. Warden is lying on the bed like before, his face in shadow. She can't tell if he's awake. Everything is so very still, but, inside, her body feels like it's been twisted and twisted and twisted and now it's just this tightly wound ball.

'Echo,' says Warden, as she reaches the bottom step. He's awake then. He tries to sit up, his face lifting into a beam of light, but she hears a gasp of pain –

'Just fricking lie still,' she snaps, her heart clenching at the sound, at the thought of The Asker's threat against him, at the thought of what she's done and what it could mean for him and…

Oh shit. Oh shit!

She finds herself standing next to the bed.

'Lie still,' she tells him again. He leans back down, obeying. 'Thank you,' she says, and her voice catches because…

Because…

'Echo, what's going – '

'I should search the room,' she interrupts. 'There could be something we can use.' If she can just find some way to contact help, something to use as a weapon even. She opens the packing boxes, but finds only books and toys and VHS tapes. Just junk, like The Asker had said. There's a wardrobe too, but it's empty.

'They took the coat hangers,' Warden tells her. 'There aren't even bed springs. Just wooden slats and foam – but not memory-foam. Why it's so uncomfortable.' He pauses. 'I don't think we can escape. We're in a box of bricks with no windows and we can't exactly fight our way out. I can't walk and there's nothing in here that you should try using against a gun, anyway. Even if there was, it wouldn't be safe.'

'None of this is safe,' says Mallory.

She has to tell him.

She has to…

The words don't come. Why are they so much harder in real life? She stays by the wardrobe, saying nothing, doing *nothing*.

'You don't have to stand,' says Warden. He shifts sideways on the bed so he's up against the wall, making space. He winces as he does and it catches at her again. 'There,' he says, 'now you can sit down without coming within a foot of me.' His tone is genuine, not mocking. She hesitates, then she walks over. She sits with her back against the head-board, careful not to jog or touch, hugging her legs into her chest and resting her chin on her knees. Beneath her, the bed still feels warm where he was just lying. The mattress is hard and lumpy.

'You're right,' she says, 'it is uncomfortable.' She glances down at him then, and there's a half smile on his face. He still looks far too pale, though. 'Did they give you more painkillers?' she asks.

'Yes.'

'But it still hurts.'

'I've had worse.'

'No, you haven't.'

'You don't know that,' he answers. 'I might get shot all the time.' He's trying to lighten things again.

'Yeah,' Mallory says, though it cuts a little too close to current reality, 'you're a real badass.'

'That's me.'

She stays silent, trying to hold it in, trying but…

'Damn it,' she says, her voice cracking.

'Echo?'

Don't cry, she tells herself, looking away from him as her eyes glass up. *Don't you damn cry.* She clings on tighter to her legs, bites so hard that her lip starts bleeding again, holding it down until pain blanks out everything else…

'Echo, what is it?' Warden repeats.

'I'm fine, *okay!*'

'Okay.' And he doesn't say anything more, just waits, waits for her to be ready, waits as her breathing slows. She looks up at the ceiling, at the cream styrofoam tiles above them, letting herself sink into the darkness. They know each other better in darkness, not as faces or expressions or sounds that complicate things in real life and make them so much more difficult.

She has to tell him.

'I did it,' she says. 'I did what they wanted. The Reckoning has gone out and it's working. I had to, Warden. I had to or they were going to hurt you. They were – '

'It's okay – ' he begins.

'No, it's not. It's not, because that's not all I did.' She takes a sharp breath. 'I told you before that I had an idea,' she says. 'Well, while I was going through the encryption, I noticed the kill switch Daedalus had written in to delete the code if The Asker missed Tuesday's deadline. The later levels were set up so that it would gradually allow you to neutralize it as you completed it… but I didn't, I left it in. I kept thinking about what you'd said and what it could do, and I kept thinking of my dad when he was in Iraq and, Warden,' she says, 'I changed the deadline to today.' Her anxiety grows, even as she says it, all the possible consequences flitting through her mind… 'The Reckoning will run perfectly for one hour, fourteen minutes, and then at five thirty, it will delete itself. It doesn't matter where it's got to by then, where it's copied to, it will vanish like it never existed.' She feels him shift beside her and finally looks down. He's watching her too, but she can't tell what he's thinking in the dim light. 'Seventy-four minutes,' she tells him, 'for the FBI to track a ping request I sent them within the virus, and to respond. There wasn't much I could do with The Asker and Scarlet watching, and there was only so much I could mess with the code anyway, but I managed to write in a single ping command and I targeted it at that IP address in the Javits Federal Building, the place the FBI tried to track me from last year. It will send again and again, every time the virus copies – and encoded inside it is our location.'

Warden doesn't say anything for a few moments, a few moments in which it feels like Mallory can't really breathe…

Then, 'You're a bloody genius, you know that,' he says.

She feels a tug of relief, but, 'Not if it doesn't work,' she replies. 'I tried to base when I released it on estimating the FBI response time – factoring in them figuring out the ping, deployment, travel – so it would be loose for the minimum amount of time possible, do the least amount of damage, but if I got it wrong, if they don't get to us in time…'

The Asker was prepared to risk everything to release The Reckoning, to complete a goal he's apparently had since long before the Forum even existed. Mallory has taken that from him. Just thinking of how he will react when he realizes, of how Scarlet will react, the apprehension wells up again, and she gets this sudden urge to reach out to Warden, to *hold* on to him…

'It was still the right thing,' he says. 'I meant what I said before. The Reckoning may only be a computer virus, but it will still hurt a lot of people. Unchecked, it would have brought chaos. I mean, with some bad luck, it could have even started World War Three. What you did was right, Echo.'

'Even if no one finds us in time?' And there is nothing left between them and that gun, and the anger that will be behind it. No one else is going to come. They haven't been missing long enough to be reported and the tracker she put on Jed's phone will be useless now hers is smashed. They have one chance.

'The Feds may not be able to catch you usually,' says Warden, 'but they're not stupid and you don't normally send a flaming beacon right to their front door. We're talking someone having cracked the common internet encryptions and made it viral, Echo. They'll follow this. It was the right thing,' he repeats.

Mallory doesn't know whether she believes him or not. In a way, it doesn't really matter now. She's done what she's done and she can't change it. She closes her eyes. Crap, she feels tired. Her body is prickling all over with swelling spikes of adrenaline, and at the same time she feels like she could collapse right where she is. She doesn't quite understand how that works.

'I want to lie down,' she says, the words just seeming to slip out.

'Sure, I,' he stutters, 'yes, sure.'

She uncurls herself slowly, careful to keep in a straight line, to not cross the invisible barrier that would be too close to him, in spite of the urge she felt to before. As her head touches the pillow, her remaining strength seems to evaporate. Lumpy mattress or not, she sinks into it. She stares up at the ceiling tiles and wonders how long they have left now? An hour? Fifty-five minutes?

'Do you know the time?' she asks.

'No,' he answers. 'My watch broke when I fell.'

Is anyone on their way yet?

'I'm sorry I got you into this,' Mallory says.

'That's bollocks,' says Warden. Mallory stiffens. 'Not the sorry part, I mean,' he adds quickly, 'just the you got me into it part. I'm not an idiot, Echo. I made my own decisions and I knew what I could be getting into. Well, not exactly, but I knew there were risks and I came anyway. You didn't ask me to. *My* decision. Yes, I was worried about you, but I cared about The Asker, too. I trusted him, too.'

'But if I'd listened to you – '

'The Asker's the bastard in all this,' he says forcefully, 'so don't go blaming yourself. You went to help a friend and that's a sodding brilliant way to be and you shouldn't want to change it or feel bad for it, and I don't either.' His voice drops then. 'I don't regret it,' he says. Mallory's fingers flex against the covers. 'I don't even regret spending the money I was saving for the Lampertz safe. No, that's a lie, maybe I do regret *that* a little bit,' he says, but she can hear the smile behind it. 'You should see – '

'I'm glad you came,' Mallory says, the words spilling out. 'Not glad as in you're hurt or in danger, but just…' Her fists ball up the fabric. 'Shit,' she says, and he actually laughs. She glares at him.

'Me too,' he shrugs. She looks back up at the ceiling, face flushing because all of a sudden she has that desire to reach out to him again, to hold on tight and never let go… She can't, though – she *can't* do that, and why is she thinking it, and why does she *want* it and…

Shut up. Shut up. Shut up!

She doesn't reach out. She moves her arm a little closer to his, though, and she knows he realizes because his breathing catches. They stay lying like that, arms closer together than the foot gap the bed could afford them to be apart, somehow, gradually ending up so close that they are almost touching…

Almost.

'It's the number of mistakes I've made,' Mallory says, speaking softly into the silence.

'What?' asks Warden.

'Six,' she tells him, 'the six in Echo Six. It's my mistakes.' She turns her head to him and he's close, and she swallows but she stays as she is. 'Whenever you do a hack,' she goes on, 'there are some things you can't account for, some security measures you could never know about – like when the Feds tried to trace me. I'm not talking about those. I'm talking about mistakes that *I've* made, things I've done less well than I could have, that could have allowed someone else to know I was there, to get closer to tracking me than they otherwise would have. I remember every single one, every time I left an *echo* of myself behind. Six mistakes. It doesn't matter what you can do, or even what you have done, you are only as good as your last mistake. So I am Echo Six, and it reminds me to be careful every time I see it.'

Warden smiles, lets out this gentle laugh – not an unkind laugh – and his eyes seem to glisten.

'So it's genuinely not your favorite scientific phenomena combined with your birthday then?' he asks.

'No,' Mallory says, 'not that.' And then she smiles a little too. 'My favorite guess was actually the *place you like to hide your destroyer in Battleship* one.'

Warden laughs again.

'Yeah, I liked that too. So what are you now then?' he says. 'Six was over two and half years ago, when you joined the Forum.'

'Still six,' she says. 'At least, I was until yesterday.'

'That wasn't – ' Warden begins.

'It doesn't really matter now,' Mallory interrupts. 'The Forum is gone. Whatever happens here, I can't be Echo any more.' The statement goes thick in her mouth.

'Hey,' Warden says, 'hey, it's just a name. The important part, the part that makes Echo matter at all, is you. Like I said before.'

'So it won't feel strange not being Warden?'

'I guess it will, but I'm still me, right? I'm still the person who was behind that laptop, whatever anyone calls me.'

Mallory looks away again. It suddenly feels too much.

'Yes,' she manages.

They're quiet a while, then, 'Why did you start?' he asks.

'What?'

'Hacking,' Warden says. 'I told you before, I did it because I liked online gaming, liked puzzles, liked figuring things out, and just sort of slipped into it. You've never told me how you started. It was always in the *ask and I'll stop talking to you for twenty minutes* questions category.'

'…I did it to find my mom,' she says, telling it to the bobbled ceiling tiles, to the Warden behind the screen. Telling it, though she's never told anyone before. 'I was eleven when my parents split. My dad got custody, but we'd see my mom once a week at first. Jed and I, we'd go over to my nana Ruthie's place across town on Sundays, and she'd be there and we'd spend the afternoon. Then she started missing a few and it became every two weeks, then once a month. Then, when I was twelve, she just stopped coming.' Mallory's nails dig in to the bare skin of her hands. 'I wanted to know why,' she says, speaking faster, 'but Roger wouldn't tell me. I asked him where she'd gone but he wouldn't tell me that either, said we should just leave it, there was nothing we could do. She wouldn't answer my calls or emails, and Ruthie said she didn't know anything, so I stopped taking Jed to see her because that was bullshit.

'I knew the name of my mom's lawyer. I'd heard her talking to him on the phone once, and I knew they'd have to keep copies of everything – things she'd said, where she was now. I didn't know how to hack when I started, so I looked things up, took my time and I worked it out.' She stops.

'Where had she gone?' Warden asks – because he's Warden and he doesn't leave asking things like that.

'I don't know,' Mallory says. 'I found the divorce documents first, and I found out she hadn't wanted custody at all.' There's an ache in her chest as she says it, an ache though she's known it so long now. 'She'd requested we go to Roger, even though she knew he wasn't right any more, knew he couldn't…' She swallows again. 'And he hadn't contested it. And when I knew that, I stopped looking, because that was all the answer that mattered. She didn't want us. We were better off without her,' she mutters. 'Jed was seven last time we saw her. He was only seven and she left him. So, she wasn't a good person. Not leaving him like that. It doesn't matter now,' she repeats. She pauses. 'I didn't find her, but in the looking I found something else that fit me, something I was good at, that I could do, that I could control. That's what I remember that day for, not what she did.'

Warden tells her he's sorry, like people say they're sorry about those kinds of bad things that happen. He sounds like he really means it, though. She shifts awkwardly, taking a deep breath… and then she finds their hands are touching, pinky to pinky, the small gap between them bridged, though she doesn't really know who did it. And she feels her heart rate lift, and feels her hand tingling, feels the skin all the way up her arm goose pimple… But she doesn't move it away, and neither does he, and they lie like that for a long time.

For too long.

To start with, Mallory feels almost safe like that, almost as if they're hidden away together in darkness. But then the minutes continue to tick by; they tick by and no one comes. They hear no sound of doors knocked in or shouted warnings or boots upstairs. And so her adrenaline starts to rise and she keeps wondering, keeps wondering what time it is… She tries not to think about it, tries not to second guess or overanalyze because there's nothing she can do now anyway, but her mind is not exactly something it's easy to shut down.

They aren't going to get here in time. She starts to think it, despite the trying not to. She starts to feel panic rising. It must be almost time. The FBI would have started receiving the ping about an hour ago. They should have been able to trace it. All they had to do was look, but...

Stupid, she thinks. *Stupid idiots!*

Now, they only have minutes. It can't be more than that, if it hasn't passed five thirty already... And she shouldn't have messed with the code... She should have just finished the virus like she was supposed to, not tried to come up with some crazy plan to fix everything, thinking she was smarter, thinking she was better, that she could control it and couldn't be beaten and now...

And now...

No, no, no...

What will The Asker do when he realizes?

What will he do?

'Echo?' Warden says, his voice cutting into her panic. 'It's probably nearly time, isn't it?' The words send a fresh chill through her body. His voice is gentle, like he's trying to keep control himself too, but she can hear the fear there now, whatever he said before. 'Echo,' he repeats. Then, 'Is it all right if I hold your hand?' The question hangs in the air, his voice shaking a little. 'I'm sorry,' he continues, just like Warden always continues through things, 'I'm really sorry. I know you don't like the touch thing, it's just that, well, I'm kind of scared shitless over here.' She turns her head and looks across at him, and he's looking back at her, and their hands seem to press closer together, even as he keeps speaking, and Mallory feels it, she *feels* it. And it's scary, but it's different because it's *him*, and she knows him, really knows him, and... 'I've been trying to be brave,' he tells her, 'you know, like you're supposed to try and be in these kind of situations in movies and things, but, truth be told, I'm a few seconds away from full on crying and I'd just rather not really.'

And she nods, even as her body tenses – she nods because she *wants* to, though it scares her. She nods because she remembers how it felt before to be closer to him, and even though part of her is screaming to run away from that, part of her isn't, and that part of her is more afraid of someone coming through that door at the top of the stairs and taking him away or hurting him and she just wants to hold on to him and protect him...

Because it's *Warden*…

And they both lift their hands at the same time and they knock together clumsily. But then their fingers find each other and they interlock and they take hold, and there is no glove between them, only skin against skin.

And it sends shivers of fire shooting right up Mallory's arm.

And she can feel her hairs standing on end, every fiber in her body suddenly focused towards her hand and the fire radiating out from it…

And she wants to let go, to get up and rush to the other side of the room…

And she also wants to grip on tighter…

'Thank you,' Warden whispers, and the relief in his voice is so powerful, so strong, that it snaps something inside of her and suddenly it isn't enough…

She does grip tighter.

And he responds.

And it feels urgent in a different way than it had been before…

And she holds his hand so tightly it must be hurting, but it's still not enough…

It's still not…

'Okay,' she hears Warden say, almost like he can tell, like he's feeling it too. 'Okay,' he says, and then she feels him turn, feels his body move on the bed, closer to her, closer…

And she feels his free hand around her waist – gently, ever so gently – pulling her closer. And her skin feels as if it's alive and buzzing, but she doesn't pull away. She lets him hold her, and she holds him back. She leans against him, wrapping her free arm around him, her other still holding tight to his hand.

And it doesn't feel like it did before. It doesn't feel safe. It feels overwhelming and sparking, and it blanks out even the new sounds of shouting from upstairs.

And she clings on to him…

And it's still not enough…

And she feels it…

And he feels it…

And their faces are so close already, and they both lean forwards, hidden in the dim light, safe in the darkness, anonymous in the darkness…

And, for the briefest moment, before Mallory even thinks it, their lips meet…

And then she's kissing him, though she's never kissed anyone before…

And it's soft and warm and terrifying and electric and…

'Warden,' she whispers against him.

Then the door to the basement bursts open.

Timing

Mallory jerks away as light spills down from above.

'What did you do?' shouts The Asker, silhouetted in the doorway. 'What the hell did you do?!'

Too late, Mallory thinks. She timed it wrong.

Everything moves too quickly from there. They come down the stairs then, all of them. She stands, putting herself between them and Warden, but he's trying to get up to do the same, and it doesn't matter anyway because arms grab hold of her – The Asker's, Weevil's – and drag her towards the staircase. Mallory yells, gasping at the touch, so different and harsh and horrible.

'Quiet,' The Asker snaps. 'Grab the boy,' he orders the others. Mallory hears Warden cry out in pain and tries to turn, but Weevil hits her and, this time, The Asker says nothing. They half drag, half carry her up the stairs, hands creeping and firm, and she's so dizzy with it by the time they reach the kitchen, she thinks she might actually pass out.

'Let go of me,' she gasps. It comes out whiny and panicked, not like her voice. She kicks out, fingers clawing against Weevil. 'Let go!'

He yells as she frees a hand and it catches him in the side.

'Hold it!' The Asker shouts. He has the gun out; one hand still holding her, the other holding it to her head. He looks blurry. Mallory realizes she's crying.

'Please, let go,' she begs him, even though she shouldn't be begging, not after what he's done. She should be shouting and fighting, and it's not even the gun that's really stopping her, it's, 'Please, let go. Just let go.' She cries it over and over, unable to think beyond their hands gripping her.

And how ridiculous is that?

Warden is being dragged after her and she should be doing something about that – she should be fucking well doing something about that – but all she does is whimper '*Please*' over and over.

The Asker finally releases her. He tells Weevil to do the same. Mallory stumbles away from them, into the corner of the room, her skin feeling as if it's writhing and rippling around her.

'Told you she'd be crazy,' says Scarlet, she and Tower supporting Warden into the room, Sneak just behind them. 'Just like Daedalus. Might be a genius, but you can't cope with all that in your little head, can you, sugar?' She sits Warden down in a kitchen chair, too hard, and his face crinkles up.

'You bitch,' Mallory spits.

'Enough!' shouts The Asker. The room goes silent and Mallory's eyes flick back to him. His whole bearing is rigid. 'Tower,' he says, 'go and watch out front again. Weevil, the back. Sneak, start wiping down everything we've used; door knobs, chairs, the bathroom – '

'But – ' begins Weevil.

'Just shut up and do it.' The Asker takes a deep breath, clearly trying to calm himself. 'She's messed with the code and that code has gone out worldwide, so we're not taking any chances till we know exactly what she did. You *watch* that street and you clear this house.' They go, the kitchen door swinging closed behind Sneak. The Asker runs a nervous hand through his hair, pacing the room. 'Scarlet, clean up in here,' he says. 'We can't stay.' She nods, and starts rubbing down surfaces with the herb-covered dishcloth.

The Asker looks back at Mallory. He knows what she did, he *knows*. She glances at the clock. Five forty-two.

Of course he knows.

'We have a problem,' he tells her, voice clipped. 'Something has gone wrong with the virus. It should have grown exponentially, but it didn't. It did at first, but then, a few minutes ago, it started deleting itself. Can you explain that, Echo?' Mallory stares at him, heart pounding. She shakes her head. 'Don't lie to me!'

'Daedalus must have – '

'No,' he snaps, 'it wasn't Daedalus. It was *you*. What did you do?

Manage to leave some of his kill switch inside?'

'No – '

'Tell me!'

Her eyes are uncontrollably drawn to the gun still in his hand. The Asker follows her gaze, then he lifts it and he points it at Warden, who looks so pale in the light, she's surprised he hasn't collapsed. Blood is soaking through the bandage round his leg.

'No,' Mallory stammers. 'No!' She steps towards The Asker. His arm swings, pointing the gun at her instead.

'Can you fix it?' he demands.

She can't…

Her mind races, desperately scrambling for some kind of solution. Of course she can't… They don't even have the source code any more. Everything on the laptop disappeared when it was sent out. She has nothing to fix. He must know…

And his gun's pointed at her…

And…

I'm going to die, she realizes, the thought piercing through her. Her limbs feel weak. No one got her message. She got it wrong. She failed. *And now I'm going to die, and Warden's going to die, and oh shit, oh shit…* Jed's face flashes up in her mind, and then Roger's, and… *No, no, no…*

'Echo,' The Asker repeats. He moves the gun back to Warden, walks right up to him and presses it onto his forehead so the metal imprints against the skin, 'Can you fix it?' he asks. Warden's jaw is clenched, his pale, freckled face sweaty, but he's trying to hold himself up straight. There are tears coming down his cheeks, but he looks The Asker right in the eye.

Lie, Mallory tells herself. *Just lie. Make something up. Buy some more time…*

Time.

That's all they need.

Just more time…

'I…' she stammers. The Asker flicks the safety off the gun. 'Maybe I could recreate – '

There's a loud thump from living room.

'What was that?' says Scarlet. No other sounds follow. The Asker and Scarlet glance across at each other. He edges towards the door.

'Tower?' he hisses through the wood. 'Sneak? *Tower?*' There's no answer. 'Who's there? Who is it? We have a gun!' Still no answer. Mallory feels the briefest spark of hope. Maybe, just maybe...

Oh please, please, please...

Scarlet takes the BB gun out of her back pocket.

'Weevil,' The Asker calls, yelling towards the back door now. 'Weevil!'

'Yeah, what?' Weevil says, hurrying out of the utility room a few seconds later.

'No answer from the others,' Scarlet tells him. She looks at Mallory. 'What did you do, you little shit? You send a message?'

The Asker lifts the gun towards her.

'Echo?' he says, and the kitchen door bursts open. It slams into him, knocking him off his feet. His head smacks right into table, the gun clattering to the floor as another man barrels into the room. Scarlet screams and dives towards The Asker, while the new man charges straight at Weevil, punching him in the face, then dropping on top of him to hit him again. Warden tries to push himself up to help, almost toppling his chair backwards in the process. Mallory grabs hold and drags him back towards the corner of the room, away from the fighting, but she can't take her eyes off the new man... She can't...

She can't, because it's *Roger*.

He's pounding in Weevil's face, in his Slayer T-shirt and military-ironed jeans.

'Roger?' she stammers. He looks up. He sees her.

'Run!' he shouts. 'Mallory, run!'

'But – '

'You fucking bastard!'

The world seems to slow. Mallory looks up, away from her dad, who is somehow *there*, and her eyes fall on Scarlet. She's holding The Asker's gun. He's still on the floor, apparently knocked out cold, but Scarlet has the damn gun and she's pointing it at Roger...

At Mallory's dad.

Mallory dives towards her. They collide and fall. The wind sucks from her lungs as they smash into the tiles. Scarlet's screaming curses but Mallory's on top of her. She swings her fist and she connects with something important because the curses get louder, but the only thing she can think is, *Where's the gun, where's the gun, where's the –*

Scarlet's looking up at her...

And Mallory feels it then, beneath her, beneath her stomach...

Scarlet fell, but she never dropped it.

No, she thinks simply.

Someone shouts her name...

Then there is other shouting...

The sounds of footsteps...

It's so noisy, but all Mallory hears, all she sees, is Scarlet – and all she feels is the metal of the gun beneath her. She reaches for it, but...

'You don't know what you've done,' Scarlet spits. '*Stupid* little girl.'

And she fires.

Mallory's body lifts off the ground a little, but she hears, more than feels the shot go off. Then arms grab hold of her and pull her backwards and her head is suddenly spinning...

She feels okay, though. A little cold, maybe.

It must have missed me, she thinks, relief fluttering. There are other people in the room now, people in navy jackets and helmets, with bigger guns than the one Scarlet was holding. *Feds,* Mallory realizes. They finally traced the virus. *Took them long enough.* She sighs. *Or maybe they got here just in time? Because Scarlet must have missed and...*

And then she sees Roger.

He's on his knees, held back behind FBI agents who are crowding round her now. They look like they're trying to talk to her but Mallory can't hear the words. Maybe it's the noise from the gun, still ringing in her ears, but...

But...

Roger is *crying*.

His face is bright red and there are tears streaming down it. He's looking down at her through the gaps in the navy holding him back, and he's rocking back and forth...

But...

Hands are pushing down against her stomach. Mallory suddenly feels very sick, like she's going to actually be sick. Her heart starts juddering and stuttering. It's not a nice feeling. Her mouth fills with saliva, only it tastes of metal. And there's too much of it. It's filling up too quickly. She tries to spit it out, tries to breathe, but she almost chokes on the liquid. She starts retching. Roger is still rocking back and forth, tears still streaming.

'Echo!'

Sound returns in a single blast.

Warden.

She looks for him, but she can't see where he is. Her eyes are all fuzzy, but she hears him again. He's telling her to hold on, to 'Just bloody hold on!'

Hold on to what?

He's talking a mile a minute, like Warden does, and she's trying to follow but suddenly there are too many sounds, too many noises... Everything becomes loud and piercing and confusing... And...

Pain rips through her abdomen.

Mallory screams, but she gags on the sound. Someone puts a breathing mask on her face. It feels like people are touching her everywhere. She feels herself lifted up...

And then she sees it...

A bullet hole in the ceiling, surrounded by a shimmer of red...

Oh, she thinks dumbly. *Oh no.*

'Echo!' Warden screams again, but the sounds are fading away, almost as quickly as they came.

Just like her vision...

Just like everything, but the hurting inside...

It hurts so bad...

I'm going to die, she thinks, only this time she really knows it, and she doesn't want to, she doesn't want...

And her eyes are going dark...

And she's so damn scared...

She's never felt so scared...

And then…
Then…
Nothing.

Echoes

Mallory is five years old.

She's sitting on a swing in a play park at Quantico that's just down the road from the house they lived in when Roger was stationed at the Marine Corps Base there. Her dad is crouched in front of her. His hair is brown and curly, no sign of grey. Baby Jed is asleep in a stroller beside him.

Roger is smiling at her.

'How are you doing, honey?' someone else asks, and for some reason that voice makes Mallory feel all caught up inside. She looks to the right, looks for the source. The sun flares in her eyes, but then she sees her, sees her mom sitting on the swing next to hers, in that white dress she used to wear a lot, with the little red flowers on it, all linked together by green stems. She looks so beautiful sitting there, all tanned skin and wide smile, long hair streaming out down her back. It's not that fake blonde yet, but black, just like her daughter's. She has the same big blue eyes, too. People are always saying how much they look like each other and Mallory likes it when they do because she likes feeling the same as Jeanie, feeling connected like that. Her mom's expression is warm, looking down at her. And there is concern there…

Mallory's eyes fall on her own small hand gripping hold of the chain. It's the middle of June and the sun is beating down on them, but both of her hands are wearing gloves. She used to make them go red raw washing them after using the swings. Usually she's all right with inanimate objects, but something about knowing the chains had been gripped so tightly by so many others… it had made her skin feel like it was creeping with bugs. Her dad had come back with the gloves that afternoon, after he got off duty. He'd driven out to a camping store in

Jacksonville to get them after he had the idea – no one else sells kids' gloves in summer.

'I'm okay,' Mallory answers her mom, and she means it. She feels calmer than she usually does in the play park. She even starts to swing a little. Jeanie laughs and the sound makes Mallory go warm inside, and Roger's grinning at her mom, stepping back to give Mallory room. And he looks happy. He looks so very happy.

And Mallory starts to smile too.

She leans back on the swing, kicking her legs out and making herself go higher, high enough that her stomach drops on the way down. She likes the feeling. She kicks back again. She starts to laugh along with her mom. She wants to go higher. She pulls back harder…

A pain tears through her middle.

Mallory gasps and her eyes black out.

No…

This doesn't belong here, not here, in this memory. Her hands let go of the chains and she starts to fall. She doesn't like the feeling this time, but she keeps falling…

And someone is shouting her name and telling her she needs to hold on, but there's nothing to hold on to…

And she just falls and falls and…

'Mallory, we have to go. *Mallory.*'

She opens her eyes. She's seated on her parents' bed back at home in Watertown. Jeanie is crouched in front of her, but she's heavily made up now, thick foundation covering any trace of skin, and her hair is the brittle blonde she'd started dyeing it the year before she left. She still looks beautiful, though, wearing the purple and white dress that she liked because it hugged tight to her figure. Mallory remembers going with her to buy it for her friend Harriet's wedding. They'd spent a whole morning looking round all the shops in town before driving out to Hartford when Jeanie had found nothing she liked. Mallory's dress is purple too. Jeanie had said she looked pretty in it, but there's the smallest spot of red blossoming out from the middle now, dyeing the fabric…

'We have to go, honey,' says Jeanie. 'We're going to be late.'

'It hurts,' Mallory tells her. The spot on her stomach is growing bigger. She puts her gloved hand against it to try and stop it.

'Oh, honey,' her mom says gently, taking a hold of her hand and drawing it towards her though Mallory tenses up. The bare fingertips are painted red. 'You can't keep acting like this,' she continues, not seeming to see it. 'People will think it's strange. You're a big girl now.'

'Mom, it hurts – '

'You can't wear these ugly things to a wedding,' she says, her voice hardening. She starts to pull the glove off and a fear grips Mallory that is greater than the pain and her worry about the growing patch of red.

'Please,' she begins, even as the first glove disappears, leaving her skin bare and exposed.

'Mallory Jeanette – '

'*Please*, Mom.'

The second glove comes off. Mallory starts to shake. She can feel tears pricking her eyes, but she tries to hold it back because Jeanie doesn't like it when she cries, especially not about this kind of thing. The door opens and Roger comes in. His hair is greying now and there are rings under his eyes that weren't there before. He looks at Mallory, then at Jeanie, holding her gloves. He says something and Jeanie starts shouting. Mallory clenches her eyes shut, clenches her hands, clenches up her whole body, even though it hurts.

'I'm sorry,' she sobs. 'I'm sorry.'

She wants to go back. She wants to go back to the play park and to the Jeanie who laughs and has hair that's black like hers. She wants to go back to when her dad's face wasn't all lined and wrinkled and afraid. She wants to go back and stay five years old...

Back before Roger went on that fourth tour, and then got sent home early, given a medal for something he wouldn't talk about, and then discharged...

Back before she realized him coming home early wasn't a good thing and meant something had gone bad – even though he'd got that medal – and that, really, he would never quite come back at all, not the same anyway, hardly speaking a single word those first few months...

Back before he wouldn't tell her what had happened, wouldn't tell her why he was different, though she asked and he'd never lied to her or hid things from her before…

Back before her mom started fighting with him…

Back before Jeanie started spending too much time down at the police station, saying she had patrol, when she didn't…

Back before that guy Lucas, a cop like she was, had started coming round more than he should, staying over when Roger was on shift, staying when he shouldn't have… when he *shouldn't*…

Back before Roger realized what Jeanie was doing and pretended he didn't, and Mallory didn't know what to do… She didn't know what to do…

Back before her mom left…

Before her dad let her go.

She wants to stay five years old. Back when they were just Mom and Dad to her, and not two grown-ups who messed things up. Back when it never came into her head that there might be someone who meant more to Jeanie than the three of them. She wants to stay there. She wants to stay there not knowing it, wants to stay there not wondering if maybe it was because of *her*, too, that Jeanie left, because of her that Jed doesn't have a real mom any more – because she wasn't quite like other children, because she wasn't really what Jeanie had wanted in a little girl of her own… Because she needed the gloves and never quite said the right things as she got older, though she tried to, she really tried… But she didn't know what Jeanie wanted from her. Not really…

Not really…

And…

It's gone…

It's gone…

It's gone.

* * *

Mallory wakes up gradually, drifting in and out of consciousness for a long time before she finally comes to. When she does, she feels groggy and nauseous, and her body aches with a bruised weariness that tells her not to move. It's soft beneath her and there are covers above. She's in a bed, but it's not her own. She knows the feel of that. She blinks her eyes open, the lids fluttering cautiously at first, and sees a plain white ceiling. There's a breathing mask on her face, the rubber pressing down against her skin. Too far to reach, though.

Where...?

Mallory turns her head slowly to the left – and it feels so sluggish – and she sees a bank of medical instruments; monitors, a drip bag... She's in a hospital. It looks like it's night time – the lights in her room are off, but she can just see from the glow of the fluorescents in the corridor beyond.

How...?

Questions trickle into her mind, but she can't quite make sense of them. Her vision swims and she closes her eyes again. So very tired...

Somewhere in the dimness, she remembers getting shot. She remembers being afraid, remembers thinking she was going to die. She remembers it hurting. It doesn't hurt now, though, and she's too sleepy to really feel afraid. She must be doped up on pain meds. She moves her left hand ever so slightly upwards from the mattress, feeling the tug of tubes in her skin and a plastic monitor clip on her index finger. She tries to shut those sensations out, disturbing though they are, and lifts higher... She finds bandages, lots of padding.

She remembers the gun beneath her...

The feeling of being lifted up...

To her right, someone snores.

Mallory turns her head again, having to think carefully about the movement, the mask shifting against her face. Roger is asleep in a chair by her bed.

Roger...

She sees him bursting through that door, then, knocking down The Asker, stopping Weevil...

He looks exhausted too, these big great bags under his shuttered eyes, head lolled against his shoulder. There's a nasty bruise on his right cheek, black and yellow, though, not the angry red of something new.

How long...?

He looks so different to the man who had smiled in her dream, slumped in that chair, forehead all wrinkled with worry lines that the memory didn't have.

But he still came for me.

He came.

'Dad,' Mallory says, using that name for the first time in a long time. Her voice is hoarse and croaky, muffled by the mask, but he stirs a little at the sound. 'Dad.'

'Wha – ' He wakes with a startled snort. Then he sees her looking at him and his face changes, furrowing with concern. 'Mallory?' he says, feverishly blinking away the sleep. 'Mallory, you're awake.'

'Dad,' she repeats, just saying the word – and she can see how it hits him then, see the breath he takes, the glass sheen that starts to form right away in his eyes. 'You okay?' she manages.

'Yeah, kid,' he answers, voice barely more than a whisper, 'I'm okay.'

And he came for her.

He came for *her*.

'Warden?' she asks. He hesitates.

'You mean Gilbert?' She nods. 'He's all right too.' Mallory feels a sharp relief, even in her drowsy state. 'Needed surgery,' he goes on, 'but it all went fine. He's fine.'

He's fine… Both fine… And Roger came…

She closes her eyes a moment.

'Sorry,' she murmurs, 'I'm so tired.'

'Hey,' he says, 'hey, you don't worry about that. You were… you were in the O.R. a long time and the doctor said you'll be tired a long while 'cause of the anesthetic, and they got you on all these medications and things. You hurting now?' he asks. 'I can call someone if you – '

'No,' she mumbles. 'No.' There are so many things she needs to ask, but it all feels too complicated. 'You found me,' she manages. She tries to think. The FBI must have finally traced the virus, but Roger…

'Tracker on Jed's phone,' he says. 'He turned it on soon as we left the house. Went dead around ten thirty. I tried calling you, but it went straight to voicemail. After the way you'd left… Took us an hour or so to get back to Watertown from the motel, and then the exhaust finally dropped and I had to tie it on with a coat hanger… I left Jed at Ruthie's.' He fumbles a little over that. Mallory hasn't let them go to Ruthie's in years, but it doesn't really seem to matter so much just now – all she thinks is how Ruthie's good at cooking, so Jed'll be fine there for the moment. 'Then I went to go see you were okay,' Roger goes on. 'I waited outside that house for a bit. I should have gone in sooner, but I didn't know what was going on. Then I saw that guy out front with all the tattoos, casing the street. And I just started moving. It sort of happened before I could think it, and he was out cold on the ground and the front door was open. I guess you never forget the training.' He looks up at her then, and his eyes are really glistening.

'When I saw you dive in front of me…' he says, voice thick. 'Mal, you saved my life, and then that gun went off and I just thought, it's the wrong way round. I've seen people shot before, but that… my wonderful, brave little girl – '

He cuts off, and, 'Dad,' Mallory says, her own eyes prickling, and she blinks and blinks, and she's overwhelmed, and she can't really think straight, and…

I almost died.

And she remembers, again, what that felt like, not just the pain, but the fear that came with it, fear like nothing she'd felt before…

And she's thinking that her dad could have died too, and Warden…

And it's all just too much…

And…

'You're going to be okay now,' Roger says, and it's fierce and determined and strong. 'I'm gonna try harder. I'm going to *do* better and from now on, Mal, it's going to be okay. You're going to be okay,' he repeats and his voice is cracking all over but he keeps talking. 'You don't have to be frightened any more. I won't let anyone hurt you, Mal. I won't ever again.'

And through her eyes that are blurring up, suddenly she sees it, sees the man before her as the man who held her hand every time he said goodbye before a tour, sees the man who was smiling at her on that swing in the park at Quantico, the same person who used to give her the cherry from his sundaes at *Franco's* and who'd read her bedtime stories and then stay up till she went to sleep when she worried there was something hiding in her closet, even though they'd both checked it.

And she remembers how he could make her feel like the safest kid in the world...

And she looks at her dad, and she finds she feels very, very young...

And...

'Dad,' she says again, her own voice cracking. 'Would you hold my hand?' she asks – hold it just like he used to before a tour, when he'd promise her he'd try, and that he'd be a good man. And maybe what he's saying is just words, and maybe it won't all work out, but it *is* different this time because they aren't just words, because he's there, because he got out that car, and went in that house and...

He pulls his chair over, legs screeching against the floor as he moves it too fast. Mallory lifts her hand from under the covers, the drip in her arm pulling, but she keeps reaching. And Roger's reaches... then he hesitates.

'Your gloves,' he says, looking round. 'I brought a spare – '

'No,' she tells him, making a choice in that moment, and his face breaks just a second, and then very slowly, so very gently, he takes her hand, enclosing it in both of his. The skin chafes and Mallory's chest tightens, but she doesn't ask for the gloves, and she doesn't let go.

Because he came for her.

And she misses him.

She misses him so very much.

'I'm sorry, Mal,' he tells her, tears rolling down his cheeks unchecked now. 'I'm so sorry.'

And her own eyes are wet and she's full on crying too, but it's not the horrible kind of crying, the kind that hurts... It feels like...

It feels like *relief*.

And, for once, she doesn't tell herself to stop.

And she doesn't want to stop.

And she doesn't need to.

Not just then.

Not when she's suddenly feeling so safe.

A Real Goodbye

Mallory's been in hospital almost a week when Warden comes to say goodbye. He's been staying in a ward on the floor above her. Like Sneak had suspected, the bullet had fractured his femur and he'd needed surgery, a titanium rod and four screws to fix it. The doctors had told him last night that he was well enough to fly back to California, though, so they're discharging him. She tells herself that's a good thing. It means he's getting better and that's a good thing, but…

I don't want him to go.

They haven't really had a proper talk since they've been there. He's come down to see her every day that they'd let him, but Mallory was pretty out of it for the first few, and then between her family and his – and all the doctors and nurses and police and FBI agents – they've hardly had any time alone. They haven't spoken about what happened between them in the basement and they haven't talked about what happens now. Mallory's thought about it, though. She's thought about it a lot. Every time she sees him, she remembers what it felt like to be that close to him and it sets her pulse racing, and it's both scary and not scary at the same time and, in a way, she's glad he hasn't said anything about it – though she wonders *what* he'd say – because she's not sure what she'd say in return. She's never really thought about… about being with anyone like that before. It always felt impossible. Whenever guys looked at her that way, it unnerved her and she was way too anxious to ever let anyone get to know her well enough to even contemplate it.

But she does know Warden.

Over the past two and half years she has got to know him without having to worry about anything like that and she never realized until she met him just how much he had worked his way in, how much he really meant to her. As she looks up at him now, dressed neatly like himself again – complete with sweater vest and side parting, and making a clunking racket at the door because he still hasn't mastered opening them while on crutches – she wonders if some feelings could maybe be stronger than her fear, if some emotions could drown out even the compulsions that tie her up inside and have just made everything so hard for so long.

Maybe, she thinks, for the first time, *maybe one day they could.* She's tired of things being hard. She's so damn tired of it.

Warden finally makes it through the door, a nurse rushing to his aid before he can further hurt either himself or the glass.

'Stupid things,' he mutters, levering himself inside. 'How are you supposed to do anything if you have to use both hands on these bloody sticks? It's a stupid system and...' His eyes meet Mallory's then, and he bobs his head – the crutch-user equivalent of a shrug. The frown softens. 'Hi,' he says, smiling sheepishly.

'Hi,' she replies. She feels it again, her pulse spiking even as he looks at her – and she tells herself to stop being ridiculous and at the same time is acutely grateful they've finally disconnected that fricking heart rate monitor. The room is empty apart from them. 'My dad's gone for lunch,' she says.

'Yeah, I know – one o'clock every day.'

He timed it, she realizes, and Warden's cheeks flush red and he suddenly becomes very interested in his feet.

'I mean,' he says, 'I just knew he wouldn't be here right now and because I wanted to say goodbye. I...' His hands grip tighter on the crutch handles – she can see it where the knuckles go white. His shoulders sag in a kind of surrender. 'I miss talking to you,' he says simply.

She nods, but no words of her own quite make it out.

For crying out loud...

He hobbles over and sits down so awkwardly in the chair by her bed that one crutch is sent clattering loudly to the floor.

'Oh bloody hell,' he snaps – and Mallory finds herself smiling. He notices. 'Glad to know my trials amuse you,' he says, but he grins back at her. He leaves the crutch on the floor, leans forward a little and,

'Mallory – ' he begins.

His phone buzzes and he jumps.

'Crap.' He looks at the screen. 'My mom,' he says. 'They've been packing my stuff up from the ward and she says they're ready to go.' He puts the phone away. 'Thought I'd have longer.'

'What time's your flight?' Mallory asks.

'Boarding four twenty, but I've got to go to the Javits Building before. There're a few last things, you know...' He trails off and Mallory nods.

The Reckoning had deleted itself after seventy-four minutes, just like she had set it to, but it still did a lot of damage and the Feds have been everywhere the past few days, asking questions, checking things over and over. Even Roger had been interrogated while she was still in surgery. Mallory understood that it made sense; the agents had entered Angeline Garcia's house to find two shot teenagers and the computer that was the source of the virus, and at first it hadn't been clear who was responsible for what... but it was disconcerting, being in the middle of it all – especially on a hospital bed, having been shot, unable to really move in the middle of it all. Mallory knew Warden had been questioned too. Like with everything else, though, this is the first time they've really been able to talk openly about it with each other.

'Did anyone tell you,' he says softly, 'they've all been charged now?'

Mallory looks down at the covers. The remaining Finders Reapers were arrested in the raid. Her dad had updated her on the investigation yesterday evening.

'Sneak, Weevil and Tower with kidnapping and cyberterrorism,' she replies, trying to keep her voice even. 'On top of that, Scarlet's been charged with attempted murder...'

My *attempted murder...*

'The Asker with accessory to that,' she goes on, hands gripping the fabric, 'and his own count of aggravated assault with a deadly weapon.' Except, he's not called The Asker by anyone else. He's Nathan, or Mr Garcia. Her thoughts start to run with the mess of it. And Scarlet's not Scarlet, she's Marsha-Jane –

'Echo,' Warden says.

You're okay. You're –

'Echo.' She looks back up at him. 'They'll be gone away for a long time. A *long* time.'

'Yeah,' she says, trying to loosen her fingers and only partially succeeding.

'It's going to be all right.'

'I know.' There's a silence then and, for once, Mallory isn't comfortable with it. She wants to talk. She doesn't want to think about the charges and what they mean, and the real names and how very real they make everything else feel.

'The FBI lady said I can pick up my laptop before I leave,' Warden says.

'That's good,' Mallory replies, seizing on it, though the new tack unnerves her for a whole different reason.

'Your dad can probably go get yours for you, too.'

She nods again. The 'FBI lady' is Special Agent Caldera. Shrewd and imposing, with a stare that's near impossible to hold, she's been heading up the investigation into the release of The Reckoning. Neither Mallory nor Warden have been charged with anything – it was clear their part in it was under duress – but their computers were taken with the others in the raid. Both had wiped themselves clean upon FBI techs trying to break into them, so the Feds have no actual evidence of any previous misdemeanors on their part either. Caldera's interviewed Mallory twice personally now, though. It was her cybercrime division that she had 'oh-so-helpfully' targeted the ping at and they'd received hundreds of thousands.

'I spoke to her again this morning,' Mallory says, still unsure how to feel about the encounter. She hadn't been very lucid during their first interview, but the doctors had taken her off the morphine yesterday and she was definitely more with it as a result. Apparently Caldera had found out. She seems to be very good at finding things out.

'Oh,' says Warden. 'What did she want?'

'Checking I said the same as you,' Mallory replies. 'At first.' She frowns. The agent had already known most of what had happened in the house. As far as Mallory could tell, Warden had pretty much told her the truth, and what Mallory had said had agreed with him. They'd both skirted around things like the bug in the nightclub – though Mallory suspected Caldera had put the pieces together on that – but the real issue had been explaining how they had met, how they had *all* met, initially. In Warden's account, the 'Forum of illegal hacks' had been relabeled as an 'online coding chat room' – that he unfortunately couldn't remember the address of. Caldera really didn't seem like a person you could bullshit and Mallory had stumbled over that too. She didn't think that The Asker or Scarlet would have given any details of the Forum away – they'd only make their own sentences worse – but she had expected the pressure to come then, had expected the agent to needle and push like she had with everything else, had had to tell herself firmly that there was no real evidence left of the group's existence or any illegal activity, trying to stop the panic that had started building in her chest…

Caldera hadn't pushed, though. She had done something completely unexpected.

'You don't remember either,' she had said carefully, red-painted lips pursing together. She had said it almost more like an instruction, than a question. Mallory had managed a negative, but the move had thrown her and she was still a little off from the meds. 'I'm going to be honest with you,' the woman had said then. 'You completed The Reckoning so I know just how smart you must be. And I can make a very good guess as to the kind of thing you might have been involved in that would have brought someone as smart as you to the attention of someone like Nathan Garcia in the first place.' Mallory's heart had almost stopped at that, but Caldera had continued, 'I also know the risks you and Mr Ward took in order to stop him. In this job, I'm all too aware of what the repercussions would have been if you hadn't.' She had paused, then, holding Mallory's gaze. 'You know, I deal with black-hats every day; people trying to steal, to tear things down, to cause chaos that my team and I have to fight tooth-and-nail to patch up. That kind of activity is everywhere and it's insidious and daily I have to make calls about what to go after and what to leave; calls about whether a person – or, let's be up front about this, a hacker – will do more harm than good if I leave them in play.' Mallory had been hardly breathing by this point. 'As it stands, I have no direct evidence of what you and Mr Ward were involved in before. Maybe I could find some if I really looked, but then you're so smart, maybe I couldn't. What I do have evidence of is that you understand consequences. You saw the consequences of something like The Reckoning and you nearly died to prevent them. To me, that understanding is the real difference between the kids who end up as white or black-hats. You're sixteen, right?' Mallory had nodded. 'Consider this is your wake up call.' Her mouth had twitched upwards. 'Be smart,' she had said.

'Bloody hell,' mutters Warden, when Mallory finishes telling him. It's kind of breathy and she can't quite tell if it's a good 'bloody hell' or a bad one. 'Then she just left?'

'Not quite,' Mallory says. 'First, she asked me if there was any chance I could remember Daedalus's algorithm well enough to recreate it.' Warden's eyes widen a little at that.

'Can you?' he asks. She hesitates.

'I told her no.' The truth is, though, that the more she's thought about it, the more she's not sure whether that's strictly true. She doesn't really forget things, and she had understood how it worked and, if she was given enough time, maybe... 'It doesn't matter either way,' she tells Warden. 'Even if I could... no.' It's not something she would ever go near again. It's possible other hackers might have picked up something about how it functioned before it deleted, but it was so complex she doesn't think they'd figure out the whole thing for at least a while. People know now that it's possible to do, though, and the FBI – and Agent Caldera – will have to deal with what happened however they choose to deal with it. She doesn't want to be a part of it. Warden nods, understanding.

'She gave me her card,' Mallory adds, 'before she went.' She points to the table by her bed where it still lies; white and plain, just a name and a number and an email address. 'She said it was for if I remembered anything, and also' – she bites her lip – 'she said, 'so you don't have to send a virus the next time you notice something we might want to know about.''

Warden smiles at that, raising an eyebrow.

'I think you made a friend.'

'I don't understand,' Mallory says. 'I mean it. Why do you think she did that?'

Warden shrugs, properly this time.

'Maybe she meant what she said,' he replies, 'she didn't think what happened was our fault and she was grateful for what you did.'

'I guess.'

'Or maybe she wants to recruit you,' Warden laughs. Then he stops. 'Actually, check that, maybe she *does*.'

'Don't be an ass.'

'No, I'm serious. I mean, you'd be a flipping nightmare for all the black-hats out there.'

Mallory feels an unexpected buzz at the suggestion. What would it be like from the other side?

'I'm still in high school,' she says, not sure what to make of it.

'Yeah, so imagine what you'll be like when you've fully grown into your powers,' Warden replies. The smile comes back. Mallory rolls her eyes. She sags back against the sheets. She can wonder about it another time.

All of it, another time.

A week, and everything still exhausts her. The doctors have said it's normal, keep telling her she's lucky to be alive – though how getting shot in the abdomen can really count as lucky she doesn't quite get yet – but it's still frustrating.

'Who knows,' she murmurs, 'maybe she even wants to recruit you.'

'Ooh, burn.' Warden grins. She finally smiles back at him, the edges of her mouth teasing upwards. And she thinks how often he smiles in real life, and how she didn't realize that before, and she thinks…

She thinks…

I'm going to miss you.

And she feels it, too, and her smile falters, though she doesn't say it out loud. Warden's face softens, like maybe he thought it at the same time… Maybe…

You don't know what he thinks at all, she tells herself.

'I've been thinking,' he says – maybe he'll tell her – 'I could set up a new chat box for us. When I get my laptop back, I could have it ready for when you get yours and make it secure, so… well, I know we won't have the Forum, but, so we could still talk like we did. You know, if you want to.' And he looks nervous as he says it, as if he thinks there's a chance she wouldn't want to, and, right then, she realizes she does know exactly what he thinks, what he wants. She does. And relief sparks through her, and…

'Yes,' Mallory tells him, 'I want to, Warden,' and his smile lights up all over again and she feels it, feels it inside.

Then, his face drops a little, lips quirking to the side.

'You probably shouldn't call me that any more,' he says quietly. 'Might hurt our 'I forgot' cover story if we use *those* names, even when we think no one's listening.' He's right, of course, and she knew it too, but said out loud it still snags at her. She nods.

'Gilbert,' she corrects, though it jars a bit.

'I'm still me,' he says, 'and you're still you, remember.' He pauses. 'Mallory, I – ' His phone goes again. 'I'm bloody coming!' he snaps at his pocket. He looks at her again, looks like he's going to say something, and then he doesn't. He shuts his mouth and reaches down for the fallen crutch instead, then levers himself up onto his feet. 'So, this is goodbye, I guess,' he says, 'for now.' He leans forward, just a little, like he wants to hug her and Mallory's heart skips and she tenses – though she doesn't mean to, and she hates herself for doing it – but he stops because he noticed.

Damn it, Mallory thinks at herself. *You fricking idiot!*

'I'm sorry,' she says, the words tumbling out.

'No,' he replies. 'It's okay. I shouldn't have.'

Mallory sends a stream of internal abuse at herself; Warden's eyes seem to be darting anywhere but at her. She doesn't want him to go on that note. She doesn't want him to. She moves her hand out towards him and he hesitates a second, but then he rests a crutch against the bed and takes it. His hand wobbles a little and Mallory's skin tingles at the touch, but she doesn't pull back because it's him, and though it's still hard, it's different with him. Their fingers brush together, moving across each other, then entwining. Mallory is grateful, for the second time, that they took her off the heart monitor. Warden smiles at her – and his phone buzzes a third time.

'I really have to go,' he says, though he looks like he doesn't want to and at the words, Mallory grips a little tighter. He pauses, then slowly – very slowly – he lifts her hand to his lips and kisses it, the softest touch. 'I'm going to miss you, Mallory Park.'

'We'll talk online,' she tells him, feeling all twisted up inside. 'We'll keep talking online, you promise?'

'I promise,' he says. 'I'll talk to you for as long as you'll listen.' He smiles and places her hand gently back down on the bed. Then he hobbles back to the doorway.

'Goodbye, Warden,' she says, calling him it, just that one last time. He stares back at her and his fists clench a little. He starts blinking too hard, too fast.

'Goodbye, Echo Six,' he says.

And with that, he leaves.

Begin Again

Mallory drives the Chevy carefully into the school parking lot. Roger had offered to take her – had wanted to, she could tell – but she'd told him no. She has to do this herself, has to start making things normal again.

'Are you okay?' Jed asks. He's been amazing these past few weeks, helping their dad take care of her, doing most of the cooking when Ruthie hasn't dropped something over, and doing it so very well, following the *100* right step-by-step.

'Yeah, I'm – ' she begins. Then she follows his eyes and realizes her hand is visibly shaking on the wheel. She stills it and turns off the ignition.

You're okay, she tells herself, trying to shut out the apprehension in her stomach. *You can do this.*

'I'll *be* okay,' she says. She looks out the front windshield. Students are flooding into the school, a few even looking her way already. 'Everything just seems so… fast.' It's not really the right word, but it's hard to explain. Her physical hurts are pretty much healed, but she feels fragile in a kind of way she never did before. She was in hospital for three weeks and didn't leave the house for another after she came home. She remembers clearly the first time she stepped outside, just to go to the store with Roger. Everything had felt like it was moving so quickly; people and bikes and cars, all seeming to whiz past.

'You don't have to do this yet,' Jed says. 'You can go back home. I'll get the bus – '

'No,' Mallory replies. 'No, I want to.' She's been home two weeks now, and, though she still feels tired, she's been the one pushing to go back to school. They've said she can take as long as she needs, but she doesn't want to take a long time. She wants to get it over with, to move forward so she can stop thinking about what happened. 'You go on ahead,' she tells Jed. 'I'll be there in a minute.'

'Mal – '

'Please, Jed.'

Four, three, four, two...

Four, three, four...

'No,' he says quietly. 'I'm gonna stay with you. We can sit here as long as you need, but you're not going in alone.' He glances at her once, then folds his hands defiantly over the backpack on his lap and settles in to wait. Mallory bites her lip, feeling something that might be pride, alongside her impatience. If he doesn't go in soon, he'll get a tardy and he knows that. She tries to steady her breathing. She just has to get out the damn car.

Why is this so difficult? she wonders. *Why does it have to be so diffi-cult?* She's been kidnapped and shot and almost died, so why does she go all rattled at the thought of just going back into school? Why does it feel like she wants to curl up in that front seat and hide – or drive and drive and drive, as far away as she can...

And why are there so many people?

Were there that many people before? She thinks of the corridors, of the jostling, of the touching... *Come on,* she tells herself, *just open the door. Just open the fricking door!*

But she stays where she is, and Jed sits unmoving beside her.

Mallory had talked to Warden – no, she stops herself, to *Gilbert* – about it all last night, admitting how nervous she was. His first day back had been two weeks ago and it hadn't exactly gone well. He'd caught a crutch in a broken drain and fallen into a hedge. She doesn't have that kind of peril to contend with at least, but the thing he'd said to expect was people staring. He'd said even kids who had ignored him before had come up and kept asking him to recount how he'd got shot. He'd told her it got better, though, that he gradually got used to things again and soon went back to being just another nerd people tried to wedgie. He'd given her this whole pep talk – some parts less helpful than others.

She looks down at her hands, bare and locked against the wheel like vices. Maybe she's just trying too many steps at once. She reaches into her pocket and pulls out a pair of gloves. She's been trying not to wear them since the hospital, like after what she's been through, she should be able to go without them now, like it's some show of strength or defiance or willpower. Some days she manages it, but it's been hard. She's still the same person inside, whatever she tries to choose, and it's not going to change overnight. Maybe it will change, eventually, just like she's been wondering if it can with Warden, but it will take time.

And she doesn't have to change it all at once.

If the gloves are what she needs to do this, they are what she needs. She slips them on to her hands and feels her body loosen a little as the familiar fabric slips back over her skin. Jed looks at her then, but he just nods, no judgement on his face.

One step at a time, Mallory tells herself. *Just one step. You can do this. Now open the door.*

She does.

She gets out of the Chevy. It's a cold morning, her breath fogging the air. She pulls Jeanie's leather jacket tighter around her. She likes it, so she's kept wearing it. She locks the car and starts across the parking lot towards the school, Jed sticking by her side, sticking past where he should branch off. People start to notice her. She can feel their eyes as she walks across tarmac and up towards the main entrance. Students stare, even teachers. They know she got shot, but due to the volatility that still exists online around Daedalus, her and Gilbert's identities have been classified regarding The Reckoning. People think she was mugged visiting New York with a friend. She can hear whispers about it as she passes. She holds her gloved hands in against her stomach and keeps walking, though. She keeps going.

You're okay, she tells herself. *You are damn well going to be okay.*

* * *

Math is Mallory's second to last class and she's already tired by the time she sits down middle right of the room. People have been asking her questions all day, crowding her more than usual, just like Gilbert had said they would. Even Morgan Hale had – and Mallory had told her straight up where she could stick it because she's not her friend and never has been. It hasn't been as bad as it could have been, though; Heidi seems to have appointed herself her unofficial bodyguard, using her all-too-intense stare to great effect against anyone who seems intent on lingering too long. She had cried when she'd seen Mallory on that first visit to the store.

Mrs Fraser-Hampton hands round a mock midterm paper at the start of the class, telling Mallory she's glad she's back as she passes her hers. It brings home how much of the semester she's already missed. She looks down at the sheets in front of her. The first question is on trigonometry. It's not an area of it they've done while she's been in class, but she can see the answer to it, see it as clearly as if it were written right there on the page with the question. She skims through the others. She could answer them all. Still, she stares back at that first for a long few minutes, even as pens scribble around her. She thinks about the decisions she made before and why she made them and, for the first time, she actually thinks about what she might *want*.

Not what someone tells her is good.

Not what someone tells her is what she should do.

Not what she does because she's afraid.

But what she wants.

And what she wants is to put the right answer. She wants to put the right answer for all of them. She doesn't want to end up dying in her bedroom like Daedalus, or an obsessive like The Asker. She wants more than that. Tiredness temporarily forgotten, she starts writing. No workings, just answers. When she's finished, she puts her hand up and Mrs Fraser-Hampton comes over.

'Is something the matter?' she asks quietly.

'I'm done,' Mallory replies. She holds Mrs Fraser-Hampton's gaze, and the teacher takes in the paper, only fifteen minutes after she gave it out. She marks it as the others work. Mallory studies her tabletop while Mrs Fraser-Hampton goes through, feels her glancing up at her within thirty seconds of starting. She doesn't comment on it during the class, though. While the others finish the test, she roots a textbook out of her cupboard, skims through the chapter listings and opens it to about halfway through. Then she gets up and lays it down in front of Mallory with a note saying '*Try this on for size.*' It's a college book on advanced calculus. Mallory starts working through the given chapter. And it's interesting. And she sort of finds she actually likes it.

When the bell goes for the end of class, Mrs Fraser-Hampton asks her to stay behind. Mallory braces herself as she stops by the middle front desk, preparing for the questions sure to follow.

Only they don't come.

'I just wanted to check how your first day back has been going,' is all Mrs Fraser-Hampton says. 'You doing all right?' Mallory nods. She bites her lip and the teacher shrugs. 'Great,' she says, 'that's it.' She sits down at her desk to start marking the other papers. 'You can go now,' she adds. Mallory nods again. She takes a step back towards the door. Then, she hesitates. 'Something else?' Mrs Fraser-Hampton says. Mallory swallows.

'I just... I wanted to ask you about applications to MIT,' she says. 'I googled you and it says you went there.' Massachusetts may be a long way from California, but Cambridge is only a couple of hours from Watertown – and Mallory's been thinking about it and maybe, just maybe...

For a moment, Mrs Fraser-Hampton looks taken aback, her mouth slightly ajar. Then she starts to smile.

* * *

By the time Mallory gets back to her room that afternoon, she is exhausted. She sits down in her grey office chair. There were good things in the day, she tells herself, but it also felt like a constant defense against assault, her mind being a pain in the ass mess for the most part. Her whole body is stiff from it. She looks down at her gloved hands. It feels like some kind of failure, but she can't bring herself to take them off again, not just yet.

One step at a time, she thinks. She wants to talk to Gilbert, but he won't be online yet. She almost texts, then she stops herself. *Damn it!*

Sometimes she wishes it could be quiet inside her head for just one fricking second, but it only ever felt calm doing one thing. She tries not to think about that. She wonders, instead, if the parcel she sent him has arrived. It should have got there this morning, although he wouldn't get it himself till he's back from school – which isn't going to be for at least two more hours. She'd found it on eBay two days ago and bid a crapload to ensure she won it; a Lampertz safe, the same model he'd been going to buy if he hadn't bought that plane ticket to New York. She thinks about what he might say when he sees it, imagines his face and his smile – expressions that she *knows* now – and she feels a little better.

Two hours, at least, though.

No point turning her laptop on and staring at an empty chat box. That would be the very definition of a pathetic waste of time. She taps her finger on the desk. Jed and Roger are out in the yard, practicing on the punch bag. She's not quite up to it yet, though she could go and watch them… She doesn't want to watch TV. She's watched so much in the past five weeks. Maybe she should start online gaming again, but she doesn't feel like doing that just now. She used to when she was younger – tactics and mysteries and lots of forums, just the less dangerous kind. Not like…

Four, three, four, two…

Four, three, four, two…

Shit.

She misses it. Even now, even after everything, her fingers itch to log back in, though nothing is there any more, even the chat box shell deleted.

Four, three, four, two…

She gets up and closes her bedroom door. She shuts the curtains, though it's still light outside. She just feels so damn tense. She sits back down in front of the laptop and stares at the blank screen and thinks and thinks and *wants*…

Echo Six is gone, she tells herself. *All of that is gone.*

The Feds think they caught everyone involved in The Asker's *other* group, but she still can't ever be that person again. It's not safe… It's not.

Even if she uses a new name…

Even if…

But her fingers are wanting to move. After today, especially, her mind is wanting to work, to release into something she understands and can control again.

Yes, she misses it.

She misses the place where the rules were clear, where everything made sense, where she could be hidden away and protected and powerful all at the same time; where people were afraid of her and not she of them. Maybe she is stronger in real life than she thought she was, and maybe she can become stronger in time, but she will never be as strong as she was there.

As she *can* be.

She misses the Forum and, if she's honest, she misses the person The Asker was to her, too. She misses Echo Six, misses being her.

She hesitates. Roger would positively freak if he knew what she was considering and Gilbert would say it was a bloody stupid idea, but…

But…

The internet is a big place. She was starting to master it way before The Asker ever found her. That's why he asked her to join those two and a half years ago. Echo Six may be gone. She made a mistake. But maybe… Maybe she could try it out, be Echo Seven by another name, just for one night.

Just one night.

She'll have to be careful. She's fairly sure she's on some kind of FBI watch list now, but there are ways around that. There are ways around everything if you look hard enough. There are always loopholes. A single phrase keeps running through her head. It's a phrase that's bigger than the man who wrote it and what he came to represent for her. Just because he fell away, doesn't mean those words mean any less;

There is truth to be shared.

And not just shared. It's not even that part that matters most to her, it's the *discovered* part. It's the finding part. It is a purpose all on its own. It doesn't have to be big or dangerous or anything people would notice, just something small to focus her, to ease away the tension.

There is truth to be shared.

The phrase repeats inside her mind. Then come the words that follow it – that have always followed it.

Let us begin.

She bites her lip. The tapping stops.

She turns on the laptop.

ABOUT THE AUTHOR

Laura grew up in Woking, England, and graduated from the University of Surrey with a degree in music. Before starting *Echoes*, she worked mainly in theatre and wrote two musicals, *The In-Between* and *Faerytale*. For more information, please visit www.lauratisdall.com.

www.twitter.com/lauratisdall
www.facebook.com/lauratisdallwriter

ACKNOWLEDGEMENTS

Thank you to God, for your saving love and for always giving me a 'next step'. Big thanks to all my amazingly supportive family and friends, especially Mum, Dad, Nan, Dave, Chris and Nat – I couldn't have done this without your constant love, belief and significant patience (and that epic car journey 'thought storm'). Thank you also to legendary proof readers Nadine, Miriam, Chrissi and James the Techie Genius (without whom Mal would have made a lot more mistakes); to Mike Butcher for all your ongoing help and for giving *Echoes* a cover that had me grinning stupidly for hours; to Jenny Glencross for massively helpful editorial notes, and to Nelle Andrew for your advice.

Finally, thank you to you – yes, you – for reading this book, and to everyone who has ever supported me along the way. You're all awesome.